A Prophecy of Ruin
The BloodBorn Inheritance
Harleigh Rose Knight

Map Design © 2025 by Danni of DandyFantasyDesigns

Cover Design © 2025 by ANKBookDesigns

Identifiers

ISBN:978-1-963934-06-9(eBook)

ISBN:978-1-963934-07-6(paperback)

This book may discuss topics that are not suitable for everyone and may be difficult for some readers. This book includes mentions of parental neglect, emotional abuse, graphic sexual content, violence, gore, blood, child death, general manipulation, murder, forced marriage, religious and political manipulation, starvation, torture.

If these topics are too much for you, put the book aside and take care of your mental health first. We will meet another time for another story.

May you find the strength to take your destiny into your own
hands, too.

Coming Soon

ComingSoon...
Origins of Cylla
Rage of Gods and Dragons, Book Four

The Bloodborn Inheritance
Hourglass of Blood, Book Two
Shadow of the Last Born, Book Three

The Bonebound Court
The Hollow Crown, Book One
Bound By Bone, Book Two
Midnight Oath, Book Three

Keep up to date with the latest news and release dates by following on social media.
FindHarleigh Rose Knight on all platforms.

Stonedale
Rubyware
Saydeean Dessert
Hollowgrove
The Alter of Time
Emberrella
Rune Hold
Lunadur
Eryndel

Contents

Act One
READY THE PIECES

Chapter One
THE FIRST STEPS ARE SMALL

Lanira

My back hit the spice rack before his rough hands gripped my thighs, and he lifted me higher in the air. His grip on me was tight as if he were afraid that I'd slip through his fingers. I ran my hands through his black hair, and my tongue glided up his neck. The salt of his skin mingled with the lingering scent of leather and steel from his armor. He slammed me down on the counter beside the rack. The speed was quick enough that the jars on the shelf still shook beside the two of us. The glass clinked together in a frantic rhythm that matched my heartbeat. He grabbed the rack to silence it while he pulled my skirt the rest of the way up with his other hand. The warmth of his fingers sent chills up my spine, and a moan slipped out of my lips.

He was one of the dumbest men I had ever met, but he was easy on my eyes. He could never entertain me if he were fully clothed, but the way my nails could glide through his skin, and he would return a tune in my ear, made for a fun ten minutes when I felt the ache between my legs.

Should we be doing this? No.

It wouldn't stop me from licking the blood from his back off my nails while his eyes were closed, either. The metallic sweetness coated my tongue like forbidden honey.

He shoved my legs apart, and the clasp of his belt clicked and clunked when he pulled his hard length from beneath it. Our groans matched when he pushed himself inside of me. He gripped my thighs again and shoved me closer to him until he fully filled me. I wished he had used more force with me, but he was insistent that he didn't want to hurt me. I thought he used the line to try steering me towards love, but he was only for now. He was simple for fun, not a future.

Any such thought was impossible. We'd lose our heads for what we were doing, let alone asking for a marriage. I would deny him if he asked. I'd still accept him filling me until I forgot about anything else. Until the world narrowed to just this moment, this counter, this desperate hunger.

He thrust harder, and I moaned louder with his rhythm. His hand met my mouth. It told me to be quiet, but I smirked underneath it as if it were a challenge. I didn't accept, despite how badly I wanted to. He silenced himself the same way he warned me to do. It was a disappointment. I wanted him to cry out about how good I felt to him, but he never would. It wasn't personal; it was the situation. He was a guard, and I was a handmaiden, a pillow talker. This was our excitement, our future. Nothing more than stolen moments between shadows.

The spice rack began to shake again, and I bit into his fingers until I drew just enough blood to feel it drip onto my lips. He was sweet and savory on my tongue. Our bodies were so close that there was nearly no telling who was who, and I pulled him closer still. It forced him to push deeper inside of me, and I felt the heat from it build like a storm gathering strength. I felt the tension inside of me brew and bubble. He felt it, too. His rushed movements spoke of it. His deepened breath told me he was getting close, and it pushed me over the edge of my own cliff.

I felt the spasms and pulses between my legs with my release, and with my carelessness, I bit into him harder. The rush of blood that filled my mouth compounded with my release, and I nearly lost complete control of myself. The world tilted, colors sharpening to an almost painful clarity. He pulled his hand back with a yell, and I wrapped my hands around his neck and pulled him back into me.

I didn't want him to see my face. I knew my eyes would be red, even if I had already tucked my fangs inside. I wasn't filled with blood, but I had gotten enough to be filled with heat. To feel full of strength and energy. Animal blood filled me. It kept me from acting out. From having erratic emotions, but human blood made me feel alive. Made me remember what I truly was beneath this carefully constructed mask.

"I'm sorry. Sometimes I get carried away." I panted against his shoulder. "You're so good it's easy to lose myself."

He chuckled with pride, and it was enough to make him comfortable again. The sound vibrated through his chest, where I rested my forehead.

"Lucky for you, it's only me. Anyone else may turn you into the king under suspicion of being a vampire," Koen murmured.

I composed myself and blinked the lenses I wore back over my eyes. The familiar weight of the disguise settled back into place like a well-worn cloak.

"You're funny." I leaned back into the wall and smiled.

I liked him, but was kept from being able to respect him for the same reasons. He was simply stupid. How many girls had he bedded that nearly slipped into a frenzy? Anyone else would have turned me in the first time I slipped. He thought I simply had a blood kink. If only he knew how close to the truth his jest really was.

He straightened his brown leather pants and looked up at me while he buckled them back on. "If you uttered the word, I'd take you away from here."

"And where would you take me?" I asked. "To live on the verge of starvation in a forest cottage you built by hand?"

"I'd never let you starve," Koen replied, his voice earnest in a way that made my stomach twist.

I shook my head, and my eyes rolled. "You know what I'm going to respond with."

"Something about keeping things casual?" He mocked, but there was hurt behind the words.

Those small gestures made me consider if the few moments of joy were worth it. At the moment, things had always been good. He clearly wasn't as skilled at separating reality from fantasy as I was. What he wanted could never happen. Not because I didn't love him. It was worse than that for him. I didn't feel anything for him if he wasn't inside of me.

The silence stretched between us like a chasm. I could feel him waiting for me to soften, to give him some sign that this meant more than physical release. But I had nothing to offer him except honesty wrapped in cruelty.

No one ran away and lived in peace anywhere.

"You really should keep yourself from falling down these trails of thought. We aren't in love. You have a nice amenity to offer me, and that is where the sentence ends." I jumped off the counter he had me placed on, and my copper heels tapped against the stone floor with the motion. "These moments are fun; let it be that way."

He leaned down to try and kiss me, but I moved just enough to ensure contact wasn't made. Koen considered boundaries more like a flagpole that could be altered at his command. I held a sinking feeling in my gut that he would become problematic later, but there were only so many ways for me to get blood. My supply was limited, and although it primarily consisted of animals, nothing was as potent as people.

I brushed down the layers of my golden-brown dress and pulled at the strings on my corset until everything was back in place. The fabric whispered against my skin as I smoothed away the evidence of our encounter. I glided my thumbs against the outer corners of my lips to clean anything that may have remained, and without a goodbye, I left the pantry.

The chefs hardly gave me a second look as they hustled to prepare breakfast. Their movements were a practiced dance around the massive hearths, the air thick with the aroma of fresh bread and sizzling meat. No one ate the same thing as the other, and they never ate the same thing two days in a row. The queen was the only one to keep a routine, and she was even on a weekly rotation. Princess Invidia was the most sporadic. No one knew what she wanted until she opened her eyes, usually in the deepest part of the kitchen's morning. It made her the bane of their day.

The same maid as every morning handed me a tray, and I gave her a half bow by lowering my head. I fought against the smirk that wanted to grow. I enjoyed the excitement of having something so close to everyone's face that they knew nothing about it. The weight of the secret was both a burden and a thrill.

I lifted the tray one-handed in the air as I passed guards rushing to meet the king before he left his room, their armor clanking in urgent rhythm. The stairs were next. The castle was decorated in plum purple, the queen's favorite color. Golden accents were the king's favorite. The décor was no testimony to the strictness of the castle. The king ruled with steel might, and the queen sat as a silent but beautiful accessory.

I opened the door to Princess Invidia's bedroom. She and I shared the entire wing of the castle, and it was spared nothing. She was the only legitimate daughter of the king and received every blessing of such a position. Silk tapestries lined the walls, and fresh flowers were replaced daily, filling the space with the scent of roses and jasmine.

"Lanira!" She stretched and groaned from beneath covers so fine they looked like spun moonlight. "I was just thinking about food!"

Her voice was as melodic as a songbird's. Her frame was as thin as her blonde hair, which caught the morning light streaming through the tall windows. It was her golden yellow eyes that made her striking. Although she was average in everything from features to breasts, her eyes were one in a million.

"I knew my princess would be hungry." I mused as I set the tray on her bedside table.

I tucked my hands behind my back and under the ruffles of my skirt, assuming the position I'd held countless times before.

"I dreamt of my future prince again. His muscles were bigger than the pile of my bed frame, and his face was as handsome as always." Invidia smiled at me, her eyes still heavy with sleep and dreams.

I knew she was waiting for me to speak. She always did this, painted these romantic pictures, and waited for my commentary, like I was her confidante in matters of the heart.

"I prefer the girth to be lower for the best results," I responded.

She giggled and took a bite of fruit. "My mother mentioned that once we are married and partake in such an act, it's best to have small and quick. She claims the faster it's over, the better."

I gave her a sly smile and allowed her to continue her breakfast. I grew so used to the smile that I held plastered to my face that sometimes, even I forgot it wasn't real. It had become as much a part of my costume as the lenses that hid my true eyes.

"I heard the guards talking this morning before they left. They mentioned Father is in a foul mood already. They remarked that Tillo turned down another marriage offer today." Invidia declared with her mouth over-packed with berries.

"He'd rather marry his horse." I made light of the situation, though we both knew the jest held more truth than comfort.

Princess Invidia finished eating her breakfast, and the other maids assigned to her morning routine arrived to help dress her. I sat on a stool by the door with my hands clasped on my lap. The stool was fine, fluffed to the brim with velvet cushions. The endless façade was exhausting. I didn't hate her, but I didn't love her. Anytime in our history together that I may have come close to genuine affection, she reminded me why I required distance from her.

I watched the maids help her slip a blush pink gown over her head while she smiled at herself in the body-length mirror. The silk rustled like butterfly wings as they arranged the layers and tied the elaborate ribbons.

It always triggered me to enter into the same memory loop. My big sister used to stand in our room and make her dresses from fabrics she found on the farm. Our brothers would poke fun at her, but our father always told them to shape up. He'd hand out extra farm work for every insult and praise her hard work. He'd ruffle my hair afterward and assure me that if I worked hard and kept honest, I could have anything I wanted, too.

The memory tasted bitter now, like wine left too long in the sun. I worked hard, but I didn't stay honest. He'd have to accept one out of two. Honesty was a privilege that I couldn't afford. I was a vampire hiding in plain sight. I wasn't surprised to exist. I should have been burned with my siblings and parents long ago.

The phantom smell of smoke sometimes still filled my nostrils when I let my guard down.

"How do I look?" The princess spun herself, the gown flaring around her like rose petals caught in the wind.

"Gorgeous." I clapped softly.

She looked like any other problem-free, spoiled royal child, the same as the other royal daughters. It wasn't my time or place to voice such observations aloud. I stood and moved to the side so she could exit first, and I followed her out. The king hated the sound of chewing in the morning. It was common for everyone to eat alone and then attend the king's breakfast.

Princess Invidia grabbed my arm while we walked and wasted no time speaking. "It will be a long morning filled with rambles and yelling, no doubt. Father's sour moods will not be sweetened easily. Tillo likely didn't have a good reason for denying another princess." She clicked her tongue in disapproval. "I simply did not like her." She mocked in a deeper voice, imitating her brother. "He will need to marry soon. Father is very on edge about the prophecy."

She kept speaking, but I hardly listened. The prophecy had always been a topic of conversation, but it became the main topic in the last month. The prophecy spoke of a kingdom ending in ruin if it was not united under a strong ruler who believed in peace and inclusion. It claimed a young vampire would rise and take advantage of the shattered kingdom, paving the way for vampires to unite and rise again.

It's a small stone tablet, hardly worth noting, and had no real power on its own. King Valen gave the prophecy more power than even he held. He spoke life into it until the entire kingdom believed it would be their downfall. King Valen interpreted it on his own and translated it for the kingdom. We were all to believe that the stone tablet spoke of his kingdom and his bloodline. He trained Prince Tillo to be the king who would bring peace and prevent vampires from rising again.

However, Prince Tillo's refusal to marry put a wrench in the king's plan. He could not be crowned king without a wife. Another foolish rule that I thought could easily be altered, though it was unnecessary. I stayed silent all the same. A good little accessory for the princess. If I were anything more, I'd be dead. If King Valen knew that I was a vampire, I'd be hung for all to see as his symbol of fending off the downfall of his kingdom.

The irony wasn't lost on me that I walked these halls freely while he feared creatures exactly like me. The thought almost made me laugh out loud.

I stood, hands clasped behind my back, behind Princess Invidia as she sat at the king's table. She sat on his left, always. The carved chair was massive, designed to make her look even smaller and more delicate than she already was.

I'd stand only for a few moments.

The room was filled with so much silence that even a mouse wouldn't dare scurry out now. The air felt thick with tension, pressing against my skin like humidity before a storm. I saw Princess Invidia shift in her seat, her shoulders tense. I didn't enjoy the silence, either. I reached up and pulled her hair behind her and off of her shoulders. She glanced back at me with a smile. It was small gestures like those that kept me in the position I wanted to be in.

Helpful and quiet little Lanira.

Queen Blair and her collection of guards and ladies entered. It created a buzz of energy in the room, like birds finally allowed to chirp after a long winter. They were all discussing something we weren't a part of, with small laughs here and there that tinkled like silver bells. The ladies helped Queen Blair take her seat, and as I knew she would, she patted the seat on her right.

I smiled and gave a slight bow before I joined her at the table. Always on her right. The wood was polished to a mirror shine, reflecting the morning light that streamed through the tall windows. Some days, I liked to think that she thought of me as another daughter. I never allowed myself to stay in that state of mind long because I was positive that, like the way the castle was decorated, I was also only a way to stab back at the king when she had no other means to do so.

A way to proclaim that he could try, but he could not control everything. They appeared happy outside of the small jabs at each other, but didn't we all? The court was full of people wearing masks, though mine was perhaps the most literal.

No one around would have suspected that I would be their end from looking at me. They had no access to my inner thoughts, no way to see past the carefully constructed veneer I'd spent years perfecting. I would still be their end. I kept quiet and carefully calculated my position to ensure it.

King Valen stormed in next. His enormous belly entered the room first, straining against his royal vest, and his laugh second, booming and theatrical.

"It is a good morning!" He bellowed, his voice ricocheting off the stone walls.

The Princess and I immediately locked eyes in silent shock. Good moods from the king were rarer than summer snow.

"Tillo has agreed to marry the princess from Saydeean! She is arriving with a guard from RuneHold." King Valen announced as he sat, the chair creaking under his weight.

"Isn't that where they still train vampire hunters?" Queen Blair asked, her voice carefully neutral, though I caught the slight tremor beneath it.

"Indeed, my dear, indeed! Things are falling into place well!" King Valen mused, already reaching for the bread. "We will also be departing."

"Departing?" Princess Invidia gasped. Her golden eyes blinked too many times, like a startled owl caught in sudden light.

"It's time to celebrate! We will be leaving for our vacation home. The Princess is already on her way there."

No one asked anything further; the king was already fist-deep in food as if he had never been taught manners. The sound of his chewing filled the silence that had settled over the table like a heavy blanket. I felt something cold settle in my stomach, though

I couldn't yet name what it was. Change was coming, and I welcomed it.

Change was coming and with it, death.

Chapter Two
A LONG RIDE WITH THE BLOOD BAG

Lanira

Princess Invidia sat on the edge of the bed and twirled her yellow hair. She attempted to force her hair into a curl strand by strand while I neatly folded her clothing. My place was confusing at first. I was her best friend some days, and my worries were none. On other days, I performed the labor of multiple handmaids. It wasn't a change based on her poor attitude. In fact, Princess Invidia was most often cheerful. It was a change dependent upon how much she wanted others around.

I was sure it was because of the king and queen. They allowed her to stay in a comfortable bubble. She never had a reason to think that anyone wouldn't want to wait on her. In her mind, friendship meant that I did things for her. The more she handed out orders, the closer we were.

She never considered me overworked. She considered me trustworthy and organized. I was built to multitask, she would insist. It had been the same since I was seven.

My eldest brother would never have agreed with her. Ash would have told me that working together would make for a better experience. That teamwork built better character than loneliness.

He'd discuss how our book of rituals and rights was made possible because so many of the vampires worked together to create it. He'd use it as a way to lecture me to be more team-spirited.

I hardly held many memories that pertained to being a vampire. I was too young. I recalled small things like having fun at celebrations, the sound of laughter echoing through stone halls, and the warmth of being surrounded by my kind. I never absorbed any of the important information. I was careless and spoiled. I thought that I had all the time in the world to learn.

Ash never pushed me. Even when father protested and declared that I was old enough to be held to a higher standard, I was never pushed. His patience had been infinite, his love unconditional.

I hadn't been able to lay my hands on the book of our rights either. It remained lost to me, along with everything else that mattered.

"I think he likes you. "The princess whispered, her voice barely audible above the rustle of silk.

She pulled me from my thoughts.

I glanced out of the corner of my eye at Koen. He was watching me as if I were his next meal. Unblinking and unconcerned with the possible consequences. He stood at the open door waiting for us, and we kept our voices low.

"Nonsense," I whispered back, though my stomach twisted with the knowledge that it wasn't entirely untrue.

"It's not nonsense. He's looked at you like he was in love with you since we were children. How have you not noticed?" Princess Invidia pressed, her golden eyes sparkling with the delight of gossip.

"Even if he did look at me in the way that you claim, I don't like him that way," I replied, focusing on smoothing a wrinkle from one of her gowns.

Princess Invidia shrugged and scrunched her face. "You're above him anyway." She nodded with the certainty of someone who had never questioned her own position. "You deserve someone better looking."

She changed her stance quickly, but she still hadn't helped get anything ready. Her hands remained pristine while mine worked.

I didn't want anyone. Koen was a blood bag and a good time. She only took the stance she did because I hadn't gushed over him. If I had proclaimed he was perfect, then she would have had many things to speak in the opposite direction.

She had never admitted it out loud, but I was sure by the way she watched Koen that maybe she liked him. It was an impossible match, but that never stopped anyone from dreaming.

Koen had been by our side since we were small. While the princes were away, Koen followed us around. He was always protective of us. Princess Invidia spoke from a guilty conscience because it was she who snuck glances at him.

The only thing she had right, she hardly knew she had right. Koen did pay me special attention when we were small. He'd present me with flowers or sneak me his dessert. Small gestures that meant everything to a child pretending to be human.

We were far from strangers, but I was just as far from being in love with him. Love was a luxury I couldn't afford.

"Let's worry about getting you a husband first," I spoke, closing the final trunk with a decisive click. "Then I'll marry whoever keeps me closest to you."

Princess Invidia smiled at me like a child who had been promised sweets.

I moved to the doorway with a bag in each arm. I handed both bags to Koen and smiled wide enough for my teeth to be visible, carefully keeping my canines hidden.

"Are you ready?" I asked.

She jumped up and grabbed my arm. "Absolutely!"

Koen went first, and we followed behind. I wanted distance between us, but the princess wanted to stay close. Her arm linked through mine like a shackle made of silk.

"You know, it wouldn't hurt to flirt with him. He clearly likes you." She pressed again, her voice carrying that tone of someone who believed they were being helpful.

"Do you want me to lose my head?" I asked, trying to hide my growing annoyance.

"No one would have to know. I've heard rumors of the guards and their activities. Some of the maids whisper about their size. Apparently, some of the guards are well endowed." The princess grew louder the longer she spoke, her cheeks flushing pink.

I hadn't seen any such truth tothe rumors. Average at best was what walked through the castle. What theyshould have whispered about was the skill some possessed. It wasn't the sizethat some carried but the skill with their hands. The knowledge of where totouch, how to make someone forget themselves entirely.

"What are you thinkingabout?" she tugged on my arm.

"Hmm? Oh, I was only thinking of how to convince the king that you should be married before you lose all your virtue with the way you're speaking. Besides, I have no interest in such things." I replied calmly, though my thoughts had been far from innocent.

The princess shook her head with a sigh and patted my arm. "He doesn't seem to share the sentiment. I've seen him glancing back at you this entire time."

"My only interest is in the princess," I declared. "You need something more to do to keep you occupied."

"All right, all right."The princess relented, though her knowing smile suggested she wasn't convinced.

In truth, my thoughts couldn't have been farther from the idea of a relationship in any capacity. I was just as preoccupied with the prophecy as anyone else. I didn't believe it. I didn't live by it. I wanted to use it. King Valen thought endlessly on the ways that it could tumble his kingdom down.

I thought endlessly on the ways that I could leverage it to feed fear into royals.

King Valen thought that if he put Prince Tillo on the throne, he would succeed in keeping it at bay. I thought his anxiety was the perfect time for me to make my first official move. The king's pressing fears gave me the chance to take things into my own hands. Prince Tillo would never unite anyone, anyway. He was too much like his father, rigid, afraid, and utterly lacking in vision.

They feared vampires and their rise because they swore humans would become extinct. That vampires were bloodthirsty and vengeful. It didn't matter that I didn't believe in the prophecy. I was going to use it to get what I wanted. I spent years looking fora way to bring back my family. I learned of a book that could show me how to doit.

The Temple of Time kept a grimoire filled not just with our history but our rituals as well. Magic older than any of us existed inside the pages, waiting to be awakened by the right hands. My hands.

I'd help distract the royal family with the prophecy, find the book, and then take over the kingdom. It was only to be the beginning. I wanted to turn the realm into rubble and rebuild it all. Create something worthy of the lives that had been lost.

No one stood up when the vampires were eradicated and displaced. None of them deserved to be in my new world.

I'd do it all in the name of my family. For my brother. Ash would mention that vengeance was like a poison. That it would eat away at you from the inside out. He'd emphasize learning forgiveness.

When we were younger, when my brother was still alive, Ash would tell me that my heart was pure and full of love. If he saw me again, he'd be disappointed. My heart held nothing but rot. I hardly knew what kindness was. The small girl I was and the woman I grew into couldn't have been more opposite.

He would have been right to observe it. I felt eroded. Changed by the hate that festered inside of me. Who I presented outward was nothing like who I was alone. How could I not be changed when I watched King Valen himself toss the burning torch onto Ash?

He was motionless even while burning. Or had he been screaming? My memory hardly served me correctly. Sometimes I heard his voice in my dreams, calling my name. Other times, there was only the smell of smoke and the sound of my own sobbing.

The warmth of the sun made me realize we had made it to the carriage. I was too distracted by my own thoughts. The golden light felt different on my skin now, not the comforting warmth it had been when I was human, but something that reminded me what I'd lost.

Koen held his hand out for Princess Invidia, and once she was inside the carriage, he did the same for me. There was extra intimacy behind his gesture to me. He swiped his thumb across my hand while I held my skirt and entered my seat. He was always too bold, too careless with displays of affection.

I saw our time together coming to an end sooner rather than later. I wouldn't risk the sacrifices of my entire life being worthless because he had no discretion. Sometimes I felt close to him, but it was only because we had known each other for so long. I didn't have any true feelings for him. That capacity had been burned out of me along with my family.

He felt much more connected to me than I did to him. It was a dangerous imbalance.

I felt the skin on the side of my thumbnail grow moist with what would no doubt be blood. I discreetly ground my pointer finger into my thumb at the idea of losing the future I had planned because of a man. I perfected small ways to release any bits of emotional outbursts so that my face stayed painted with a smile.

I was seven when I realized I was alone. Seven, when I mourned my family in secret. Seven, when I learned to sneak into the stables and drink from rats, their tiny hearts beating frantically against my lips.

Seven, when I started laying out the chess board that we would play on.

I swallowed hard before I pushed the thoughts back down. I closed them into a small box and tucked it away. My heart raced, but I hushed my breath. Emotional control was my best skill, maybe my only skill. It was what kept me alive in a world that wanted me dead.

Koen took his seat, and Prince Tillo entered last. He closed the small door, and the carriage took off with the sound of horses neighing before Prince Tillo was comfortably placed in his seat. The entire vehicle rocked with the motion, wheels grinding against cobblestone.

"Are you excited?" the princess wasted no time asking, her voice bright with anticipation.

Prince Tillo sighed loud enough that I thought he had to be in physical pain. The sound spoke of a man carrying burdens far heavier than his years should allow. I moved the purple velvet curtain over the small window to take in the view while we traveled. I wanted to look busy, to avoid being drawn into whatever conflict was brewing.

"I am excited that Father will allow me some peace," he grumbled, his voice heavy with resignation.

"It's a noble position you'll have. You shouldn't take it for granted. It'll be you who saves us fromthe vampires," Koen, our guard, spoke with resentment that surprised me. There was something darker in his tone than I'd heard before.

I kept my head pointed out of the window. I wanted to remain a backdrop. I did not miss the shock on Princess Invidia's face, just as I saw the frown move across Prince Tillo's thin lips. Koen spoke too brashly, too boldly for his station.

"Tillo is the eldest son and has been specifically training for the role his entire life," the princess defended, her voice carrying the authority of her birth.

Her eyes were soft, but her brows furrowed in offense. She didn't like anyone questioning her family's right to rule.

"Although I appreciate your services as our guard and would defend the kingdom if such an event did occur, I hardly see the chances as high. My father made sure to kill every single one. Lanira would know better than any other." Prince Tillo paused and looked at me. "If you'd like the role, I'd give it for a moment's peace."

I had always been grateful for the style in the kingdom, which was long-sleeved no matter the temperature, because if my thumb hadn't bled from my picking before, it wasn't far away. The fabric hid more than just scratches.

"Correct." I mused as if the conversation didn't offend me to my very core. "I owe my life to King Valen and Queen Blair. My entire family died that day. I don't know where I'd be now if it weren't for their kindness."

The lie tasted like ash on my tongue, but I spoke it with the same conviction I'd practiced for years.

Princess Invidia cut me off, all too happy to finish speaking for me. "I'll never forget how we found you mixed up in all of the bodies. You were crying and alone. So small. Unusually small, even for a child." She paused to linger on the thought before she shook her head. "Just like a vampire to kidnap human children."

My hands clenched into fists beneath the folds of my skirt. I wanted to scream at her, to tell her that those bodies were my family, that I hadn't been kidnapped but born among them. Instead, I nodded along with her narrative.

"I remember the commotion in court when everyone laid eyes on you," Koen mentioned. "No one understood why you weren't killed. Alliances between every kingdom were so shaky. Still, the queen was adamant that you stay. She mentioned she wanted another child, and the king owed it to her. I was scared of where you'd be sent if they denied you. No one knew where you belonged."

"I'd have been terrified to be alone as a child," Princess Invidia frowned, her sympathy genuine but misplaced.

I hadn't been alone. I had begged to whatever high power there may have been for my life to be taken while I was with my family. I pleaded to whatever may have been bigger than us to end things for me so that I could have been reunited with them. With Ash. I wasn't done learning the lessons that he had to teach me.

They didn't want to hear that. They wanted to feel something good. They wanted to be portrayed as saviors instead of the murderers they truly were.

I rested my hand on the princess and squeezed. "It was as the universe saw fit. I found my sister that day. I was given the chance to grow with my best friend, and I couldn't have asked for a better family. I hope to remain with you until my end."

"I hope to serve you until my end as well," Koen told the princess, but his eyes were on me when he spoke.

The idea brought bile up my throat. Eternity as the princess's toy when she was bored, when she didn't feel like lifting a finger on her own. Forever with Koen as the only source of real blood. I couldn't imagine a worse eternity than being placed with them forever, without my family. Trapped in this gilded cage, pretending to love the people who had destroyed everything that mattered.

If Koen and I were caught, we would die. Loyalty was prized above all else for King Valen. If we were sneaking behind his back as lovers, then we weren't loyal to him. He was strict with all of his rules. If I were to risk death, I'd rather it be for a hundred other reasons than supposed love.

Koen was only a means to better blood than old, half-drained animals. He was far too careless to be trusted with anything more than my flesh.

I had no intention of being caught. Not when I was so close to everything I'd worked for.

"Do you really mean that?" Prince Tillo asked, his voice cutting through my thoughts like a blade.

I looked up at him without moving my head, meeting his gaze through my lashes.

"Do you really want to remain with her forever? You aren't curious about the life you had before? Even a little?" Prince Tillo narrowed his eyes on me. There was something calculating in his expression, as if he could see through the mask I wore.

As I anticipated, I didn't have to respond myself.

"Of course she means it!" Princess Invidia cried, her voice rising in defense. "She loves me, and I love her."

Prince Tillo nodded, but his raised brow and crooked lips suggested otherwise. He saw something the others missed, and that made him dangerous.

"Not all of us wish to runaway from what's in front of us. Some of us look forward to facing life head-on," I responded with a smile, though the words felt like a challenge thrown down between us.

I held Princess Invidia's hand to boost her confidence and turned my gaze back to the window. Outside, the countryside rolled past in shades of green and gold. Soon, we would reach the vacation home. Soon, I would be one step closer to finding what I needed. The landscape blurred as we moved, and I allowed myself a moment to imagine it all burning. Every field, every village, every reminder of the kingdom that had stolen my family.

The thought should have horrified me. Instead, it filled me with a warmth that had nothing to do with the sun streaming through the window.

Chapter Three
An Escort to a New Life

Ravi

The scent of vanilla hung in the air. The incense burned in every corner, filling Niyla's chambers with a sweetness that couldn't quite mask the underlying staleness of confinement.

"Why write a request to join me?" I asked, though I already knew the answer would break my heart.

She sighed at my words. Not in annoyance but in longing. She twirled the small silver teaspoon in circles until there was a liquid tornado inside of her teacup. The porcelain clinked softly against the silver, a gentle rhythm that had become as familiar as breathing.

She was adamant that, if done right, it kept her looking young. She heard it from a traveling witch. She'd have been sent to the dungeons if the king knew. The irony wasn't lost on me; she feared growing old in a room where time had already stopped.

"If it were that easy, I'd have sent request after request until I had traveled to every town and castle in the land," I lectured, though my words lacked conviction.

"I knew it wouldn't be approved. I know that Orn won't allow me to leave. Was it not worth a try? Why also make me feel worse? Given the situation, it'll be up to you to bring me back memories.

A flower, or a rock!" Her eyes lit up like candles in a dark room. "Maybe a pet!"

I couldn't help but smile at her. At the way, even though I knew she wanted to scream, she remained level. She was always gracious. She was never granted freedom as the only daughter of RuneHold. Niyla was considered a valuable resource. Her marriage would grant King Orn anything he desired. A chess piece in silk and jewels, too precious to risk but too valuable not to use.

Niyla was the best royal I had met. She was kind and considerate. It was a loss to the world that she was locked away. When she sat at her desk, surrounded by paper and ink, her fingers stained with words that would never be sent, I imagined what our life would have been like if she were in charge.

When the two of us were small, she was the one to clap for me. To share her desserts with me. It was she and I who played together while others called me a bastard child, their whispers following me like shadows.

"I'll bring you back everything I see that makes me think of you," I promised, and I meant it with every fiber of my being.

I gave her a kiss on the forehead and allowed myself one last lingering look. Her big green eyes were filled with such potential. She never judged anything I did or proclaimed. Still, I felt like a monster around her. She and I felt like yin and yang, light and shadow dancing together until one consumed the other.

I closed the door to her room behind me, and King Orn waited on the other side. Floating lanterns waved in the air around him, casting shifting patterns of light across his face like a mask that never stayed still.

"It is time for you to depart," King Orn announced, his voice flat as stale bread.

"I needed to say goodbye to my sister," I replied, meeting his gaze without flinching.

"Half-sister," he corrected, and I could hear the satisfaction in his voice.

His words made my blood boil. He did it on purpose. I knew he did. He enjoyed the rise he could get from me. He reveled in the response he was able to pull from people, feeding off their reactions like a parasite.

She was my sister. No matter what percentage of blood flowed, she was my sister. Just as he could be thrown from a watchtower, and I'd not claim him as a brother. I felt as strongly about both subjects.

His golden hair moved as if there were no weight to it as he walked. I could have ripped each strand from his head. It was a symbol, and I'd learned long ago that symbols held more power than weapons. Sure, it was seemingly meaningless if you only looked on the surface. It was a poor habit to have, only peering at the highest layer. Everything, no matter what it was, had deeper meanings.

His hair was the only thing allowed to flow freely within the castle walls. It was an extension of him, so it was free. No eyes watched it from the shadows. Everyone else, everything else, ran on the expectation that they were as rigid as a nail. As unbreaking as he demanded. He was free because he was a king, and only a king was free.

King Orn moved ahead of me, and I knew he meant for me to follow. I kept my steps one behind his. Perfectly in sync, as I should be. The sound of our boots on stone echoed through empty corridors. He didn't deserve his title.

"You will be escorting the only daughter of Saydeean to her engagement celebration and handing her off to the king of Emberrella. Don't lose sight of who and what you are. If you see a vampire, I want to know. If you hear someone whisper of the prophecy, I want to hear of it. Even the tiniest crumble can be of the most importance." King Orn lectured, his voice carrying the weight of paranoia. "The prophecy will be at the front of so many minds now. I've heard the king of Emberrella is practically feral over it."

I gripped my blade handle a bit tighter. He sounded like a fool. He spoke to me of doing my job as if I hadn't done it better than anyone else in his court. As if I hadn't dedicated my life to him without question. As if I didn't prioritize my sister and her well-being above my own. I went through more than he could have imagined to earn my position in the court.

I did everything that I did for the sake of the kingdom. For loyalty to my oath. Yet each day, that oath felt heavier, like chains around my soul.

"If you feel that anyone doesn't fear the prophecy, kill them," King Orn finished, and the casual way he spoke of murder made my stomach turn. "Our alliances need to grow, but not at the cost of losing sight of our main goal. As long as this mission moves with success, then we will be moved into a pleasant position with Saydeean and Emberrella."

"Of course," I acknowledged, though the words tasted bitter.

I held my eyes on the floor beneath us, which emitted a small colorful glow under our footsteps as we walked. The magical stones responded to our weight, creating ripples of light like disturbed water.

After all, it would only take one seed to sprout thoughts of doubt. He couldn't allow such a thing. Once, I admired our way of life. I thought that we were so far advanced, not just in our kingdom but in our way of thinking as well. The more we slaughtered in our dungeons, the less I could convince myself of that.

At the bottom of the chain, it was easy to see only the good. It was easy to have admiration for people. The higher one moved up the chain link, the less true that became. The view from the top was often obscured by the corpses you'd climbed over to get there.

My thoughts were painted true by the events of my last mission.

I couldn't find a way to put reason behind King Orn demanding the death of every child and witch that we managed to pull out of a ship that set sail for RubyWake. Their faces haunted my dreams, their cries echoing in the silence of sleepless nights.

I wanted to remain loyal to my kingdom, but a part of me could never sleep again without seeing those faces.

Children with tears in their eyes and their mothers' names on their lips.

I wanted to present reform, but I knew the idea of change would not be welcome. If Niyla were the ruler, then she and I could have sent RuneHold in a direction of change. Instead, Orn was the ruler. He and I were never more than rivals. At first forced by everyone else, it didn't take long until Orn decided it was the backbone of our relationship.

Orn went silent and stopped at the entrance of the castle. He stood aside and watched me with eyes that taunted me. He used the smug smirk on his face to tell me he was in charge and gave me permission to move past him. The morning sun cast long shadows across the courtyard, making everything look like a chessboard.

"Do not disappoint me, Ravi. You may have impressed the council of hunters and moved up, but you've yet to impress me the same way you never impressed my father," Orn warned, his voice dripping with inherited cruelty.

If he wanted to claim that man, he could do it without concern for what I may have felt. Orn was only half the cruelty of his father. Maybe that was why I hated Orn so much. Maybe we could have been close if he didn't have so much of his father in him. It was even in the way that he smiled with his eyes when he thought he had found the soft spot inside of someone.

Maybe that's why I loved Niyla so much. She reminded me of all the good that had once been in my mother.

I wanted to tell him that the way he spoke to me was inappropriate. Every fiber of my being wanted to tell him that he may be king, but he helped set up a system inside his kingdom that admired the hunters more than him. That if he kept on the path that he was on, he'd have a kingdom so divided he would never get it back. That one word from me, and I was confident I could spark an uprising.

Even if we didn't speak of it out loud, I knew in the way glances were exchanged that I wasn't the only one who questioned the way our land moved. The doubt in people's eyes was becoming harder to ignore.

I didn't voice any of this. Even if in my mind I was defiant, I was loyal to my oath. I was loyal to my land. To the hunters. We swore to take our orders and protect our people, and I would. Even if those people sometimes included the ones giving the orders, I despised.

"I won't disrespect the kingdom," I responded, and it was the best compromise between truth and loyalty I could manage.

It was the best I could do not to lie or fight.

I moved into the open light of the sun before the two of us could start a back and forth. I glanced back at the castle before I took a deep breath of fresh, light air. The scent of jasmine and morning dew filled my lungs, washing away the stale tension from inside.

The sight of the castle was beautiful when it was left behind. It was covered in bright flowers and trees, vines crawling up the walls like nature trying to reclaim what man had built. Nothing like what went on inside the walls. The castle was carved on every piece of trim with runes and designs. Great care went into making our home look presentable, hiding the rot beneath layers of artistic beauty.

I climbed inside of the carriage and shut the door with a decisive click that felt like sealing my fate.

Anything that I had to do this time, I'd not let my emotions get in the way.

Inside the carriage sat the princess of Saydeean. Just a girl covered in yellow fabric. She wore silk over every inch of her, the material so fine it seemed to glow in the filtered sunlight. I wondered how she was able to breathe, but it wasn't my place to question her traditions. It was noble of her to stick to them even when there was no one to enforce them.

The air between us was thick with unspoken fear. I had to assume it had nothing to do with me and everything to do with her situation. She spun her fingers under the cloth. If the jumping fabric wasn't enough to tell me of her nervousness, then the sound of her nail slipping off skin on the side of her opposite nail would.

"Do you need to speak, your highness?" I asked, keeping my voice gentle.

She shook her head, and the jingle of jewels moved with her like tiny bells marking time. Her silence was palpable, heavy as a stone dropped in still water.

"There's no one to hear but me, and I am not in a position to share secrets. It's part of my oath to hold them," I tried to assure her, leaning forward slightly to show I was listening.

She was but a bird in a cage, like so many of the rest of us. If I could have offered her even a sliver of relief, I wouldn't deny it.

"My father tells me that marriage is not for love. My mother tells me that I can learn to love anyone if I try hard enough. I wonder what will become of me if the prince of Emberrella is cruel or refuses to allow me to love him. My father never allowed my mother to try to love him." She spoke as if the words had been building pressure inside her for months. "What if he forces us to keep our distance and I'm never anything other than a girl who had a baby?"

Her words were like a slap in the face. The way she strung her sentences together as if she had to spit them out or they'd never come sent my heart skipping beats. There was desperation in her voice that reminded me too much of Niyla's quiet resignation.

It was a tragedy to see so many people with so much potential fear being so little forever.

She got to choose as much of her life as I did, which was to say nothing at all. Part of me thought I might halt the carriage, fake an attack, and let her go free so that she could choose. Even if she chose to stay on her path, at least she would have had the choice.

Would it have brought her peace? Or would freedom be just another form of cage for someone who had never learned how to use it?

My loyalty, my oath, kept me from acting on the thought.

"Are you free to marry?" She asked, breaking the silence that had settled between us.

"No. I'm a hand of the king. Sworn to him and my home. It is my sole focus," I answered, though the words felt hollow. "I'll live and die for him."

"Are you satisfied with that?" She pressed, and I heard an echo of my own doubts in her question.

"We all have to find a way to be satisfied with our future or drown in misery," I replied, though I wasn't sure I believed it anymore. "It isn't what I wish to tell you. I wish that I could offer you something more comforting. If I had a story to tell you with a happy ending, I would. All I can offer you is an ear to listen and the hope that you get to be the exception to your fears. I hope that he lets you in, and the two of you grow close so that this is the only time you fear for yourself."

Our conversation was too complicated to give any answers with so much simplicity. Life rarely offered clean solutions to messy problems.

No matter the words spoken, I knew that in the end, I'd still deliver her to the destination she was sold off to. The weight of that knowledge sat heavy in my chest like undigested food.

In the end, she would likely fade away and be the girl who birthed the next king and nothing more. Just like so many before her, her story would be written by others while she watched from the sidelines. The thought made me grip the hilt of my sword a little tighter, though I wasn't sure if it was to protect her or from the growing urge to change everything.

Chapter Four
Fun in the Mountains

Lanira

I took the extra time to take in the view while voices rang out against each other.

"What? I don't believe that," Prince Tillo scoffed, his voice cutting through the afternoon air.

"It's true. Saydeean has a king, but it's run entirely by women. The king is more of a second thought. It's why the idea that she is marrying outside of her kingdom is so shocking. Normally, a prince would be brought to her. She's being escorted by the highest-ranking vampire hunter to ensure her safety," Koen assured him, leaning forward with the authority of someone who prided himself on knowing court gossip.

"I agreed to this so that I'd feel less pressure for a little while, not to hold even more weight," Prince Tillo sighed, and the sound carried the exhaustion of a man twice his age.

"If that's what you wanted, you made the wrong choice," Koen laughed, but there was an edge to it.

They spoke too loudly for me to fully enjoy what I wanted to take advantage of during our journey.

The mountainside was beautiful. After a long day of traveling, we were on the correct side of the mountain to be able to see our second sun. Bright and pink, it tinted the rest of the sky in shades of rose and gold. The air was thinner here, carrying the scent of pine and something wild that made my vampire senses sharpen.

I thought it had to be one of the best ways to ring in the arrival of change and new beginnings. If there was one thing I brought, it was change.

"What do you think, Lanira?" Princess Invidia asked, pulling me from my contemplation.

"Hm?" I sat up straighter. "What do I think of Saydeean?"

The carriage came to a halt, and the horses neighed in relief. Their breathing was labored from the mountain climb, steam rising from their flanks in the cooler air.

"Yeah, I mean it is a much bigger deal than it's being made out to be, don't you think?" She pressed me harder with her eyes, seeking validation for her own confusion.

I think if it were me, I'd never have sent my only daughter outside of my walls and break a long-standing tradition on the idea that an untrustworthy kingdom would suddenly be on my side. The move reeked of desperation disguised as diplomacy.

I wouldn't voice it out loud.

"I think it shows a deep trust already blossoming between your two kingdoms," I replied, the lie sliding off my tongue like silk.

I shoved the door to the carriage open and moved down the small steps quickly. I wanted to move before another question was asked. I had no interest in being cornered and forced to discuss such nonsense.

I didn't care about any of it. I had no intention of either kingdom standing soon enough. Saydeean having a daughter or who they were run by was of no use to me. They could have been run by horses for all I cared. The only fact I'd be interested in hearing is if they had burned to the ground, or their royal family had died. Preferably both.

I couldn't recall the last time my emotions were truly engaged for anything. Taking in the maids running around to prepare for a wedding before we even entered the mountain castle was the first string played on my heart in years.

I caught myself smirking and pushed it back down before anyone could see me. I needed to hold it together a bit longer. Seeing my plans come to light in front of me was my happiness. The sweet taste of revenge finally within reach.

I had finally arrived at the starting line of getting my home back.

I grabbed the princess's two bags but was halted nearly immediately. Koen snatched them from my hands in what he was sure to have thought was romantic. It was only a show of his immaturity and his desperate need to impress me.

"You shouldn't be doing such things," he insisted, his voice carrying that patronizing tone men used when they thought they were being chivalrous.

Prince Altair, the younger son of King Valen, stepped in. "He's right. You shouldn't be doing these things. Enjoy the brief break we are receiving. Things are sure to become hectic soon enough."

I gave Prince Altair a slight bow. "I'll listen to you this time, but we are sure to have this same conversation again. I want to be helpful, and I really don't mind." I spoke in a gentle tone, letting just enough breathiness creep into my voice.

I fidgeted with my hair and shifted my eyes from one place on his face to another. I wanted to look caring, even nervous. The perfect picture of a humble servant girl overwhelmed by princely attention.

I wanted to look as naïve as he wanted me to be.

He held his chin high, and I knew I had convinced him that I was beneath him. Exactly where I needed to be to remain invisible.

"You know, this entire thing has me thinking of my own marriage," Prince Altair mentioned, his voice taking on a contemplative tone.

He motioned me with his calloused hand to follow him inside. The scent of beeswax and mountain herbs drifted from the castle's open doors.

"I hope that you find a good match. I hope that match arrives exactly when you need them the most," I responded as I followed him inside, my heels clicking softly against the polished stone.

"Have you thought about yours?" he asked, and there was something calculated in the casual way he posed the question.

I shook my head without hesitation. "I have no desire to marry. I am happy to stay by Princess Invidia's side. I ask for nothing more."

Prince Altair brushed his hand against my own while the two of us walked over the red velvet carpet that led us inside. The action made me realize what he hinted at. I looked him in the eye when he slowed his steps to a halt. My stomach turned at the thought, and it helped my cheeks flush. Though I knew it was from disgust, he would consider it a blush. I covered my smile with my hand, and the reaction caused a smile to form on his rounded cheeks.

He bore a resemblance to his father, except for his shimmering green eyes and slimmer physique. The same weak chin, the same entitled tilt of his head.

"Maybe it's unrealistic, but—" he sighed as if he had shaken his thoughts away. "Your lipstick looks nice now. This morning, it was a bit smudged. As if you had been up to something."

"I had hoped no one noticed. I woke late and was rushing to get ready in time," I chuckled lightly, adding just the right amount of embarrassment to my voice.

"You and I could be perfectly matched, if it were to come to that. Both of us are second place, and neither of us has any space in our hearts for love. We are both good at putting on a show. So good, maybe you also forget who you truly are sometimes. If for no other reason, a marriage between the two of us could offer stability and a kind of comfort only last place would understand," Prince Altair declared, his words carrying more weight than I'd expected.

His words took me by surprise. I'd never accept his offer; it didn't fit into my plans, but it shook me the way he spoke, all the same. I hadn't cared to consider that he may have felt the same sort of way that I did because he couldn't have.

I felt loss, and he felt jealousy. He placed himself in a competition with his siblings, and I set up my chess pieces to achieve checkmate before he knew I was playing. Prince Altair compared us, but he and I were nothing alike. The idea that he considered us not just similar, but equals, filled me with disgust.

We were both performers, perhaps, but our stages and audiences were worlds apart.

"Lanira! She's going to be here soon!" the princess called from somewhere inside the castle.

My shoulders relaxed, and even though I held a smile on my lips, my inner sigh was loud. Princess Invidia was my savior. Not that I truly had anything to worry about. The arrangement would never have occurred. King Valen hardly let his sons out of his sight. Although the biggest set of plans were for Prince Tillo, Prince Altair still had a detailed future planned out for him.

"There is to be a ball! Father planned a full schedule of events to celebrate. The vacation castle is to be packed to the brim!" Princess Invidia already had her fingers intertwined in mine as she mused, her excitement radiating through her touch.

Prince Altair still held a small smile in my direction. I couldn't care less about King Valen's long list of plans. We could have been surrounded by gold. The rarest animals could have danced around my feet. It wouldn't have changed anything for me.

I turned my attention back to the scene in front of me. The things that mattered. I'd use the commotion to my advantage. The extra strangers, the distractions. They'd be the perfect setup for what needed to happen.

Prince Altair excused himself and left first. Princess Invidia used the fact that we were hand in hand to drag me behind her. I took in my surroundings instead of focusing on where she led us.

Maids rushed around with fabrics and sunflowers. Kitchen staff ran outside with buckets of feathers from the chickens they prepared. Everyone in attendance carried more stress than joy. The air buzzed with nervous energy, thick enough that I could taste it.

Just as every day, the only true face of joy would be on King Valen's face. The king was the only one to ever feel truly free. Sure, he'd cry out over a problem or two in his court, but in the end, his word was law, his hand was the only justice we had, and he'd get his way until he was happy again.

"We must change!" Princess Invidia stressed, her voice pitched high with anticipation.

I nodded with a smile. To the world, we would have looked like two girls enjoying the chance to dress up. Two girls without a care, only fluttering with joy at all of the love in the air.

She was so naïve that she didn't question the conversation between the prince and me because what could the two of us have spoken of other than innocent small talk? I hardly spoke of anything to anyone other than Princess Invidia. She had no reason to ask questions because what could I be if not her loyal sister?

"I know exactly what you're going to wear!" she squealed, her voice echoing off the stone walls.

She shoved me into her room first and used her silk-covered foot to close the door behind us. It moved so quickly that I heard the air hiss before the slam of wood on wood. She was in her walk-in closet, rummaging through things, but I only noticed the flowers.

Vases were scattered all over the floor and tables. Sunflowers filled every available surface, their bright faces turned toward the windows. Sunflowers were rumored to help keep vampires at bay. Something about the scent being too strong for their noses. The land they came from was too cursed to grow such a beautiful flower; the men at court would prattle on about it.

We only didn't grow sunflowers because they didn't thrive in our kingdom, that was true. It wasn't from a curse or a fear of the petals. It was simply the soil. A fact any average person would understand. It was the same reason that not all places grew pineapples.

It was too complex a thought for anyone who lived above the average person to have. Members of the court, or advisors, didn't think the same as anyone else. They didn't have to. They lived separate lives in a separate world. It was easy for them to not just spread such a foolish lie, but to believe it.

Those average citizens who wanted too desperately to belong in the same world as the royal court would believe anything they proclaimed for just a chance at being like them. Most average people thought that, if even by proxy, similar was still similar.

A small piece of velcro, after all, still stuck the same as a larger piece.

I plucked a sunflower and stuck it behind my ear. It was a bit of defiance, but also my favorite flower. The irony wasn't lost on me, adorning myself with the very thing meant to ward off my kind.

"Yes! Exactly!" Princess Invidia exclaimed as she shoved a dress at me. "Golden will look so good against your black hair and brown eyes! You'll be glowing."

I held the dress against myself and stood in front of the wall-length mirror. The neckline was low but covered in sheer lace. I liked the golden color, and who was I to deny the princess what she wanted? The fabric was rich silk that caught the light like liquid gold.

Could I not also look good on a night of celebration? I could allow myself a small slice of indulgence.

"Maybe I'll put my hair in a bun and add the sunflowers to it," I suggested, already envisioning how the yellow blooms would contrast against my dark locks.

She nodded in mindless agreement as she lost herself in the choices of baby pink fabric and lavender lace. My dress was enough to look the part. It was enough for people to notice my attendance, but it wasn't so elaborate that I couldn't kill Prince Tillo in it. Silk would wash clean, after all.

The event would be filled with many faces from more than one kingdom. There would be so many fingers to point, and his sudden death would come before the marriage could become official.

No alliance would be formed for King Valen.

It would be the first of many of his pawns to be removed from the board and sit beside me, marking the first move in his descent into madness.

His first loss would be a mighty loss for him. It would be the biggest blow I could give him. I wanted to start strong, and he loved nothing as much as he loved his precious Tillo. The golden child, the heir apparent, the one who could do no wrong in his father's eyes.

King Valen would have such a brief amount of time to bury his son and renegotiate a marriage to his younger heir. The heir that he ruled out so entirely of ever having a say in anything. If the idea of the lesser son sitting on his throne didn't drive him insane, then the prophecy moving one step closer to reality would.

Perhaps Prince Tillo's death would be so sudden and devastating that the king would stop holding anything else as a priority. Other rulers would see him as weak and incapable. After all, he would be the first ruler to lose a child or a prized heir under such circumstances. Others would look at him as I did, long past who he used to be. Long past the man he was twenty-two years ago when he slaughtered my entire village.

He'd be a washed-up king, not worthy of such a prized marriage or alliance, destined to sit on a collapsed throne of madness. And I would be there, patient as a spider in her web, ready to help him fall the rest of the way.

Chapter Five
THE NEWEST PIECE ON THE BOARD

Lanira

Princess Invidia held tightly to my arm. She acted as if she were an excitable puppy. Distracted by every small glint of stones that were used as accessories on every woman around. The jewelry caught the light from crystal chandeliers, sending sparkles dancing across her face. She left me behind when she saw a jewel the same size as her hand. She was speaking to the girl before she was entirely in her presence.

It was her entire personality to be a free spirit. She never considered anything she did before she did it. It looked like an enviable position to be in. I couldn't imagine what it must have been like to live without considering every breath I took. Another part of me thought it must have been its own prison. In the end, she was so carefree that she wouldn't have been able to survive if it weren't for having others to take care of everything for her.

I let her go without a struggle and continued through the crowd to the inner room. Small tables lined the halls with more flowers and candles. Their flames flickered in the gentle mountain breeze that drifted through tall windows. The vacation castle was a contrast to their home. It was a place where the king reigned supreme, and gold was the highlight of the rooms instead of an accessory.

My own castle would be soaked in emerald and crimson. I'd not have passive battles with the others who lived in my court.

The rooms were lively. Filled with laughter and drinks. The scent of wine and roasted meat mingled with expensive perfumes. The ballroom was too big to see the other side, with too many bodies swirling in silk and velvet. Portraits of older kings lined the walls, and the ceiling was decorated with stained glass flowers that cast rainbow patterns on the floor below. Perfume smoke curled in the air from incense holders on tables with golden cloth covering them.

A group of men sat elevated above the rest of us and played instruments to keep the crowd lively. The melody was light and celebratory, washing over conversations like honey. The center of the room was reserved for dancing. There wasn't a care in the world inside those walls.

"I can't believe they brought the help to a ball," a girl moving past me whispered, her voice like a blade hidden in velvet.

"And they let her dress so nicely," the other agreed, their disdain practically dripping from each word.

They spoke loud enough that I could hear them on purpose. If I had forgotten my own home and my family, it wouldn't have mattered. Hardly any court ladies would allow me to forget where I came from. I didn't allow myself to join their happiness because I already knew that I'd be treated with resentment.

I held my dress up and bowed. "Maybe I can also attend your engagement celebration one day. You are considerably older than I am, so it would be an honor to dress for that occasion and show my respect."

"Perhaps no man will have her because of how her tongue wags," Princess Invidia interjected, appearing at my side like a golden-haired guardian.

"Hmm. I suppose you are right," I agreed, though inside I smiled at their flushed faces.

I had already spoken out of line enough. I'd not push my luck. Instead, I pulled Princess Invidia further inside. I caught the Queen in the corner of my eye and knew I needed her to see me. She held a soft spot for me, and I wanted to use it. After I killed her son, she would defend me if there was suspicion, and I needed strongly aligned voices in my corner willing to speak out in public to defend me. I had to play my pieces well and keep the valuable ones close.

We moved to the Queen, and she held her hand up from a smaller chair on the right side of the king's throne and used her fingers to gently wave. The rings on her fingers caught the light as she gestured.

The sound from the musicians playing carried well enough to drown out individual conversations. They muffled the sound of footsteps and the whispers of lovers stealing moments in alcoves.

"Queen Blair, you look magnificent. The purple makes your blonde hair glow," I gushed as I stepped down from her throne.

I made sure to always remain lower than she was. It was a subtle and passive way of ensuring she always felt above me. No one ever considered someone they felt above a threat.

Her already pink cheeks flushed further, and she patted her hand over the French braids on her head. The truth was that she looked old and tired. Her hair was thin at the bottom, brittle from years of elaborate styling. It was as if she lacked something vital in her diet. She refused to cut it, citing that she needed the length. She refused to listen to anyone who tried to tell her that broken length didn't make it look good.

I thought it was a testament to the way she held onto a boxed-off idea of youth and femininity. She wasn't able to adapt to the idea that she was aged. She could have been strong and beautiful if she had accepted that things change with time, and it didn't make them less valuable.

I thought that there was a beauty in aging; time could have made her wiser and beautiful in a different way. In a way that perfect wrinkle-free skin could never understand. She could have embraced the healthy aspects of her hair and her life and moved forward as a teacher.

Instead, she was a wasted space covered in signs of stress and exhaustion.

"You girls look wonderful, too," Queen Blair proclaimed as she stood, her joints creaking slightly with the movement.

She moved us to the side of her seat, where the princes of Saydeen stood and chattered. Their conversation halted as we approached.

"Princess Sala. These are my daughters," Queen Blair declared with a smile that didn't quite reach her eyes.

Both princes glanced at me without their smiles when the words left her lips. Of course, I noticed. I noticed everything. I wouldn't let them throw me off my path. Their unacceptance was not a shock.

"It is nice to meet you, Princess Sala," I murmured as I bowed again.

I was the only one to do so. I was the only one who would have to continue to do so all night. It was a clear indication that I was not her daughter. If I did not bow, the king would have my head.

I wasn't firmly against the act of bowing because it was also a joy that I was allowed to hold in silence. It was a way that I could announce that I wasn't part of her family. A small act of defiance that I could claim was out of my control.

I wasn't her daughter. I was the girl they took in. The child that should have been tossed into the fire just to make sure. I was openly kept at a distance as a reminder that although I was close, I was never near. I had to bow or be punished by the king. He'd claim I was spoiled and thought of myself as an equal. I also had to please the queen, which meant that late at night, I'd be the one to help take her hair down and brush it out while her blood daughter lived in her own world.

She'd forgive me for the bow, then, while she no doubt thought of the daughter who had no time for her.

"You're beautiful!" Princess Invidia exclaimed, her enthusiasm cutting through the tension.

Princess Sala blushed and smiled without parting her lips. "As are you."

The princess of Saydeean had strongly defined features and dark brown eyes that seemed to hold secrets. Her hair was so black that it was nearly blue in the lights, styled in an intricate pattern with tiny diamonds woven throughout. She was covered in diamonds from her wrists to her ears, each stone catching light like captured stars.

"I'm excited to have you as a part of our family. What is it like in Saydeean? Your family didn't join you? Will they meet us in our kingdom?" Princess Invidia asked the questions tumbling out in a rush.

Princess Sala shook her head, and her jewels chimed softly. "My mother is not to leave our kingdom. She can't risk her life in such a way. It was months of convincing for this alliance as it was. I do hope to go see them once we have settled, but that is a conversation for another time."

Princess Sala spoke with such confidence that it was hard to remember that both girls in front of me were princesses of the same age. One felt so much more experienced. It was like seeing both princes side by side. A sharp contrast in wisdom and maturity.

"Saydeean is a beautiful land. It's much different than here. You have mountains, and we have sand dunes. Our castle is made of glass. You can see inside every room from the outside. Rainbows appear in ways you wouldn't believe!" Princess Sala gushed, her eyes lighting up with genuine warmth.

A glass kingdom would be easy to shatter. The thought made me smile behind my carefully neutral expression.

"That sounds beautiful," Prince Tillo interjected, his voice cutting through the moment like a blade.

He walked slowly into the group and stood between the two princesses, inserting himself into the conversation with the entitlement that came naturally to him.

"You two have already met?" Princess Invidia asked, her brow furrowing in confusion.

"Of course, it would be strange for this to be the first thing we discussed," Prince Tillo scolded, his tone dismissive.

"Give him a bit more credit," I nudged Princess Invidia gently.

I had stood as a quiet listener for too long.

"I have heard much about you," Princess Sala observed, looking in my direction with curious eyes.

"I'm sure none of it is true," Princess Invidia blurted, always quick to defend me.

Prince Tillo shrugged with calculated indifference. "Some of it probably is."

"I heard that you were there that day in Lunadur. That you saw the slaughter. I heard whispers that you were cursed by a witch. That you've got a lock placed on you, hidden somewhere safe to keep prying eyes away from finding it." Princess Sala also shrugged, but her eyes remained kind. "It is likely not true. But word of you travels farther than your feet have ever stepped. I want you to know that I think it is shameful the way so many high advisors carry a young girl's name on their lips as if they have nothing better to do. My home thrives off of fairy tale stories passed around. It's common for a whisper to be picked up and turned into a fantasy."

I only noticed the way Prince Tillo furrowed his brows at her, his expression growing darker by the moment.

"I thank you, princess. I dare not speak ill of anyone above my station, but I'll do my best to return your kindness," I responded with a smile, though her words had struck closer to home than she knew.

"I'll speak it for you. You are to be part of my family also, are you not? Where I come from, family is a bond not created only by blood. It is stronger than blood, and we take care of each other no matter where the fruit was borne." Princess Sala placed her hand on my shoulder and squeezed gently.

I held a bit of pride for myself for just a moment. If I had wanted her trust, I would have been one move closer to having it. I was quiet enough to feel harmless but enough of a presence to be noticed.

"You'll need to worry more about the children you will need to bear," Prince Tillo interjected, his words dropping like stones into water.

I felt the pressure on my brows and knew all of our faces were imitations of the next. Shock and disgust pointed like a light straight at him. The air around us seemed to crystallize with offense.

"Does she look like a cow to you?" My mouth fell open in disbelief.

"I have to agree. You only just met, and that's what you have to offer? Father may have given you the best education tutors could provide, but he clearly slacked when it came to manners," Princess Invidia shook her head in disappointment.

I nodded in agreement, watching as his face flushed with embarrassment and anger.

"I only meant we all have a duty to fulfill and a role to play. It should be our focus. Friendship won't matter if we don't uphold our given agreements," Prince Tillo defended, though his voice lacked conviction.

Princess Sala lifted a glass of wine from the passing maids with serving trays and drank it in one swift lift. The liquid caught the light like liquid ruby. I wanted to join her.

"If you'll excuse me, I think that I've worn out my welcome for now," Prince Tillo declared with a small bow before he left us.

It was an act of mocking, and I felt my nostrils flare with barely contained rage.

"I'm sorry for his manners. He's nervous," Princess Invidia pleaded, her voice small with shame.

Princess Sala smiled, though something distant flickered in her eyes. "There's no need to apologize on his behalf. We have the rest of our lives to get to know each other. There's no need to let one nervous interaction set any uncomfortable tones."

Despite her words, the air was uncomfortable between the three of us. I took a bit of relief in the thought that Prince Tillo and Princess Sala did not seem like a good match. It made what I was going to do easier. I wouldn't be breaking up a potential love. I'd be saving her from a life of misery.

Perhaps it was King Valen's gaze that made me convinced there was tension. His eyes rested on us as if he were analyzing every smile, cataloging each laugh and gesture. The weight of his observation made my skin crawl.

King Valen watched who smiled too widely and who didn't laugh hard enough. I'd seen the look before in the eyes of predators before they lunged. His focus was the heaviest on the princess of Saydeean. He looked as if he were already suspicious of her. As if her efforts to fit in and act as a princess should made her something to be threatened by.

I seemed to be the only one with eyes on King Valen. Even Queen Blair had her eyes forward, focused on the dancing couples swirling across the marble floor. I allowed my gaze to paint over the sight in the golden ballroom until it landed on what everyone else focused on.

A new figure had entered the room, tall, imposing, with the bearing of a warrior. The crowd seemed to part around him like water around a stone, whispers following in his wake. This had to be the escort from RuneHold. The vampire hunter who had brought Princess Sala safely to her new life.

The final piece was sliding into place on my chessboard.

Chapter Six
THE BISHOP HAS FALLEN

Lanira

Queen Blair moved in front of us all. She had the spirit of a young girl meeting the man everyone wanted. Her eyes lit up, and she grabbed his hand with an enthusiasm that seemed genuine for the first time all evening.

"And this is Ravi. He is the First Blade of the Hunters," Queen Blair announced with pride. "Was your journey easy? Should you need anything while you're here, my staff is your staff. Do not hesitate to ask them anything."

The First Blade was supposed to be the head of the vampire hunters' guardian section. He was second only to the Commander of the Hunters, who led the army of RuneHold.

"You're too kind, your highness. My room already has everything I could need during my stay here. I intend to see you all back to your home and then head back to mine," Ravi responded, his voice carrying a formality that felt rehearsed.

He didn't look as if he were the head of anything. There was hardly anything impressive about him. He didn't show any hint of muscle mass beneath his clothing or a single scar to show he had been through anything. His build was lean rather than imposing, almost scholarly in its slenderness.

The only prominent thing about him was the two shades of green inside his almond eyes. One was much darker than the other, as if there had been damage to one. His brows spoke for him while his mouth was still tightly shut. Thick things that rose on one side as he trailed his gaze up and down my body.

I bowed again. "It's nice to meet you."

"I assume you are Lady Lanira," Ravi acknowledged.

I glanced at the Queen. No one had added 'lady' before my name. I didn't have a title in any official form beyond the princess companion.

"She is simply Lanira," the Queen declared with a feigned laugh.

The twitch that spasmed on the corners of her lips was a shock to see. It was the first time since I met her that I had witnessed her show any sign of resentment at the idea of me being a titled member of the royal family.

"It is strange, isn't it?" Ravi rubbed his bare jaw thoughtfully. "To have her treated as and act like a maid, but be allowed to join and speak as a royal? I apologize for my mistake. I assumed that she would have some sort of title to her name."

The Queen gave a second forced laugh, and it still took me by surprise.

"She has no title because when the time is right, she will be titled as the second princess of Emberrella. In the meantime, please don't disgrace her name with such a low status again," the Queen proclaimed with unexpected steel in her voice.

She reached up and stroked the hairs that flew away from the bottom of my hairline. Her nails trailed the base of my skull, and I half expected her to dig them in with the way she started the conversation.

Still, she never applied pressure. She was gentle and smiled at me with the eyes of a mother. They were as soft as her touch was.

I smiled in return, but I didn't speak. It wasn't a good time for me to insert anything. Even if it was a comment about being grateful. I knew when to shut my mouth.

Ravi held his arm out for me to take. "I've created a tense situation, I can see. Care to dance? Consider it my apology for an incorrect greeting."

I looked to Queen Blair for permission before I made a move. She nodded with a smile; she waved me off and whispered 'go'. I took his arm and allowed him to take the lead. The warmth of his touch was unexpected; most people ran cold compared to my vampire metabolism.

The trick was to ensure the smile met your eyes. If only your lips smiled, then it was a failure. Everyone depended on their eyes for the final true conclusion. If you could fake your emotion with your eyes, even your lips didn't matter.

He wrapped his arm around my waist and pulled me tightly into him. His other hand took mine, and he led our footsteps with surprising grace. The music swelled around us, a waltz that seemed to echo off the high ceiling.

"The sunflowers look good in your hair," Ravi observed.

"Thank you. They are my favorite flowers," I replied, wondering if there was hidden meaning in his comment.

"Hmm." He nodded, studying my face. "It's not a flower that someone would normally wear to a celebration, unless you're expecting to run into a vampire."

"There weren't many other options," I responded carefully. "They didn't set up much variation in the garden or vases."

He leaned closer to me and inhaled near my exposed collarbone. He trailed his nose up and stopped near my lips before taking another breath. The intimacy of the gesture made my skin crawl, though I forced myself to remain still.

Could he smell the blood?

"That is a beautiful scent you're wearing," he murmured, spinning the two of us through another group dancing before he spoke again. "Princess Sala is excited for her marriage tomorrow. She thinks she will be marrying into a lovely family."

He phrased the sentence as a question, waiting for my response.

"She is right. The LeBlancs are a noble family with high morals and values. She won't find someone to treat her better than Prince Tillo," I answered, the lies flowing smoothly from my lips.

"I haven't seen much, but I already disagree with your sentiment," he declared.

He took my fingers and twirled me again before he placed his hand on my back and dipped me to the ground. The two of us were so close that I felt his breath on my lips. The scent of mint and something sharper, steel, perhaps, filled my nostrils.

He never took his eyes off mine, and I wondered how he moved so easily around the others without looking. "Did you know you have small red flecks in your eyes?"

He shouldn't have been able to see anything in my eyes. The lenses should have hidden everything.

"Did you know that your bottom lip is fuller than the top?" I responded, deflecting with observation of my own.

He chuckled, a sound that was warmer than I'd expected. "You are quick on your feet."

"Is that supposed to be a compliment?" I asked.

He didn't speak in response, but his brows did move closer together while he continued to study me. He didn't seem as if he were anything special, but the way he looked at me began to chip away at a deeper part of myself.

A part that was so confident in my ability to blend in. Red eyes were for vampires; there was no exception.

There was no other reason to have such a thing.

His duty was to kill me if he suspected me.

I couldn't allow myself to squirm under pressure and hand him a reason to be suspicious. I was good at covering my tracks. Even if he was skilled enough to be the First Blade of the Hunters, I was still better.

"If you only brought me out here to dance so that you could question me on the marriage, then you are far from the gentleman that your title suggested. Prince Tillo will treat the Princess well because he wants to please his father. There's nothing you need to worry about. I'll excuse myself now." I dropped his hand and tried to pull myself from his body.

He did not drop his arm from my waist, and although he didn't appear as though he was much, his grip was tight around me. There was strength hidden in that lean frame after all.

"I didn't mean to offend you," he offered, his voice softening along with his expression.

"I am not offended. I simply want to go. You look at me as if I'm a meal and question me as if I am a prisoner," I allowed my own brows to furrow in practiced irritation. "I don't know anyone who would enjoy such a thing."

"I apologize, Lady Lanira. You simply seem to be more complex than most of the others here." He dropped his arm from my waist and offered me a bow instead of waiting for mine.

"You'll see my head separated from my body if you continue to put lady in front of my name," I grumbled.

I returned the gesture with a quick bow of my own. I made my way back to Princess Invidia, weaving through couples who were becoming increasingly unsteady on their feet. She had not wasted a single moment of time while I danced. The liquor was pure and strong on her breath. I hadn't gotten close enough to take a whiff myself before I knew it was her that reeked of it.

If they really wanted to chase vampires away, they didn't need to use sunflowers; they could have just increased the amount of liquor they drank. The scent was unbearable, and the blood tasted even worse when tainted. If everyone stayed drunk, the vampires would die off for fear of the sickness that we would get if we drank from them.

Princess Invidia hardly noticed my arrival back at her side as she laughed with Princess Sala. I wanted it to remain that way. I had done enough speaking and smiling for one day. I wanted the evening to hurry along. For the drinking to intensify.

I wanted everyone in attendance to have blurred memories of their evening because it would change the course of the months to come.

I wanted Ravi, the First Blade of the Hunters, to take his eyes off of me. I wanted him to busy himself elsewhere before he ruined my evening as well. I wouldn't have another moment so perfect again.

"It seems you've noticed it, too," Koen mentioned as he moved beside me.

I glanced at him in silence. One must never speak first. It's a rule to live by. It's how you get caught in something you may otherwise have avoided. You always allow the other person to reveal what they mean first.

"The drinking is out of hand so early in the night," Koen shook his head. "They arrived thinking that they'd be in attendance until the sun rose, but they'd all surely be sprawled across barren floors before long."

"Should you not be joining them?" I asked.

"And miss such an opportunity as to spend an evening with you?" His smile was crooked. "If only the staff is half sober, imagine how easy it would be for the two of us to sneak away."

"You dream while awake," I replied dismissively. "Should you not be with King Valen?"

"I've been watching you stand alone all night. I wanted to tell you that you look beyond beautiful in that dress. I can't stop thinking about what's underneath it," Koen whispered, his words slurring slightly.

He spoke to me, and he spoke sweetly. It still meant little to me. It meant even less when my eyes were still locked on the man who called himself a vampire hunter.

"Koen, you must get back to the king before you pull suspicions onto us," I urged.

I did not allow him the chance to speak again. I moved forward to Princess Invidia and took the drink from her hand. She hardly held it well, the crystal glass trembling in her grip.

"Lanira!" She squawked in protest.

I set the cup down on the chair that was beside her and took her hand in mine. Princess Sala paid no attention to either of us and instead focused on finding a new group to celebrate with. I checked my surroundings a second time, but Ravi was gone. A small part of me was on edge, but a bigger part of me did not see him as a threat.

Princess Invidia mumbled on about what, I was not sure. The words slurred together into incomprehensible sounds. I hardly understood anything that she spoke of. When I laid her in her blankets and removed her shoes, she stopped mumbling. She stretched as if she were a cat and made no other sound.

I ruffled my side of the bed and tucked pillows around to create the impression of a sleeping body. If the princess were to stir and look, she'd think I slept beside her. I removed my own shoes and changed into a nightdress. It was much more casual. Plain black silk from my ankles to my wrists. The ball gown exposed more skin, but this would be better for what I needed to do.

I used my hands to apply pressure to the door and allow it to open quietly. The hinges made no sound, a blessing in this old castle. I used my bare toes to sneak through the cold hallway toward Prince Tillo's room. The candlelight gave away my shadow, but what did it matter when no eyes were around to see it?

Prince Tillo was not in his room. He would no doubt be soon enough, probably stumbling back from another attempt to charm someone. I pushed things around his already cluttered desk. I didn't understand how he had the time to make such a mess when we had only arrived that same day. His outward appearance would never have allowed anyone to think he was so disastrous when alone.

It seemed I wasn't the only one hiding something on the inside. Prince Tillo and I hardly had time to grow a relationship. I supposed I couldn't speak of him being a deceiver. I hardly had anything to go off of for such a conclusion.

He would die with a good reputation among the citizens, and another kingdom would be sent into ruin for killing such a well-organized future king.

"Until tomorrow, my princess!" Prince Tillo called out to Princess Sala before he slammed his door.

The motion was hard enough to knock things around on the tables. I shoved myself under his desk. I wouldn't have had the time to move anywhere else. He stopped and stood in front of my hiding place and stripped his clothing off piece by piece.

My lip curled downward at the sight of him unbuttoning his shirt. His being half-dressed would help things look a bit more natural, but the sight of him was unappealing. He was pale where he should have been bronzed. Ravi likely had more to see beneath his clothes. His grip had been strong, which meant there had to have been something lurking beneath that fabric.

Unbelievable. I was unbelievable. Here I was, hiding under a desk with a knife, thinking about a vampire hunter's physique.

I needed to focus. Prince Tillo struggled with his buttons and had only one shoe on. His look could have easily been mistaken for someone who was in a fight or even an intimate encounter. He turned to face me, and I pulled out the knife I kept around my ankle.

It was small, and I had to press a button to release the blade, but it was important to me. It was hand-etched with the design of a sunflower by my brother. I'd help his soul rest and ease mine by using it to kill Tillo. The metal was cold against my palm, a comfort I'd carried for years.

I moved from under the desk, and he stumbled back. He opened his mouth and furrowed his brows, confusion and alcohol slowing his reaction. His balance was his biggest challenge until I plunged my knife into his chest.

The blade slid between his ribs with less resistance than I'd expected. I watched his face change from harsh contortion while he looked at my hands around the knife to soft and falling. His lips drooped, and he coughed blood that spattered across my night-dress. I felt the beating of his heart on the sides of my hands that were against his chest.

I wanted to enjoy watching him die. I wanted to give him a speech or teach him about my siblings. I had planned to let him die, knowing that his family would think he was murdered by another kingdom. Maybe even his bride-to-be.

Instead, I was distracted by the sound of his heart and the smell of his blood. Thump, thump. It was the only sound that filled my ears, drowning out everything else. The need that grew inside of me, I was unable to ignore.

"Your eyes," he grunted, his voice wet with blood.

They must have already turned red. I never could hide them while in a frenzy. My hands shook around the knife as I watched the blood pour like a waterfall down his chest. I didn't understand why I was so affected. I had blood from Koen. It should have helped me remain in control.

If I bit him, there was nothing that I could have done to cover the bite marks. I fought against myself with every ounce of willpower I possessed. There was a vampire hunter in the castle. He already spoke to me as if he knew something more. The bite marks would send me spiraling into the spotlight.

My fangs were tearing through the skin on his chest before I was able to consider resisting further. The warm liquid filled my body with fire that rushed through my veins like lava. I gulped like a starved calf. Like I hadn't seen or smelled blood in years.

I gulped as if I were going to drain him completely.

He scratched at me. Hard at first, his nails digging into my arms, but he was quick to become motionless.

Even with all the alcohol, his blood tasted sweet. I should have felt sick from the liquor in his system. He must have faked how much he drank.

I felt his pulse stop while I still drank, and it's what pulled me back to my senses. The silence where his heartbeat should have been was deafening.

He was dead. I was covered in his blood. They would know it was a vampire, and I would have a lot to cover up and get rid of. My breath came in short pants as the reality of what I'd done, what I'd lost control of, settled in.

My black gown was wet with the blood that had drained from him before I fed. I'd have to clean myself up and destroy my clothing before I slept. But first, I had to make sure no one would think to look for a vampire.

The knife was still embedded in his chest. I pulled it free and wiped it clean on his discarded shirt before tucking it back against my ankle. Then I forced myself to focus, to think like the predator I was rather than the starved creature I'd become.

I had work to do.

Chapter Seven
Burning Embers

Lanira

The sun had hardly peeked over the horizon when it woke me. It wouldn't have on any other occasion, but I slept lightly last night. The golden light filtering through the heavy curtains felt different, somehow warmer, more promising. Trying to sleep when I knew there was a momentous event only hours away had resulted in tossing and turning.

Maybe I should have been restless because I killed the prince. I thought, before I had done it, that it may have haunted me. I feared that I may have had a softer side of myself that wouldn't make it through such an event.

It was a waste of my time. I hadn't ever felt more alive. I had never felt more satisfied. The blood still hummed in my veins like a song of victory.

I felt as though my family was one step closer to peace or revival.

My eyes felt heavy, but my spirits felt high. I stretched in my blankets and let my smile push itself forward. It was only I who would know it was there. Princess Invidia snored on her side of the bed, completely oblivious to what had transpired mere rooms away.

I had my own room, but sleeping beside her after a drunken night felt as if it was a good alibi. She slept through all my movements anyway, lost in whatever dreams alcohol had gifted her. I pushed the blanket off just enough to slide out of bed. I wore a white slip. It was not as modest as the others. Thin straps allowed me to see that I was scratched by Prince Tillo.

Three of his fingernails had torn through the top of my forearm, leaving angry red welts that would need explaining. I moved to the fireplace, grabbed four more logs, and placed them inside, where I had burned my other slip from last night. The flames danced higher, consuming any evidence. I used the poker to move debris around before I added the rest of the logs. Any evidence had spent the night in flames, but I couldn't risk letting it die down yet.

If anyone went through the ash, they might find a sign or two of what I did. I'd make sure to keep adding logs myself until we left to prevent it. It wouldn't look suspicious if I dumped the tray of ash myself. It was within my duties.

It was the best I could do to clean up my own mess. I didn't want to worry about my bloody clothes when I needed to focus on hiding the scratches on my arm.

During the ball, Ravi never confirmed anything aloud, but he sniffed me as if his nose were made for the scent of old blood. If that were why he was so interested in my scent, I'd have a lot of trouble ahead. The memory of his breath against my collarbone made my skin crawl.

I left the logs to burn and crawled back into bed. I wanted the scene to be as believable as possible. Princess Invidia and I needed to wake up together. She and I needed to experience the pain of finding out together. I wanted to watch her eyes as she fully digested what the evening brought to her doorstep while she carelessly drank and enjoyed her time.

I kept myself distant from all of them so that when the moment they all died came, I wouldn't feel sadness.

Despite wanting to stay awake, I dozed off again and was woken a second time by screaming. I knew it was time. There was a difference in the scream from a startle or a bug and the scream of agony. This was the latter, raw, primal, the sound of someone's world shattering.

Princess Invidia shot up beside me. The blankets were ripped off my body by her sudden movement. I had to pull myself together because the smile on my lips didn't want to leave.

It was no time for another slip-up. I already used the one mistake I was allowed to make when I drank from Prince Tillo.

I shot up and turned to her. "Are you okay?"

"Did you hear that?" She asked, her voice small and frightened in the morning light.

A second scream sounded from another voice, and the Princess was on her feet. I jumped from the sheets to follow her out. My heartbeat was faster than the sounds of her bare toes hitting the stone floor as she rushed toward the commotion.

I rounded the corner and bit my lip to hold down the emotions threatening to burst out of me.

Guards gathered, and two maids cried into each other's arms. They pointed inside the room with trembling fingers, but it wasn't the guards who followed; it was Ravi. His presence commanded attention even in chaos.

I had hoped that enough people would have been in and out of the room to disturb as many things as possible. He entered the room first, and the guards followed. The princess spoke to the maids and set her sights on me before she finished speaking.

Her eyes gave me exactly what I wanted. I watched the slight movements of her lips as they quivered. The small, almost imperceptible blinks of her eyelids as she processed what they may have seen.

I watched the water well up on the inner corners of her golden eyes.

My heart fluttered. It skipped a beat, and the child inside of me who cried over her family cracked a smile as well.

I forced a frown and moved closer to her. I rushed and pushed another maid aside to hurry and stand by her side. I grabbed her arm in the same way we so often did and leaned into her.

"What's wrong? You look as though you're about to cry," I whispered, making my voice soft with concern.

Her chin quivered before her words left her. "It's Tillo, he. He—"

I looked at her and forced my brows to push in on themselves, creating the perfect picture of worried confusion.

I pulled myself into my imagination for a moment. I was a child again. I was small, and I had fallen while trying to wrangle the animals; I had failed. Ash would lovingly tuck my hair behind my ears before he spoke.

I reached up and tucked Princess Invidia's hair in the same way, mimicking my brother's gentle touch.

Carefully, I moved it all away from her face. I traced my fingers gently over her skin to ensure that she felt loved. That she never felt suspicious of me, because I was so delicate with her.

I lowered myself down to look up at her the same way one would a child. "What is it?"

"He's dead," she rasped, the words catching in her throat. "They think it was a vampire attack."

I gasped and pulled her into my chest just as my brother would have done to me. My fingers went through her hair as if they were a comb. The blonde strands were a matted disaster from sleep, and it made my fingers catch.

It was less of a loving gesture and more of a bother, but she wouldn't know the difference.

"How could this have happened?" I murmured against her hair.

Ravi exited the doorway and cleared his throat, the sound cutting through the morning air like a blade. "We will be holding interrogations and testing the blood of everyone inside these walls. Please do not try to leave or resist. I will consider you guilty and take you back to my kingdom with me as a suspected vampire. We think it is likely a woman, as the scent of perfume is still in the room. We will start there."

My breath caught in my chest. I hadn't considered that I would need to avoid such a test so soon. I thought I'd have more time. I hadn't prepared any blood or emptied the ashes in the bedroom.

Ravi moved too quickly. I hadn't planned my next step until I brought the princess her breakfast.

"Let me go get you some tea. It will help you stay calm until we know all of the details," I offered, my voice steady despite the panic clawing at my chest.

She tried to resist, but I stopped her. I had to leave her. I had to find a mouse. I needed blood that wasn't mine before Ravi's eyes fell on me.

"Please, sister." I paused to clear my throat and pretend to shove down my tears. "Let me mourn him by taking care of you if you fall sick or or—"

"Okay. Tea will be nice," she agreed, her voice hollow with shock.

I smiled at her, and instead of making a small gesture, I pulled her into an embrace. I buried my head into her hair until I could hardly breathe. From her or any other passing eyes, the two of us would appear as mourners.

What I needed was her scent. Her perfume on me to cover my own. Hers was more expensive, bolder, layers of jasmine and rose that would mask my simpler lavender. It should have had no problem covering my own perfume. It was the only move I could make. I had to prioritize my scent, which Ravi already noted at the ball, or be able to hide my blood if it were tested.

I let go of her and turned in the direction of the kitchen. It was easier to show genuine emotion when my heart raced so hard I felt it in my throat. I walked as casually as I assumed one would after hearing such grisly news. I watched the ground with a frown on my face and water in my eyes.

"Have you heard? They've decided that it's the princess of Say-deean or Lanira."

"Lanira? The Saydeean, I understand, but Lanira?"

"The King blamed Lanira, and the Queen blamed the princess."

The maids whispered as they scurried past me, their words like arrows finding their mark.

My vision tunneled for a moment before my eyes blurred. My heart pounded in my ears before I sorted out my sight and pulled myself back.

It was then that I noticed I didn't have shoes on. The cold stone bit at my feet, grounding me in the moment. It was then that I felt the sinking feeling of an eye heavy on me. I tried my best to resist the glance, but the feeling was too strong.

I allowed my eyes to shift upward, and Ravi met my glance. He had already watched every step that I took from the shadows that he stood in.

Did he suspect me? His face was too barren to tell what he thought. He could have been thinking anything from the morning being chilly, to being set on my guilt, and I'd not know.

My stomach dropped, but it wasn't quite fear or excitement. I felt somewhere in the middle, nervous yet ready to prove that he wasn't as smart as he thought.

I wanted to challenge him. I wanted to prove that I was smarter, tougher than his title. That, even nameless, I could slip under his eye.

I shifted my eyes back to the ground and away from the shaggy black hair and thick brows that pressed against me from the hallway. He looked the part of a hunter. He stood tall and examined everything, but I wouldn't allow him to outmaneuver me.

My plans were fine. A few hiccups would not halt me. That's all they were. My hunger may have gotten the best of me, but it meant that I would be beyond satisfied and able to continue without worry.

I walked on the tips of my bare toes across the cold floor of the kitchen. Chaos had reached every corner of the castle before I arrived. The chefs and maids cried together with hardly a scrap of food in sight. Pots sat abandoned, fires left unattended.

Maybe King Valen would get so distracted by the lack of duties done that he'd be too busy with their punishments to think of me. I should have known he would consider me so quickly. I was foolish for not considering how much he disliked me.

I grabbed a kettle and set it on the open kitchen fire. I had no idea what I grabbed from the herb collection, but it smelled good enough to make a sweet tea. A maid glanced over at me, and I stirred the liquid and pressed the sleeve of my dress into my palm. I wanted the fabric to stay close and hide my arm. There wasn't a tear in sight, but I'd make the motion all the same.

I couldn't risk it.

She lingered on me for a moment as if she weren't convinced. I kept my head facing the kettle but allowed my eyes to drift. She stepped towards me, and I bit down on my own tongue until it caused tears to well up in my eyes.

I only ended up angry when she was pulled away by a higher-ranking maid and tossed orders. My mouth throbbed for nothing. I resisted the urge to toss the teacup and pot onto a tray. Everything was set. I only needed to find the mouse.

I had to find a way to calm down. I'd only draw suspicion to myself if I acted suspicious. If I were confident that I had nothing to do with his death, others would believe it, too.

I moved into the pantry and pretended to shuffle through nonsense on the wooden racks stacked against every wall. The scent of dried herbs and preserved meats filled my nostrils. I checked my surroundings before I lowered myself to the ground. I knew the mice hid in the lowest part of the shelving. They were left undisturbed, and there was food. Two mice squeaked and played just as I knew they would.

I reached my hand out, and they both ran. My arm wasn't long enough to reach where they'd scurried. It was only the first group I saw. I had no need to panic so soon. I stood and moved to another corner and bent back down.

Barren.

I circled my pointer fingers against my temples, feeling a headache building behind my eyes. A backup plan wouldn't be too hard.

I just needed time to think.

Where else would have easy access to blood?

Chatter sounded loudly from outside the pantry. Guards had arrived, their boots echoing on stone.

I grabbed a small glass jar no bigger than my finger and snuck with my bare feet out of the pantry. A pig sat on the middle counter. It waited for dinner, still untouched, its pink flesh pale in the morning light. I held the jar under its neck and sliced it with my nail.

It didn't need to be deep or pouring. It only needed to be enough for what Ravi might demand.

"Lanira! There you are. The vampire hunter wants you. He declares you should be publicly tested," a familiar guard announced, his voice cutting through my concentration.

I furrowed my brows with confusion. I only needed to buy a few more seconds for the slow drip to fill the vial.

"Lanira, move!" He commanded, impatience coloring his tone.

"I don't understand what I did," I cracked my voice and shifted my eyes down to the vial, watching the dark liquid gather drop by drop.

He marched closer to me. "I didn't come here to chat. I came to take you where you're required."

"Can't you understand why this stranger scares me?" I pleaded, letting genuine fear creep into my voice, though not for the reasons he'd assume.

I glanced down at the vial; it needed a bit more. It was small, discreet, but the cut wasn't deep enough to fill it quickly.

"Can't you understand why I wouldn't want to get in trouble for you lingering?" He shot back. "We're both in a predicament. If you hurry up, it'll be easy to get out of!"

I glanced down again, and the jar was nearly full. I only needed a few more seconds.

"Lanira!"

"Okay," I relented and tucked the vial into my sleeve, feeling the cool glass against my skin. "I don't want any trouble."

I moved ahead of him with my hands placed flat on my skirt, the weight of my deception hidden in silk and determination.

Chapter Eight
The Vial of Victory

Lanira

I'd never voice it out loud, but being escorted by guards that I knew well, being practically herded through halls that I helped prepare for many celebrations inside of, I felt a sense of exhilaration. My skin prickled, and my lips wanted to lift in triumph. If the face I wore inside could have been seen by everyone, I'd never have stood a chance. I'd have been caught right away.

I'd bought my time, and I'd planned every step I'd take for so long that it was hard to believe the pieces were moving. I was excited. Would King Valen have tears streaming down his cheeks? Would he be so distraught that he sent the Queen to deal with me? Would he be forced to skip a meal out of sorrow? The thought of his pain made warmth bloom in my chest.

The candles did not flicker bright enough to match the rise in my joy, but the sun did.

Prince Tillo was a perfect place to kick off the prophecy they believed so deeply in. He would be missed, but not by me. He would be considered the first pawn to move across a board that many more would journey through, and nothing more to me.

I kept my head down and my palms just as flat when we entered the iron hall. It was as close to a dungeon above ground as a room could get. Anyone thought to have committed a crime was sent there first. The walls were lined with cold metal that seemed to absorb warmth and hope alike.

Blood tests occurred in small or large quantities depending on the king's mood. Sometimes, they took a head just to be sure of the person's innocence. Alchemists of RuneHold traded truth serums and other tools to aid in whatever the king desired. In exchange, he sent rare fruits and herbs.

I didn't care about a truth serum or hypnosis. The alchemists were skilled, but nothing was ever perfect. Their vials and serums failed as many times as they succeeded. The king depended on them for his ultimate orders, and we citizens depended on them to fail in our favor.

I was scared to lose my head before I made any real progress. I had a chance to return from a lot, but not from losing my head.

A part of me suggested Ravi may be worse than losing my head. Still, I'd hold it high until someone proved to be smarter than I was.

Minala, the priestess, stood behind King Valen. I felt a smirk linger under the surface of my lips. The sight of her gave me a second wave of confidence. If she were to be the one who determined my innocence, then I'd have an even easier time leaving alive. Her faith in magical rituals was absolute, and her critical thinking nonexistent.

"Lanira," Queen Blair declared. "I'm sorry to have you come to such a place. You don't belong here, but you can understand how we need to rule you out."

I met her with a slight bow. The bow made my demeanor slip for a moment. My heart sank as I noticed a few pieces of red fall and shimmer beneath the brown dye I kept on my hair.

That's what would get me caught. No one had red hair unless they had vampiric blood in their veins. I swallowed harder than usual and let my breath out slowly.

For the first time, I was fearful.

I stood back up and tucked it behind my ears in hopes of hiding the treacherous strands beneath other strands.

"It is I who should apologize to you, ma'am. I'm hardly decent. I still wear night clothes and have nothing on my feet," I ended my words with a sniffle.

"Why are you so indecent?" King Valen demanded, his voice cutting through the air like a whip.

"Invidia and I." I paused and watched the ground. I forced my lip to quiver. "The princess and I were awoken by screams. When we went outside, we, we—" I stumbled over my words, let them crack in pitch. "The princess was inconsolable. I wanted to find her a tea. A tonic. Anything to alleviate some of her pain. If I could have taken the weight myself without leaving her side, I would have. I didn't worry about my feet or clothes after I saw the hurt in her eyes." Tears ran down my face.

They were real. I allowed myself to slip back into the way I felt when I first carried the sting of my own family's death.

I did what I always did. I slipped back into my memories. I forced myself back to a time when I watched my sister, who was only two years older than I was, become impaled by a spear. A spear that carried the colors of King Valen. I floated back to a time when I watched blood drip from the corners of her mouth.

When she didn't notice me watching her. She only saw the foreign object inside of her that drained her life. Her eyes were filled with shock and confusion.

It was the rattled sound of her breath that I'd never forget.

"Do you expect me to take pity on you, girl?" King Valen slammed his fist into the arm of his chair, the sound echoing off the metal walls.

"No, I—"

"Nonsense! Tillo was like a brother to her!" Queen Blair snapped. "You go too far with this. I'll permit you to test her, but I won't sit beside you while you belittle her loyalty to us!"

Ravi moved closer to me himself. His brows were crunched together with no space left between them. It seemed to me that maybe looking irritated was his natural stance.

His eyes were focused on my hands. He looked as if he had the goal of checking me, but he stopped nearly as fast as he started. He watched me with his head slightly tilted before he motioned a guard with a small dagger and a rune over to me. I watched the motions from the corner of my cloudy eyes.

Why had he stopped? I couldn't read him. Had he noticed something? The uncertainty gnawed at me like hunger.

"There is no reason for the two of you to argue. Discourse between the two of you will only look as though the royal family is weaker than it is already believed to be in the wake of Prince Tillo's murder," Priestess Minala interjected, her voice carrying false wisdom.

She was the fakest one in the royal court. Hardly divine in any sort of way. My knowledge of that meant nothing to King Valen. He trusted her beyond anyone else. Her opinion was vital to any choices made.

If the rune declared that I was innocent, she would stand by it, and so would he.

I would be free.

I sunk my shoulder and slouched. Body language was more important than any words one could ever speak. I could have told anyone that I was the happiest girl in the world, but if my eyes never lit up, I'd never be believed.

I could protest and claim I didn't enjoy all eyes on me, but I'd be called a liar if my chin stayed raised and I looked confident in the center of a group.

I could tell King Valen all day long that I was distraught over Prince Tillo, but if I didn't allow myself to look submissive and broken, he'd never believe me.

"Just as there is no reason for this!" Queen Blair demanded. "She has been raised as our daughter. Tillo as her brother! You think she would kill him? That she is some sort of vampire in such disguise that we have missed it the entire time she has lived with us? You have a home filled with outsiders, strangers, many people who would love to see your kingdom fall, and you ignore them all for her. A girl who has been loyal for fifteen years?"

The guard moved closer to me with the rune written on parchment. I felt his shaky breath. He didn't know what it meant to be nervous. I could have made him truly nervous.

I was nothing compared to the vampires written of in stories. They were quick, strong. They felt like a fairy tale. I was a small step above average, but still high enough to put fear into the guard. True fear.

I could have ripped his throat out before he knew it had happened.

There was a power in the thought, but there was a true high behind the idea that I was his nightmare in the shadows, and I was truly in the shadows in front of him. He trembled in front of me at the wrong thoughts.

He was scared of the king, the rune, and the possibility that he would lose his head because he messed up the ritual.

He should have feared me.

The idea made my heartbeat quicken with anticipation.

I desired above anything else to be what was feared. To have more power than those around me. To never be made helpless again.

He moved close to me because I allowed it.

"Isn't that all the more reason to test her? If she is truly loyal, she should have no problem with doing it! Why do you fight me so hard?" King Valen yelled back.

"He's right," I proclaimed.

I snatched the blade that the guard held and pretended to slice my finger as I dropped to my knees. I kept the blade close to me.

"I'll test my loyalty as many times as I need to," I added.

The vial of blood that I filled was pushed into a small bracelet on my wrist. The band held it tightly against my skin. As I dropped to my knees, I pushed the small jar into my palm. I wanted it to look like I had sliced my finger when in reality I only moved the jar.

The guard leaned down with the rune on parchment, and I pushed the cork off the vial. The king and queen still fought and screamed at each other, but Ravi's eyes were locked on me.

His gaze made my blood cool and rush through me. His feet stomped towards me, and I was hit with an instant sinking sensation.

I shoved my hand onto the rune until it was soaked in the blood from the vial. The rune glowed white in what was sure to have only been a second or two, but it felt as though it had been ages of slow motion.

Maybe it wasn't that the glow of the rune moved slowly. Maybe it was that my mind wasn't on the situation in front of me. Not fully.

My mind was elsewhere.

My thoughts flashed back to when I was seven. To my mother's burning flesh, filling the air with acrid smoke.

My mind pushed me back to the sight of my sisters, piled on top of each other. Lifeless. Long gone.

To their blood running like a river, and my cries ringing out in the empty air.

"See!" The Queen yelled triumphantly. "She's innocent!"

I snapped back into the moment from her words.

"When I was told this was happening, I could hardly believe it!" Princess Invidia shouted as she entered the room, her voice cutting through the tension like a blade.

I moved my shoulder until my gown fell off the side and sank down. Another small detail that felt nonessential but was important to looking the part that I needed to play. Helpless and hurt.

Princess Invidia, my uncertain chess piece, had shown up in time. Ravi still marched toward me with his eyes fixed on my hand. I cradled it to my chest. The act smeared blood across me, but it also slid the vial down my arm, and I pressed my arm tighter so that the vial stuck.

If he wanted to see my arm, he'd not see the vial. Princess Invidia wrapped herself around me and put a halt to Ravi.

I should have used the time I had to embrace her and look grateful. Instead, I rolled the jar and quickly shoved it inside my breasts. If there was one place I could be certain something would stay hidden, it was there.

"That rune confirms she is innocent! You can all do something useful instead of harming my sister. One more finger on her, and I swear, I'll, I'll—"

"Enough," King Valen commanded. "My sweet, you have to understand—"

"No, I do not! You know she wouldn't hurt us," Princess Invidia shouted back.

"It's the perfect cover! If she wanted to kill one of us and be free, then this is exactly how she would do it!" King Valen pleaded.

It was the first time I'd ever called him smart.

If anyone had listened to him, the rest of his family might have been saved.

"She's not some soldier or assassin! She's a companion, a hand-maiden. She is my sister, and if you ever would have allowed it, she would have been your child too." Princess Invidia helped me to my feet.

I cradled my hand to my chest and leaned into the Princess. I wanted her to feel like a hero. I wanted her to think that without her, I'd be dead now, too. I didn't move until she stepped first.

"Tillo would be ashamed of you. He would be embarrassed to know that his father used his death to hurt Lanira," Princess Invidia shook her head. "He considered you a sister, you know."

"I didn't want to cause a problem. If hurting me made Tillo's death easier, I'd accept it," I cried from beneath her arms.

"I know you would. I'm glad I got to you when I did. Stop allowing them to hurt you to keep peace. Let them bicker on their own. You aren't a dummy to be taken advantage of," Princess Invidia lectured me.

I'd never consider them my family, but there were moments when I felt a bit of emptiness inside. There were small moments where I felt as though betraying Princess Invidia was the only hardship in my plan.

I hoped she died before learning that she was my knight piece.

"Are you all right? Do you need a tonic? Bandages?" Princess Invidia moved me around to look me over.

I leveraged her movements to run the blade that I still held against my finger. I sliced it all the way to my palm. I would need to cut away the proof. I already had to ensure that my blood wouldn't touch another rune with her around.

I shook my head. "I'll be okay. I just need to clean myself up," I assured her.

She pulled me in closer, and the two of us left the rest of the royal family and guards behind. As we walked away, I felt the weight of Ravi's stare burning into my back. He suspected something, but suspicion wasn't proof.

Not yet.

Chapter Nine
A Matched Move

The castle was surprisingly quiet. The morning was so rushed and filled with noise. I assumed that the afternoon would have been filled with funeral plans or rushed packing to get home. There were many plans to make in order to bury the prince with honor.

Instead, there was hardly a mouse around. The silence felt unnatural, like the calm before a storm.

Princess Invidia was called in to meet with King Valen, and I was not allowed to follow. No word was given as to what they needed to discuss, but it was safe to assume that it had to do with the morning's events and her abrasive words. She'd receive no real punishment. She was the only prize the king had left.

The worst thing King Valen could face was only Prince Altair to depend on. He was called a spare more than he was called by his own name.

To King Valen, Prince Altair was supposed to lead Prince Tillo's army in silence until he faded away in battle or old age. Forced into the backdrop and hushed.

Maybe King Valen would take a page from Saydeean and turn his kingdom's rule over to the princess.

I stood outside the iron hall and saw a copy of the rune that priestess Minala was so sure would catch any vampire in its sights. I knew that I shouldn't push my luck. I didn't need to move as far as I had to mess it up on something foolish.

I relented and gave in despite the fact that I knew better. My fresh and clean white gown traced the ground as I ran inside to the stand. I bit my finger and dripped blood onto the rune.

My heart pounded in anticipation.

Nothing.

Not a simple glow, or a shudder, came from the rune. I shook my head. I knew it was useless. I still took a deep breath at the sight. The idea of the unknown scared me. It shouldn't have. Priestess Minala had always been useless.

"Lanira, what are you doing here?" Koen asked, his voice cutting through the silence.

"Koen? What are you doing here?" I startled, spinning around to face him.

"If it were anyone else who saw you here, it wouldn't look good for you," Koen observed, stepping closer.

I moved closer to the door in a hurry to leave. "I know. I just, I just can't make sense of how they haven't caught whoever did it yet."

I had no other story as to why I was wandering in rooms I shouldn't have been in.

Koen slid to the side and blocked my exit. "Do you know what's being said? There are whispers that you were the first to be checked. That you grew jealous and ungrateful of the king."

"Koen, that's—"

"I know how it sounds. It's a lie, but you of all people should know how a lie can ruin someone if it's spread far enough. What were you doing last night?" His ocean eyes stared down at me.

The room was cold, void of furniture beyond seats for the king and queen. Weapon racks with still-cold steel. Koen, he was warm.

He looked at me with concern. With possession. He watched my reaction to him with demand.

"I was with the princess. I took her to bed and slept with her. We shared a bed from the time I took her to it until we were awakened by screams, together. I can't believe you'd even consider me capable of such a thing." I quivered my bottom lip.

"Stop," he commanded and pressed his thumb over my lip. "I only needed to hear you say it. My offer still stands. I can take you away from here. I can save you before there's a chance anything can happen to you."

I didn't need saving.

"You know I can't leave the princess. Especially not at a time like this," I shook my head. "She needs me, and I need her. The prince was a brother to me."

"Don't you care what I need? I don't know if I would have made it. If word had spread of your death in this room today. I can't fathom what I would do if you left me," Koen's breath shook with emotion.

"Someone may think there's something between the two of you," Ravi observed with crossed arms as he stood behind Koen, his presence like a shadow suddenly given form.

Koen's body jolted, and he stood up straight.

"I asked him if he could assist with extra watch of the princess and her room," I replied with a bow.

"Of course, we will be giving extra care to the rest of the royal family. In the meantime, allow me to escort you back to them. The princess has requested you," Ravi held out his arm for me to take.

I took it quickly and spared no further glances at Koen. I wanted him to seem an afterthought to me in front of Ravi. It wasn't the hardest thing I had done. Koen was an afterthought to me.

I could hardly read Ravi to know if it worked or not. His face was made of stone. His brows spoke the words he didn't, but he still had such control over them that I was sure they only revealed what he purposely allowed.

Our steps were in unison, as was our breath. The sound of our footfalls echoed softly in the empty corridors.

"I can't seem to figure you out," he broke the silence. "When I arrived, I swore that I saw red in your eyes. I thought to myself, 'a vampire in the royal family. Not just the royal family, but the man who made his life about slaughtering them all?' Surely, I had to be wrong. Then I saw you with the sunflowers, and it confirmed that I had to have been mistaken. I danced with you so that I could see better the color of your eyes. When you left, I followed you. I saw you tend to the princess with such care and devotion that I second-guessed myself again. It was your perfume that sent me on high alert. I smelled it all over Prince Tillo's room. I knew that you had to be tested. I was sure that if you had enough time, you'd find a way to cheat that test. Your clothes they were so thin and left little to the imagination, and you bled so much, there was no way you could have done something to the rune."

My heart skipped every other beat the longer he spoke.

"As long as the correct rune is used, it's always accurate. It's made to pick up even the slightest hint of vampire blood. Hunters are one of only two exceptions. Hunters have a small amount of vampiric blood in them to allow them to use rune magic. The only other way to not light the rune up is by having a very special rune somewhere on your body that will cover every trace of vampiric blood. Only high-ranking individuals can use the rune." Ravi finished. "Or you could be a witch trained in the ways of a fate sister. That's even more unlikely than you being a vampire."

My chest hurt from how much he spoke. From the words he declared. I wanted to shift the conversation. I wanted to feel less pressure laid on me by him. He was speaking of things I didn't have much knowledge of, but I understood too well that he was on my trail.

"Do you think that I'm a vampire set on the collapse of the royal family, or are you looking at how thin my clothes are and smelling my perfumes?" I asked. "You seem to be unsure of which way you sit, and I feel uncomfortable for it."

His sun-kissed cheeks flushed ever so slightly. I shifted my eyes forward again. I saw enough to know the comment had worked the way I wanted it to.

"I appreciate that you think so highly of me, but I love the prince. I care for my Princess as a sister, and I consider the king and queen a mother and father."

He stopped my speaking. "You've proclaimed that, and you're very convincing, I admit. I nearly believe you. Understand, Lanira, that if I find proof you are a vampire, I won't listen to soft words. I'll have your head."

I smiled. "Sir, you need not threaten me. I don't fear you; I have no reason to. I'm confident of my innocence," I declared.

He allowed me to enter the room first, where the entire royal family sat along a table. I took a seat beside the princess, and she leaned into me.

"He's coming with us," Princess Invidia whispered, her breath warm against my ear.

"What?" I nearly choked.

"He's coming back with us," she repeated.

My heart sank. I thought I'd be rid of him soon. I thought that he'd not have a chance to meddle in my plans if I just waited a little longer.

"Ravi will be escorting us home, and we will be leaving after he clears everyone in attendance," Queen Blair announced.

I nodded but kept my lips tightly closed.

"Where is Princess Sala?" I asked. "How is she?"

I asked partly out of curiosity and partly out of the need to change the topic.

The king looked at me with rage burning in his eyes. "She doesn't matter! We only have seven days to bury my son!" King Valen yelled.

"I promise to be prompt and thorough in my investigation. It's my duty as a vampire hunter to ensure justice is brought to anyone who makes such a bold move as what happened here. We will arrive at your home in time for your burial rituals," Ravi assured him.

There was something about him that interested me, too.

He had already gotten such a read on me and my moves that he made me uneasy. For the first time, I doubted the solidity of my plans. I wondered if my moves were as strong as I thought they were.

Sitting beside Princess Invidia and seeing Ravi talk to the king about his vows made me consider that maybe Ravi slipped in his plans, too. If he was so sure that I was a vampire, why hadn't he already killed me? It was his duty to do it, even under strong suspicion.

If he saw the red flecks in my eyes, he had already gained enough evidence against me to do anything he wanted.

"He's my son, too. I want to see him buried properly, but I also want to catch whoever did this to him. It is possible for us to do both, Valen," Queen Blair argued.

"I'm here to work for you, not against you, sire. I offered the Princess of Saydeean to your second son so that even this tragic death cannot stop what's best for your kingdom. Peace will still be your future, and justice will accompany it. My recommendations are for your best interest," Ravi urged.

"Your time is limited! I will have my son home in time to proceed with his death rites," King Valen got to his feet in a messy scurry.

There was no grace to King Valen or his movements. He left in a crash of what he considered intimidation. The king only looked like a foolish cup of lard.

The Queen left after him, but Prince Altair lingered on with the two of us, as though he had many things to say, and then left without speaking.

One by one, the room emptied.

"Are you going to ask me?" I turned to the Princess.

Her jaw sat open, and she shook her head more times than needed. "I would never ask you."

She was as much of a fool as her father. If she had any sense to her, she would suspect me. She would consider me as guilty as her father does. Her loyalty to me was stronger than any emotion I felt for her. Only occasionally did I consider her a friend.

"I trust you as my sister. Father is only overcome by grief. When we go home and bury our brother, and he has time to see reason, things will get better," she ran her hands through my hair.

I became suddenly aware of the fact that I still had red showing in my hair.

"Princess Sala has been ordered to remain inside her room. Father has proclaimed he can not risk even the smallest chance she becomes injured," Princess Invidia mentioned.

I nodded in acknowledgment.

"For now, I'm going to go to our room, you are going to get us something to drink because my ability to stay strong is dwindling," Princess Invidia offered me a smile, but her yellow eyes were tired.

"I'll meet you upstairs with something to help you relax," I smiled.

I stopped before I reached the kitchen when I heard raised voices. The castle was still quiet and lifeless. So, I stood in place and listened.

"I'm telling you, they are sure there is a vampire here. We are staying so they can find it."

"Disgusting to think I'm under the same roof as one of those things."

"I heard someone mention that it's the princess."

"The one sent to marry into our kingdom?"

"Exactly. They claimed she was sent with the vampire hunter to look innocent."

"Do you smell that?"

"Perfume."

Two men rushed through the doorway and came to a halt in front of me.

I needed to stop the perfume.

"Are you spying on us?"

The second guard placed his hand on the hilt of his sword at his waist.

"No," Ravi stated as he moved from the shadows. "She's on her way to the kitchen at my request. It can't be helped that the two of you are gossiping and doing it loudly."

My eyes shifted between the three of them, and my heart sat in my throat. The guards matched my inner sentiments when they paled at Ravi's voice.

"I'd suggest the two of you get back to guarding the royal family instead of talking about them," he pressed.

"Yes, sir," they responded in unison.

Ravi looked me up and down, slower than just a casual look, but he remained silent. I wanted to ask him why he had followed me, but I didn't speak either.

Why had he helped me?

"We must stop meeting like this," Ravi observed.

"As long as you stalk me from the shadows, it seems we shall keep meeting like this," I sighed.

"Do you not enjoy being watched?" He asked.

He lifted his hand and rolled his fingers through the ends of my hair. It was messily draped over my shoulders.

I slapped his hand away. "I do not."

He pushed air through his teeth. "You'll have to find a way to enjoy it. Everyone will remain under watch until I'm ready to say otherwise."

"There are many others besides me that you may investigate," I replied.

"None so pretty," Ravi smirked.

"I feel as though I may need to request a guard to follow me so that I have protection from you," I declared.

I pulled a member of the kitchen staff between us and turned to run. It would allow me enough time to put space between us.

Did he think that he was funny? I thought he was foolish. But as I hurried away, I couldn't shake the feeling that there was more to his game than I understood. The way he'd helped me with the guards, the way he watched me with something that wasn't entirely suspicion, it made me wonder if Ravi was playing a game as complex as my own.

Chapter Ten
A Break in the Sunshine

Lanira

Koen followed behind us by only a few steps. He was assigned to Princess Invidia's every move for the foreseeable future. He was normally a general guard for the royal children. Now, it was one guard per family member.

I had planned for such changes, but I wished he followed more than two steps behind. He seemed satisfied with his proximity, close enough to catch every whispered word.

"I can see you noticing him," the princess observed.

Being pressed between Princess Invidia and Koen was agonizing, but I still smiled all the same.

"Everything seems to make me feel nervous now," I forced a laugh.

Princess Invidia wanted to go for a walk through the garden. The doctor mentioned it would help her feel at ease and allow her to find some real rest. It made little sense to me. Sweat, bugs, guards. It hardly seemed like restful ambiance.

A hot bath filled with lavender. The only sound would be the ripples of water from my feet popping up and making a splash. Scalding hot chicken broth steaming in a porcelain bowl.

That sounded relaxing. That sounded like exactly what someone would need after a long day.

"Koen is taking our safety very seriously. Tillo would have loved him. Tillo would have praised Koen for his courage and determination," Princess Invidia's voice cracked as she glanced at me.

I squeezed her hand. "Prince Tillo was far braver than any of us could hope to be. He would have loved the view of the mountains from here, too," I sniffled.

She stopped and took in the view in front of us. The sun was bright, and snow sat on the tips of the mountain like white crowns. The grass closest to us was covered in purple flowers, and the scent of lavender filled the air.

Prince Tillo wasn't as brave as I expected. I thought that he would put up much harder of a fight. I felt like he saw death and called it an easy way out.

He didn't feel like someone with a strong need for life, to me.

Princess Invidia wiped her face with the back of her hands and moved us forward. Her face dropped and paled when both of our eyes landed on a group of women in the center of the garden.

"Can you believe she protected her?" a woman not from our court whispered.

"I would have had her beheaded just to be sure," another agreed.

"I agree, one single maid is not worth the risk of letting a vampire inside."

"The kingdom was only a few days away from ensuring the prophecy didn't begin. I'd sacrifice anything to stop that."

"Mhm. I can't believe we were around to witness the beginning of the end for their kingdom."

"They should have trained the prince better. If he were from my land, the prince would have been strong enough to fend off any attack."

"He wasn't the better brother, anyway."

Princess Invidia left us behind and stomped forward, "That's my brother's life you're so carelessly discussing!"

The group of ladies jolted apart and stood straighter at her sudden arrival.

"Princess! We were just wishing for your peace of mind!"

"I heard you!" Invidia pointed accusingly.

She stormed towards the group as though she were going to hit them. I'd rather be on cleaning duty than have to get in the middle of such a petty squabble.

They were right after all.

I'd look beyond suspicious if I allowed her to go at it alone. I may even add credibility to my name with Ravi if he knew I defended the dead prince and princess Invidia.

I marched behind her, but Koen grabbed Princess Invidia and picked her up, tossing her over his shoulder.

"I can not stand by and watch. Your father would have my head if I allowed you to fight. It's not just out of character for you, it's reckless. He will have theirs too if he hears what they said," Koen spoke loudly.

"Oh, he will hear of it!" I blurted to the group.

My words were loud and annoyed even me.

"He didn't deserve to die!" The princess cried louder. "And he doesn't deserve to be the center of your gossip!"

Koen gripped her tightly enough that she couldn't reach the group.

"I should take her back to her room," Koen declared.

I nodded. "I'll find the doctor and ask him to prescribe her something."

I couldn't have asked for a better outcome from our walk. Her constant crying would be out of my ear for even a little while. It would only have gotten better if Prince Altair were here and ready to die as well. I could have faked a second attack while the two of us were alone.

Sure, I'd have more suspicions on me, but it would have been worth it.

When I killed Prince Tillo, I knew that I'd have to spend time consoling the princess, but I expected to also be busy. To have enough things in motion that I'd only be with her half of the time.

I watched Koen leave carrying her as if she were a child, and turned to watch the women scurry away. Instead, my heart jumped out of my chest at the sight in front of me.

"Lanira, it's funny we should meet again like this," Ravi mused.

I had never been so tested. So, on display and dependent on the skills I picked up trying to survive. I could have jolted or hit him. Instead, I only offered him an extra blink. I was proud of myself for the amount of control I held.

Bright green almond eyes smiled at me. His lips sat still as if he were unamused, but for the first time, I could read his eyes. He seemed to enjoy what he was doing.

"Funny? You're following me. Of course, we are meeting again," I remarked. "It's truly no surprise."

"Walk with me," he requested as he held out his arm.

"Am I allowed to refuse?" I asked.

"No," he smirked. "I do have a bit of leverage given my position."

I relented and took his arm. "Lead the way then."

"Are the two of you sleeping together?" he asked.

His sight was straight ahead, but given his words, he could have offered me the decency of a glance.

"I can't see how that's any of your concern, hunter." A wave of nerves washed over me.

Why was I suddenly worried?

"I'm only asking for investigation purposes. I've had time to think about it, and I know that I smelled your perfume in the prince's room. Maybe his death was a lover's quarrel. Two men fighting over a beautiful woman," Ravi patted my arm, which was intertwined with his. "It is common for guards and princes to lie with maids. It's even more common to have bastard children and squabbles."

If he were going to insult me, if we were to play a game instead of being direct, so be it.

"Did you just compliment me twice?" I held my fingers up around his arm and counted on them. "I smell good, I'm beau-tiful," I shook my head. "It seems to me that you come to this conclusion because you are guilty of such things yourself. You hardly know me, yet you follow me and insist on meeting alone."

He stuck a finger between the collar of his blouse and his throat. He circled the rim to loosen the fabric, and my smile grew too wide. I had struck a nerve. Pressed some sort of button that he didn't like.

I cleared my throat and tucked the smile back away. Just as I was proud of myself for my composure, I broke it.

"You speak carelessly for a maid under investigation for the murder of an heir to a throne," Ravi glanced at me from the corner of his eye.

I sighed. "You're right. I'm sure you're very professional after years of training. I must be mistaken," I replied. "There's no such lover's quarrel occurring between me and anyone."

"If not a lovers' quarrel, then I'll have to try again. I think I'm not yet ready to cross you off my list," he declared.

"If I were guilty, I'd not be so bold as to take your arm," I offered.

"In that we are matched. If I were sure of your guilt, I'd have not offered you my arm," he responded. "Maybe both of us are right on the edge of the truth."

I hardly wanted to look away from him. I spent so much time reading every word off his lips, every breath, with such ease that his challenge felt electric.

"Why not just kill me and be sure?" I asked. "You have the authority."

"I try not to make it a habit of killing those who could be innocent," he responded.

It seemed his weakness was wanting to be painted as a kind and gentle man. He was right, both of us were matched in pretending to be something that we aren't.

I saw an opportunity that I couldn't miss when we neared the yellow rose bushes. I wanted to keep him guessing. I wanted him to be uncertain of how much pain I was in. I stopped walking in front of them.

"These were his favorites," I paused. "The prince used to collect one for each of us any time that we were here. I have a collection of them at home. I've never been so happy to have dried them out," I spoke in a low whisper. "I'll at least have memories of him."

Ravi leaned down ever so slightly to see my eyes and the way they welled up. It was only a half lie. Ash used to bring me flowers anytime he left. I kept the tradition on my own. I did have a collection of dried roses. I liked their look, but if ever they were to have a use, this was perfect.

"The petals on most of them are wilting. Take comfort in the idea that you do not mourn alone," he whispered back to me.

I hadn't noticed that he turned to face me. He wasn't built as I would have thought. His shoulders were not massive or weighing him down. Still, he held a sense of protection and command. He wiped the water away from my eyes with his thumb in a slow, gentle motion before he cleaned the moisture off on his pants.

"I think I may smell of you for a while after this, too," he murmured. "If you are guilty, you're going to make this hard."

"Hard? I'm just a maid that you know nothing of," I responded.

"A part of me thinks that I may want to know more about you," Ravi whispered under his breath.

He spoke so low that I couldn't hear what he said clearly.

Our eyes were still locked on each other.

I became aware of how close we had become when my thoughts drifted to how soft his lips looked. When his eyes suggested that he may kiss me, and my chest indicated I may let him, I became fearful.

It was outside of the plan.

He was outside the plan.

"Stay still," he commanded, and got to his knees in front of the rose bushes.

Two older ladies of the court walked past the two of us and whispered. They clearly spoke of us. We must have looked indecent. He tried to hide from them, but he only made things look worse. The vampire hunter was on his knees in front of me.

"Do you usually help those you find guilty of high crimes look even worse before you kill them?" I asked.

"You can worry less. I can't ruin my ability to punish you correctly," he remarked. "I wouldn't allow you to be locked away for something so small by anyone else."

I met him with a smirk. "You will be disappointed in the time you waste on me."

He stood, and we walked the trail of the garden again.

"If I am to be forced to spend time with you, am I allowed to ask questions?" I turned to watch him.

"Sure."

"What makes a vampire hunter any different?" I asked.

"Hunters aren't monsters who kill innocence to live, for one," Ravi replied. "We have the smallest amount of vampiric blood in our veins, so we have a natural connection to magic. It allows us to freely use runes."

"Aren't you?" I may have regretted my words, but it was too late to take them back. "You don't drink blood, but you kill the innocent to live the life you decide is right. Do you not? You get to decide who is good or bad and, in turn, who is worthy of life and death, so that those you deem good enough can live in what you consider peace. That feels monstrous to me. You don't know who I am, you know nearly nothing of our kingdom, yet you've become the rule that gets to alter our lives."

He dropped my arm and looked as though he were ready to give me a lecture. As though he couldn't believe I had spoken something so wrong.

I gave him a bow. "Now, I need to get back to the princess if you don't mind."

He returned the bow and gave me one last glance up and down before he turned to leave. He felt as ready to leave me as I felt to do the same.

"Oh, I did forget something," he announced and grabbed my hand. He set a small sunflower hairpin in my palm. "I think that this is yours. I found it in the prince's room."

I kept my gaze on the pin as my vision narrowed and blurred. The delicate metal felt cold against my skin, a piece of evidence

I hadn't even realized I'd lost. "It must have fallen out when we arrived, and I had to put his bags away."

I didn't look to see his expression. I could feel the weight of his stare, the satisfaction he took in this moment. It was time for my exit.

The game between us had just become far more dangerous.

Chapter Eleven
A Queen and a Knight

Lanira

I was happy to have a bit of peace. To be alone and able to freely think without feeling as though I stood on a cliff by the tips of my toes. Playing games with Ravi was entertaining, but he was the only one to have me where he wanted me instead of the other way around.

I couldn't get the idea that vampire hunters were made with true vampires out of my mind. How did they do such a thing? The thought made my skin crawl.

The castle halls were dimmer since Prince Tillo's death. Lit only by smaller candles that cast long shadows against the stone walls. The light seemed to retreat from the grief that filled every corner.

An image of a dungeon with vampires locked away flashed through my mind. Used as blood bags for RuneHold and its desires. The idea was sickening. Enraging. It made the hunger gnawing at my insides feel even more pronounced.

There had to have been another way. Something else they did. There were traitors in every group, everywhere. There is no doubt that there had to have been a vampire or two who had fled and exchanged themselves. Blood for life. If they had seen the same things as I that day, then I couldn't have blamed them.

I was allowed an education, to a point. It never included anything outside of King Valen's land. I was not allowed in his study or the separate library. Ravi could have told me they ate rocks, too, and I'd have no choice but to believe him.

Princess Invidia wasn't allowed the knowledge either. It was the only reason I was never argumentative. If she wasn't receiving it either, then I had no leg to stand on for myself. I had a feeling they'd soon regret the choice for the princess.

The king and queen would have choices to make once both of their sons were dead.

Either way, it was an odd experience knowing those who knew so much about the past walked around, and yet I wasn't allowed to interact with them. There were still members of the court who met with vampires in peace once. There were those who knew details of the rituals and customs of my life that I didn't hold, and I couldn't ask them about it.

I often wanted to ask if King Valen had met my brother. It only made sense that Ash had been inside the same walls as he was.

The two of them eating together, sharing laughs. Only to be betrayed.

Carrying next to no knowledge of my home, yet being surrounded by it, was a pain that I couldn't put into enough words. I could almost touch the only thing I ever really wanted, but it was always just out of reach. Just a hair too far for me to hold.

I pulled too hard at the skin on the side of my thumb and jumped at the sharp pain. Blood welled to the surface, and I quickly wiped it away before it could tempt me further.

I sighed and dropped my hands so that I wouldn't use them to distract from my emotions. If I caused myself pain, I'd not have the time to focus on sadness.

I wanted my focus to be on pain. I wanted it to be on justice. I wanted my thoughts to be tunneled on King Valen.

I knew that King Valen could hurt more. He could lose more. Prince Tillo was only the first step.

I'd lose too much, too, if I didn't get a break from being followed. It had been three days since Tillo's death. Three days since I had eaten anything that I needed to keep me full. Three days of hoping that the meat I was served was raw enough to drip blood.

The castle was covered in mirrors, and every time my image slipped into one, my cheeks were paled and my eyes sunken. I had to find a way to eat. First, I had to meet the queen. She requested me for the first time in three days. I waited patiently for my chance, and I couldn't let it pass because of a bit of blood.

I was stronger than my needs. My slip-up with Prince Tillo didn't change that.

The thought brought back the memory of his taste. He had done a good job at pretending to be drunk. The sweet copper tang filled my memory, making my stomach clench painfully.

I shook myself from my thoughts. My mind was shifting to the wrong place while I was so hungry.

I straightened my red lace skirt and pulled my silk sleeves down. I fixed my hair as soon as I had a chance and added more dye to the lenses I wore over my eyes.

They were easy to make. It was the one thing that I had managed to get my hands on from the king's study. He kept a book with writing from the alchemists placed on his desk as if he had no discretion. The halls were empty.

It was as if my brother had come back from the dead and set up the most perfect combination of events. Until then I had hidden alone under filth and darkness to not be seen with red features.

Inside the pages, writing taught me to dye my hair, color my eyes, and cover freckles if I wanted. The book spoke of fashion in their kingdom and its importance. An innocent enough book had helped me hide my appearance in a place that would have killed me otherwise.

I took a deep breath and let it out with another sigh to try to help center my thoughts.

I hardly had the chance to enjoy what relief I could have felt when I was slammed against the wall of the common halls.

Koen's face brushed against mine before he kissed my neck. I didn't feel it. I couldn't have counted how many times his lips touched the skin between my chin and shoulder. It didn't matter how I was touched, I wouldn't feel it.

Instead, I counted every beat of his heart. The sound of his blood pushing through his veins screamed out at me. My eyes grew heavy, and the rhythm became a song. My mouth drifted closer to his shoulder.

I couldn't have felt his touch because all I felt was the beating in his chest. My body pulsed with its rhythm. The hunger was a living thing inside me, clawing to get out.

"I've been watching you and that hunter. The two of you look to be getting close. I don't like it, Lanira. You're mine. You belong to me," Koen whispered against my ear. "I can't keep watching you from a distance and not touch you."

The words broke me from the trance that I was in. Being repulsed was stronger than being hungry. When I opened my eyes, they landed on Ravi. He stood with his arms crossed and his eyes burning into me.

It seemed that I wasn't the only one repulsed by the sight.

"You aren't the only one who's been watching me, and he's watching us now," I whispered.

"Let the hunter watch," Koen growled.

He tried to pull at my skirt, but I used both of my hands to shove him off of me by the chest.

"Not only do you look as though you don't know what to do with a woman. You're breaking laws in front of an enforcer. Do you expect that I will turn a blind eye? What is the punishment in your kingdom for such a situation? I think it's sterilization?" Ravi questioned, his voice cold. "With the state King Valen is in, it may even be death. He has been in quite a rage."

Koen stopped in front of Ravi. Their shoulders would have hit if neither had moved. The situation was hardly amusing to me. Ravi already considered this exact thing he witnessed as the reason for the prince's death. He was a far cry off of the truth, but I couldn't tell him that.

I couldn't assure Ravi that my killing spree had nothing to do with Koen and everything to do with the very thing he was sent to shut down.

No, First Blade of the Hunters. It's no lovers' quarrel. It's a scorned daughter seeking to ensure her family gets the vengeance that they deserve. How could you be so far from the truth? You've failed, go home.

Surely, he would tuck his tail and go about his business.

Of course not.

I could only wiggle like a worm stuck inside a bird's nest.

The way the two of them looked at each other, as if they were stags ready to bash antlers, under any other circumstance, it would have been worth the laughter. Both of them had shaggy black hair, but they were as opposite as they could have been from there.

Koen was large in size, broad shoulders straining against his uniform, but Ravi had to be something if he had gotten to a top rank. There was a lethal efficiency in his lean frame.

Koen moved past Ravi without a second word. It was the only smart action I had seen him take.

"Consider that the only time I do you such a favor," Ravi declared.

"Your kindness is unmatched," I smiled, not bothering to hide the sarcasm.

"My wrath will indeed be worse. You lied to me!" Ravi pointed accusingly.

Did I owe him something, and the terms were kept secret? I hardly knew him to owe him any truth.

"Sir, I am only a woman in a kingdom of men. What would you have me say? Would you have me fall into your arms and tell you of how all the women of my station are treated? Would you defend me if I mentioned that I was forced to use my body for a bit of peace? Would you consider me not guilty if I told you that the only happiness allowed is what can be stolen in the dark? What you saw does not make me a liar. You asked me if there was a love triangle, and there is not. The prince and I are as siblings. Of course, signs of me are around him. You'll find them everywhere. I live with them and see them every day," I sighed and took a few breaths, heavier than normal. "We all have choices to make, Sir. Some of our choices are much smaller. My body is the only bargaining chip that I hold. Be it for happiness or safety."

My hunger had made me too emotional. Too loud. The words tumbled out with more truth than I intended.

He looked at me with concern, pity even. If he were anyone else, I'd rip him open and drink until he was empty. I hated being looked at the way he had.

It was true that the chips I had to play were small, but I chose to play them in the end. I didn't need his pity.

"Don't look at me like that. Do your duty, hunter, and I'll do mine," I bowed as quickly as I could.

I wanted him to feel some small semblance of disrespect. I stomped harder down the hall than I had before my interaction with them. The peace I had just dipped into felt far away. The ache in my belly felt closer than anything. I had never gone so long without the ability to sneak something.

I was only shown that I was right. I was never alone.

Ravi's steps were still behind my own, and it filled my body with fire. My ears rang with the pounding of his heart. Saliva formed at the corners of my lips.

"I'm sure you have a busy schedule," I remarked.

"Not at all, actually. It's pretty easy here for me. At home, I'd have a strict schedule and activities, but here it's all people watching and food. I imagine it's pretty relaxed for you, too. If you have time to be fondled in the halls," Ravi challenged.

"I'm at the mercy of the princess," I snarked back. "My day depends on her needs."

Ravi shook his head. "I don't think that's true. I think you have a wide variety of freedoms that most do not. Some you may want to use soon. You look a bit pale. Maybe you're stressed?"

"I am in mourning," I snapped.

He nodded. "Where I'm from, mourning means rising before the dawn to fit in extra training. There's no time to worry about the mind's exhaustion if the body is worse off."

"Sounds awful for you," I sighed. "Perhaps you should go do some of that training?"

I stopped in front of the Queen's doors, and he placed his hand on my shoulder to stop me. The warmth of his touch made my skin tingle.

"If I were a vampire and I killed someone of importance, then sat on the brink of starvation. I think that I would look pale, too," he tapped his fingers on my shoulder.

"If I were in charge, I'd send you back home the first chance I received. You are clearly obsessive, and it's keeping you from finding the one responsible for causing such a tragic event," I snarled.

"I'd have to argue that I think I'm on the right track," Ravi removed his hand from my shoulder.

He walked away with his hands behind his back, his pace marked by a smug ease. He was despicable. Infuriating. I took in a deep breath and held it until my chest hurt, and let it out before I turned the doorknob to Queen Blair's room.

"Lanira! Oh dear, you look so pale. Are you ill?" Queen Blair exclaimed.

"I'm doing as well as I can," I bowed.

If one more person mentioned me looking pale, they'd be my next meal.

Queen Blair studied me for a moment before she spoke.

I studied her room. It was a stark contrast to the rest of the castle. She looked sad, but her room was bright, and the breeze from the windows whipped inside, stirring the gauzy curtains.

Her room smelled of jasmine and pomegranate, the scent so rich I could almost taste it.

It wasn't the sight I expected to see her surrounded by.

"You know that I've not been able to put you on the same pedestal as Invidia in public, but that I love you as a daughter all the same. As my daughter, I trust that you will be honest with me.

I know you had to have seen something," she narrowed her eyes on me.

I built such a wall that her words felt hollow. She attempted to play a game with me that I had already been playing with her.

Both of us used the idea that we cared for each other to play a game.

"I don't think I saw anything more than everyone else did," I responded.

"Lanira, whatever you say here, stays here. No one will know anything came from your lips," the Queen leaned closer to the edge of her seat, her eyes imploring.

I dropped to my knees and placed my forehead on the ground. "I'm sorry," I pleaded. "I love the prince as my brother, and I've been eaten alive by my position and the inability to do anything useful that comes with it."

"You can be useful right now! Think hard and speak honestly," she urged.

She rushed down the three small steps that held her seat above me and pulled me into her arms. Her blue eyes were exactly like Prince Tillo's.

I flashed back to the shock on his face when he saw me in his room. He looked healthier there than the Queen did in front of me. Her face showed that she had also not eaten or slept. Dark circles hung beneath her eyes, and her cheeks were hollowed.

I wished that I had a way to hand that image to her. To the king. They'd never see his last moment like I saw my family's. They'd suffer, but they'd never know that kind of agony. I wanted so badly to hand her the look on Prince Tillo's face when he took his last breath.

"Is that why you look so ill? Guilt of shouldering secrets?" She shook my shoulders.

"I didn't want to point fingers in the wrong direction. I meant no harm. When I took Invidia to her room, I had to go back into the hall and get her shoes. When I did, Tillo was taking someone to bed, but it wasn't his betrothed," I whimpered under her shakes.

The sound of her heartbeat was the true cause of my whimper. I was starving and only hoping I made sense. I planned this story so well that it had to have been burned into my mind.

I would repeat from muscle memory as she stood so close I felt my palms sweat.

"Tell me!" She urged.

"It was the Princess of StoneDale," I whispered.

"StoneDale? You're sure that it was not Saydeean?" Her breath was on my face.

I smelled blood from her biting her lip while she talked, and I felt my eyes grow heavy again. The scent of it made my head swim.

"I'm already in a negative spotlight," my words slurred. "I didn't want to make waves. If what I saw was true, then—" My knees buckled under the weight of my body.

"Then it means the kingdom of StoneDale doesn't want us at peace. This was an act of war by their Princess. An act of jealousy," the Queen drifted off into thought. "I need to go. I won't tell anyone these words came from you for now, but if I request it, will you repeat in front of King Valen?"

"Of course," I agreed.

What choice did I have in the end?

Queen Blair let go of me and instead held up her skirt to run out of the room. The noise of her heels pounded against my own skull like hammers.

My nostrils flared at the still lingering scent of blood.

It wasn't the Queen any longer.

There was something else. I allowed my nose to guide me to a bird in a cage above the queen's bed. It was small and brilliantly colored, its feathers a mix of blue and green. I couldn't tell where it bled from, but I smelled the blood.

Without a thought of my surroundings, I opened the cage and grabbed the bird. Its small heart beat frantically against my palm. I bit into it, and the warmth filled my mouth. It was as though I sat in front of a feast.

Small and hardly satisfying, but enough to allow me to hold clear thoughts again. The hunger receded just enough to let me think.

I tucked the bird's body under logs in the Queen's fireplace. I left the door to its cage open. She'd consider it a runaway. A small tragedy in the midst of greater ones.

I'd consider it a small smudge on the way I viewed myself when I looked in a mirror.

I'd be ashamed of myself for the low that I reached, and yet proud for the war my words would ignite once the Queen repeated them to the king.

A small price to pay for the beginning of the end.

Chapter Twelve
Uncomfortable Sardines

Lanira

"The vampire hunter has cleared the names of everyone in attendance as well as can be done from our location. We have three and a half days to bury my son. Everyone will be ready to leave by this afternoon. Accommodations have been made to bring the vampire hunter back with us so that he may keep investigating and moving towards justice," King Valen announced from his seat.

He sat on his throne and looked worse than I did when I was starved. His skin had taken on a gray pallor, and his eyes were sunken into dark hollows. The Queen sat beside him and carried bags of shadow under her eyes. She glared at the king with a fury I hadn't seen from her before, the heat of it almost tangible in the air between them.

It seemed the idea of Ravi coming with us upset more than me.

"Don't look so upset," Ravi whispered through King Valen's continued words.

He stood beside me, dressed in all white. Black trimmed his corset and pocket watch. The contrast made his eyes seem even more piercing.

"You seem to have allowed your inner thoughts to become outer expressions, Lanira," he smirked.

"I was only thinking that between a renowned hunter and a great sorceress, it's strange to not have the culprit," I replied.

"I do agree. It's a stain on my reputation. Which is why I'm coming with. I want to keep my eye out for any little clues. As for the sorceress, I think we both know that she is false," Ravi remarked.

"I'm beginning to think you are as well," I challenged.

"Enough standing around! I want to bury my son!" The king yelled, his voice cracking with grief.

I gave a bow, held for several seconds, and excused myself. I felt as though I were a mother duck with the way that I was followed out by Ravi and Koen. I kept my gaze ahead and focused on the etched decorations that lined the walls' crown molding, the intricate patterns giving me something to concentrate on besides my unwanted company.

"You aren't going the right way," Ravi remarked.

"I'm going exactly where I mean to be," I responded, not slowing my pace.

"Aren't you meant to be packing?" He asked.

"Guardian Koen, did you place the bags in the carriage as I asked?" I turned my gaze to the other man.

"Yes. They are there," Koen responded, his eyes darting between Ravi and me.

"The princess is also already inside the carriage. I knew we departed today some time ago. I only just learned that you would be joining us. So, no. I am not going the wrong way," I didn't want to look at him.

"If you keep only looking at Koen, others may learn what I already know," Ravi taunted.

I should have been free of him. I should have happily waved him goodbye as the carriage pulled me away to set their entire kingdom ablaze. Instead, he still followed me. I stopped and turned to face Ravi instead. I felt the heat on my ears.

"Don't you have somewhere to be?" I pointed. "Bags to pack. A carriage to prep? Anything other than breathing down my neck?"

He smiled at me, and it became even more apparent that his upper lip was thinner than the bottom. His teeth were white enough that they were a distraction. King Valen, Tillo, even Altair hardly brushed enough to have the same shimmer.

"Lanira, I think you'll love to hear that I'll be traveling with you. The king and queen thought it best to have someone highly trained in the carriage with their children. In case disaster strikes on the road," he reached up and fixed the sunflower pin in my hair. "Though you don't smell as strong today. I was looking forward to your perfume."

I felt my ears heat further. My cheeks grew hot next. I turned on my heel and marched outside. Koen caused me enough problems while we were away. He was sure to act up even further with Ravi breathing down my neck. I'd starve to death or I'd lose my sanity before my plans had their time to succeed.

I lived off of a small bird and the raw meat that I managed to get ahold of from the kitchen. It wasn't nearly enough, and the hunger was making me careless.

"There it is. I knew there was some real fire in you somewhere," Ravi chuckled. "Maybe I'm not so wrong about you."

His words shot me full of fear. They stung like sharp and silent teeth. I had slipped too far. Showed too much with my outburst. This man was unraveling me, thread by thread.

I opened the white wooden carriage door and climbed the steps inside. Princess Invidia and Prince Altair already sat next to each other. Which meant I had to sit beside Ravi. I stood still and looked between the empty seat and the two of them, dread filling my stomach. Prince Altair must have felt the pause because he switched sides.

"Here," he pointed to the spot beside his sister.

I smiled and took the seat with joy. Ravi wasted no time crawling inside and sitting beside the Prince. Ravi nearly shoved me with his pace.

He knocked on the carriage, and the coachman sounded the reins. The carriage lurched forward, beginning our journey.

What was his rush?

"The king and queen will be following soon. They assigned staff to gather belongings and head back at their leisure. The carriage with your dead brother will be behind us," Ravi declared.

"Don't speak of him that way. As though he has no name or value now that there is no breath in him," Princess Invidia demanded, her voice sharp with grief.

Ravi nodded. It was the last movement before silence sat between the four of us like a heavy blanket.

I took the princess's hand and held it. I needed to recover my image from the outburst. I'd blame it on grief and frustration.

Ravi would be the only one who wouldn't let it go. If he told the king, the king wouldn't let it go. No one else would consider it odd. I'd have to speak to the king before Ravi. I needed to stick to my plans. I'd have to force the narrative that Ravi is the outsider.

That maybe he was the one against us.

"If I may break the quiet up. I was curious how Lanira became part of your family. It's something everyone likes to whisper about but no one keeps straight," Ravi asked.

Princess Invidia squeezed my hand and perked up. She sat straighter than she had in days, eager to share a story that always made her feel special.

"She was found alone and crying during the battle of Lunadur," she answered, pride in her voice.

Ravi crossed his legs. "How did you know she wasn't a vampire? She really should have been killed on the spot."

"She was a child!" The princess shouted, her face flushing with anger.

"Sister and mother were very much against the idea," Prince Altair interjected, his voice calmer. "We tested her and she came back clean every time. There were many in the court who also felt the same way as you. They wanted her dead, child or not."

"Luckily, they did not get their wish. She's been with me since," the princess smiled. "She's never given us a reason to believe that she was a monster like those vampires. She takes care of everyone. She sacrifices herself to do it. She can't be a monster and love us the way that she does."

Ravi nodded. "If she were, I imagine you calling her a monster would elicit some sort of emotions. Since it does not, you must be correct," his tone was tinged with sarcasm. "Your adoption day must have been wonderful. I imagine it was a big celebration."

The princess shook her head. "She doesn't have our last name. Father said LeBlanc's are born, not created."

"So, then she isn't a member of your family. Only a maid," Ravi observed.

"I see what you're trying to imply—" Princess Invidia grumbled, her fists clenching.

"I am simply Lanira. I'm happy to be of service to them. You are going too far," I interjected. "A name doesn't change anything to me."

My family name is not for his knowledge. I saw right through him. He wanted to know what name my family went by so that he may try and trace me. He would never get such a thing. Ambrose is for my lips only.

"I mean no offense. I simply find it odd that a man so concerned with the prophecy would ever take such a risk. Consider me a fool from another land, only trying my best to learn," Ravi bowed his head to the princess before he turned his gaze back to me. "What do you think of the prophecy?"

"I don't. I do not think of it. I do not have any thoughts about it. I'd give my life to protect my sister, and that's as far as it matters to me," I lowered my gaze back to the princess's hands in mine.

"Well, I think it's nonsense. I think someone made it up to keep people filled with fear. People will always walk a straight line if they're scared that taking the curve will mean death," Prince Altair announced.

He crossed his arms and leaned back into the carriage wall. His casual appearance made me realize that I was far too stiff. I forced myself to relax my shoulders.

"I think you're wrong," Princess Invidia disagreed. "I think it's not about the ruler of our kingdom, like Father does. I think it means we unite by pulling kingdoms closer. If I marry someone strong and smart, then Altair does the same, and then we've already united three of the five kingdoms. We all have to stay strong so that together, with care and love, we can keep everyone safe."

She was nauseatingly sweet.

If I allowed myself to be honest for a moment, it was why she hadn't died first. A part of me had grown close to her after fifteen years. The thought made my chest tighten uncomfortably.

"Isn't it amusing how we can all interpret it differently? I think a little closer to the prince. I consider the prophecy a tool. It is so simple yet so powerful. I think someone left it to fuel anxiety and panic in kingdoms. What better way to break something from the inside out? If everyone is scared or fighting over a meaning, then someone on the outside would hardly need to lift a finger to start a collapse," Ravi leaned back with the prince. "Holding people where you want them always starts with words, not weapons."

"Does everyone from your land think the same as you?" Princess Invidia asked.

"No. Most of them believe in it wholeheartedly. Our entire lives are dedicated to being ready to fight the chosen vampire that will rise and destroy everything," Ravi answered.

There was something different in his face when he spoke. Something that I hadn't seen before. His nostrils flared when he answered, and a muscle twitched in his jaw.

Had he lied?

"That sounds like an empty life," the princess frowned.

Ravi gave a small chuckle as if he had agreed with her sentiments. I hadn't considered someone with such a heavy demeanor to be so empty. He seemed to be filled only by the thought of killing monsters that never existed.

I nearly felt bad for him until the scent of blood was in the air. I glanced at his finger where he pricked himself and squeezed at the blood. The copper tang filled the carriage, making my throat tighten.

Our eyes connected as he pushed more blood from beneath the skin. He taunted me, watching for any reaction, any slip.

"If we're going to openly speak, then whispers have been circling of the problems your presence is causing," Prince Altair mentioned, oblivious to the silent battle happening across from him.

The two men sat together, relaxed and leaning back as if they had not a care in the world. If I didn't cry, I was guilty, but Prince

Altair looked as though he had forgotten Prince Tillo, and no one gave him a second glance.

"Indeed. The King was more than happy to allow me to come. He wanted more of us. His idea was for me to send word to the king of my land for a full platoon or more. His desire for vengeance would have had that entire castle slain if it were up to him. Your Queen, however, denied my every word. She said my presence was enough. That the King disgraced her by not allowing her the time she needed to grieve. In the end, the fighting of your land is none of my concern. I only take orders," Ravi spoke casually.

"I think mother is content with this. I think she is considering what her life would look like if I were on the throne instead. She is right, I would be softer on her than my brother would have been. It brings me no surprise to hear she was against causing an uproar," Prince Altair admitted.

"Enough!" Princess Invidia snapped. "They are both upset, and grief looks different for all. Don't speak things that you wouldn't want to swirl around the court."

"It is just nice to be able to be honest for a moment," Prince Altair argued. "Everyone has a reason to spread every word they hear. He doesn't. He's bound by honor and an oath."

"So are all the members of your court, but they speak freely," I inserted myself.

Ravi sat up straight and lifted his hand to move the curtain on the small carriage window. He smeared the blood from his fingertips on the wood beside my head as he did it, deliberately letting the scent of it fill the confined space.

His eyes were on mine. They searched for any sign of a slip at its scent.

I held his gaze, refusing to break or show any reaction despite the hunger clawing at my insides. The small bird had done little to sate me.

I was ready to be back in the kingdom of Emberrella. I was ready to be back where all of my plans were set up and waiting. I was ready to be rid of Ravi, even if it meant that I had to kill him myself.

The thought surprised me with its intensity, but I knew it was true. Ravi was becoming too dangerous, too perceptive.

And I had come too far to be stopped now.

Act Two

The Knights' Reckoning,
Paved in Blood.

Chapter Thirteen
The Return

Lanira

We arrived at the kingdom, and it seemed that I wasn't the only one ready for separation.

I walked behind Princess Invidia through the halls until we arrived at our wing of the castle. Her door was left open, and she walked inside without needing to wait for me to push it open for her.

She sat at her pastel pink and golden desk but ignored the mirror. She didn't want to look at her own tired reflection. Her yellow hair and eyes usually created a glow around her. The more days from Prince Tillo's death we moved, the grayer she flickered instead. The light that had once radiated from her seemed to dim with each passing hour.

I hadn't expected the small tug at my chest the sight created.

I felt a conflict I didn't anticipate. I didn't feel particularly close to her, but I still felt a small wave of sadness.

Maybe it wasn't sadness because we were close. Maybe it was sadness because I saw in her what I felt inside of myself. I glowed once, too.

It slowly burned out of me, too.

As I watched her sit at her vanity, I knew what she wanted from me. I picked up my skirt and hurried to her back. I grabbed her custom-carved wooden brush like I had done so many times before and gently raked it through her hair. The familiar motion was almost comforting in its routine.

"Do you think that he suffered?" She whispered, her voice barely audible.

My eyes shot up to her reflection in the mirror. She still hadn't looked at herself in it. My heart dipped a little lower in my chest at the sight. Her mourning was still as raw and fresh as when the first screams sounded during the discovery. She was always smiling and happy, or spoiled, until she wasn't.

To see her so deeply embedded in darkness wasn't something I expected. Her eyes were still puffy, rimmed with red from constant tears.

He did suffer. He felt pain; he choked on his own blood. It wasn't quick enough, and I enjoyed it.

I still enjoyed the thought. It overrode the tinge of sadness for her.

"No. They said it was fast," I answered her. "Soon we will send his soul to the afterlife, and no matter what, he will be at peace."

Her chin shook before tears moved down her cheeks. A part of me hated to see her that way when we were supposed to be sisters. Another part of me loved to witness her cry for her brother in the same way that I cried for mine. Even if the guilt that I felt was small, I hadn't expected any.

She was still privileged even in her suffering. I had to mourn behind closed doors, alone. I was expected to forget my past and merge into their family so quickly that, for a while, I did believe the lies I told myself.

For days, I was questioned and told to eat my tears. For days, I was held as a criminal and screamed at. I was convinced that it was the reason for my memory. Such big emotions for such a small body, something had to have come of it.

She at least held onto all of her memories. She at least held onto his belongings.

I held onto flashes of memories and dreams that slipped away like smoke when I tried to grasp them.

"Do you think he is with the gods? Do you think even though they abandoned us, that they still comfort the dead?" Princess Invidia asked, her golden eyes searching mine in the mirror.

This time, I wouldn't lie.

"No, I don't think so. I don't see why they would have left the living but coddled the dead," I replied. "Do you know why they abandoned us?"

I shouldn't have asked, and I doubted she knew, but I was kept in such a box that I had to try with such an opportunity in front of me.

She shook her head. "You could have lied to me."

Of course, she focused on that. I held my sigh in.

"I would never lie to my sister. We are both hurting, and the Prince would want us to use such a time to become closer, not create a relationship of deception," I said as I still brushed her hair, the strokes rhythmic and soothing.

Her breath shuddered as she tried to hold her tears in.

"Who are we to pretend to know the ways or the thoughts of beings so far beyond us. Maybe he is with them and they are watching us now," I tried to comfort her.

The bits of guilt or sorrow that I felt for her faded during our talk.

"Mother never allowed my education to be filled with talks of these things. She said it was beyond anything that I'd have to worry about," Princess Invidia admitted.

The Queen kept the two of us equal in the one thing that I wished the princess had received more of.

A knock sounded at the door.

"The king wants you, Lanira," a guard announced from the doorway.

I set the brush down, and Princess Invidia nodded me out, assuring me that she would be fine with her forced smile and silence.

When we arrived at the main hall, King Valen looked as if he were a bowl filled with slop being pushed around as he trudged to his throne.

I remembered his younger days and the man he had been then. It was a bright contrast to who he had allowed himself to become. I remembered being a child and the sight of him in his silver steel armor. I thought he was something much more once.

I recalled the way his long, golden hair gave him a halo, the same as his daughter. I thought he had to have been a god. A being of higher power that had arrived to save me.

I also recalled the way that image of him shattered when I learned he led the assault on my home. I could recall the exact moment when my strong admiration for him turned into disgust. On that day, the scent of pork and tomato hung in the air. Giggles and cheers for a new beginning sounded out, and mugs clashed in a slow motion that changed the path of my future.

No one would believe that he was the same man. Once strong and intimidating, and now fat and hardly sane.

"Lanira and Koen will escort the hunter. Koen will give him a tour of any room or item he may need, and Lanira is to ensure the room is cleaned and he has proper linens. The rest of you will stay with me. I want the funeral planned by the end of the day. I want the heads of anyone who tries to stop progress," the king's fist slammed into the arm of his chair.

I bowed and backed out of the room. I didn't care what else he had to say. I didn't need to hear anything else. I stepped on a cloud and rode the high of his emotions. He had no time to enjoy the pleasures of being a king. He was consumed by rage and grief.

The constant frown on his face made my stomach flutter. The anger in his voice and the desperation in the words he used. It let me know that he felt everything slip through his fingers in the same way I felt once.

I could have danced off into the night.

"Do you have something to say?" Ravi asked.

I stood straight, caught in my moment of pleasure.

"You look as though you have something to say," Ravi walked past me while he spoke.

Koen moved past us and led the way. He radiated annoyance. It was in the way he dodged hitting shoulders with Ravi on his move past.

"Nothing?" Ravi pressed.

"Is this part of your investigation? If so, I'll need you to be more specific with your questions. If it isn't, then I'll need to tell you that I'm only a handmaid and we have no reason to keep speaking," I kept my eyes low and my voice soft.

It was time that I got back on track. Time that I followed my plans. He and I had played enough.

"You don't want to speak to me as a friend? The look on your face just now was so happy. You seem stressed now, crushed by the weight of responsibility and rules. Maybe I can take you back to my kingdom. I have tools there to make this quicker than you can imagine, so you can live freely," Ravi suggested.

Koen stopped walking, and Ravi hardly dodged him in time. Koen turned back, and the two men were face to face. There was a spark at the idea that the two of them were willing to fight over me.

A small, nagging voice accompanied it, saying I was a fool. It wasn't me; it was the ownership of property that the two of them fought over.

"Koen, the king needs you!" King Valen's guard called out.

The two men didn't open their mouths to speak, but they fought with their eyes.

"Koen?"

Koen locked eyes with me, and I did my best to shift my eyes in a signal to leave.

With a huff, Koen marched away from Ravi. He paused at my side.

"At your request, I'll kill him," Koen threatened in a low voice.

Koen marched the rest of the way down the corridor, and the two of us watched.

"He's going to be your downfall, Lanira," Ravi whispered. "I'll ignore the threat he made and pretend he was skilled at whispering. An average guard is no threat to me, but to you? I can feel the slip-up from a mile away."

I cleared my throat and moved forward to open the door, but the distance didn't deter him.

"If I were anyone else, or even a sliver more convinced of your guilt, then he would be what delivered your final nail. He'd be what sealed you inside your coffin," Ravi moved quickly inside behind me.

He gave me no opportunity to leave him behind or ignore him.

"Explain to me then, what it is that keeps you from hammering that last nail?" I commanded.

"This kind of thing. You're so bold, and I've never seen someone who was filled with guilt ever be so bold," he replied. "The sunflowers as well. I keep thinking back to them. If you are a vampire, then it means what we know is a lie."

The pedestal he put himself on was obnoxious. The idea that anyone had all the knowledge without mistakes made him too full of ego. I felt my lips fold down.

"I don't believe you," I shook my head. "You're supposed to be a top hunter. Ruthless and intelligent beyond a simple maid. I wouldn't be the first life that you took simply on suspicion of guilt."

"I'm curious," he spoke with a nod. "No one has ever avoided me like you are. I've always picked the guilty ones out in hours. A day at most. I can't decide with you."

I allowed the disgust to move across my face for only a moment. "May I never know what it feels like to struggle with a choice simply because I can't accept my own faults. I didn't expect someone with your title to struggle only when faced with a choice that would make you admit to a fault."

I set my steps back into motion. I had no desire to stand around and talk to him. I wanted to show him the places that I had to and move on. I'd do what was asked of me and put the distance back between us.

"May I never presume to know someone so deeply after only a few conversations," Ravi remarked.

My eyes twitched, and I bit my tongue. The game between us was infuriating. I was forced to be silent. If I mentioned things like him taunting me with blood, I'd give myself away. If I pushed too far with my snark, I'd surely be held in a cell.

"I didn't expect it to be so easy to silence you," he chuckled.

I sucked in air through my teeth. "Are all men in your land so like you?"

"I've been told that I'm not allowed to speak to you about my kingdom, so you'll just have to guess," he smirked.

The action caused the dimple on his cheek to become clear.

My heart skipped a beat before my thoughts ran over his words.

"Who told you that?" I asked.

"Your king," Ravi tilted his head ever so slightly. "Or should I say father?"

The words sent a bolt of rage through me. I let the silence hang and directed him to follow me. We had tasks to finish that involved silence. I guided him out and through the castle.

I couldn't come up with a single reason why King Valen would order Ravi not to share information with me.

I felt Ravi's eyes burning through me while I showed him from place to place. He had little interest in his own room or the kitchens.

"Show me to the baths so that I can get cleaned up," Ravi requested from behind me.

I felt the frustration grow behind my eyes as I resisted rolling them.

I walked him to the baths and stood outside the entrance. Ravi placed his hand on the small of my back and shoved me through the large black column entryway. I hadn't realized that I was cold until every piece of my skin prickled and tingled at the warmth behind his palm.

The room opened up to a large black marbled floor. Silver swirls decorated the black. Nearly the entire room curved down into a dome that was filled with steaming hot water. Milk and honey swirled in the baths and filled the air with a sweet aroma. Braziers held fire that lit the space and added extra warmth.

Ravi's belt buckle unclipped and filled the air with the sound of metal. The sound sent a shiver down my spine. He looked me in the eyes when he unclipped each button on his trousers. His green eyes didn't waver when he allowed them to drop to the ground.

I became aware of how hard I swallowed my own saliva when he took off his corset vest and tossed it to the ground with the rest of his clothes.

I became all too aware of the sound of his heartbeat when he used one hand to unbutton his blouse while he moved closer to me. The rhythm of it quickened as he approached.

I nearly cracked when the sound of his blood pumping through his veins played for me as he leaned into my face. He hovered so close to me that I felt his breath on my lips.

"You should consider cleaning up as well. There's enough room for both of us," he whispered against my ear.

He moved himself away from my ear and back to staring me down with his green eyes. He blinked one slow time before he shifted his gaze to my lips. My heart nearly jumped out of my chest.

I could nearly taste his warm blood in my mouth.

"I don't know what kind of game you're trying to play right now, but I don't want any part in it," I whispered.

I wasn't convinced by my own voice. The way it shook gave me away.

"It's only a bath," he said, still locked on my lips.

His finger made contact with my throat, and he trailed down my chest. My body set fire at his touch, the warmth spreading through me.

"I'm not interested in love or games. I've done my duty; I'll take my leave," I stumbled over my words.

"I didn't say that I was in love with you. I said I wanted to see what was under your dress. Consider it part of my investigation. I'd be able to report that you have no markings," he smirked.

Images of his mouth on my body had already begun playing out in my mind, and I squeezed my thighs together at the idea.

"You're staring at my lips as though you agree," he said through a smirk.

I knew he had to be playing a game with me. If he was attempting to cause me to slip and release my fangs, I wouldn't.

He closed the distance between us, and his lips were on mine before I had the chance to take a breath. He wrapped his arms around my waist and pulled me into him until there was no space left.

The throbbing between my legs felt nearly as loud as his heartbeat sounded when I felt the hardness that he held pressed against me.

I realized what his game was when I tasted the blood coming from the inside of his bottom lip. He tasted bitter. I shot my eyes open, and his were already watching me. He had watched me the entire time. I placed my hands on his chest and shoved until he stumbled back into the bath. I hadn't ever encountered someone who could taint their blood.

"This isn't appropriate," I mumbled as I backed away.

I doubted he heard me. I hadn't heard him come back up from the water. I jogged away from the bath. I needed the distance. His blood tasted as if he had eaten something to make it resemble a pile of lemons.

I had never tasted anything so sour in my life. The taste wouldn't leave my mouth, no matter how many times I swiped my tongue across my teeth.

He couldn't be sure that I was a vampire even after that kiss. He couldn't guarantee that I tasted blood. I could have just denied him.

I was mindlessly walking through corridors in the maid's wing, but my mind spiraled too hard to fully realize that I needed to turn around.

If he hadn't tasted so bitter, he might have ended the same way Prince Tillo did. I would have drunk him until he was dry. It had to be because I wasn't eating enough. Ravi was nothing to me.

"Lanira!" Koen pulled me into the maid's bedroom that he stood in and shut the door behind us. "I've been dying to get you alone."

His mouth was on mine faster than Ravi's had just been. He moved to my neck and chest just as quickly. After Ravi's slow movements and agonizingly hard gaze, Koen felt so rushed and clumsy.

A chore, no, a necessity felt so different to desire.

"I keep seeing him make excuses to be close to you, and it's driving me crazy." he slipped his hands under my skirt and onto bare skin. "You're so wet already, Lanira. I knew you missed me as much as I missed you.

He slipped one finger inside of me, then two, and I gasped. I licked away the blood that still lingered on the inside of my lip. I wanted to taste it. To feel a part of Ravi inside of me. Even if it were bitter.

"Tell me that you missed me. Tell me that I'm better than Ravi. Say you're wet for me and not him," Koen whispered between thrusts of his fingers.

I opened my eyes at the feeling of my heart skipping beats. "What?"

Koen scrunched his brows and stared at me. I moved his hand from me and stood straight.

"What's wrong?" He asked.

"What did you say?" I asked again.

"Lanira, I thought you'd be into it." he shook his head and backed up. "Wait, are you upset because you're into him?"

"Of course not!" I shouted.

"Then what is it?" He pressed.

"I just wasn't expecting to hear another man's name while your fingers were inside of me," I scoffed.

"I've known you for your entire life, and I've never seen you act like this. You do like him, don't you?" Koen's brows couldn't have been raised any higher.

I didn't know what to say. Of course, I didn't like him. I had only known him a short time, and he wanted me dead. There was no way someone could be interested in anyone they had just met. Even if there was, I couldn't be.

The conversation was foolish, but no words came from my lips. The weight of my silence filled the room.

Koen looked at me with disbelief. He wasn't the only one reeling and trying to process.

"Your silence has said enough. I'll kill him, Lanira. Then it won't matter which words you pick to speak or hold onto."

Koen stormed out of the room and slammed the door behind him.

I needed to eat, and I'd think clearly. I'd get back on track with my plans. This distraction was becoming dangerous.

Chapter Fourteen
The Cost of Progress

Lanira

I stood behind Princess Invidia for the length of the royal's break-fast. Queen Blair didn't invite me to sit beside her. She occasionally glanced at me as if she had something to say, her eyes lingering a moment too long before darting away.

She never said whatever sat on her lips. She never furrowed her brows hard enough to tell me she was angry. She never softened her eyes enough to tell me she was sorry.

I was in the dark about her thoughts.

She never gave me eyes filled with an apology or a soft smile. The woman who had once brushed my hair and whispered that I was like a daughter to her now regarded me with something I couldn't decipher.

I had no hint or clue as to what was on her mind.

I didn't understand why I cared. It wasn't as if she hadn't acted that way before. There had been many times, more than I could count, when she was cold to me simply because it gave her a bet-ter position with the king. Some days, forcing him to watch her mother, I got her further with him.

Today seemed to be a different kind of day. I was only concerned because I allowed my guilt to take the forefront of my thoughts. I was supposed to be in control.

Yet I was panicking. I was letting myself slip under my own mind. I needed a good meal and the chance to pull myself back together. Ravi thought that Koen would be my downfall, but at this rate, I'd be my own worst enemy.

There were too many small but unignorable things happening. The Queen felt somehow different, as if her grief had changed her. The King ordered me to be surrounded by silence.

"We've nearly finished our investigations. Ravi has been a great help. He has techniques we've never seen before. Powerful runes that do things beyond our means," an advisor informed the king.

"We're certain the last man is guilty, at least in part, but he won't give names of those he's working with," another added.

"When Ravi returns to his kingdom, we think that you should request that other hunters take his place. We know that you didn't want to pay the cost before, but after seeing them in person, we think it's worth it. Our kingdom would be better protected than it ever has been."

"Unless you're here to tell me you've found Tillo's murderer, I don't want to hear it," King Valen grumbled through eggs. "You disgrace our guard in front of me and think nothing of it."

If they sent another Ravi, I'd risk it all to kill him on the spot. One was enough. The thought of more hunters prowling these halls made my blood run cold.

Princess Invidia leaned back and signaled me with her finger. I leaned down to listen, grateful for the distraction.

"Can you tell the maids to prepare a bath for me? Milk and lavender. I'd also like the kitchen to have my lunch ready early," she whispered.

"You're hungry?" I responded, unable to hide my surprise.

She hadn't eaten hardly anything since Prince Tillo's death.

She met me with the soft smile I had waited for all morning. The smile that allowed me to leave the tense air they gave off. I bowed and silently left the room. I felt as though I could take a deep breath. Everyone would be condensed in that room for a little longer.

My first stop was to be the kitchen. I needed to get back to who I knew that I was. I needed to remember my brother. My plans. My hopes for a future. I needed to get back to reality instead of whatever it was that I was doing.

I was Lanira Ambrose. The last of my family and I was in the kingdom of Emberrella so that I could get vengeance for my family. I was going to tear the world down so that it had to be rebuilt from rubble.

From that rubble, vampires would rise again. I would make sure of it.

The castle felt as if it knew change was on the horizon. Banners with the royal crest were hung outside of the castle, and although the golden stitches were new, they had already dulled and hung limp. Maids grew quieter and advisors grew increasingly nervous at what the king's next move would be.

Outside of the kitchen, three maids knelt in a corner. They drew runes on their arms in black. The runes were a tradition that was meant to help a soul pass peacefully. Some of them also protected people from being haunted by shadows. Souls of the dead that never passed onto an afterlife.

Traditions that were given by RuneHold to Emberrella. It was one of the only small insights into RuneHold.

It was said that when an important soul was to pass on, shadows would receive extra length on their chains and be allowed to roam further and louder than normal to receive the soul.

The entrance of the castle was painted in runes to protect against it. King Valen wanted his son to join the gods, not other souls.

I entered the kitchen, and it was lively again. Nothing like being in the mountains. The air was thick with the scent of roasting meats and baking bread, a stark contrast to the somber mood elsewhere in the castle.

"Princess Invidia would like her lunch brought to the baths. She'd like to eat early," I announced to the chef.

The room was buzzing with life. Preparations were being made for the send-off meal. Despite the grief written on the king's face, deaths were considered a celebration. A send-off on the next journey.

"Got it," the chef mumbled.

He continued under his breath about how her timing couldn't have been worse. They all looked stressed and distracted. Just as I hoped they would be.

Maids came in and out for more crushed herbs to burn. Rosemary was to be burned for four days in remembrance of the prince.

I entered the back pantry. I was hidden from sight and the coming and going. My heart fluttered at the sight of the blood buckets. Two pigs hung from the ceiling and drip, drip they went. I could taste the warmth before I even touched it, the copper scent making my mouth flood with saliva.

I reached behind a container of flour, and my ladle waited for me. I gulped at the bucket as if it had legs and could move away from me. I scared myself at the pace I gulped. I hardly drank. It was far from sips. I had nearly drained the bucket by the time I gasped for air.

I had never been so hungry for so long in my entire life. I reached for the second bucket and put my mouth to it. The ladle wasn't enough. The heat that ran through me felt like home. As if little stitches put me back together bit by bit with every gulp. I could feel the vitality returning to my limbs, the strength flowing through my veins.

I slammed the second bucket down and huffed in the air. I knew my eyes were red, and I had to have signs of what I had done on my face. I shoved the ladle back on the shelf and ran with confidence. I felt brand new. Strong. Full.

I felt ready to play their games and introduce my own again. There was a bathroom only around the corner from the kitchen. It made things easy for me for a long time. I rounded the corner of the hall, and the door was in sight.

"Lanira!" Ravi called.

I should have been scared, but I rode such a high, I nearly welcomed the chase.

I pulled the bathroom door open and slammed it shut, clicking the lock.

"Lanira!" Ravi pounded on the door.

"You ask much of me, hunter. You cannot have my personal time to use the facilities, too," I called out.

The mirror showed me exactly what I felt. Blood soaked my face, rivulets running down my chin. I cupped water from the basin and washed my face as gently as I could. Once, twice. I still saw hints around my lips. A third cupped hand of water sloshed against my face.

The bathroom smelled of milk and roses from the bars of soap sitting around. A sweet scent to contrast my harsh look.

"You've already seen so much of me; it hardly seems fair to shut me out," Ravi laughed.

"I never asked to see such a thing," I called back, scrubbing harder at my skin.

I tossed the basin of water out of the small window. The water was tinted red, but the ground below held brown dirt. It would keep my secrets close. I pulled out my small vial of perfume from the garter on my thigh and dabbed it from my chin down to my chest.

I needed to cover any hint of blood from him.

The mirror showed me someone with more color in their cheeks. Someone perky with not a drop of blood in sight. My eyes had changed back to their disguised brown, and the pallor that had haunted me for days was gone.

"You never looked away, either," he hummed.

I took a deep breath and opened the door.

"Why are you here and not busy being useful?" I crossed my arms.

"I noticed you left the meeting. I felt it proper to check on you. See if you were all right," Ravi explained.

"The princess asked me to leave," I pushed past him.

He followed me without missing a beat. "Were you close with the prince?"

I audibly sighed. It was natural for anyone to feel annoyed by him. I could release a bit of my inner thoughts without looking out of place.

"As close as any of us are," I replied. "If you are trying to imply that I'm not sad enough, then you should become more acquainted with the rules. I am not allowed to show an excess of emotions. I'm a companion, not a person." I walked faster.

"Would you cry if you could?" Ravi asked.

He sounded less accusatory than anything he had asked me before. I wanted to say no. I wouldn't. I wasn't sad that the prince was dead, not even a little.

"I need to go, sir. I have things to do still. Can you let the maids know that the princess would like a bath? Milk and lavender," I bowed. "Thank you. You've held me up and set my schedule behind."

"I'll do it, if you agree to speak with me again," he smiled enough to show his single dimple again.

"You phrase it as if I have a choice," I blinked.

"Of course you do. If you deny me on a personal level, then I'll follow you out of duty," he countered.

I rubbed my forehead before I turned to leave him without a word.

Ravi followed me from the bathroom to King Valen's throne room. He didn't walk inside with me. The king sat alone when I entered. His fists were clenched on the armrests, knuckles white with tension.

"Lanira. I called you for two reasons. I think you know something that can help. I think, no, I hope that because of how you were brought up, you hold loyalty to us," the king declared.

I bowed, "Of course I do. I only felt it inappropriate to discuss such things while you grieved." I pleaded.

"Then you do know something?" He perked up, leaning forward in his throne.

"I did. I overheard a group discussion at the ball. They spoke of how the prince was weak. They spoke of how the princess from Saydeean should have married into StoneDale instead. I only want to help, but I also didn't want to fuel rumors," I kept my head low and my gaze on the ground.

"We knew other kingdoms would have words to say about the marriage, but I never imagined they'd be so bold," King Valen muttered.

He spoke as if I weren't in the room. As if he talked only to himself.

"Prince Tillo was a good man, and he would have made a great king," I offered.

The king sat in silence for several moments before he sighed.

"The second reason that you're here won't be as fast, but it should be as simple," the king paused.

Koen brought in a man in chains and a bag over his head. He forced the man to his knees between the king and me. The chains rattled against the marble floor.

"This man has been suspected of being a vampire. He was found saying things similar to what you claim to have heard. You are to kill him. Not just in the name of Tillo and avenging him, but also to prove where your loyalty lies," the king leaned back on his throne.

I looked between Koen and the king. He was serious. My shifting eyes were already too much of a giveaway to my internal emotions. It had to be a trick. One of them would say stop as soon as I tried.

It was one thing to kill the prince. He deserved it. The king deserved it. It was justified. It was needed. There was logic in it.

Koen took the bag off the man's head, and he looked me in the eye. His face was bruised, one eye swollen shut. The man was no vampire. He was just a man. I could hear his heart pounding with fear, smell the sweat beading on his skin.

I didn't believe he had actually said anything I claimed, either.

I made the claims up myself.

The king nodded to Koen, and Koen moved to me. He picked up my hand and placed a knife in my palm before he backed up. The weight of it felt wrong, heavier than it should be.

"Use that and finish the job," King Valen commanded. "You're either with us, or you'll burn in the war that I'm going to start as a traitor."

I took a step closer. I knew that the longer I hesitated, the guiltier I'd look. A part of me said that if I killed that man, then I'd prove to them that I was capable of killing. That it was possible for me to have killed Prince Tillo.

It felt as though either side was a losing side. There were to be heavy consequences either way.

I took another step, and the man began to squirm and shake his chains. His eyes widened and shifted between his chains and my knife. I could smell his fear, hear the rapid beat of his heart.

I took another step and tightened my grip on the knife. My palms began to sweat, and I thought I might have dropped it. I stopped in front of him, and he begged for his life.

"Please, I didn't do anything! I have children, I have a family!"

The ringing in my ears was too loud to hear all the words he said.

I took a breath in and held it as I slashed the knife through the man's neck. The blade met resistance, then gave way. Warm blood sprayed across my dress, my face. The sound of his final gurgle would haunt me.

My knees buckled, and I thought for a second that I might have puked. I wasn't sure how I managed to keep it from happening. The knife slipped from my fingers, clattering to the floor.

"Take him away," the king commanded Koen. "I knew you'd be loyal."

The man may have been innocent of that single crime, but how was I to know if he had been truly innocent? He could have done any number of horrible things in his past.

He was part of the cost of progress.

He was the cost of what had to be done to get to the end. To get to peace.

I knew that I'd have to make sacrifices and that not all of them would be easy.

Ash would want me to keep going. He would see what I had done and understand my reasoning.

Wouldn't he?

He would see that it was the man or me.

He would understand. Even if he wasn't proud, he would get it.

He would want justice.

But as I watched Koen drag away the body, leaving a trail of blood across the polished floor, I wondered if justice was supposed to feel this hollow.

Chapter Fifteen
A Burial to Celebrate

Lanira

Tillo looked unrecognizable while he was being prepared for his final day. He was hardly a shell of skin on bone. I hadn't left a drop of blood behind when I fed from him. His throat was torn apart, the flesh ravaged in ways that made my stomach clench. The destruction was underplayed in conversations around the castle.

I was in such a haze when it all happened that in my mind, I had only left two small marks and a lifeless body behind.

The reality was much darker. I had acted as if I were an animal. An animal with no sense of restraint.

I considered myself as close to an average human as I could be. Only two small things made us different. They drank water, I drank blood. My teeth could retract, theirs couldn't.

I had never considered myself a monster until I laid eyes on Prince Tillo's corpse.

I tucked a golden coin under his tongue and closed his mouth. It was to buy his silence in the afterlife.

Prince Tillo wore the clothes he was to be crowned king in. He didn't look the part inside his straw coffin. Even if he died worse than I recalled, it was better that he died before he was able to see the world burn.

The realization that I was capable of much harsher things than even I knew, though startling, didn't quite outweigh the sense of pride I felt as I stood over his body. He would be put in the ground, and I would walk away from him, still free.

"Do you see why I'm having such a hard time?" Ravi asked, walking up behind me. "I don't think that you're capable of such violence, but I do think you had something to do with it. Koen isn't smart enough to stay hidden if he were a vampire. Maybe it's the Princess you're trying to protect. Maybe her sweet smile is an attempt to cover up how dark she can be. It would make more sense than assuming she is as sweet as she portrays herself to be. I've never seen anyone so locked inside of a bubble that they were able to genuinely be so, so." He moved his hands as if they were spinning with his thoughts, "So naïve."

"Don't be ridiculous," I snapped. "She's many things, but she is not a monster."

"You are, though?" He asked.

I turned to look at him. He watched me with genuine interest. There was no part of his face that contorted into blame or judgment. He looked at me as if I were a person and he wanted to hear not just my voice but my words.

"Ravi, do you ever consider the consequences of your pressure? If I were a vampire capable of this level of violence, aren't you afraid? If I did do this, in a place so crowded, wouldn't I do worse to you in a place I was more at ease?" My eyes shifted between his green eyes.

His skin was perfectly golden tanned. It complemented the color in his eyes well.

He smiled and ran a few fingers through my hair. "I think maybe that's what I'm pressing you for. I only need to find the right button to push, so that you show me if I should fear you or not. Part of me does hope you're innocent. I wouldn't mind getting a little closer to you," he ran his fingers through a few more strands with a smirk. "Sometimes the light gives your hair red highlights."

I pushed his hand away. "I'm going to urge you to remain professional. Touching me is against the rules. You may act ill-mannered in your own kingdom, but not here."

Ravi's laugh rang out with a sharpness that startled me, but I turned to leave without another remark.

He wouldn't get anything further out of me. The sight of Tillo startled me, but not enough to deter me from my goals. If Ravi wanted to die so badly, maybe I needed to grant that wish sooner rather than later. Before he had the chance to truly be in my way.

The only good thing that Ravi brought to my life was the ability to ignore other things. He pulled me from letting my mind linger on the guilt of what I had done.

It was hard to wrap my thoughts around the emotion. I didn't know what to name it. I did not feel bad for killing him. I felt bad for myself, and the way I was revealing that I hardly even knew who I was. I didn't feel bad for the tears that the queen and princess shed, but I did feel guilty for the way my mother must have cried watching my sisters.

I felt strange because I only felt bad for myself. I didn't want to get caught in a swirl of grief and claim that I was done, and Prince Tillo's death was for nothing. It was good that I wasn't lying in my own bed crying, but a new thought started to wiggle its way into my mind.

Was I a bad person?

Was I slowly becoming everything that I hated?

The image of the prince's body wiggled into my mind. He was a necessary death, and there would be more. I need to keep my mind on that track. I had to repeat it and believe it. I was on the right path. I had known it for fifteen years.

I'd keep marching forward. For my mother, who had to have cried the same tears as I saw for Prince Tillo.

After all, my family died just as horrifically, and they received nothing in return.

Had they grown into trees? Flowers? Were they still ash sunken into dirt at Lunadur? Had anyone gone back to burn incense for them? Did their souls still wander our old kingdom?

I had lost the name of our temple. My memory was scarred with the faces of the dead and the screams of the dying. It didn't hold any space for names or traditions. I was too young to be taught most of them. I was at an age where I was still allowed to pick what I wanted to spend my days doing.

The horns of rebirth sounded in the air. A relic from the age of vampires and a signal that things were progressing. They were a gift left behind by the God of Rebirth. King Valen's land once had rituals and deities, too.

When the Gods left, so did most of the knowledge of them and their customs. Thann, the God of Rebirth, was one of the only known deities simply because he taught burial rites. It was one of the last traditions still held in Emberrella from the age of vampires.

His horn was the sound that would alert the shadows that they needed to pick up a soul.

Villagers gathered inside of the palace walls. Something only done when a member of the royal family died. They were covered in runes, the same as the court members of the castle. The symbols glowed faintly against their skin in the afternoon light.

Small children held candles coated in rosemary and sunflowers as they watched the proceedings. Their eyes were wide with the solemnity of the occasion.

I hurried my steps until I found the other maids and companions. It was my place. Another reminder that even though I was called sister or daughter when the times needed it, I truly wasn't.

Torch holders guided Tillo's body in front of the royal family. They were dressed in their most expensive clothing. Jewels shimmered brighter than any tears. Incense holders walked behind them. They carried rosemary for remembrance.

It was our turn next. We walked in rows of three with our heads down. My heart pounded hard enough that I heard it inside of my ears. I was happy to be back in a situation where I was no longer allowed to show large amounts of emotions.

If I were to break down in sobs in public, I'd be punished.

I only wanted to laugh. To look King Valen in the eyes and ask him how it felt to bury his favorite child. To tell him that I picked his favorite as the first to die on purpose.

The other maids and I stood to the side while the guards brought in the tree. Guards lowered Tillo into the ground, and his personal guard and maid crawled inside the hole with him. They'd go with him to help him in the afterlife. Koen helped shovel dirt over the top of them, his face grim with the finality of it.

The forest that bordered the kingdom of Emberrella was planted entirely by death. Every tree was grown by pulling nutrients from a dead royal. Each trunk stood as a monument to lives that had ended in service to the crown.

A small golden sign was hammered below each tree with the name of the royal that was buried beneath it. No plaque mentioned the ones buried with the royal; they weren't notable enough. The trees were rich with life. Birds nested and trees grew fruit that no one dared to eat.

One day, I'd build from the tree that grew out of Valen's corpse.

"Prince Tillo was a great member of our kingdom. A top student and a wonderful contributor to our royal court. His ideas would have launched us to new heights," Minala, the priestess, spoke to the crowd as they crashed the roots of a half-grown tree into the hole.

She stood in front of the tree on a small metal stand until the king shoved her off it. He took her place with his eyes and lips sagging.

"I know my kingdom well. Tillo knew his subjects well. If there were a traitor in our midst, he would have known it. No one could have hidden from Tillo. I trained him better than that. I've heard many confessions and testimonies since his death. I've had many loyalties proven to me as well," King Valen took a moment to compose himself, his hands trembling as he gripped the edge of the stand.

The supposed vampire's face that I knew King Valen referred to flashed in my mind. The way the blood ran down his chest. The way his eyes pleaded with me not to kill him.

"It has come to my attention that StoneDale is not an ally of ours. They've grown jealous of our success. My investigation has uncovered facts. They killed Tillo to ruin the marriage alliance and bring the prophecy crashing down on us. They want to see us in ruin so that they may take our place as the center of rule and trade. In Tillo's name, on the day he is laid to rest, I am declaring war on StoneDale. We will show them the might of our army and help Tillo rest in peace," King Valen finished speaking.

It was hardly enough time for everyone to exchange looks before shouting began.

"We can not go to war!"

"How do you know it was them?"

"Please reconsider!"

"How many soldiers will die?"

"Where is the proof of this claim?"

I was tired of being passive. I was tired of not moving pawns on my own. I was sick of the slow pace at which things progressed while I starved. I was ready to force hands again. I was ready to make the waves instead of moving with them.

I pushed past maids and guards. I gave a smile to the princess, and I moved past her, too.

"The only reason to protest your King is if you think his armies are too weak to fight and win. Is that what you, as his advisors, are suggesting?" I looked between them. "Do you not also want the prince to rest in peace? What would you have the king do instead? Allow someone to roam free after killing a member of the royal family? Is that the image you would have drip from your king's name? Does Prince Tillo's death mean nothing to you?" I kept my chin high and my words sharp.

One man moved forward, "Damaged relations are harder to rebuild than an army or castle. If we declare war on the grounds that they killed a royal family member, we can not just take it back. What proof is there? No one who sees through the lens of grief and vengeance ever sees clearly."

"Why would we want relations with them, ever again? If your King has proof, that is enough for me," I demanded.

"I am your king. I do not need anything other than my decree. We go to war as soon as preparations can be ready," King Valen shouted.

King Valen stepped off the metal stand and placed his hand on my shoulder. The pause was only a few seconds, but it felt like a lifetime with his disgusting hand on me. He looked at me as if he were proud. The act sent shivers of disgust down my spine.

I'd never get the scent or memories out of the fabric.

"My lord! I have to disagree," Priestess Minala announced as she stormed her way to us. "This girl is an enemy to us all. She is a dark shadow that hangs over your kingdom. If she considers your move well-positioned, then maybe it is time to consider it a poor choice."

King Valen let his eyes linger on me for a moment, and I softened under his gaze.

For the first time, he looked at me with compassion. I was getting exactly what I wanted.

"Are you challenging my judgment?" He asked as he turned to Minala.

"I'm merely trying to do my duty and tell you when a decision is ill advised," she urged. "She is a snake. A vampire who lurks until she can take a second bite out of us. I've seen her out late at night when the rest of the world sleeps."

"Didn't she pass your rune test?" Ravi inserted himself into the conversation. "If I recall, it was your idea, your rune, and your words that claimed it was foolproof. Which means she can't be a vampire in waiting. This feels," he paused for a moment. "It feels as though maybe you need a closer look."

"What?" Minala yelled.

Her gaze shot to King Valen immediately.

"Someone as close to me as you are would have the perfect opportunity," the king pointed at her.

King Valen was further gone than I thought he was. I never imagined that I'd see the day the king turned on his favorite member of the court.

"My lord, don't let them get into your mind! I am loyal only to you!" Minala dropped to her knees.

"A simple test should be no problem then," Ravi declared.

I kept silent. I didn't know why Ravi would interject.

I didn't want to consider what the cost of his help would be. The more pressing worry was that I knew when to speak and when to shut my mouth. It was a time to shut my mouth.

"Guards, I want her to be tested," the king commanded.

The guards took a struggling Minala by each arm. She didn't relent even when the two of them shoved her face into the dirt.

King Valen watched with wide eyes and an open mouth as a third guard sliced Minala's hand open and pressed it into a piece of parchment. The same rune used on me was drawn on it.

How many pages did they have lying around?

The guards dropped her limbs and allowed Minala to lift her head when the parchment cleared her name.

She gazed up at King Valen with watery eyes and a trembling lip. She was correct, and yet no one listened to her pleas. She was the only one to see what I had done and call out my name, but she pleaded to deaf ears.

If King Valen was allowed to keep feeding his rage and delusions, I'd be safe.

She'd be shamed.

My game of chess was even better than I could have imagined it to be.

King Valen walked past Priestess Minala without glancing down at her. He had seen that she was clean and loyal, but still left her in the dirt.

He cared for no one but himself.

Ravi grabbed my arm and pulled me into him. "Next time, keep your mouth shut."

I smiled, just slightly enough for him to see. "If you are so happy to be my hero, should I not give you reasons to be?"

"Lanira, I won't do it again. I've clearly spoiled you with the idea that you may behave any way you please," Ravi grumbled.

"Perhaps so," I agreed.

He dropped my arm when Princess Invidia ran to my side. She pulled me in closer to her as if she were going to save me from whatever may have happened, even though it was already over.

The irony wasn't lost on me. She was trying to protect me from the very man who kept protecting me from myself.

Chapter Sixteen
Plans Must Go On

Lanira

I stood, dressed in my best white gown, in the middle of King Valen's throne room. A place I seemed to be called to often lately. I was surrounded by advisers and the entire royal family. Princess Invidia stood beside me with her hand clasped in mine.

They were freezing. Near death temperatures from her neglect and fear. The room reeked of old men who considered basic hygiene something too time-consuming. The light bursting through the stained-glass window and filling the room with rainbows was the brightest thing among us, a cruel contrast to the darkness of the proceedings.

"My army is already in the depths of preparation. They will be ready to march in a few more days. Unless there is a much better reason, I won't stay here and listen to this," King Valen declared.

"It won't cause any harm to halt the army for a few days. You need time to consider your choices," an adviser urged.

"You can't take this kind of choice back," another interrupted.

"Making such an action based on the instigation of Lanira is beneath you," Priestess Minala pressed.

Princess Invidia squeezed my hand harder. "Whatever it is that you have against her, you need to stop letting it affect your judgment."

"Princess, I have never given ill advice before," Minala replied.

"There's a first time for everything, priestess. I'd say that it's easy to see you have a bias," Princess Invidia stood with her chin held high.

She proved to be an even more valuable asset than I had imagined her to be. I was called to be put on trial, again. Yet I had not spoken a single word in my own defense.

Ravi moved forward. "I have to agree with the princess. It seems that priestess Minala has a special interest in Lanira. Lanira has more than proven herself. Her blood, her loyalty. At what point does this stop?"

"It stops when her vampire corpse is on the ground and we abandon the idea of a war! We are supposed to be united. Pulling the kingdoms together! We are meant to be gathering strength and rising against her!" Priestess Minala screamed.

Her words had me sitting on edge. She spoke only the truth, and I had to hope that I had just enough grace in those around me, that I'd walk free.

How much luck could I have?

"Do you have anything to say, Lanira?" Queen Blair asked, her voice cutting through the tension.

"I think instead of pointing fingers at an innocent girl, we could focus on things of importance. Priestess Minala is half right. We should be focused on the right things, like uniting the kingdom against our foe. The army is nearly ready, and I think seeking vengeance for a man I considered my brother is the only appropriate next step. It is possible the one who killed the prince is or knows the vampire of the prophecy. I think after that, we still have the marriage between the Princess of Saydeean to consider. She can marry Altair," I was interrupted before I could continue.

The Queen watched me as if she were content with my answer, though something flickered behind her eyes.

"That's a worse idea than this war!" Priestess Minala yelled.

"I've considered the same thing. We can write an agreement that all of the choices for the kingdom still rest in my hands while Altair and the princess sit on the throne," the king mumbled to himself.

"This is what I've been talking about! She is planting seeds of corruption!" Priestess Minala pointed accusingly.

"The King and I spoke of this already. It isn't Lanira who spoke of this idea first," Queen Blair interjected.

"Maybe it's you that wants our downfall," the princess suggested. She spoke calmly in comparison to the chaos around us.

"We can marry them and sit the two on the throne for everyone to see, Altair is not as good as Tillo, but for the prophecy's sake, he can still unite the kingdoms under my guidance," King Valen still rambled as if he were alone.

"That won't fulfill the prophecy. If Altair and the Princess aren't fully in charge, then it defies the prophecy!" Priestess Minala argued. "This should show you that Lanira is sowing corruption."

King Valen slammed his fist on the armrest of his throne. "We will send the army and still hold the wedding! We will stave off the prophecy and enact revenge. My idea is a great one, and anyone who doesn't agree will be labeled a traitor."

Advisors and Minala all yelled in unison their protests. Princess Invidia still held my hand in the midst of the chaos. I didn't hear anything they yelled because my eyes were locked on the queen's. She watched me as if taking in every little thing about me. As if I were someone new. Someone she had never met before.

She twirled the rings on her finger as if deep in thought.

Maybe it was my eyes playing tricks on me. Maybe it was my guilt slipping out again. Maybe I was sabotaging myself.

I pulled the princess closer to me and backed us up from the chaos. The old man was deep enough in his thoughts that I couldn't imagine he even remembered I was there. The Queen did. She watched every move I made.

I would prove to her that I was innocent and protected her daughter.

"Princess, I think we should go. You shouldn't be here. I thank you for defending me, but you don't need to put yourself in the middle of things for me. I'd give my life for you. It should never be the other way around. Let's get you out of this and somewhere peaceful," I spoke softly.

She smiled at me, and I guided her out of the room with a matching smile. I took her through the candle-lit halls and past the always bustling kitchen. The princess slowed at the smell of apple pies, the sweet aroma cutting through the tension that had followed us.

I still heard the sound of raised voices echoing behind us. Men panicked at the thought of losing their power. Each one of them fought to have the king's ear and be the wisest in the room.

"I'm sure they'd offer you some of the pie," I whispered.

She smiled and guided me into the kitchen. She pointed, and the maid smiled with a nod as we knew she would. They wouldn't say no to her. The two of us climbed onto the stools placed at the wooden island in the center of the kitchen, and the plates were placed in front of us.

Eating pie didn't give me the same high or energy as blood did. It was nowhere near the experience, but it was edible all the same. Some of it tasted divine. Even my favorites were never as good as warm blood. I still required food to keep up with all of the same things that anyone else did. My diet required blood along with fruits and vegetables.

"This was exactly what we needed," the princess declared.

I nodded in agreement. "Thank you for what you did."

"You don't need to thank me," she replied through a mouthful of food. "I stuck up for my sister in the same way I know that you would do for me."

I wouldn't do the same, but I smiled.

"Can I ask, do you remember any of your old family? We don't speak about it," she asked hesitantly.

I remember more than she'd like to hear. More than she'd be able to handle hearing.

"Only small bits," I responded.

"Can you share with me?" She asked.

"I don't have much to share. I recall only brief bits of having a dinner table and a pink blanket on my bed," I offered.

I wasn't going to give her anything further. I recalled the devastation that her family caused to mine more than anything else. She wasn't going to have my memories and hold the blame for taking the chance of making any more away from me.

"It must be hard for you. Now that Tillo is gone, I can't help but wonder what kind of grief you must feel. How heavy it must be to not remember," she pushed the pie around her plate. "I'm sorry that I never asked before, but I want you to know that I'm okay hearing about your memories or loss."

Her words should have made me feel better, but they only enraged me. She needed the death of her own brother to feel anything for me. Soon, she'd be able to feel closer to me still when I killed her second brother, and she was all that was left.

Even in the moments where she looked so innocent and genuine, I found it hard to see her as a true sister. I knew what that felt like. It wasn't someone who only thought of me when they were backed into a corner. It wasn't someone who gave me permission to share who I was or where I came from.

Even in the moments that I nearly felt close to her, there was something in her eyes that reminded me she wasn't truly on my side.

If she knew who I was, if I didn't serve her, she wouldn't consider me a sister.

"Do you recall when we were children, Tillo used to sneak us into the back courtyard with the training dummies? He was so adamant that we know how to protect ourselves in case he couldn't be around. When father found out, he had Tillo take twenty-five lashes," she paused and pushed her food around. "It's that memory that makes me so determined to ensure your safety. You tried to take his lashing for him. You were so loud about it. You demanded that Father give them to you as if you didn't fear the king at all. The rest of us shook too hard to move our lips. I thought you were so brave. I can't imagine that nine-year-old girl grew up to be a cold-blooded killer." She set her fork down and smiled at me.

"I do remember that. King Valen wanted to give both of us the lashings and it was the Queen that wouldn't let him punish me. She mentioned that leaving scars on my skin would lower my worth if it were ever needed," I chuckled, though the memory tasted bitter.

Princess Invidia frowned. "You know she didn't mean that. It was only what Father needed to hear to spare you."

I found myself fidgeting with my skirt under the table. "Of course."

The princess took both of my hands in hers. "Lanira, I want you to know I never meant to treat you as anything other than my sister. I'll keep defending you if I need to."

Her words felt like a bee sting. They were empty, but they stung with the promise of what could have been if only she were a bit less selfish, and I were a bit less angry.

She'd call me her sister, but still order me around.

I'd call her my sister, but I still would kill her entire family.

Maybe in another life we could have been sisters. In another life, I could have shown her my home, and she could have grown me sunflowers. We could have shared our homes in peace without silent betrayal.

In this life I'd smile at her with a sticky sweet layer of praise, and she'd reason that keeping me below her was just how things worked. That it didn't mean anything, and we were still as close as wallpaper and wood.

There was cruelty in the question, but I'd ask it anyway out of curiosity.

"When things are set right again, what do you plan to do? If Prince Altair takes the throne and you're clear to do anything, the prophecy is halted and the world is free," I took a bite of the pie.

Princess Invidia watched me while she thought. She blinked more times than I could count. As if the thought never occurred to her before, I asked it.

"I think I will ask to travel. Maybe I will ask to study the hunters. I'd want to do something useful, noble. I'd want to protect people," she replied. "If I were free to pick then I'd want to do anything more than remaining inside of the same walls and simply existing until I died. I pretend to enjoy the way we live, but—" Princess Invidia set her fork down with a frown. "I haven't been happy since we were children. I try to be, but I've never felt as useful as my brothers. There's no future ahead of me, no carefully thought of instructions like they received. I'm only the princess who will remain to play with a sewing needle."

It was strange to see her have a desire outside of a spoiled child. She talked about a side of her that I had never seen before.

"Sometimes I imagine that one of the kingdoms has magic, and I go to learn it. Like in the fairy tales the maids tell. Other times, I think maybe I would be allowed to wear armor and go fight for a cause with everyone else. I wish Tillo were still here, but I think a part of me broke further when I realized that even in the death of my brother, I remained in last place. Only an angel to be looked at. I haven't become an option to help in anything still. If Altair isn't fit for the throne, what about me?" Princess Invidia lost herself in rambling.

"Have you spoken to Queen Blair? If she heard this, maybe the two of you—"

She stopped me with a laugh. "She doesn't like me. She likes you. It's always been you."

"That's not true. She speaks often of how badly she wants the two of you to grow closer," I replied.

"I've tried. She likes the way you brush her hair or the way that you listen so well. She tells me often that I cannot live up to you," Princess Invidia admitted.

"I had no idea," I confessed.

"It is not your fault. Although I am a bit jealous of you," Princess Invidia smiled, but there was sadness behind it.

I picked up my fork and scooped a bit of pie and fed it to Princess Invidia. I had known her a long time to only see a real and vulnerable side of her after I killed her brother.

She took the bite and sat back up straight. While she chewed, she plastered the smile back on her face. The moment of vulnerability disappeared like it had never existed, buried beneath years of practiced performance.

For the first time, I wondered if we were more alike than I'd ever imagined.

Chapter Seventeen
A New Pawn Placed

Lanira

My room was only a wall away from the princess, but a wall was enough for me. My room was exceptionally modest compared to hers. Both were filled with pastel colors at her request. The only thing I wanted was sunflowers and a thick fur blanket. They were two things that I never received.

No one had time to consider my two requests. Simple desires that seemed too small to matter yet meant everything to me.

I did have plenty of time to silently observe and learn instead.

I studied things that didn't always seem worth it at the time, like who ignored what foods, and who couldn't ignore what drinks. I collected skills that seemed like they might be useful later, even if I didn't know at the time what I would use them for.

I was glad to have stuck with handwriting observation. Understanding the little things that made the king and queen's handwriting unique was a skill that ended up being beyond useful, even if I didn't see it at the time.

My wooden desk had enough space to lay out both of the letters that I needed to write. A war was going to rain down on StoneDale and thin their army and ours.

It seemed that the princess of Saydeean would still marry into King Valen's family, which meant Saydeean would be forced to get involved in any war that involved Emberrella. Three kingdoms would be at war and busy, their resources stretched thin and their focus divided.

King Valen's kingdom wasn't yet burning hot enough.

When I put the first war into motion, I'd have time to focus on the last two kingdoms and the last son of Emberrella.

I only picked StoneDale because they felt the easiest. RuneHold had vampire hunters. RubyWake had never been spoken of in my presence. I didn't know even the smallest detail to plan for. They had to wait.

I wrote a letter in the king's handwriting. It would state that he followed through with the plan. That the boy was removed as promised and he was waiting for word of their next move. I wanted it to stay ambiguous. The less detail included, the better. It would feel real that way. It was enough that anyone who read it would think he had involvement in Prince Tillo's death.

That, at the very least, the king conspired with someone outside of his own court.

The entire kingdom was on edge, and the King even turned on his priestess. It would be easy to plant any seed that I wanted.

I wrote a second letter in the Queen's handwriting. It would mention that the useless pawn was removed from the board, and to proceed as planned.

Both letters would be similar, but worded in the way they each spoke. I wanted the same seed to be planted on both sides.

They'd both be painted as a traitor, and both would have reasons that it was believable.

The Queen always did favor Prince Altair, and perhaps King Valen grew jealous of everything that Prince Tillo grew into. Maybe he wasn't ready to give up his position after all.

I sealed the king's with gold wax and the queen's with purple wax. They'd not question if they were authentic with the wax. I tucked both letters inside the skirt of my dress and flattened the skirt back down.

I wished that I knew Ravi's handwriting. I could have written something about the Priestess. I could have set things up to make it appear that Ravi was suspicious of Minala but afraid to voice out loud that she was a vampire. I doubted Ravi would not confront the idea head-on, but once a whisper started, there was always a hint of it in some corner.

I doubted that I'd ever be rid of Priestess Minala. She had been around longer than I was. She was born in the castle under King Valen's watch. She should have died with the vampires. Priestesses, witches, they were taught by my old home.

She only received a pass because she had never stepped foot out of the castle walls. She was groomed to be loyal to King Valen, and loyal she was. She would lick his feet if he so asked it.

It was a shame, but I need not grow greedy. Some things would happen naturally over time.

My door creaked as I slowly pulled it open, and I rolled my eyes.

Of course, it made noise when I needed it to be silent. I never knew when I had eyes on me, and even the door betrayed me. The hour was late enough that everyone should have been sound asleep. My feet were bare to aid in my silence.

I walked through the halls as close to the wall as I could move my body. I wanted to blend into the shadows left between the flickers of torch fire. I felt a calm kind of high until the footsteps of a guard sounded in the air. I shoved myself flat against the wall and listened to their stride draw closer and closer.

Footsteps pounded against the marble. They became filled with a sudden rush.

One. Two. Three. Four. They bolted in a full sprint in my direction.

My heart raced, and I pushed myself tighter against the wall.

"Damn those hounds," he muttered as he ran past me.

My heart sank, and I slowly let out my breath. His ears had to have been trained for those dogs because I still hadn't heard them as I watched all three of them run through the firelight. They should have been in the kennels outside.

I started my steps slowly back in motion. There wasn't another guard or person in sight.

I took a path not often traveled to ensure that I was not seen. A closed-off wing of the castle that had once been used for vampiric visitors. They'd sleep there as guests when they arrived to discuss trade deals.

Dried sunflowers hung from doorknobs to ensure no wandering vampire tried to take advantage of the empty beds.

I visited the wing often as a smaller child. It was the only way I had to be close to home again.

Some walls were covered with paintings of old deities and important vampires. One portrait was a goddess with crimson hair and eyes. Her skin was as pale as the stars. Some doors had their own runes carved into them. Runes I had never seen translated.

A thick layer of dust coated every surface, just as cobwebs sat in every corner. Every surface of the wing spoke of deities that were no longer concerned with our well-being.

Outside of the wing, on the edge of the king's study, I had to hold myself against the walls again as another guard patrolled. I waited for his footsteps to sound distant before I made my move.

I slowly turned the knob and pushed the door open. King Valen was confident enough in the fear he gave everyone that he never locked his doors. His cocky nature was what made it easy for me to crumble him and his sanity.

I moved around the desk and set the note inside his top drawer. I left a small piece of paper with scribbled words. I wanted it to look as though an uneducated guard had written it. The small note left a simple message.

You need to know the truth.

It was simple, but meaningful.

I closed the desk and moved away from it. I wanted to stay longer. I wanted to go through all of the things that sat on his shelves. His study was covered wall to wall, floor to ceiling, in books. Their leather spines created a mosaic of knowledge I was denied. I would come back soon.

Inside his study sat everything that was left of my past. A book sat somewhere inside his study that told exactly how to bring it back. It told our history and all of our rituals that I was too young to absorb. It told how to revive the dead, and it would be the thing to tell me who I was.

It had to tell me why I wasn't like any vampire ever spoken of.

I was closer to a human than any whisper ever sent into the wind of my family.

That was for another day. A day soon to arrive.

I left his study and slowly closed the door. I'd need to go to the queen's bath next. I'd hide her letter where I knew she spent all of her time. She didn't have a study of her own because Valen didn't believe her place was reading or working on matters of the kingdom.

She educated herself outside of his permission, all the same.

Every morning, she cleansed herself before heading out for the day, and every evening she soaked the shame of King Valen away. She was bound to find the letter soon enough. The king would find his first no doubt, and she'd be confused over his rage.

I cracked a smirk. I was alone; I could let one slip. I didn't allow it to linger, but I did allow it to show.

The small moments I had to outwardly be myself were so important to me. Sometimes I didn't feel real. Some days, I felt hollow. I feared that I'd eventually forget how to feel true emotions.

My feet froze every time they touched the ground. The sensation and being so close to another step down felt like a rush of adrenaline. I slipped into the bath, set the letter and the note by her hairbrush, and slipped back out of the doorway.

My heart dropped into my stomach when I looked up from my steps through the hall.

I was stopped by a face that I knew well.

"I watched you enter, and I thought that you'd notice me following you and wait for me. You're leaving so fast that I get the feeling you didn't realize I was watching," Koen observed, stepping out of the shadows.

"Koen, I thought you were guarding the king tonight," I replied, forcing my voice to remain steady.

My chest still pounded.

"No." He watched me with narrowed eyes and parted lips. "What is going on? You and I used to meet nightly. Sometimes midday as well. You used to be obsessed with me. I spent more time inside of you than I spent inside of the king's chambers. Now that Ravi is around, you've become distant." Koen growled.

"It has everything to do with being a suspect. I had little to worry about before. I'm the subject of nearly all conversations these days. It's a heavy weight to carry. You'd have no idea what that's like," I snapped. "It's nothing to do with Ravi."

"You aren't the kind of girl to let that affect you. I've known you too long for this. You think that I don't see you, but you're wrong. If it's not Ravi, then there's only one other reason why you'd decide that I wasn't good enough for you anymore. You've set your sights on the throne."

He paused to watch me, and my heartbeat sped up. I hadn't planned to kill him yet, but if he had guessed my motives.

"You plan to marry Altair, don't you. You want to become the queen. I won't allow it. I won't allow anyone else's hands on you, Lanira. I haven't forgotten how close you stood beside him in the mountains. I'll tell everyone that we've slept together. I'll help them lock you in the dungeon myself," Koen hissed.

"You'll be locked away too," I pointed out.

I did my best to keep calm despite my shaking hands.

"I don't care. They can lock me in the cell beside you. I'm willing to lose everything that I have if it means that you do too. If it means that no other man will see you the way that I have," Koen's face hovered above mine, his breath hot against my skin.

"I'm not sure when I gave you the impression that I was your property to speak to any way you want," I growled.

Koen grabbed my arm and pulled me closer to him. "You became my property the first time you opened your legs for me."

I hadn't planned to kill him yet. I had considered him too dull-witted to truly be a problem. If he kept threatening me the way he was, as if I were property that belonged to him, I'd have to leave his lifeless body behind with the letters.

"I cannot keep pretending that I don't see this," Ravi declared from behind us.

Ravi grabbed Koen by the back of his shirt, and Koen nearly pulled me with the two of them before he let go of my arm.

Ravi pulled Koen with such force that Koen's head hit the wall before his back slammed against it. Koen's nostrils flared, but Ravi's face was as calm as the night air.

"I've given you enough chances. I draw the line at seeing your hands on her. You'd better be sure of those words before you end up locked away and filled with regret. It's your final warning," Ravi threatened.

Koen ran his tongue over his bottom teeth before he pushed himself up and off the wall.

Koen shifted his gaze back to me. "Think it over, Lanira. You know where to find me."

Koen shoved past Ravi with a kind of confident anger I'd never seen from him before. I wasn't as confident in who would win as Koen was in himself.

"I may arrest him before I arrest you," Ravi mentioned with crossed arms. "Care to explain?"

"It's none of your business," I replied and tried to shove past him, too.

He grabbed my arm and pulled me back to him. "I think that it is. Do you think that I'm under an obligation to stay quiet? Or that I care for you enough to defend you like I have to do for the princess?"

"I think that you're doing to me exactly what you were so out-raged to watch a moment ago. I think that even if I don't have your loyalty, I have your curiosity. You've lost yourself right now. As such, I do think that it's enough to keep you quiet," I took the risk.

Ravi dropped my arm. "Tell me this, then, are you in trouble?"

"I'm not in anything that I cannot handle," I assured him.

"I've seen many women taken down by a jealous man," he sighed.

"How would you know anything about a woman's life in court?" I moved past him while he gave me the chance to move.

I didn't want to feel trapped. I didn't want to remain looking as though I had just come from the king's study.

"I learned plenty through the trials and suffering of my mother before I was ripped from her. I'm only warning you that my silence is wearing thin," Ravi sighed and straightened his top.

"I never asked for your silence," I mumbled.

"You'll learn the hard way that moving alone is never successful," he looked me over one last time.

I expected him to remain hard while he gazed at me, but his eyes were soft in a way that made my stomach flutter.

Ravi marched in the opposite direction, and I was relieved that he left. I still had one letter to leave. There was a part of me that was sad to see him go. A small part of me wanted more time to speak to him.

I heard Princess Invidia's voice in my head.

He's cute, what's one time? It may end in a marriage!

Her voice squealed, and I grimaced at the thought of it.

I tucked my brown hair behind my ears and lifted my skirt. I was lucky to have had the interruption, but I had one more letter to leave in a bath house before the castle was booming with life again.

The night wasn't over yet, and neither was my work.

Chapter Eighteen
A Thorough Investigation

Ravi

Lanira's hair was brown, but it still managed to make a bright halo around her head. The sun always touched her as if she were the morning's gift.

She stood in front of the window that sat at the top of the double staircase. Stained glass held an image of the king and queen who founded the kingdom of Emberrella. The sight of Lanira in her cobalt-colored skirt and white lace-up corset would stay in my memory for eternity.

She held her hand out with a letter for me to take. Her fingers were long but thin. She had perfectly rounded nails as if she had never done a hard day's work. I knew she had. I watched her do task after task. I watched her make beds and clean rooms.

I watched her while she helped the kitchen staff clean up at night. I watched her for the better part of every day since I arrived. It was hardly work. It had become more of a hobby. I had memorized the way her lip would twitch if she had to lie too many times in a row. It was burned into my mind the way she picked at her thumbnails when she was lost in her own thoughts.

"Why do I need to take this?" I asked her.

Her voice was as beautifully soft as her face.

"I was asked to have you deliver it to Koen, "Lanira replied. "A guard made it seem like it was urgent."

She wore a soft smile and big brown eyes. Did she think that I'd do anything she asked simply because she looked at me that way?

"Who? I need more information than that," I demanded.

"I don't have further information. Please, Ravi. I'm not you. I don't have a position that allows me to ask questions," she pushed the letter closer to me.

I took it with a sigh. "If you recall who it was, point them out to me. That will be enough. I'll question them myself."

I may not have felt so conflicted about her if I didn't know what she had to go through living in court.

My mother went through the same things Lanira had to go through. My mother was at the mercy of the men of the court in RuneHold. There were only so many ways to guarantee yourself safety or information.

The crown protected whom it wanted to, and a bastard son and his mother were never on the list. I watched the king call my mother a maid during the day and a whore by night. He never admitted it to the end, even as I was put into hunter training, he denied my paternity.

It was only on his dying breath, when I had become First Blade of the Hunters, that he claimed me, and by then I resented him too much to care.

My past made me soft to her.

I would stick to that thought. The alternative was that I liked the girl.

Lanira bowed before she casually walked away. She didn't rush as if she were nervous or fidget as if she were guilty of something.

There was something about her that had me convinced she was someone different than who she presented herself to be. Her lips smiled as they should. Her skin flushed at the correct times. She was exactly as she should have been.

Her eyes failed her. Even when they lifted with her smile. Even when I was nearly convinced that she was just an innocent girl doing her best for her position, her eyes told me differently.

They were so empty. Sad. There was something that lurked behind them, and I wanted to talk to it.

If she did turn out to be a vampire, I'd have a hard choice to make. I didn't dare dwell on it.

I wanted to meet the girl who hid herself. It was so hard for me to remain in their kingdom. I should have gone home with a success story already. Lanira was right, I could have sentenced her without evidence. She wouldn't be the first that I killed without proof. If I had done it, she would no doubt not be the last.

There was something that stopped me. Something that tugged at me. A voice in my head that screamed, she could very well be innocent. I never thought twice about killing without proof before because I could read their guilt in their eyes. It never haunted me because I never doubted my choice. I knew that I was right in the choices I made.

That I was the hunter's hand of justice.

Not with her. When I watched her, there were times when she truly looked innocent. The scent of her perfume led me to her. The cork left behind after her rune test convinced me she lied her way through it. The strong defense she mounted convinced me otherwise.

I've tempted her, I've poked and pushed her. I've tainted my blood to taunt her. If she panicked, I hadn't seen it shine through yet. I saw a few small glimpses of what may have been fear, but I talked myself away from them.

Of course, she was shaken when I kissed her.

Was that fair to hold against her?

I was taught about vampires for my entire life. They were red-eyed, hungry monsters. They didn't smile and help kitchen staff with their duties. They fed and caused chaos to their surroundings.

Maybe it was less her and more about me. Maybe it was the way I left my own kingdom. I didn't agree with having a hand in the things going on. I was told my emotions were irrelevant. I was trained to be loyal to the king of RuneHold. I had a duty but more important I had to prove my worth.

The king of RuneHold wanted me to escort the princess of Saydeean for the high payment he'd received from her father. I wasn't allowed to leave until she was married off peacefully.

No matter how long it took.

The king of RuneHold had to prove his worth, too. If he had the strongest hunters, he'd have to show it.

My stay was extended when King Valen sent word of a vampire. I was assigned the task of flushing it out and told both things must be completed before I was allowed home.

I was to leave with a married princess and a vampire in hand.

Lanira frustrated me. I knew in my mind that she was a vampire. She had to be. There were many sympathizers inside King Valen's court. More than I expected. They walked silently but carelessly. Lanira, however, gave me a pit in my stomach that filled me with doubt.

I needed to find something concrete. Something as solid as catching her feeding.

It may be the only thing that I'd believe.

I opened the letter Lanira gave me, and it was written too well for me to believe she had done it herself.

I received word of you meeting with a maid in secret. If you don't want me to kill her myself, wait for my second letter with a list of demands outside the princess Invidia's door.

I folded it and put it back inside the envelope. I warned her that he would cause problems.

I handed the letter to the first guard I saw and directed him to keep it closed and hand it off to Koen.

I'd have it delivered to Koen if only to see it play out. If it were from Lanira, it told me that I severely underestimated her.

I passed advisors tucked away, caught up in whispers. Maids shuffling to their duties. The castle had become louder since the king's announcement of war. Everyone felt the need to pick sides.

Whispers of the king agreeing with Lanira were loud, too. Most couldn't believe that he sided with her over his priestess.

I was shocked to see the man who condemned and killed the supernatural have such a girl by his side.

I believed the king listened to Lanira. It wasn't about her. It was about the king's need for anyone to say he acted within reason. He wanted validation. He didn't care where it came from. He only needed one voice to agree. The fact that it was her voice made little difference to him.

I stopped outside of the Queen's personal garden, and her guard didn't say a word before he went to alert her of my arrival. I already interviewed the kitchen staff. They had nothing to say. They called her helpful and quiet. They were surprised to see her at the center of so much attention. They all considered her a backdrop to daily life.

I wanted to speak with the princess, but after the way things unfolded, I felt she would be hostile and not just withholding, but she would tell Lanira that I was asking about her.

The guard motioned me in and took his post back.

"When you asked to speak to me, I was happy to hear it," Queen Blair declared.

I sat beside her on a stone bench. She tossed nuts to the birds in the grass beside us. Their chirping created a peaceful backdrop that contrasted with the tension in the castle.

"I thought you'd be the best to speak to about Lanira," I mentioned.

The Queen nodded. "Although I'm happy to know that you are clearing all possibilities, I don't think Lanira is worth so much focus. There is no way she would betray us. I can't see a single reason for her to do it."

"If she were guilty, I think that's exactly what she would want everyone to think," I replied.

The Queen sighed. "I admit, some of the current events made me doubt her a small amount for a brief moment. I've had some time to consider, and I think she is only driven by the same guilt that my husband is. That I am. To understand her reasoning, you'll need to understand her. Lanira once had a mother and father, siblings. They were farmers. She was sent out to gather their sheep when the attack happened." The queen's voice drifted off for a moment.

She spoke as if she weren't there. As if she didn't approve of the king's actions. But she did. She approved so well that they made it a family event. When the king gathered armies and marched on the vampires, she brought his entire family to witness the triumph.

"She lived in a small village on the border lands. We had heard of the villagers who lived too close to the vampires before our arrival. There was an effort made to keep them clear, but when the vampires scattered, there was nothing to be done. Lanira hardly remembers the events, but when we found her, she was a tiny girl covered in blood, hugging her brother, who was long passed. I couldn't leave her there, so frail and scared. She was supposed to work in the gardens originally, but Invidia and Lanira became so close that they were inseparable. If she lashes out, it's from the fear of losing another family." The queen wiped a tear from her eye.

I wasn't convinced her tears were for Lanira. They felt like the tears of shame and regret. Agreeing with her husband and seeing the devastation she agreed to must have created very different emotions.

If I were in her position, I'd be obsessed with bathing as well. No one escapes the dark touch of court life, but the filth that she'd been part of was something that wouldn't wash away easily.

"How do you know she was from the village and not a vampire?" I asked.

"If she were, she would surely be dead by now, "Queen Blair laughed. "All this time and no blood?"

I didn't crack a smile.

"Do you think she harbors any resentment towards you?" I asked. "For the king?"

The Queen's eyes shifted down. "The King treats her well some days and badly on others. Lanira is not one to hold a grudge. She isn't violent. She is a sweet child. She understands that the king is in a difficult position."

She's twenty-two, hardly a child. I kept my sigh internal. Feeling disgust for the queen was not how I thought I'd feel during our conversation.

"I admit that I've kept myself from getting as close to Lanira as I could have been for fear of the king being upset. I always wanted more daughters. I even allowed Invidia to help teach Lanira privately to makeup for it. Lanira knows how to read and write.

Even when my husband refused her an education, she received one to match a royal child, all the same. Altair and Tillo spent a little time showing the girls how to fight, and Lanira still practices late at night. She does it to be able to defend Invidia." The Queen rambled. "She is devoted to our family."

"So, if you consider her innocent, then who would you say is the vampire hidden among you all? Who would you consider so filled with rage as to kill your eldest son?" I kept my gaze on her.

I wanted to see even the smallest hint of a slip.

"Priestess Minala," she proclaimed. "She has many reasons to want my children out of her way. Once the king retires, she has to hope my son will want her around. Neither of my boys believe in the power she claims to have."

It was a foolish choice. The priestess had already been cleared. It's not as if she were hiding runes in her body to cover up being a vampire.

A spark lit up in my mind. A thought hit me like a bolt of lightning.

"You mentioned Lanira knows how to read and write?" I asked.

"Yes, as a mother, how could I deny her something so basic? I'll do what I can to help you investigate, but I think Lanira is not the one that you should look into. She's just trying her best in the same grief we are all swimming in," the Queen urged.

I nodded in agreement, but her words faded out for a moment before they tuned back in.

My heart pounded in my chest. I read the letter that Lanira handed me, and had it sent off under the assumption that she was too simple to have created something so perfectly written.

"Thank you for your time, Your Highness. I'll consider everything you told me," I replied before I stood.

I bowed and left the garden with haste.

My ears rang while I ran to the princess's wing of the castle. Had she set me up to be the one to have killed Koen? Had I fallen for something so simple?

I had to be wrong. Lanira had not set up a scheme. It was believable that they had been seen. I had seen them too.

I rounded the corner of the entrance to Princess Invidia's wing and stopped with relief when I saw Koen alive and well in front of the princess's door. A maid handed off a tray of food to him. Their exchange felt a bit stiff. The maid walked as fast away from him as I had sped away from the queen.

Koen removed the lid with shaky hands.

The scent of eggs lingered in the air beside the sound of a hiss.

His eyes widened, and a small snake shot out of the tray at him. It dug its fangs into Koen's lip. I recognized the bright red spots on the snake. Koen screamed and ripped the snake off of him, but it was too late.

The venom from that snake was as fast-acting as a snake could become.

I arrived too late to save him, but fast enough to look guilty.

Koen's body hit the floor and convulsed as the door he stood beside opened. Princess Invidia screamed, and the sound echoed through the halls and my mind. Lanira moved out of the shadows and stood beside the princess.

Her eyes locked with mine. They were blank, but her face quickly turned to panic.

I couldn't believe how bold she had been. How calculated the move was. How she managed to get me to lower my guard on the assumption that she was too uneducated to pull anything off. Too scared of me to make any major moves.

I couldn't believe how far off I was about her. The panic on her face showed me how good she was at hiding her emotions. I wished mine had been hidden as well. I wanted to be able to lie and claim I wasn't shocked by the feeling in the pit of my stomach.

It was clear she set it up. She had killed Koen. Yet, in that moment, out of all of them, I wanted to protect her so that she could befree of him and his ability to ruin her.

I was the most upset that she had killed him and not me.

I was somehow proud of her bold behavior.

No, I was envious of the way that she knew exactly what she wanted and did not hesitate.

Chapter Nineteen
LATE NIGHT LOVE

Lanira

I was excited for the cool night air. The scent of fresh-cutgrass still lingered in every corner. The castle was quiet, and even the flames on the torches whispered. My walk to the courtyard was filled with pride in myself.

I was peacefully able to take blood from the kitchen. Princess Invidia requested a hot bath and an early night. She was prescribed atonic to help her sleep. I felt good for more than one reason; I felt peace.

I picked up my wooden axe and slammed it into the neck of the dummy in front of me. I wore the biggest smile. My cheeks throbbed underneath it. The look on Ravi's face as he pieced together the situation still satisfied me.

Koen was out of my way. Ravi would look guilty if anything came to light. He played into my plan even better than I could have imagined. The guard that Ravi gave the letter to was terrified of what he had accidentally become a part of.

There was a clear trail from the guard back to Ravi. If Ravi tried to point a finger at me, I'd have several pointing back at him. The princess, the queen, they'd never believe I'd hurt Koen. If they protected me over Prince Tillo, it would be even easier to do it for Koen.

Koen had been by our side for too long. It would be easy to spin things back with the guard and claim maybe Ravi was the guilty one, and that's why he hadn't found the vampire. Maybe Ravi was sent to kill Tillo and tear us all apart from the inside out.

I pulled the axe back and slammed it into the straw dummy again. Proud of myself wasn't enough of a statement for the way I felt.

The moon shone bright, and the air felt as if spring were on the horizon. It carried my win on its back.

Any stress left inside of me, I'd let out on the dummy in the cool night air.

The snake was a bit dull of a way for Koen to go, and I'd lost my only small source of human blood, but the loss still outweighed the stress. I was proving that even in my doubt, I was capable of moving alone toward my goal.

That I was smarter than the royal family and Ravi.

I was at my best on my own.

A wooden sword was placed on my shoulder, and I shifted my eyes to it.

"This seems inappropriate already," I whispered.

I spun around and met his wooden sword with my axe.

"I'd still consider it less inappropriate than your day," Ravi retorted.

"My day?" I shook my head, "Do you mean the trauma of seeing a close friend die so soon after the last loss? I suppose itis fitting to see you here. This makes a second death on your watch."

Our wooden weapons parted, and they immediately clashed again. The sound of wood on wood echoed in the night air.

"Don't play dumb with me. It's the two of us and the moon. I know you killed Koen. I don't think it's your first time either. I think you killed Tillo, too." Ravi put more pressure on his weapon. "Koen, I understand. Tillo, I still don't."

"I think that there's a guard who is a witness to you giving Koen a letter that told him where to wait," I replied as I returned the pressure. "It seems the evidence is set up to show your guilt, not mine. If you were guilty of Koen, well, it may be easy to claim you're guilty of Tillo too."

He moved to the side and took his weapon with him. It caused me to fall forward.

"I think I was a fool for not holding onto that letter, but you were thoughtless if you were confident that I'd just take the blame silently," he declared as he moved for me again.

I dodged and slammed my weapon into his knee. Wood still hurt.

"If I knew what you spoke of, I'd think maybe if you stopped picking on a poor defenseless girl, no one would press further about Koen."

"So that's your play, hmm? Force me into silence by threat? Did you think this would truly allow you to be free and clear of the prince's murder?" Ravi tossed his weapon to the ground. "I underestimated you. I'll admit that. I should have killed you the moment I smelled your perfume in Tillo's room. Everything pointed to you. You have the perfect position for this. Everyone I've asked claims that you're loyal and quiet. Harmless if not next to useless."

"You've been asking about me?" The smirk slipped past my lips.

Ravi let out a deep, annoyed chuckle before he lifted his arm into the air. "You know what else I think!" He used a small pocketknife to slice his arm until blood dripped freely. "I think that this will make you slip more."

My ears rang at the scent. Shivers ran through my entire body, and my nose no longer smelled anything but iron. The metallic sweetness filled my senses completely. Even if I sat on the edge of no control, it was still an edge with the chance to back away. He wasn't the only person to bleed in front of me, and I was blessed to have had my fill just moments before coming outside.

I tossed my axe to the ground and stepped closer to him. He moved a foot back as if he had forgotten that he had asked for this.

"You've tried this before," I whispered.

I held the shake in my voice down. The remembrance of what he tasted like the first time. Bitter and cold. The thought made things a bit easier to handle. I stepped closer again, but he didn't back up a second time.

"What's it going to take for you to leave me in peace?" I whispered again.

His eyes shifted to my lips. He had already glanced at them more than once, but this time was different. He looked at me as if he wanted to give in. As if I were in charge of the game board and he were only a pawn.

I wanted to give in, too. I wanted to give in to the blood that dripped beside me. To drain every last drop of blood from him.

"I want to remind you that proof is a grace and not a requirement. I can kill you right here if I want. The only thing I need is suspicion. I can send word to my kingdom, and their entire army will rain down on your home. I can send word that the royal family is proven vampiric sympathizers and have them all hanged," Ravi smirked as if he had a winning hand.

I wanted to be the one to push my luck. To stretch my hand thinner. I wanted to have just a moment of true open defiance.

I leaned into him until our lips hovered over each other and whispered into his mouth.

"Do it."

My chest pounded against my ribs, and I heard his do the same.

Ravi backed away and wrapped a cloth around his arm. Once it was in place, he lowered himself to the ground and sat. He leaned back as if sunbathing under the moonlight.

"Sit. I've had enough for now. Do you know how to talk casually? Or are you only filled with spite?" He asked.

Against my better judgment, I sat beside him.

"If it weren't for you, your kingdom would be the dullest place I had ever been to," Ravi observed. "Things are so passive here. It's nothing like my home. Everyone is only friends in order to have someone to pull the rug out from under."

"It sounds exhausting," I replied. "Then again, I think it would be a better experience to know that everyone was out for me than to wonder who was being true."

Ravi nodded. "I hadn't considered it that way. I do imagine it would be more of a challenge to question everyone, to always be paranoid. I imagine there would never be a moment of peace unless you found away to sneak out at night." Ravi chuckled. "The idea that Priestess Minala considered you a traitor for this alone is beyond amusing."

I gave a breathy chuckle. "She spoke simply what she thought King Valen wanted to hear."

"In the same way that I haven't moved past you, I haven't wrapped my head around the idea that she is here at all. I'm aware of the surface-level idea that she never left, she was never tainted by outside sources. It still felt as though he had broken something sacred by having her. Then again, you all feel strange to me. You're much less black and white, and far more filled with grey area," Ravi sighed.

He spoke as if he were writing in a journal. His shaggy black hair hung freely with the way his head was tossed back. He felt like an entirely different person from the hunter who had been pursuing me.

"I wonder if it's regret that keeps her around. If it's his way of atoning for what he did. A last piece that he can nurture for forgiveness when he dies. An apology of sorts to the vampires that used to roam the castle," Ravi mused.

"I never considered such a thing," I responded truthfully.

"Do you wonder what it was like before? When vampires walked freely?" Ravi turned his head to look at me, "We're speaking as friends. Nothing leaves here."

"I wouldn't know. I'm not allowed that knowledge, "I answered.

"But have you ever wondered?" He repeated.

"Hasn't everyone? It's natural curiosity. You paint them as monsters, but the wing that was left behind by them reveals they were artists, writers." I cut myself off.

Even as friends, we only needed to say so much to each other. Nothing would truly stay buried. He was likely using it as a way to pull something out of me.

"I walked through the halls left behind by them, too. It's where my thoughts came from. I have to be honest, my thoughts fell to you, not painters. If I were you, surrounded by the last real parts of my family." His eyes widened. "I'd have done the same as you. It must be a hard burden to keep quiet. No mourning, no speaking. I imagine you couldn't even write your thoughts down. A whisper to the night sky would even seem risky. The joke sits in the idea that the ones living call you family while ordering you around. While you know what a real family is like. I imagine Minala has peace in that, if nothing else. She only knows what she has, so there is no longing for her. No emptiness inside her heart." His shoulders lowered with his thoughts.

"You speak as if you hold your own thoughts close to your chest," I observed.

I wanted to give in and speak freely. He felt so sincere. There was a barrier inside of me that was too high and too heavy. It stopped me from speaking freely.

It didn't stop his words from penetrating a part of me I kept behind lock and key. I had no time to dwell on anything deeper than duty or plans.

"Vampire hunters know what peace is, too. We know what family is, and the peace of a mother's love. We enjoy home-cooked meals and the grace of being allowed to spill a cup of water and be greeted by a smiling face. Then we are ripped out of those arms and tossed into a dark abyss. We are weeded out by strength. We are starved until we kill each other. Only a specific number of us move forward, and the alchemists need us to prove durable before they take us. Some start training when they start walking, just to increase their odds," Ravi revealed.

"By the way you speak, I assume you don't agree with it?" I asked.

I was entranced by his voice. He spoke with such raw emotion. It was a rarity I found overwhelming.

"There are many willing to do the job once they are old enough to understand. So, no, I don't support the idea of how it is done. I hope to change it," he answered.

There it was. The reason why he didn't kill me despite knowing what I was. He wasn't as committed to his kingdom or their cause as he claimed. He wanted change and reform, just as I did. Killing me when our thoughts were so closely aligned would be a betrayal of himself.

He made excuses not to kill me, like I made excuses not to look at him.

"I want change, too," I agreed.

The day that the two of us would have to stand off would be an unfortunate day. I hadn't ever gotten to breathe so easily around someone. Or hear something so close and personal. He would be the one that was hard for me to kill.

It was foolish of me to be so sensitive about someone who was still closer to a stranger to me than a friend. I was becoming careless. But in this moment, under the moonlight with his guard finally down, I understood why I found it so hard to see him as just another enemy.

We were both products of systems that had shaped us into weapons, both yearning for something different than what we'd been given.

Chapter Twenty
Another Tantrum

Lanira

Princess Invidia spoke even through the gasps she let out while I tightened her corset. I pulled the strings harder than I needed to, more than once, for my own amusement.

"I knew father was slipping, but I hadn't expected mother, too. They fought all night long. Screaming and throwing things. Both blamed each other for Tillo's death. I don't understand it. It's as if Koen was the last of the news that mother could handle before she snapped. I've never seen her this way," Princess Invidia dropped her arms as I tied the last of the ribbon. "Do you recall when you spilled the red wine on mother's favorite dress? She didn't even scream then! She's been screaming all night! She won't tell me what's wrong, but a maid mentioned she found a letter meant for Father. She read it and has been on the war path since."

I sat on a chair beside her. The cushion was filled with feathers and still preserved as if hardly sat in. "We all process grief different-ly. Even I'm starting to feel less like myself. So much loss seems to be happening at one time. Even the castle grows quieter with the advisors being sent to the dungeons. Staff being beheaded under suspicion of anything. Things are tense, and we all just want you and the prince safe. It's breaking to feel so useless," I slouched as if to look defeated.

"I feel different, too," Princess Invidia sat on the edge of her bed, still half dressed. "I wish that I knew how to fix it. How to fix them."

I wished that I could fix how slow things moved. I still needed to find the correct book in the king's study. I won't need to kill alone once I can find it. It was supposed to help me raise vampires from the afterlife and bring them back. If I couldn't get to it, then Prince Altair would have to be the next death by my hands.

I knew the first time that I heard the King speak of the book that it had to be important. He kept the knowledge of it from me, which made me want to learn of it that much more.

The king had already sent his army away. They'd be thinning out soon enough. Another notch in the board.

Princess Invidia grabbed her fur jacket and threw it over herself with a sigh. "I have my violin lessons now, but I will see you straight away after."

I met her with a smile, "Of course."

The two of us left the room together, but in two different directions. I was tasked with Princess Sala. She was locked in her quarters since our arrival. She was kept such a secret that most of the castle had nearly forgotten she was with us.

I was to check in on her and offer her anything she may need. Her usual set of maids had come down with an illness. The herbalist claimed it was only a common cold. Still, she needed someone to offer her new sheets and clean bathing water.

I knocked on her door before I opened it. I didn't know what I would be walking into. My heart raced with possibilities. I was nearly afraid that I might walk in on her lifeless body with the lack of noise that came from the room.

Princess Sala was sitting in her window. She pressed her knees into her chest and took in the view from outside. Her black hair hung around her like a curtain, creating a barrier between her and the world.

"Princess Sala, I've come to see if you needed anything," I announced as I closed the door behind me.

"No," she replied simply.

"New blankets? A snack?" I moved closer to her.

"Can you sneak me out? Can you send me back home? If not, then you cannot help me with anything," she leaned her head onto her knee.

"Would your family accept you if I did? If I sent you out this very night, would they let you stay or send you right back?" I asked.

I grabbed her side chair and pulled it closer to her. It was common for ladies of the court to use maids as personal journals. Princesses, Queens, ladies. They all considered us secret keepers.

"If they didn't allow me to stay, I'd simply go to another kingdom. Anything would be better than this. I'm locked away in a place that still smells of vampire filth, surrounded by weak men who can't make a choice and stick to it. I have no freedom, no future. What I could have had, I left behind," Princess Sala still looked outside while she spoke.

"The kingdom was formed on the backs of vampires. As for your future, whatever you dreamt of, your parents didn't see you in the same light. If they did, you wouldn't be here," I snapped.

Princess Sala finally lifted her head. "What?"

I cleared my throat. "It's a poor choice to speak ill of the dead while sending off a soul to them. Prince Tillo deserves a chance at a good afterlife, does he not? As for your position, if you dwelt less on what could have been and focused on pushing forward, you may have everything you wanted here."

I spoke too carelessly.

"What if I proclaimed I was happy Prince Tillo died? What if I wanted him to have a poor afterlife? What if I wanted you all to suffer in life and death?" Princess Sala spat.

She stood up, grabbed the tea cups from her side table, and threw them at the wall. I stood and moved myself back. I didn't want to be in her way. I didn't want to step on porcelain shards that glittered like broken promises on the floor.

"What if I declared that as soon as I was let out, I'd be the one to kill your king? Hmm?" She screamed louder.

Princess Sala grabbed another cup and threw it at me. I lowered myself just in time to dodge it hitting me in the face.

"I don't want sheets, I want out! I don't want another meal in my room, I want freedom!" She wailed.

A knock sounded at the door, and I didn't hesitate to open it.

Princess Sala had lost her mind. She wasn't meant to live court life outside of her home if she was so easy to shatter. She would need to pull herself together and do it quickly.

"I'm sorry, ma'am, but guards are here to speak with you," they pushed open the door and held me at spear point. Two other guards entered and held Princess Sala. They slammed her into her bed before a maid ran in with a new cup. A guard held her jaw open while the maid poured the steaming liquid down her throat.

Princess Sala sobbed as she tried to resist drinking, the liquid spilling down her chin.

"What is the meaning of this?" I demanded from their grip.

"King's orders, your highness," one guard replied. "Princess Sala needs her prescription, and you are needed elsewhere. Another maid will take over for you here."

They each grabbed my arms as if I were as poor off as Princess Sala. I didn't struggle, but they walked fast enough that my feet dragged behind me. They shut the door on the Princess and locked it from the outside. A guard took his place in front of her only exit.

The king meant to put me in the spotlight without defense this time.

The guards pulled me through gaze after gaze. Whisper to the next whisper. Pointed fingers and gasps of court members and staff until we were in the throne room. They shoved me to my knees and held spears to each side of my neck. Ravi stood in the center of the room with a blank expression.

"I called you here to get the meaning behind the things you've told the king and queen," Ravi declared.

"I don't understand," I forced my body into shaking.

"I'm to have you explain why you told the king and queen that you saw members of StoneDale leaving Prince Tillo's room in the mountains," Ravi repeated. "It seems that they've learned you met with both of them separately, and they are both convinced you must have lied."

I let tears well behind my eyes. "I don't understand. I only told them what they asked me to. I only wanted to speak the truth. I wanted to see revenge sought out for my brother. I thought holding in such a thing and keeping it a secret would be worse than participating in gossip." I sobbed and bowed until my head touched the cold floor.

Ravi sighed and moved closer to me. He bent down and lifted my head with each of his hands on my cheeks. "A truth tonic," he explained as he held my cheeks and poured it down my throat. "It wasn't my choice or idea."

I was no stranger to the tonic. It was used on me more than once.

Princess Invidia and I used to accompany the king when he would go hunting, and I would feed the hounds until they were too spoiled to help in hunting. I was caught quickly, and of course, I lied about it. I was too young to understand the importance of covering my steps. Priestess Minala enjoyed using the tonic.

I was caught and not allowed back to the hunt. Every hound was slaughtered as a result. The king would declare,

Once spoiled, they can never be brought back.

"Answer again," Ravi demanded.

"I only want the truth to be revealed," I spat out.

"And your family?" He pointed.

"I only want to ensure the safety and well-being of my family," I responded.

He'd think that I spoke of King Valen. Ravi wasn't specific enough in his question, and it allowed me to be ambiguous with my answer. It was all the truth. Every word of it. I couldn't lie under the potion. We only spoke of different truths and different families.

"Lanira," Altair spoke low, but the way he moved forward dripped with confidence.

I hadn't noticed that he entered the room. I assumed it was only Ravi and the guards.

Prince Altair held up a letter I recognized well. It was the letter I planted for the Queen that set the king up as Prince Tillo's killer.

"There was nothing that I could have done to calm the rage once this letter was found. Inside is a message to the King. It seems he may have been involved in Tillo's death. The Queen wanted to make sure that what you told her was true. It seems there are now two solid pieces of proof in the matter. Be assured, this will be the last time you get pulled into something like this. I'll make sure of it," Prince Altair assured me.

It may have been the first genuine smile I saw from him since I was a small child. The act tugged at my heart in a small way. Not for him. But for my own brother. For the reminder of what I had once so long ago. For what I remembered only in pieces and small flashes.

For what they stole from me.

Prince Altair glanced at Ravi and gave him a nod. One that spoke of release before he left the room. The guards removed their grip from my arms and followed the prince out.

"Let me escort you back to the princess," Ravi offered.

I didn't want to speak to him. I didn't want to part my lips. The truth serum was far from worn off.

Ravi sighed. "Let me be kind to you just once."

My nostrils flared, and I kept my frowning lips pressed close. I moved ahead of him. I didn't want to be seen too close. I didn't know why I was suddenly so aware of eyes on the two of us. Might they think there was something between us?

Of course not. Why would they?

"Fine, if you won't speak to me as a friend, then let's speak of business. The king and queen are distracted with each other, but I haven't forgotten Koen. The other guards have already replaced his position, but I haven't forgotten."

"What would you have me say?" I snapped. "This is a cheap way of getting me to speak to you."

Ravi held my gaze. "Don't you feel anything? Any guilt at all?"

"Why should I? I did what I had to do. It was him or me. He had made it very clear that my body would remain his or my life would be," I whispered to ensure no one overheard me.

"I've done what I had to do, too, but it was never murdering the innocent in cold blood," Ravi challenged.

"Wasn't it? How many vampires have you killed, Ravi? How many of them committed any crime other than being alive and in your sight? Hmm? How many were just average people? From where I stand, it looks like we aren't that different. From my perspective, it seems like one of us lies to ourselves to sleep at night and the other accepts that sometimes things are more complicated than black and white," my words were sharp as broken glass.

I gave him one last passing glance. From his green eyes to his sword on his hip before I turned and left without regret. He didn't move to try to stop me.

The truth serum was still in my system, and every word I'd spoken had been true. We were both killers, both products of broken systems. The only difference was that I had stopped pretending otherwise.

Chapter Twenty-One
MISSION AFTER MISSION

Ravi

The king's study was far from comfortable. I had expected something far different after seeing the rest of his castle, but his personal study reminded me more of a dungeon than a room for the most powerful voice in his land. He was reluctant at first to allow me in, but after some thought, he decided that I was the only one trusted to enter.

It showed that he held little trust for outside sources and the room itself. The air smelled of mold and decay. Some of the books' pages were browned and looked as though something had eaten through the paper. There were no windows, no true light. It was a cave of dust and regret.

I opened the letter that King Orn sent me from RuneHold. He grew impatient for my return. I knew he grew restless at the idea that he was unaware of my daily comings and goings. My chain was too loose for his happiness. I grew restless at the idea of leaving.

King Valen's study was abysmal, but RuneHold was colder still. In Emberrella, so many freedoms were afforded to people that they grew complacent. Most of them saw privilege as an everyday right.

In contrast to the court officials, I knew better how Lanira felt because it's how I felt every day in RuneHold.

I would write back to King Orn and ask for another extension. I knew I had to be running out of them, but I wasn't ready to leave.

I tucked the letter into the pocket that sat inside my vest and buttoned my top. I grabbed a stack of books and carelessly fumbled through them.

King Valen's latest idea was to use vampire magic against StoneDale. He tasked me with going through the writings in his study for anything that I or the other hunters may be able to use. Most of the books he held were as useless as he was.

A book on crops, I tossed it to the side with a sigh. A book about marriage rites sat beneath it, and I tossed it to the other side. A book teaching the seasons and recipes. I leaned back into the chair with a sigh, and my foot kicked another stack of books. A thick, old book slid from the pile, and I leaned down to pick it up.

I flipped the pages, and inside most of them were empty. The book looked so much different than the rest. The pages felt different, too, older, more substantial. The only thing that held my interest was the rune that read vampiric curse. I wouldn't pretend to understand why it was placed on the book.

I opened the drawer and shoved the book in and under some scrolls. I knew that I didn't have time to figure it out then, but that it could use some closer attention. It seemed as though the writing that had to be inside was hidden somehow from normal sight.

I wanted to speak to the man that King Valen was when he rode out to the vampires. I imagined that man and the one today would not agree with each other. One was bent on eradicating any hint of vampires, and the other was willing to use their teachings to tear another kingdom down.

I couldn't understand King Valen's thought process. I knew his mind had to be degrading when he picked me instead of someone that was supposed to have been trustworthy from inside of his circle.

I got to my feet and moved to the shelves that lined the far wall. Floor-to-ceiling books and scrolls. There was hardly a comfortable amount of space to walk. If Lanira were with me, she would no doubt make it look like an easy skill she naturally had, to be able to dance around the clutter as if it didn't faze her.

She was able to dance around most things as if she had perfected carrying the calmest mind.

I grabbed a scroll and opened it; the edges were tattered and ripped. I held it up to the candlelight so that the writing was clear.

The God of Rebirth is an awful being. He is no deity to be worshipped. He is a curse, a soul so cruel that even small children aren't safe from him. We tried to offer him what he needed at first, but he always needed more, so soon after. Enough became too little, and too much became only a burden for us. His appetite for knowledge grew to become insatiable. Thann, the God of Rebirth, discovered that one line of vampires had enough natural magic in their blood to use witches' runes. The witches refused him their teachings, but the happiest he had been was when he found a way around them. Helia, the Goddess who quickly went from our nightmare to our peace, never stepped in to stop him.

A dagger felt like a gift when compared to an axe.

If you find this. If you can read our words. Please, send us a weapon that can defeat a god. The two of them have no intention of sparing us otherwise. Bleed on an orchid and call to the sisters of fate. Ask for the one painted in white. She walks the crossroads. She may hear us. She may help us.

I closed the scroll and moved it far from my immediate space. Reading it filled my mind with the sound of crying children and pools of blood. Our realm was built from horrors even I couldn't imagine, and they continued on as if it were tradition. I grabbed a second scroll with the hope that it would be light enough to wash away the first.

I was relieved to know, for once, that the gods had abandoned us. I opened the second scroll and held it up to the candlelight.

The sister of fate and the witches use bones to summon souls of the dead. Although witches know how to wield the power well, not all witches follow their own rules. A coven broke law and bonded bones together. It is unnatural magic.

It has had a profound effect on not just our realm but also another. The coven was beheaded and boiled until the flesh on each melted away. Their bones were crushed into powder so that they may not be raised again. The outcome of bone binding can be madness, curses, or possession.

We are announcing our sixteenth law; any witch practicing for-bidden bone binds will be crushed to powder along with every member of their blood kin, living or dead.

I closed the scroll and put it back on the bookshelf. A shiver ran up my spine. A part of me thought that maybe the scrolls weren't real. I had never seen such parts of our realm's history written anywhere else.

I moved back to the desk and rummaged through the rest of the drawers. There were four on each side. The top left hardly held dust. The middle drawer held a secret compartment. Nearly invisible if it weren't for the corner of the desk, wood rotting away from moisture.

I lifted the corner, and under it was a small letter with a broken wax seal. It was a rune. It stood for soul-bound. Did it mean that whoever the letter was intended for and the writer were soul-bond-ed to each other? Was the letter bound? I was too unfamiliar with the rune to say for sure.

I opened it and it was still in perfect shape. It appeared as if it had only ever been opened once.

Ash,

Saydeean and RuneHold no longer want an alliance with the vampires. They say the blood you offer isn't enough, and the trade treaty is unfair to them. They've called a meeting of houses so that the other three kingdoms can be included in talks of new trade agree-ments. They intend to persuade all kingdoms to move against you. I'm writing you as soon as word reached my ears. I should be invited to the meeting; I've worked my way into the king's ear. I will not delay any further news as I have it. Move quickly, my brother.

Vex.

Who was Ash? I folded the note back into its perfectly square shape. This Ash had to be a vampire. The letter was clearly intended to warn the vampires of tense alliances.

I tucked the letter into my inner chest pocket, where I kept everything of secret importance. The letter was the most valuable thing I found since my arrival in Emberrella.

The letter had nothing to do with helping King Valen but everything to do with the bigger picture. A part of me still yearned for something else. Something better than the way things were. A part of me tugged at my chest when I thought of all the ways the kingdoms could have grown and lived at peace.

I was loyal to my oath as a hunter. I was loyal to my home.

It seemed that the more freedom I felt, the more of life I saw, the more I had to be disloyal to myself to do it.

If the letter was real, it meant that there was a bigger picture to be seen. I needed to find out who Ash was. I'd start with living vampires before the massacre. All kingdoms kept a ledger with detailed family lines that would help me.

I used my feet to push around books on the floor and ran my fingers over the shelves. I knew the symbol I was looking for on that book. It would be a tree root with orchid petals surrounding it. The king's collection of secret scrolls and books made no sense to me. He held close any book that taught of outside kingdoms. It didn't make sense to me why he would keep such things from his people, let alone his children.

I shoved another book and saw it, the symbol I was looking for. I slammed the heavy book on the desk and opened the pages. I thumbed page after page until I reached fifteen years ago. I had to keep moving back until I reached two years before the massacre.

Ash Ambrose came from a line that held control of the temple of time in Lunadur since the age of the Gods. His place in his family line and his job as high priest were intact in the book, but everything after him had been altered. Black ink blobs erased any information about the rest of his line. He had at least four siblings, but anything beyond that was far from legible.

The name Ambrose sent a chill through me. I stared at the page longer than necessary, trying to make sense of the deliberate destruction of information. Someone had gone to great lengths to hide this family's legacy.

I opened the door to the study and welcomed the fresh air. I pulled the air in like I had suffocated. Too long in that room made me feel like I was losing my mind, likely from mold spores.

I walked the halls to the throne room. I had to report back to King Valen what I found before my day could get back on track.

I wanted to follow Lanira. I wanted to find a reason to still be lingering in Emberrella that made sense. I made excuses for myself at every turn.

King Valen looked up at me with raised eyebrows as I entered the room.

"Have you found something?" He asked.

I shook my head. "Nothing."

King Valen got to his feet and shoved the maid who stood beside him with drinks to the ground. The crystal goblets shattered against the marble, sending shards across the floor.

"How useless are you?" He yelled.

"Your highness, I do not believe anyone would be so careless as to leave outlines for deadly weapons in what you collected and held in a study," I replied. "Fifteen years have been spent trying to gain access to any information they may have held close. I'm not going to find something that those who have been tasked with this for so long haven't found."

King Valen's chubby fingers reached up and grabbed his jeweled necklace and pulled it off. The sound of the clasp snapping filled the air, and he threw it across the room. He looked foolish. His tantrum was not intimidating, but pathetic.

The sight was sharp to see. Power and rule never went to those who would better life. It only went to those willing to stoop low and take from even the smallest lives. They were corrupted further the more power they were extended, when no one pushed back, and the rulers never had to pay for what they took.

King Valen, the most powerful man in his kingdom, broke his own things to throw around in rage because he simply wasn't used to the word no.

Priestess Minala ran into the room and straight to the king. She placed her hands on his shoulders and spoke to him as if she were his mother.

"Your highness, what is it? Do you need a tonic?" She placed her hands on his pink, flushed cheeks.

King Valen tried to rip off another piece of his jewelry to throw it, but his priestess stopped him. She cooed and hummed to him as she pressed his head into her chest. I couldn't stop my lips from the downturn they formed.

"You're all right. They will feel your wrath soon enough. Shhh. You will make them pay," Minala whispered while she stroked his hair.

The king's eyes met mine as if he had forgotten that I was still in the room. Priestess Minala followed his gaze back to me.

She met me with red eyes.

"Get out! Haven't you done enough? He wouldn't be this way if it weren't for your failures!" Priestess Minala pointed at me.

I had never been so pleased to follow a command. But as I left the throne room, the name Ambrose echoed in my mind. Something about it felt important, though I couldn't yet place why.

Chapter Twenty-Two
The Garden of Accidents

Lanira

I grew frustrated with myself. I moved too casually. I let Ravi slow me down and become a distraction.

"Prince Altair will marry in two days and ascend the throne in title only. He will marry the princess of Saydeean as Prince Tillo would have. She has been checked to ensure she's still intact. Priestess Minala has confirmed she is still a virgin and eligible to be married. We will ensure our kingdom follows the necessary steps to prevent the prophecy. I will not allow any vampire to rise from nothing and overthrow our realm! Anything not prepared in time will not be part of the ceremony," King Valen announced.

The king stood at the end of his war table as if he were still young and ready to charge into battle himself. No horse would carry him in his new state. Even if one did, he looked exhausted. Pale and on the brink of death. The only thing he didn't look like was starved.

The king leaned into Prince Altair and spoke in a lower voice. "Don't sleep with her too soon. I can't hand back a princess who's lost her value or risks carrying a child with no husband if you die too soon."

Prince Altair's face flushed pink before it lost all color as he took in the words.

"If you are not part of my advisors, then get out. You've received your orders. Get to it. We need to discuss the messenger from StoneDale that should arrive tomorrow," the king declared.

I left with the crowd, but the king did not wait to yell about his demands.

"There is to be no mercy, no matter the offer brought to us. We are winning. StoneDale's army is already halved, and Saydeean will send in more soldiers once the wedding is complete."

The king's voice trailed off as we all moved further away. The castle was once filled with brighter light and chatty voices. It was no longer that way. The day went on in silence. The only communication was what needed to be uttered.

The wedding would hardly be beautiful or joyous. Advisors, maids, ladies in waiting. They had been halved, too. Even gardeners were suspicious and beheaded. There was too much work to be done and not enough hands to do it.

Sometimes I wondered when the deaths happened. It felt as though we woke up, and people were just gone.

The day passed in a haze of fabrics and food. We had to trust the measurements that Minala provided us. No one was allowed to lay eyes on the princess of Saydeean since I had witnessed her decline. King Valen could not risk her and his alliance if whispers spread.

Princess Invidia went to bed early, and I ventured outside for a moment of true peace and quiet. Flowers wilted in the front gardens, the same way the inside dimmed of life. I needed them all the same. The flowers in the front garden could be mixed and crushed into the paste I needed to keep my hair dyed.

I knelt down and started to pick one after another, when I nearly jumped out of my skin. Prince Altair knelt beside me and helped pick the flowers and place them in my basket.

"I didn't mean to scare you. I saw you in the halls and thought you had the right idea. There's something about the inside of the castle these days that's suffocating and stagnant," Prince Altair observed.

He kept his eyes on the flowers, their petals soft between his fingers.

"I'm sure the weight of internal affairs is heavy on your shoulders now," I replied.

"Second best son, second best option. Second forgotten death," he sighed as he created his list out loud.

I looked at him beneath furrowed brows.

Prince Altair pressed his brows just as hard in challenge. "Oh, come on, Koen was a faithful guard who had been with us all his life. He was murdered, and he hardly had two words spoken about him. His position was filled hours later." He sucked a breath through his teeth and let the air out hard. "I know I'll die soon. I can feel it every breath I take. It's like I'm already choking. They'll pass me over the same way they did Koen."

My chest tightened, and for the second time, I felt complete pain for someone who was in my way. He was right, second place received second-rate treatment. He'd hardly be treated as well as Prince Tillo when he passed. He didn't deserve what I'd do to him. He didn't deserve what his father put him through. He deserved many more hugs from his mother and an easy afterlife.

I placed my hand on his shoulder in an attempt to comfort him. "He loves you. He's just awful at showing it. Fair treatment has never been his shining quality," I offered.

"You don't need to feed me nonsense, Lanira. It's only us in the darkness. Please, just let me have a moment of feeling like a human being," his voice cracked when he spoke.

The sound hit me in a place I didn't know existed.

"You've always been better than Tillo. It's why the king chose him and not you. If you had been trained properly and placed on the throne, you'd have made his legacy look like nothing but a murderous tyrant. He couldn't risk it. Even if he had gotten past that, Blair favors you. He'd never allow her closer to power than she is. You are simply caught in the wrong place. There's nothing you could have done to change it," I declared.

It felt nice to tell the truth. To voice something that I honestly believed out loud.

Prince Altair nodded. "You deserved better than what you were handed as well. My mother has spent your entire life trying to make up for the guilt she holds for approving the slaughter that happened back then. She saw you as a way to cleanse herself of guilt. Whenever she's feeling the weight of her actions, she treats you differently. You should never have witnessed the things you did." Prince Altair set a few more flowers in my basket. "I should have treated you better, too."

I didn't have the words to understand why his comments made me feel more than anyone else's. Maybe it's because I believed him. I did believe that he was sorry. I did believe that, like me, he was only doing the best that he could to survive in a place where that's all we had.

We were both deemed and marked as a certain worth and had no opportunity of changing it.

There was a piece of us that could understand each other.

The thing about viewing it from that lens was that it also fed me the confidence to be certain that when I killed him, he'd understand that too. Coming to such a conclusion had a sour taste.

If he had been elevated after Tillo, then he and I wouldn't have had that moment. I'd have remained beneath him and in the dark, to his thoughts. I wasn't a confessional. I wasn't a priestess who would hear him and offer him forgiveness.

I had to remind myself that it wasn't out of friendship that he and I spoke, but because it was easy to feel safe around someone deemed lower than his own position.

I was simply a girl born into a random position. Even the sweetest food tasted bitter when I looked at the bigger picture. When I considered that even I was as fake as the smiles around me, and my family rotted in ruins.

The truth may have been that he was sorry, but it did little to alter the past. The idea of what he did wrong may have been heavy, but it wasn't heavy enough to change anything; only power was.

Hooves pounded dirt, and a horse stopped in front of us in a cloud of dust. A man in silver armor jumped off and stood in front of us. Prince Altair got to his feet first.

My heart skipped a beat, and a rush ran through me. The emissary showed up early. He must have pushed himself and his horse.

"The hour may be late, but I need to meet with the king now," the man announced.

He held a letter in his hand with a grip so tight he might smudge the ink inside with sweat.

"You're from StoneDale?" Prince Altair asked. "I'm the prince."

The man nodded. "I am. I came as fast as I could."

I stood slower than the prince had. I took my time to scan our surroundings. Sometimes I felt alone. Other times, I felt as though someone watched over me and agreed with my plans.

I was standing in a moment that I could not let pass. The second son and the messenger of StoneDale.

Double the profit. I could set a new fire to the war, and push the king into madness.

I stood on my tiptoes and leaned into Prince Altair's ear.

"I saw fangs in his mouth. I saw them Altair. Please—"

He didn't let me finish before he unsheathed his sword from his hip and plunged it into the emissary's chest. It was so simple, so easy to use him because he had enough trust in me to not question my words, but just as much life training in accepting orders without question.

Prince Altair grabbed me and pulled me into an embrace. I felt his body shake as I heard his sword hit the flower bed we still stood beside.

"I killed him," he mumbled.

Our surroundings were still silent and empty. Prince Altair still tried to pull his thoughts together. My winning moment was held frozen in front of me.

I'd ensure that, unlike his wedding, his funeral was what he deserved.

"You did what you thought best," I comforted. "It's all any of us can do."

I pulled the small purple-lined dagger from its holder on his belt and pulled myself back from him. He tilted his head to look at me in the moonlight.

If he had been taught even a little better, this would have been harder.

If he had been a bit less kind, he'd never have been in this situation.

I pulled my arm back and shoved the gift from his mother into the center of his throat and left it there. Prince Altair reached for his throat as he dropped to his knees. I moved to the side as fast as I could. I didn't want even a drop of blood on me.

He was confused, reeling, and trying to piece together the events that occurred, but my mind was as calm as the night sky. I lowered myself to my knees while the sound of him choking on blood still held strong in the air. I pulled the letter from the emissary's hand and opened it in haste.

"We did not make a move on your son. We wave a white flag. We will aid in finding his killer."

What a useless letter. I ripped it up and shoved it inside my blouse. I pulled out a small pad of paper and my small charcoal pencil.

"The price of peace is the heart of every royal child, even the bastards." I tossed it on Altair as he still tried to dislodge the knife.

"I took the emissary's head. Let this be a message of our future dealings." I shoved the paper back in the envelope and tucked it into the bag on the horse.

A hard slap on the horse, and he took off back into the night.

Prince Altair grew silent and still. I no longer heard his heart-beat.

If I were to spare any of them, it would have been him. There was nothing to do moving forward but burn the evidence of the letter in the fire of my room.

I moved quietly and swiftly through the halls with my flower basket held close. I had considered that they may have left a trail of petals if I wasn't careful. I had the sinking feeling that I was being watched. I knew it wasn't just a feeling I created.

I closed my door quietly behind me and tossed the flowers on the ground by my side.

I pulled the letter out and ripped it to shreds in a messy rush and shoved them into the bottom logs of the fire. The heat nearly burnt my fingers, but the thrumming in my chest was harder to ignore than the pain in my fingertips.

Once the fire was settled over all of the tiny pieces of paper, I scrambled to my bed and flung blankets over me.

My heart raced hard enough that holding my breath silently was complicated.

The door to my room swung open, and though I thought it was going to slam closed, instead, it closed with a softness that spoke of secrets. I gripped the knife I kept under my pillow and closed my eyes to listen to the footsteps.

One, two. Slow, calculated, and quiet movements closer to me. Three, four.

Hands touched the edge of the bed, and I opened my eyes. I waited until I felt the presence of their body over me to turn myself and held the knife at their chin.

"I imagined you had a few more lives to go before it was my turn to kill you," Ravi murmured.

"This intrusion feels as though you want to be next," I whispered and pressed the knife harder.

"Then you admit it? You know why I'm here?" He asked.

"Men usually only enter the rooms of maids in the early hours for one reason," I snapped.

"Don't insult me in that way, Lanira," he shoved my hand and the knife away.

I pushed the knife back under my pillow and stayed in place.

"Ravi, I am in my bed. You are positioned over top of me, on my bed, and the sun hasn't even climbed over the horizon yet. I can feel your breath on my lips. I wonder what else I would offer you if not the idea that you are here to take my virtue," I smiled.

He did look good in the position that we were in.

"I found the bodies," he didn't shift himself or acknowledge my words. "Both of them. The King will be on a rampage by morning." Ravi's words were filled with anger, but his tone had pleading in it. "If you expect my defense—"

"I never asked for your defense," I stopped him. "I never asked for a single thing from you."

His eyes shifted between mine for several heartbeats of silence.

"I can't figure you out," he shook his head. "Is death what you want? Their throne? Are you a half breed? What is your goal?"

"Do you expect me to hand over my secrets simply because you ask for them?" I asked.

"Yes," his voice begged me to relent.

"You're even more naive than I thought," I chuckled.

"You're right. I can't decide if I want to kill you or kiss you. You've single-handedly made me doubt my life's teachings. You've already had me stand to the side of my own lines. The ones I swore I'd never cross. You didn't ask for my defense, but you made it look so tempting. Every time I spoke up to assist you with whatever your plan was, I felt equal regret and fire. The worst of it? I didn't come here to turn you in. I was relieved when I realized that I was the first one to find out what you had done. That I moved fast enough after you that I had time to make sure you were all right. I felt sick to my stomach, being unsure about your condition."

I heard his heart beating in his throat at such a rapid pace, I thought it might have exploded.

Mine matched.

"Even right now, I can see the red in your eyes. The red that you can only have if vampiric blood runs through your veins, and I'm talking myself off a ledge because of it."

"What happens here can stay here. I'll allow you the chance to see if you want to kill me or kiss me."

He hesitated as if he were going to change his mind, but I also realized I wasn't sure which outcome I wanted.

I grabbed his face and pulled it to me until our lips met.

He didn't pull away to resist.

He kissed me harder the second time his lips connected with mine. The movements between us became so natural that he was fully on top of me with unnoticeable motions. I only realized when the blanket that separated us fell away, and his body was flush with mine.

Another kiss, and my hips ground into him. I felt the hard length of him press against me at the same time as I heard the rush of blood through his veins. He wanted me more than he was willing to admit with words.

Another warm kiss, and his tongue slipped past my lips.

There was nothing bitter on his lips this time. Only heat that I wanted to fan higher.

Another harder kiss, and I reached for his belt.

It was the action that pushed him back to reality. His lips parted from mine as fast as they had touched.

"Enough," he mumbled to himself.

He ran both of his hands through his hair, and it made him look a mess. My lip stain tinted his mouth, and nail marks sat on the back of his neck.

"This can't go any further," he whispered.

I sat up and looked at him in silence. He sounded as though he spoke to himself more than to me.

"Lanira, you keep pushing me past the boundaries of who I am and what I was trained to do. I felt your fangs slide off my lips more than once. You keep begging me to hurt you. I keep rationalizing my thoughts and jumping through hoops that don't make sense to convince myself I'm wrong. Whatever your plan is, whatever you're doing. I can't keep letting it slide and be responsible for you killing an entire royal line."

Ravi left my room without allowing me to speak. He walked with defeat in his steps. It was likely for the best. I wasn't sure what I would have said to him. I hardly knew what to say to myself.

Koen was the only person that I was close to on any romantic level. I never felt even a hint of emotion for him. He was something that, although fun and fully my choice, was not romantic. There was no passion wrapped in lust.

Ravi set me on fire.

And that terrified me more than any blade at my throat ever could.

Act Three

The Lake of Crimson Kings

Chapter Twenty-Three
The Fall of the Final Pawns

Lanira

I stood outside the throne room as instructed, the cold stone wall pressing against my back through my dress. Princess Invidia had urged me to stay out of sight as much as possible. She had cried into my shoulder while the sun rose, tears dampening the fabric as she whispered about how she couldn't lose me as well. They were looking for anyone to put the blame on, and Princess Invidia just knew she felt it in her gut; she had murmured that the blame would be placed on me.

I listened as instructed because I also had no further interest in being in the spotlight. The memory of too many eyes watching, judging, still made my skin crawl. I didn't agree with her assessment, though. I was sure the spotlight would be on other kingdoms, on a war that would build only losses upon losses.

Still, I had caused enough fires to burn in enough places that I could move on to my next set of plans. The acrid smell of smoke seemed to follow me everywhere now.

Maids suddenly burst from the throne room, shoving each other in their haste to escape. The sight startled the villagers, who were also being ushered through the halls like cattle. The wooden floors creaked under so many hurried footsteps.

The king threw a vase at them as they fled. It crashed and crumbled against the doorway, porcelain shards scattering across the stone. I lifted my hands over my head and walked further to the side to avoid any debris. Silent and unnoticed, that was what I wanted, no matter the tantrum erupting around me.

"I won't hear any criticism or ideas!" The king's voice boomed through the corridors. "I refuse to listen to anyone who thinks they can defy me. I want every citizen of my kingdom who is twelve and older, even if they're ninety-four, prepared to join the war. Do you hear me?" Another item crashed into the walls, the sound echoing like thunder. "I'll send you too if you argue. No, I'll have your head and hang it at my entrance until it's rotted away all the flesh!"

Several advisors fled the room as well, their robes billowing behind them. They mumbled about how nobles would not take well to the idea of being rounded up to fight. I agreed. None of them knew how to fight their own battles, let alone survive a war.

"Enough!" Queen Blair's scream cut through the air like a blade. "My son needs his funeral proceedings planned more than you need a war! If you must keep busy, go meet all those bastard children Minala has dug up so that you may pick a new heir!"

"I'll take your head, too! All of your value died off!" King Valen bellowed before he marched out of the room, his heavy boots pounding against the floor.

He took the opposite end from where I stood. I may as well have been a statue for all the attention he paid me. The irony wasn't lost on me.

My heart stopped with the jolt of my body when the Queen's scream hit the air again. She sobbed with the howls she released, the sound raw and animalistic.

"My baby. My little boy." Queen Blair rocked back and forth, her voice breaking on each word.

I smirked before I lifted myself off the wall. The cool stone had left an impression against my shoulder blades. I kept my distance from everyone, but I wanted to see the fallout, needed to know what was happening around me, so that I could plan how to move. The castle had been so quiet for so long that the sudden rush of movement helped me feel alive again, blood pumping faster through my veins.

Guards trained children throughout the halls, and maids ran as if they had lost something precious. Like ants scattered from their line, chaos replacing order. A small boy with chocolate-colored hair was slapped in the back of the head for his poor form while he struggled with a sword as long as he was tall. The metal gleamed dully in the torchlight.

The guard left him behind to aid a boy much larger and stronger. It infuriated me to watch him take the easy student and abandon the rest. I pulled a shorter, thinner sword from the rack the guards had hastily set in the center of the villagers. The situation was so disorganized and driven by King Valen's whims that they were fitting and half-heartedly training villagers in hallways and dining rooms anywhere they could find space.

I offered the smaller sword to the boy, but he didn't consider it a gift. His small hands trembled as he looked at the weapon.

"You'll be able to hold this better," I offered, keeping my voice gentle.

"I don't want to hold it at all." His lip quivered, and I could see tears gathering in his young eyes. "I was supposed to be learning math today. I really like math."

The simple innocence in his words twisted something inside my chest. "If you practice well with your sword, then you will still have time for math left in the day." I pinched his cheek softly, but he found no relief in my words.

I wouldn't have found relief in any of my own words, either. I knew when I put my plans into motion when I set up these kingdoms to tear each other apart, that it would mean full casualties. That more would die than just the guilty. It was the only place I felt true guilt settling like a stone in my stomach. Prince Tillo, Prince Altair, for them, I felt more pity than anything else.

The king and queen, I felt joy course through me like wine. Princess Invidia stirred a mixture of sorrow in me, but she always found a way to remind me why I shouldn't dwell on such feelings.

The boy, though, I wished I hadn't seen them with my own eyes. It was so much easier to pretend that things not in front of your sight simply didn't exist.

King Valen's voice carried down the hall as he walked with his personal guard and priestess Minala. He continued to bellow about how he would take over StoneDale if it were the last thing he did. He ranted about leaving the Queen and marrying the princess himself, spittle flying from his lips in his rage.

I glanced back at the boy, condemned to a fate he never asked for, and pushed the emotions back down where they belonged. It was too late for me to turn back, even if I felt the weight of regret pressing against my ribs. Deaths would be in vain, no matter what future I choose now. I still held the chance to make all of the deaths worth the loss, though. That had to be enough.

I followed Valen with a renewed sense of commitment flowing through me, my footsteps silent on the stone.

"She will resist the idea, but of course, your word is the ultimate voice in the end." Priestess Minala's voice carried the practiced tone of someone who had spent years perfecting the art of agreement.

"She will marry me. No protest will be enough to convince me otherwise. I don't need you to assure me of that!" King Valen's voice echoed off the walls. "Blair is washed up and cannot give me back what she helped take from me. She is a traitor! Princess Sala is in her prime; she can produce many heirs. I dare whoever has the gall to kill my children to come after me! I dare them!" The last words came out as a roar.

Heads turned in the opposite direction, necks craning away from the spectacle. No one wanted to be seen looking at him while he threw his tantrums. Priestess Minala was the only one brave enough to watch him, and she did so with a sadness in her eyes that I recognized as the same look I had seen in Princess Invidia's gaze.

Both women looked at their respective men with loss and long-ing etched into their features. They saw things that they would never be able to touch, love that would never be returned. I was happier than I had ever been at the sound of his words, though. Princess Sala would have the worst kind of setup waiting for her. At least the princes had received death, and their worries were gone forever.

If King Valen ever dared to touch me, I'd end his life without a second thought. I could only hope that Princess Sala saw it the same way. I'd be blessed by whatever invisible force watched down on me and granted me the kind of luck I'd been having if it meant one more person on my list was out of the way, and I had a clear alibi on my side.

I stayed far enough back to remain unnoticeable, but close enough to catch every word that might fall from their lips.

King Valen slammed open the door to the room where he had left the princess locked away. He did so without mercy to the hinges, the wood splintering slightly under the force.

Minala let out a sharp scream, but Valen's face turned deep red as he took in the scene before him.

I leaned out from the hallway just enough to peer inside the doorway. Princess Sala dangled from a stone pillar used for ceiling decoration, ornate pieces that formed stars and held candles. They were only meant as a touch of unique aesthetics for the room, a request made by King Valen himself years ago.

Today, they held the perfect image of life in the kingdom for anyone but the king himself.

They held the encapsulated picture of King Valen's failures, even in the smallest choices.

They held my bright future spread before me like a feast. They held one more piece on Valen's board that was now removed and sitting on my sidelines.

I pressed my hand to my mouth, if only to cover the smile that broke free from my lips despite everything.

"Princess Sala was locked away and felt a false sense of pressure for a situation she couldn't have changed until it drove her mad." The handmaid's voice rang clear and strong through the room. "She couldn't go home, she couldn't even walk the grounds of what was supposed to be her new home. The dark wishes of a failed king touch everyone here. You should be hanging instead."

King Valen hardly had time to respond before Priestess Minala pulled the sword from the guard accompanying them and shoved it into the girl's stomach with a wet sound. The girl dropped to her knees, but somehow a smile still played across her lips.

"Killing me to hide from the truth?" She coughed, blood spattering across the stone floor. "I'll see you again soon."

I kept myself tucked in the shadows, my back pressed against the cool wall. I wanted no part in the scene unfolding before me. Princess Sala hardly deserved anything that had happened to her; her maid was right about that. Nothing I could do or say would alter what the outcome of the day's events would be. The die had already been cast.

A second maid rushed into the room after the King pointed her inside with a trembling finger. Guards cut the rope with careful movements and placed the Princess on the ground with surprising gentleness. The maid whispered words I could not hear before she turned back around to meet the king with wide, horrified eyes.

"It's too late," she whispered, her voice barely audible.

"Our alliance! We have to try and bring her back!" Minala's voice had turned frantic, higher pitched than usual.

"What does the note say?" Valen demanded as he pointed at an envelope that lay at the princess's feet like a final accusation.

His guard walked inside and called back, his voice hollow, "Two dead. I am cursed. No more empty walls. No more death."

"She's right. She's cursed. That's what it must be!" Valen's words came out in a rush. "She brought devastation to my kingdom. She must have been the trigger for all of this. Burn her body! She will have no funeral. She will grow no new life from her corpse. We will split our army and send half of the soldiers to Saydeean! They'll pay for cursing us!"

The smell of fear and desperation hung heavy in the air like incense.

Ravi suddenly brushed his hand through my hair as he walked past me to enter the chaos that played out before us. It was a silent message that he had seen me lurking in the shadows, and the brief contact sent an unexpected shiver down my spine.

"King Valen, your army is already thin," Ravi inserted himself into the conversation with calm authority. "If the Princess isn't sent back to her father, his army will be sure to come this way instead of marching toward StoneDale."

"You!" The king pointed his fat finger directly at Ravi. "Maybe you're cursed, too. Your arrival sent us into a spiral as well!" King Valen's voice climbed even higher. "I have the strongest army in the land! I cured the land of the vampires, me! I did that! I can take Saydeean and StoneDale both!"

"I only want to help you and your land prosper," Ravi replied, his voice steady as stone. "If that idea isn't sufficient for you, may I remind you of my home? It is far from similar to StoneDale or your court. The movement upon my loss would be swifter than any motion you could imagine."

The way Ravi spoke with such quiet assurance, with such a measured drawl, made my heart skip a beat. I realized I was biting my lip hard enough to taste copper.

I shook my head and sank back deeper into the shadows. There was nothing special about Ravi, I reminded myself firmly. I needed to refocus on what mattered.

King Valen's ears reddened at Ravi's words, the color spreading down his neck. The king opened and closed his mouth several times like a fish gasping for air before he decided against whatever sat on his tongue. "Figure this out!" he finally demanded.

Ravi bowed to King Valen with practiced grace. The king marched past him and continued to berate Minala, but Ravi's eyes found mine even through my careful silence and distance.

"This may be your easiest assignment yet," I chuckled softly as he approached. "She did it to herself."

He looked at me with disappointment etched into every line of his face as he moved closer. He was clearly unamused by my comment, and something in his expression made my stomach twist unexpectedly.

"Are you happy now?" Ravi whispered, his breath warm against my ear. "Is this what you wanted? To drive them into madness and risk the entire kingdom?"

Ravi was smart, too smart for his own good. He was clever enough to pick up clues and piece together guilt like a puzzle. He clearly wasn't smart enough to understand that he couldn't change someone, though. He and I both understood the loss of loved ones, but we did not share a common understanding of what to do with that pain.

He had hoped people could change for the better, and I knew they were all in need of a harsh lesson.

He took orders and asked no questions. I wanted to die knowing I had served the hand of justice myself.

We shared a similar foundation, but our homes were built of entirely different materials.

I leaned closer to him so only he could hear my words, close enough to smell the leather and steel that seemed to cling to his skin. He looked at me with something that might have been hope flickering in his green eyes, as if he believed his words had to have struck a chord somewhere inside me. He was wrong. I felt cocky, reckless.

I felt as though testing my boundaries was worth the risk.

"Yes," I whispered, placing my hand flat against his chest where I could feel his heartbeat. "It's exactly what I wanted. Death isn't the worst fate one can suffer, anyway."

"You're one step away from falling off the cliff and into your own grave," Ravi whispered back, his voice tight with warning.

"Would you save me?" The question slipped out before I could stop it.

"Would I save you?" He repeated my words slowly, as if tasting them.

"If I were about to be buried, would you step in and save me?" I kept my voice low, barely above a breath. "You seem to have a fondness for me, do you not?"

His body went rigid at my words, muscles tensing under my palm. I took full advantage of his stillness. I ran my hand up his chest until it rested around his neck, and let my other arm join it. He didn't embrace me back, but the realization hit me like cold water. It wasn't my boundaries I was testing.

It was his feelings for me. It was my own feelings for him that I was putting to the test. I wanted him to embrace me back with a desperation that surprised me, but he remained still as stone. He shifted his green eyes back and forth between mine, studying my face. His brows pinched together at the center, and he brushed loose hairs away from my face with fingers that trembled slightly before he grabbed my arms and carefully moved me away from him.

The rejection stung more than I had expected.

"I would not," he said simply.

He moved past me then, and it felt as though he left a dagger behind, buried deep between my ribs.

I stood there in the shadows, finally understanding what I had been blind to before. There were fates worse than death, like finally having something in front of you that you desperately wanted, and discovering you could never reach out and touch it.

Princess Sala was at least free now, free from watching others live the life and enjoy the freedom that she never would. In that way, perhaps she was luckier than the rest of us who remained breathing.

Chapter Twenty-Four
The Book

Lanira

Instead of spending my evening outside, breathing the cool night air, I was going to spend it inside the king's study, surrounded by dusty tomes and forgotten secrets. I turned the knob until I heard the soft click and slowly pushed the door open, wincing as the hinges creaked in protest. There was hardly any light in the room, just like the last time I had visited. The heavy curtains blocked out even the moonlight. It must have been a while since the king had stepped foot inside; the air smelled stale and unused.

I closed the door behind me with careful precision and lit a small candle that sat on a side table, wax pooling around its base from previous use. The flame danced, casting long shadows across the walls lined with leather-bound volumes.

The idea that he hadn't been reading in a while wasn't a surprise. He hardly made the time to bathe anymore, the longer things went on. The smell of unwashed flesh seemed to follow him through the halls now. There were fewer secret rendezvous with women behind Queen Blair's back, too. If it weren't for her children dying in exchange, it may have been the happiest time of her marriage.

I ran my hands over book after book, feeling the worn leather and embossed titles beneath my fingertips. I wished that I had the time to read them all, to lose myself in knowledge instead of schemes. I had spent so much time thinking about all of the secrets that could have been hidden in that very room that being inside, able to grab anything I wanted and run, was overwhelming. My pulse quickened with the thrill of finally being so close to answers.

I sorted through a pile of scrolls that sat on Valen's desk, their parchment yellowed with age, and tucked them carefully into my corset where they crinkled against my ribs.

I didn't know what was inside them, but that was a mystery for later. They looked old, important, the kind of documents that kingdoms went to war over.

Next, I needed the book. I moved around the desk and opened the drawer, the wood groaning softly under my touch. I pushed aside loose papers and scrolls until I saw the leather-bound book with a rune drawn on top, which sat undisturbed like a sleeping secret. I picked it up and flipped through the pages, the scent of old paper and ink filling the air, musty and rich with history. The only problem was that half of the pages were blank, their emptiness mocking me. The other half felt somewhat useless from my quick glance.

"So, this is what you wanted?" Ravi's voice cut through the silence like a blade. "All of this death for a book?"

A scream tore from my lips as I lifted my candle in the direction of his voice, hot wax dripping onto my hand. He leaned against a corner bookshelf as if he had been there for hours, watching me like a predator studies its prey.

"What are you doing here?" I huffed, my heart hammering against my ribs.

"I want to know the same thing." He stepped closer to me, his boots silent on the thick carpet. "All of this destruction for a book."

"It wasn't just for a book," I replied, clutching the tome tighter against my chest.

"Don't insult me by lying now." He pulled the king's chair closer and sat down, making himself comfortable in my moment of vulnerability.

"Stop. Don't get any deeper into this than you already are." I backed toward the door, feeling the cool wood against my spine. "Go home. Kill me. Whatever it will be, just pick a side and be done with it before you're involved in something that you don't want to be part of." I shrugged, though my shoulders trembled slightly.

"I don't think I can kill you." The admission fell from his lips like a confession.

The words hung in the air between us, heavy with implications I wasn't ready to examine.

"Then go home. Pretend you did a good job. Let me deal with the consequences that I signed up for." I tucked the book inside my cloak, feeling its weight settle against my hip.

"I can't do that. I'm here until I receive word that I can go home." He leaned against the desk, close enough that I could smell the leather and steel that clung to his clothes. "Instead, maybe I can help you. We can call it our first move as friends."

"You can't help me. I don't want friends." The words came out sharper than I intended. "Don't consider it. Don't think of me. Don't care for me. I'm content to die at the end of this."

"Die? At the end of what, exactly?" His green eyes searched my face in the candlelight. "I can't stop thinking about you. About how much you must be hiding. About how perfectly you do it. I think you've planned every step that brought this kingdom to the brink it's teetering on. I think I didn't give you the credit you deserved." He paused, running a hand through his dark hair. "You aren't just a vampire. You're a chess player. You set up a war to dwindle an entire kingdom, no, two kingdoms. You've killed two princes. You beheaded an innocent man at the king's request and called it a necessary move."

Ravi stopped to take a breath between his observations, and I could see the pieces clicking together behind his eyes.

"The things you've done, that you're still doing, they're awful. Still, in a strange way, I can't help but admire you for it."

The look in his eyes wasn't one of disgust like I was used to seeing. Or fear, like I expected from most people when they truly saw me. He looked at me as if he were begging for something I couldn't name.

"I read that book before you arrived here." He gestured toward the tome hidden in my cloak. "There's nearly no writing inside the pages. Are you trying to resurrect vampires? That's all I could gather from the few legible sections."

My blood went cold. He had been in here before me, had seen what I was after.

Ravi stood up from the king's chair and walked around the desk, closing the distance between us. "I'm already a witness to your theft. Either I turn you in and you tell the kingdom the truth, or I keep your secret, and you explain to me what it is you're really doing."

"Are you threatening me?" The question slipped out before I could stop it.

"I'm—" He moved even closer, near enough that I could feel the warmth radiating from his body. "I am threatening you, and I'm willing to raise the stakes if I need to."

Fear and something else I refused to name twisted in my stomach. I turned and reached for the door, but his hand closed around my arm first, fingers warm through the fabric of my sleeve.

"You are smart. Brilliant, even. But you will reach a point where you can't keep going alone. You will need someone on your side." His voice carried a warning that felt more like concern.

"If that time comes, I'll carve a way out of it." I pulled my arm from his grasp, skin tingling where he had touched me.

"Stop." He released me immediately, stepping back. "Let me escort you back to your room."

"I'm not leaving the book behind," I declared, my chin lifting defiantly.

The sigh that escaped from Ravi was nearly silent but heavy with resignation. "Take the book. I've gone through it a hundred times, there's nothing in there that you can do anything meaningful with."

His words struck me like a physical blow, but I kept my expression neutral. I stepped aside for him to go first and guide me back to my room, the silence between us thick with unspoken thoughts.

When my door came into sight, I rushed my footsteps into a run, my cloak billowing behind me. When I reached my room, I closed my door as quickly as I could without slamming it, the soft click echoing in the quiet hallway.

I needed to be alone with whatever disappointment awaited me.

I threw myself onto my bed and moved further down until I was tucked into my blankets like a child hiding from nightmares. I set a candle on each side of my bed, their flames creating a small circle of warmth in the darkness, and pulled out the scrolls first.

They were rough to look at, tattered and clearly much older than any of us. The parchment felt brittle beneath my fingers, as if it might crumble at the slightest pressure.

Temple designs covered the first scroll; it must have been used when the temple was originally created. Intricate archways and detailed stonework were sketched with careful precision. A list of names filled another scroll, written in faded ink; they were meaningless to me, just ghosts from a forgotten past. An image of a crow sitting on the shoulder of a young girl adorned another, the drawing surprisingly detailed for its age.

None of it meant anything to me. The scrolls felt like puzzle pieces to a picture I couldn't see.

I set them aside with growing frustration and reached for the book. My hands trembled slightly as I held it, and I hesitated to open the cover. Inside were supposed to be all of the things that I would have already been taught by my brother if life had moved a little differently. Inside was supposed to be the life I should have been living, the answers to everything I had questioned in the lonely hours of night.

Or at least, that was what should have been inside.

Worry settled in the pit of my stomach like a stone when Ravi's words replayed in my head. If there had been endless important information inside, he wouldn't have let me leave with the book so easily. I had known from my quick flip-through that there were blank pages, but my hope hadn't been completely dashed until Ravi spoke with such certainty.

I opened to the first page, and it displayed a rune painted into the parchment with what looked like dried blood. The symbol was intricate, meaningful in a way I couldn't decipher. I didn't understand what it meant. I hadn't been able to study runes, like so many other things that should have been my birthright.

I turned to the second page and felt my hands grow shaky as I saw paragraph after paragraph stretching before me. The text was clear, written in the same dark ink. Maybe Ravi couldn't see the words because he didn't have the eyes of a true vampire, I thought with desperate hope.

Yumi, the Goddess of Starlight, created our world and gifted it to Helia, the Goddess of Time. Helia did not have the power to create life, so mortals were brought from another realm and taught to live here. We were promised that if we succeeded in cultivating a special kind of people, we would be taken back to the realm of paradise where they all lived.

Years passed, and we failed. The Goddess injected us with magic, blood, and curses that she brought from another realm. She altered our bodies with no success. A God arrived to aid her, and together they created surges of magic. They filled a young girl with enough strange magic that she glowed white. She died and sent a surge across the land that killed everything. Our realm had to be rebuilt, regrown. We considered it a sign that things were happening that should not be. Helia considered it her success.

A curse was triggered. Some of the Temple of Time members left and formed the alchemists with the teachings the God of Rebirth had shared with us. Others still longed for the other realm—a realm of supposed peace.

The Goddess did succeed after the curse. The next young girl wielded blood from her fingers, but she also fed on blood. We learned the only way to create more was to breed them, and so the young girl was bred repeatedly.

The words made my stomach turn. Ink ran together for several pages after that, making the text no longer legible. Smudges and water stains had rendered entire sections unreadable. The book was horrifying rather than enlightening. I had thought that it would bring me peace to know my history, to understand where I came from and what I was meant to be.

But it hadn't. It only filled me with more questions and a sick feeling in my chest.

A few pages later, the ink became clear again, and I continued reading despite the growing dread.

High priest Dominic and his trusted friend Dimitri were sworn into positions in the promised land with the other Gods. Goddess Helia claimed they would run the temple there. She selected seven girls to accompany them as well. High priest Dominic left us guidelines for rituals before departing. They joked that we'd be on our own now that they had so many girls with bloodlines strong enough to wield the magic of blood.

We asked what their purpose was, and she told us of a Great War between the Gods that was approaching. The blood magic was to be used against other Gods as a weapon. We were finally told the truth—that she needed a realm away from the eyes of the other Gods so she could freely experiment on mortals in secret. She was never going to take us all with her.

She left us, and though we waited, she never returned for us. The bloodline grew stronger still.

Our priests spoke of the LastBorn—a descendant far enough down the line to wield the power to reconnect us with the gods.

I turned the ink-smudged pages again, my fingers leaving small marks on the ancient parchment, until I found the next clear section.

We were shaped by moonlight, stolen by starlight, and corrupted by time. The sisters of fate had yet to answer our calls. The Gods abandoned us.

I sighed heavily and turned another page, my chest tight with disappointment. The book wasn't what I had thought it would be, wasn't what I had needed it to be. I had expected it to tell me how to be myself, how to control the darkness inside me. I had wanted it to show me how to be acceptable, how to change what I was into something better.

I had wanted it to teach me more than an origin story filled with abandonment and betrayal.

I turned more pages, but I only skimmed the words now, tears of frustration beginning to blur my vision. Hot drops fell onto the ancient parchment as the reality sank in. I had fought and killed for a book of bedtime stories, tragic ones, but stories nonetheless.

The last readable page contained a revival ritual, and it was the only thing that made my pulse quicken with interest. It detailed every step of how I could bring someone back to life, complete with diagrams and ingredient lists. But even that felt hollow now, another piece of magic I didn't understand and couldn't properly use.

My door opened suddenly, and I jumped, slamming the book closed and shoving it under my pillow with guilty haste.

"Are you crying?" Ravi asked softly.

He closed the door gently behind him and sat on the edge of my bed, the mattress dipping under his weight. I shook my head, but more tears spilled down my cheeks despite my denial.

"I haven't been right about much lately, but those are definitely tears." He reached up and wiped a tear from my cheek with surprising gentleness, his thumb warm against my skin.

"I'm fine," I whispered, though my voice betrayed me.

He continued to clear the drops from my face with his thumb before taking out his handkerchief and finishing the job with careful attention. The fabric smelled like him, leather and something clean I couldn't identify.

"I won't tell anyone else that the ruthless Lanira shed tears," he murmured.

He was attempting to lighten the heavy air around us, but my heart still felt like it was made of lead.

"Did the book not tell you what you needed?" His question was gentle, without the 'I told you so' I had been dreading.

I sat in silence, not trusting my voice. I didn't trust him either, but I felt unexpected relief that he wasn't gloating over being right.

"Why are you asking me so many questions?" My voice still quivered like a child's.

"You're right. It's none of my concern." He paused, and I could feel him studying my face in the candlelight. "If I had to guess, though, the answers you wanted from your past weren't hidden inside those pages. I lost a lot when I was young, too. The current king of RuneHold is my half-brother. My mother was a maid who was swept away by promises from a king who never meant to keep them. When whispers swirled about my parentage, she was taken, murdered, and buried with no further words spoken about her. I was sent away to be trained as a weapon. I've never gotten those pieces of myself back. I've never found anyone willing to speak of her or tell me who she really was."

His voice was raw with emotion for the first time since I had known him. There was no undertone of sarcasm or carefully maintained distance. I hated hearing that pain because it cracked the lump in my throat that I was barely holding down. I could imagine his suffering because it echoed my own; the screams of my brother crying out for our mother before I was able to reach them still haunted my dreams.

I could imagine his loss because it was all too similar to the gaping hole in my chest that never seemed to heal.

He reached up and wiped at my cheeks again, catching tears I hadn't realized were still falling. His eyes were soft in a way I didn't know he was capable of achieving. He didn't look at me with pity, which would have made me recoil. He looked at me with understanding, with recognition of shared pain.

With that hope that both disgusted and drew me to him. He had some thread inside him that I didn't possess, whatever he clung to that gave him hope for a bright future, mine had been severed long ago.

Our eyes shifted back and forth, memorizing the details of colors and patterns, etching them into each other's minds before our lips met. Both of his hands cupped my face, and I tasted the salt from my tears mixed into our kiss. The warmth of his mouth against mine sent shock waves through my entire body.

I nearly got lost in that warmth, in the way his hands stayed respectfully on my face and didn't wander. In the way he kissed me for connection rather than conquest, in the spark filled with electricity that arced between us like lightning.

For a moment, I didn't hear the usual sound of his blood calling to me or the steady beating of his heart. I only felt the thread of passion that formed between us, fragile and terrifying in its intensity.

I pulled back, and he rested his forehead against mine, both of us breathing heavily. I swallowed hard at the intimacy of the gesture, more personal than the kiss itself. My heart felt so low in my chest that I thought it might fall from my ribcage entirely.

"Go home, Ravi," I whispered against his lips. "You won't change me, or what I need to do."

"I think I'll stay." His breath was warm against my face. "I'll pretend this meant nothing and that you were only caught up in emotions, so you can continue to feel in control."

I didn't find comfort in his words. I wanted him to leave, needed him to go before something inside me broke completely. He scared me for the first time since I had met him, and not because of his dangerous background or his skills with a blade.

He terrified me because, for the first time since I was seven years old, I thought maybe I didn't want to die.

Maybe, just maybe, I could allow myself to care for someone again.

And that was the most frightening thought of all.

Chapter Twenty-Five
A New Chess Board

Ravi

"Ravi?"

I jumped from my stance against the wall and sat up straight, blinking away the fog of sleep. The stone had left an imprint against my shoulder blade through my shirt.

"Did you sleep the entire night out here?" Princess Invidia asked, her voice carrying a mixture of amusement and concern.

I got to my feet and tried to look outside, wanting to pretend I had been awake and alert. The stained glass in their wing made it difficult to gauge the time. I couldn't tell where the sun sat behind the giant painted flowers that cast colorful shadows across the floor.

Princess Invidia regarded me with clear doubt written across her face. One raised eyebrow and a knowing smirk directed my way told me my deception wasn't working.

"Don't tell her," I relented, running a hand through my disheveled hair.

She looked at me with equal parts confusion and understanding, as if she were piecing together a puzzle she'd been working on for some time.

"I'll keep this to myself for now. I wouldn't mind being filled in on what exactly I'm keeping to myself, though." She took my arm and pulled me forward with gentle insistence. "Walk with me."

I wasn't sure how to handle the situation; it was territory I had never navigated before. Was I supposed to tell her that I had kissed her supposed sister, and it wasn't the first time? That I wanted it to be far from the last time? Was I meant to confess that I thought I needed to return home and offer myself up for punishment because kissing Lanira was only the beginning of the things I found myself thinking about?

Would she want to hear that I was breaking all of the rules I had been raised with? That I harbored a deep, growing desire to be close to a vampire?

That I was certain that woman had killed both of her brothers but had done nothing about it?

That I feared my afterlife would be filled with difficult questions I couldn't answer?

Of course not. Even if I was willing to push the boundaries of my oath, I didn't have a single desire to push the boundaries of trust with Lanira. She was hard enough to try to reach as it was.

"She was distraught last night. Nightmares about both princes plagued her sleep." I chose my words carefully. "She's been doing her best to hold herself together for your sake. I know it's not my place, but I couldn't leave her alone in her sorrows, not with the kind of misfortune that's been following this castle."

Another lie spilled from my lips for Lanira's sake, one I'd no doubt have to answer for at some point down the road. It was becoming too easy in Emberrella's kingdom to forget what awaited me back home and the price I'd pay if the choices I made here ever became whispers in RuneHold.

"It's strange to witness." She sighed, her breath visible in the cool morning air. "I must admit that I'm jealous of you."

The comment caught me completely off guard.

"I've known her for so long, and I've never seen her truly distraught. Not since we first found her." Her voice grew softer with memory. "She had nightmares then, too. She hardly slept or ate for weeks. Then one day she just turned it all off, like snuffing out a candle. I've never been able to coax her to turn herself back on. Even when she tries to be vulnerable with me, it feels the same as those polite little smiles people give because they feel obligated to."

We passed a window where early morning light filtered through, warming the side of my face.

"When we found her, my mother reached her first. They spoke for quite some time, and when Mother brought Lanira back to the castle, Lanira was covered in mud and crimson from head to toe. We couldn't even tell the color of her hair beneath all the grime." The Princess patted my arm gently. "My mother insisted that she be the one to care for Lanira until she settled in. I've never experienced a real or raw version of her, only glimpses of her deepest grief and her most impenetrable mask. What is it like?"

I considered her question carefully, thinking of Lanira's tears the night before, the way she had trembled in my arms.

"Sad," I admitted, my voice barely above a whisper. "It's like watching an ocean filled with the brightest coral and the clearest waters, but it never moves to make a wave because it doesn't recognize its own potential. Like a prized hand-carved vase that you dropped, even after gluing it back together in the perfect places, something is still off. It's beautiful, it's hardly noticeable that you dropped it, but if you look closely enough, the inside remains cold and forever changed. It's worth polishing and treasuring, but you know it'll never quite be the same."

"Maybe it's because even though the outside appears perfect, the inside has no paint to cover the crack lines," she mused thoughtfully.

The halls were bustling again with men who barely knew how to hold a sword attempting to teach children how to wield ones twice their size. They all looked hollow-eyed with hunger and exhaustion. The contrast between the life we lived and theirs was stark and uncomfortable.

"Do you think that she is guilty?" The Princess asked suddenly, her voice dropping to barely audible. "I've spent countless hours thinking about it. I can't bring myself to believe it's true, can you? I cannot see her as capable of not just trying to hurt someone, but actually taking a life. Yet it's the thought of those cracks deep inside, the ones that only she controls, that feeds me a spoonful of doubt."

It was precisely her ability to shut down and hide everything away that both scared me and fascinated me. The control she wielded over her own emotions was something I'd never encountered.

"If she were guilty, I would have handled it myself," I replied, the lie tasting bitter on my tongue.

How many more lies would I tell for her sake?

"What is it you want?" I asked, desperate to shift the conversation away from territory that made me feel like I was betraying Lanira's trust. "If life returned to normal right now, what would be your deepest wish?"

It felt wrong to keep discussing Lanira as if she were afternoon gossip between courtiers.

"I want to get married. I want to have children, lots of them." Her voice took on a dreamy quality. "I want peace, true peace. I've spent my entire life waiting for it, watching my brothers prepare for their grand destinies. I thought my turn would come soon after Tillo was wed. I know it sounds utterly ridiculous, especially by comparison. My brothers had such elaborate lists and ambitious dreams. I'm sure if Lanira shared hers, they'd be just as grand, perhaps even grander." Princess Invidia watched me carefully as we walked. "I truly do look forward to the days when I'll be sent away to live in quiet contentment with a husband who tends to my needs after fulfilling his duties. What about you?"

I had dreaded her turning the question back on me the moment I asked it. Yet part of me longed for just a small moment of honesty with someone who seemed to be opening herself up to me.

"I thought I knew the answer to that once." I paused, choosing my words carefully. "I only wanted to serve my kingdom and ensure they were moving in the right direction. I wanted to make changes that would better their lives, make their training more effective, and fair. I do still want those things, but I think maybe I've felt things recently that make me realize I don't want to do it alone anymore." I sighed with instant regret at my admission. "I've spoken too much."

"Not at all. What you've shared stays between us." Her smile was gentle and understanding. "She is special, isn't she? She has a way of making you look at strength differently. At life differently. I'll give Lanira that much."

She did exactly that. Knowing Lanira made me feel as though I could see a whole new spectrum of colors I hadn't known existed before. At first, she had merely interested me with her mystery. Then she confused me with her contradictions. I had graduated to admiration for her cunning and resilience, and now, the more I caught glimpses of her vulnerability, even the tiniest hints, I found myself obsessed with the idea of truly understanding her mind.

"To the King! To the King! We're under attack!" A guard's panicked scream echoed through the corridors.

I turned to the princess with a mixture of concern and relief at the interruption, while the color drained completely from her cheeks.

"Go back to your room and stay with Lanira. She will protect you if needed." I gently but firmly pushed Invidia back in the direction we had come from.

I ran toward the castle's entrance, pushing past confused farmers and frightened children to get a clear view of the situation outside. The acrid smell of fear-sweat filled the air.

Reanimated corpses lurched toward the castle with unnatural, jerky movements. They might not have posed much of a threat under normal circumstances, but the king had sent everyone capable of handling such creatures off to war. His home was now entirely defended by men who played with wooden toys or herded sheep for a living.

I bit down hard on my finger until blood welled up, then drew a rune in the air with the crimson liquid. I combined the symbols for summon and sky, feeling the familiar tingle of magic coursing through my veins. A golden ray of lightning cracked from the heavens and struck a group of the undead with devastating force. The bolts shattered and arced to hit all four of them, their bodies dropping to the ground. Though they still twitched and writhed, they were now harmless.

As I moved closer to examine them, I noticed they wore the sigil and armor of soldiers from StoneDale. Runes were carved deep into their foreheads, the same symbols used by the alchemists in my kingdom.

Had I missed something crucial? Had RuneHold picked a side in this conflict? Had StoneDale somehow stolen our sacred runes?

I pressed harder on my finger wound and released more blood. Drawing another rune in the air, I felt the ground rumble beneath my feet in response. Thick vines tore up from the earth and wound around the remaining undead's feet and legs, rooting them in place so they could not advance.

I drew my sword, the familiar weight comforting in my hand, and systematically removed the heads from the remaining group. The blade cut through decaying flesh and brittle bone with sickening ease.

It was hardly an attack that any competent guard should have struggled with, but King Valen apparently surrounded himself with cowards.

I turned to walk back inside, wiping my blade clean on my cloak, but before I reached the stairway, King Valen came bellowing out of the entrance like a charging boar.

He wore pieces of armor that were clearly too small for his expanded frame, metal plates straining against leather straps. A sword hung awkwardly from his belt, obviously unfamiliar in his grip.

"Out of my way! I'll handle them myself!" he roared, spittle flying from his lips.

My lips curled in disgust at the pathetic sight. Even in Emberrella, the King used his people as shields and only showed up in time to pretend he had been useful.

"They're already dead, Your Highness," I replied as I climbed the stone steps. "They were StoneDale soldiers raised from the grave."

"Dead soldiers?" The King blinked at me with confusion clouding his features. "Reanimated soldiers? So that princess was cursed after all! Her death brought this curse upon my land!"

I tried to suppress my sigh of frustration. Whatever part of him had once been worthy of respect had degraded beyond redemption. He spoke like a fool and looked like an overfed pig stuffed into armor.

I would get Lanira out of his castle before he had the chance to turn his paranoid sights back on her. I needed to discover what was happening in my own kingdom, and I would take her with me when I left to investigate.

"I believe it's more likely the result of the war you started, and not some supernatural curse," I replied evenly.

"If you're so clever, what would you have me do?" King Valen mocked, his voice dripping with false bravado. "If you claim to know more than a king, prove it!"

"If I were a king, I would admit that I was wrong. That I made my move too hastily." I met his gaze steadily. "I would call for talks of peace. I would investigate what was directly in front of my face instead of chasing fantasies. I would start by examining those closest to me, because if I were a king surrounded by people who refused to tell me when I was making mistakes, I would consider them failures rather than trusted advisors, Your Highness." I paused, letting my words sink in. "In this war, you are not cursed, you are simply wrong."

I didn't wait for his response; I turned and headed toward the castle entrance.

"If I were you, I'd have your head for such insolence!" he called after me, his voice shrill with impotent rage.

If we were both kings, I thought grimly, I would have ended his reign before his descent into this madness had begun.

The weight of that truth settled heavily on my shoulders as I climbed the stairs, leaving him to rage at my retreating form.

Chapter Twenty-Six
THE OCEAN OF FIRE

Lanira

I snuck out of the back of the castle and into the fresh night air, the cool breeze carrying the scent of jasmine and damp earth. I took off running through the grass, my bare feet silent against the soft ground, and plunged into the Hollowgrove forest. I ducked and dodged branches from the ancient burial trees as quickly as I could, their gnarled limbs reaching out like skeletal fingers in the moonlight.

I felt as though my brother had to be looking down on me with approval. Things had worked so perfectly for me that even when I had to think on my feet, everything fell into place. The timing was almost supernatural in its precision. I hadn't known how I would manage to slip away from all the villagers making war preparations, or the maids bustling about to keep up with them, and still have enough time to perform the ritual written in the book.

Yet somehow, I had managed it all. I snuck around the castle without a single hiccup, not one eye had noticed my departure.

The undead soldiers from another land had shown up at precisely the right moment to provide the continued distraction I needed. If I had been an afterthought to the royal family before, I was completely forgotten now. I didn't know where the creatures had come from or who had sent them, but even the universe seemed to be conspiring in my favor with how seamlessly events aligned.

King Valen continued his descent into his own downward spiral, muttering and raving like a madman. I doubted he even remembered who I was anymore. He spent all his time bellowing about curses on his land and how the prophecy was fighting back, though he'd still emerge victorious in the end.

His tumble into darkness was deeply satisfying, but it could taste even sweeter still.

I stopped running and stood before the ocean that bordered the burial forest. The trees and sky hung in perfect silence, even the wind didn't stir so much as a whisper of breeze. Every star in the vast expanse above seemed to be watching me, waiting.

I opened the vampire's book with trembling hands and set it down in the dirt at my feet, the ancient pages rustling softly.

Lowering myself to my knees, I pulled out my knife from the small hidden pocket inside my dress and sliced my finger open. The sharp pain was immediate and grounding. I held my bleeding finger over the water and glanced back down at the book as crimson drops fell into the dark ocean.

"Moonlight and Time. Blood of the Sun. Collide the Stars under Insanity."

The blood shimmered like liquid gold before it burst into flames, transforming the water from unmoving crystal blue to a towering blaze higher than I could stand. The fire spread across the entire ocean's surface, illuminating every inch of the night sky with dancing orange and gold.

My heart raced as I realized how far these flames could be seen, the light probably visible for miles. I needed to move faster before someone came to investigate.

I glanced back down at the book, my pulse thundering in my ears. I only needed to read one more incantation before all of my family would be brought back. One more line before my people would be alive again, before I could finally have a home worth returning to.

"I call upon the sisters of Seed, Water, Clock, and Death to bring back what was wrongfully taken."

The fire shifted dramatically between emerald, cobalt, crimson, and pure white before burning all colors at once in a spectacular display. Then, just as suddenly as it had begun, the flames went out completely.

Nothing happened. No familiar faces greeted me from beyond the veil. I sliced a second finger with desperate urgency and dripped fresh blood over the water, but it remained cold and dark; no fire sparked this time.

I grabbed the book and frantically flipped through the pages, searching for something I might have missed. My hands shook as I scanned the ancient text.

I should have been greeting my mother, feeling her warm embrace. Shaking hands with my father, hearing his proud voice. I was supposed to be hugging my brothers and sister, whole and alive and real.

Instead, there was only silence and the taste of failure bitter on my tongue.

My mind suddenly exploded with agonizing pain, and the shock sent me face-first into the dirt. I felt my body begin to convulse violently. First, my feet cramped with excruciating pain, then my legs shook uncontrollably. Before I had time to process any other changes, I was being pulled at impossible speed through a swirling vortex of images and memories that weren't my own.

No matter where my eyes shifted, I saw only fragments of someone else's life, brief clips of moments in time where I had never existed. I felt my body stretch and contort as it was dragged through time and space before being violently spat out on the other side.

I was in the same place, beside the same body of water, but everything felt different. The air tasted of ancient magic and old blood.

A girl knelt before the water, her wrists bound with chains that glowed with ethereal light. Her short pink hair hung in tangled strands around her face, and even from behind, I could sense her defiance.

A man stood over her holding a massive claymore, his long grey beard and matching hair wild and unkempt. Beside him stood a woman with flame-red hair and eyes like fresh blood, her skin so pale it seemed to glow in the moonlight.

A circle of robed figures surrounded them in complete silence, watching the scene unfold. One lifted their head just enough for the moon to catch the gleam of elongated fangs.

"I'll give you one last chance to change your mind. One final opportunity to reconsider," the red-headed woman spoke, her voice carrying the weight of divine authority.

"Helia, I'll tell you one more time." The pink-haired girl's voice rang with unwavering determination. "If you take me with you, the moment we set foot in the other realm, the very second our feet touch that ground, I will ensure every God knows exactly what you've done here. There is no price you could pay for my silence. No bribe I would accept to protect the atrocities you've committed in this realm."

The girl spat defiantly into the water, the sound sharp in the still air.

"Alio, please. Your mother is serious about this," the grey-bearded man pleaded, his voice heavy with sorrow.

"Thann, don't." Helia's tone grew cold as winter. "If this is the choice she's decided to make, then so be it."

She pointed at Thann, and he reluctantly lowered his blade toward Alio. The girl with pink hair looked up, and I saw her crimson eyes blazing with fearless resolve. Just as I thought she was about to lose her head, something extraordinary happened instead.

A blinding ray of orange light erupted around her, lifting her from the ground and hurling her through the air into the water with tremendous force. The impact sent waves crashing in all directions.

"Let this serve as a lesson for what happens when you betray me," Helia declared, her voice echoing with divine power. "She isn't the only god now imprisoned at the bottom of an ocean."

She tucked her hands into her robes and disappeared into the darkness, leaving only the sound of lapping waves behind.

I was yanked back through the swirling vortex of images and slammed into my own body with jarring force. I gasped for air, feeling simultaneously weightless and unbearably heavy.

A small section of water began to separate in front of me, and out flew a raven unlike anything I had ever seen. Its feathers were mostly gone, replaced by burnt, scarred flesh. The few remaining feathers were embedded deep into its skin like black needles.

The creature was grotesque yet somehow beautiful in its horror. It released a cry like a war horn and took flight, circling above me as if studying every detail of my form.

"Look what we have here." A guard's rough voice cut through the night as his hand tangled painfully in my hair. "The king won't be pleased to hear about this midnight adventure, but he'll be delighted to have proof of your sneaking around."

I struggled against his brutal grip and jerked my head forward despite the searing pain. I would rather lose hair than be captured. I hadn't had nearly enough time to recover from whatever supernatural experience had just occurred.

The guard shoved my head under the icy water without warning, and I reached back desperately to scratch and claw at him.

I hadn't gotten a chance to catch my breath or prepare before he forced me under. My mind went completely blank with terror as water filled my nose and mouth.

He yanked me up by my hair, and I barely managed a partial breath before—

"I have the entire night to wear you down and drag you back," he growled.

He shoved me under the water again, this time holding me down longer. I couldn't tell if the warmth running down my scalp was blood or water, but the sensation was equally terrifying.

I stopped clawing at his arms because it accomplished nothing; he didn't even flinch. My vision began to blur as my lungs screamed for air, and my heart hammered painfully against my ribs. I reached frantically into my pocket for the knife, but it was gone. He pressed harder on my head, grinding my face against the rocky bottom.

He intended for me to pass out, to push me as close to death as possible without finishing the job.

I searched desperately through the water for a rock, a stick, anything I could use as a weapon against him.

A loud splash broke the surface above me, and something heavy sank to the bottom beside me in the water.

Suddenly, I was pulled up, gasping so loudly it was nearly a scream of its own.

"Breathe!" His voice shook with unmistakable panic and fear.

I coughed up water for what felt like an eternity, my entire body convulsing with each painful expulsion.

"Are you alright?" The desperation in his voice was palpable.

I managed to hold my thumb up before I fully opened my eyes. In front of us floated the headless body of the guard, dark blood clouding the water around it. I took in the gruesome sight while I struggled to fill my burning lungs with air.

Had Ravi actually beheaded a man to save me?

"Look what you made me do!" Ravi's voice carried a mixture of anger and something that might have been regret.

"Me?" I choked out, spitting up more water. "I didn't force you to do that."

"I had to do it to save your pretty neck," he replied, though his usual cocky tone was strained.

"This is no time for flattery or attempts to cope with distraction," I managed to say.

I threw myself onto the muddy ground, still soaking wet and shivering. I needed time to process everything: the failed ritual, the vision, the near-drowning, and now this.

"You owe me," Ravi declared as he dragged the guard's body deeper into the water.

I didn't answer, only closed my eyes and tried to stop my teeth from chattering. Ravi removed his overcoat and tossed it on the ground beside us before lowering himself down. He reached for me and pulled off my soaking jacket, then moved to remove my top as well. I had to slap his hands away; he seemed intent on stripping me completely.

He relented at just the jacket and picked up his coat to drape it over my shoulders before pulling me against his chest. He wrapped both arms around me, trying to warm my chattering form with his body heat.

"What are you doing out here?" he asked quietly.

"What are you doing here?" I countered, though my voice lacked its usual bite.

"I followed you." The admission came readily. "The princess went to check on you and discovered you missing. The king also alerted the guards that he was missing a book of great importance. It was assumed that you stole it and fled. King Valen wants you in a cell immediately."

"Why did you kill the guard then, if you're planning to arrest me all the same?" I met his gaze directly, wanting him to admit his true intentions.

Ravi looked down at me with an expression I couldn't quite decipher. "No one gets to lay hands on you in front of me."

I opened my mouth to argue, but he placed his hand gently over my lips.

"You have two choices now, Lanira. Trust me, or run." His green eyes were serious in the moonlight. "I know you'll immediately choose to run, but at the very least you can trust that I won't let you be hanged or beheaded by anyone but my own hands, if it comes to that." He removed his hand from my mouth. "You can trust that I want to be the one to catch you red-handed, if you can trust nothing else I tell you."

"That was truly inspiring," I replied flatly, though something warm flickered in my chest despite everything.

"Stay. Hand the book over to me and I'll keep it safe. We'll do what we have to do, and I'll have you free again." He squeezed me tighter against him. "I will get you out of this in one piece."

"It doesn't seem like I have much choice. Don't think—" He cut me off.

"I know. You're going to give me the 'rough lone wolf who doesn't need anyone' speech." He fixed me with a steady glare. "Despite all the resistance you're going to put up, you do need someone this time. The entire castle is awake and searching for you."

He pulled out a set of iron chains from his belt and grinned from ear to ear. I hadn't even noticed them before in the darkness. He really had come to arrest me. I would make him pay for this deception, double.

He locked my hands in the shackles with what looked like genuine satisfaction.

"This will be the only time something like this happens, so enjoy it while you can," I grimaced, the metal cold against my wrists.

"I certainly hope not," he laughed, the sound rich and warm despite the circumstances.

He made jokes, but my stomach churned at the thought of being locked in a cold, moldy cell. My head still pounded from oxygen deprivation, and my thoughts raced, trying to make sense of the vision I had witnessed.

Who was the girl named Alio? And what did her imprisonment have to do with my failed ritual?

The questions multiplied as Ravi helped me to my feet, the chains clinking softly in the night air.

Chapter Twenty-Seven
A Crimson Knight Beside the Crimson Queen

Lanira

When we arrived at the castle, Ravi shoved me roughly to the ground, forcing me onto my knees in front of King Valen's throne. The stone floor was unforgiving against my kneecaps, sending sharp pain up my legs. Ravi played his role with theatrical boldness, as if he genuinely enjoyed every moment of my humiliation. If he expected that I wouldn't make him pay dearly for the way he was performing, he was gravely mistaken.

King Valen rose from his throne and strutted toward me with obvious relish. His multiple chins jiggled with each deliberate step he pounded down, the sound echoing through the silent throne room. The king grinned at me as if he had been waiting years for the day he could see me at my absolute lowest. His small, piggish eyes sparkled with malicious glee as he no doubt imagined all the creative ways he could separate my head from my shoulders.

I fought back the overwhelming urge to tell King Valen that no matter what tortures he inflicted upon me, it wouldn't restore even an ounce of his lost worth or dignity.

Queen Blair sat in stony silence behind him, her face a mask of carefully controlled emotion. She lifted her gaze toward the ornate ceiling as though refusing to witness what was about to unfold would somehow make it less real. As if she could avoid carrying guilt as long as she didn't actively watch the proceedings. It was exactly like her, always choosing willful blindness over difficult action.

"I found her outside the castle walls, but she had nothing on her person. No book or journal of any kind," Ravi reported, his voice crisp and professional.

"Did you search her properly and thoroughly?" King Valen snarled, spittle flying from his lips.

"There's nowhere such an item could be concealed, Your Highness," Ravi assured him with conviction.

"Where is my book, Lanira?" King Valen bellowed, his voice bouncing off the stone walls.

"I don't know what book you're referring to. Most of the castle knows I take walks at night, it's hardly unusual behavior. I haven't done anything wrong!" I cried out, letting genuine desperation creep into my voice.

"You've done wrong if I declare you've done wrong! You're nothing but a thief and a cursed child!" King Valen's accusatory finger trembled as he pointed it at me.

The way he screamed filled my stomach with ice-cold dread, though I felt simultaneously void of everything except pure, burning rage. My jaw remained clenched so tightly I thought my teeth might crack.

King Valen raised his meaty hand and slapped me hard across the cheek. The sound cracked like a whip through the throne room. My head whipped violently to the side, and my breath caught painfully in my throat. Still, I refused to wince or give him the satisfaction of seeing any reaction beyond the physical impact.

Ravi immediately stepped in front of me, his body creating a barrier between the king and myself.

"Allow me to lock her away for now, Your Highness. Let's remove her from your presence so we may focus our efforts on locating your missing book," Ravi offered diplomatically.

The king ground his teeth so loudly in my direction that the sound was audible throughout the room. He waved his hand dismissively. "Get her out of my sight before I do something we'll all regret."

Queen Blair suddenly jumped to her feet in desperate protest. "You must not do this! Valen, she hasn't done anything to warrant imprisonment!"

The King completely ignored her pleas, turning his back on both of us.

"How many more of our children must die before you've had enough of this madness?" The Queen kept pleading, her voice breaking with each word.

Princess Invidia suddenly bolted from the doorway where I hadn't realized she'd been standing and wrapped her arms tightly around me. Her embrace was warm and fierce, smelling of rose water and desperate tears.

"I'll get you out of this. I promise on my life. If I can't manage it, Mother will find a way. We won't let you stay locked away in that horrible place," Princess Invidia sobbed into my hair.

She cried hard enough that I could barely understand her words through the broken syllables. For a startling moment, I lost myself completely to memory and found myself somewhere else entirely. My real sister was clinging to me and crying just like this, telling me she hadn't meant for me to get in trouble. She gripped me tightly after some petty dispute we'd had, a foolish argument that had stolen the place of what could have been a happy memory.

I could almost smell the lavender oil that my true sister always wore in her dark hair, could almost feel her smaller hands clutching at my dress.

Ravi gently but firmly grabbed Princess Invidia and moved her away from me. He took hold of my arm and pulled me to my feet with practiced efficiency. The princess remained in the throne room as Ravi guided me out, her sobs echoing behind us until the heavy doors closed with finality.

"When I'm free from this place, I'm going to make you suffer for this performance," I whispered low enough that only he could hear.

"I'm genuinely looking forward to it," Ravi whispered back, and I could hear the smile in his voice.

They left me completely alone in the dungeon's oppressive darkness. I tried my best to find sleep, but the rest I managed was broken and far from satisfying. Every time I began to drift off, the cold would wake me, or some distant sound would jolt me back to consciousness.

The stone floor was colder than even I had imagined possible. The air hung thick and stale, heavy with the scent of decay and despair. Old bloodstains had seeped so deeply into the walls that they looked like abstract paintings of violence. The iron bars had rusted until they were more orange than black, and everything felt damp with moisture that never quite dried.

I had thought I knew nearly all the comings and goings of the castle, but the horrific state of this dungeon told me I had been painfully wrong. Far more atrocities had occurred than my ears had ever heard whispers of.

Aged signs of long-term use were evident everywhere, but so much fresh evidence of recent torture and death lined every surface. My stomach turned violently at the thought of how many innocent people had been falsely condemned and brutally killed in this very space.

The realization hit me like a physical blow: no monsters surrounded me down here. Only average people had been forced to suffer horrifically at the whims of a mad king.

I allowed myself to sit with that disturbing thought for only a moment before forcing my mind back to practical matters. I had to think clearly. I needed to plan my next move carefully. I had never seriously considered that I might end up in the dungeon myself. I had thought I might come close to imprisonment more than once, but I had always been confident in my ability to talk my way out of such situations.

I pulled my hair around my shoulder and brushed my fingers through the tangled ends, using the familiar motion to help me think.

Breaking out wasn't realistic given the circumstances. Even if I somehow found a way to escape, I would have to spend the rest of my life on the run. Changing my identity completely was too drastic a step, and it would mean abandoning everything I had worked toward. I was so tantalizingly close to bringing about Valen's kingdom's complete collapse. I only needed one or two more carefully calculated moves.

I sighed heavily and let my head fall back against the cold stone wall.

"You don't look like you belong in a place like this," Ravi's voice cut through the silence. "Even though I know without a doubt that you do."

My eyes shot open to find him standing just outside the bars.

"Neither do you, considering you've killed far more people than I have, after all," I replied simply, meeting his gaze without flinching.

"Do you never think about them? The people whose lives you've ended?" he asked, his voice carrying genuine curiosity rather than accusation.

He stood outside the bars as though he occupied some kind of moral high ground. For a brief moment, I had thought that he and I might have developed some mutual understanding. At least a little.

"Do you think about the ones you've killed?" I countered. "I didn't force that guard to attempt murder, just as I didn't force you to remove his head from his shoulders. We both made choices in moments when decisive action was required."

Ravi shook his head slowly and rubbed a weary hand across his face. He licked his lips thoughtfully before speaking again. "Who taught you to behave this way? You're so mechanical, so calculated, that sometimes you don't even seem real. You always have the perfect response ready, the exact expression needed for any occasion. I find myself believing your performances most of the time." He paused, studying my face through the bars. "The only problem is that behind every flawless smile or carefully placed gesture, you completely lack emotional weight. Your eyes are always utterly empty."

I lifted my head from the wall and rose to my feet, moving closer to the bars. "My eyes may be empty, but I would rather carry zero emotion than bear the crushing weight of self-righteous falsehoods. The only real difference between you and me is the way we choose to tell ourselves the truth." I wrapped my hands around the cold iron bars, feeling the rust flake off under my grip. "You look at me and convince yourself that you could never become what I am. You tell yourself that you walk some kind of just and noble path. I refuse to pretend there's any moral goodness behind the choices I make. I make them knowing full well that I may have to pay dearly for them someday."

I leaned closer to the bars, close enough to see the conflict playing across his features. "I will get out of this place. With or without your assistance. When I do, I will continue pursuing my goals. Not because I have some sense of false moral superiority, but because I have consciously decided to enact my own version of justice in this world."

He watched me silently for a long moment, his expression shifting as if he were sorting through complex thoughts. His brows furrowed deeply as he stared at the stone floor between us.

"What exactly is your plan, then?" he finally asked. "If I were to decide that perhaps you've made some valid points, and I wanted to help you succeed, what would you even do from here?"

"Pufferfish," I announced, snapping my fingers with sudden inspiration.

"Pufferfish?" He scoffed, clearly confused by my seemingly random response.

"Exactly! The kitchen staff will be blamed for the contamination, and the king will be permanently out of our way. The queen would have no choice but to free me, even if she harbored doubts, and she would do it for the princess's sake. Then I will offer myself as a diplomatic bride to make peace and atone for being the supposed curse that Valen claimed I was." I smiled at my own cleverness.

I knew I could devise something workable if I just applied myself to the problem.

"I don't understand why you look so pleased with yourself. Your entire plan only functions if I agree to help you execute it," Ravi pointed out.

"I'll find another method if you would feel more comfortable not involving yourself," I replied with a casual shrug.

Ravi clicked his tongue thoughtfully. "What if we negotiated a deal? I'll provide the assistance you need if you promise to leave this kingdom with me and come to RuneHold."

"Absolutely not," I responded immediately.

"That was an remarkably fast response," Ravi observed. "What if traveling to RuneHold were a way I could get you out of here without requiring anyone's death?"

"We sabotage the king's meal with pufferfish, wait for the paralysis to set in. Death won't be far behind for him after that. We blame the kitchen staff, I'm freed from this cell, and we accomplish our goal without unnecessary killing and without any trip to Rune-Hold."

"I am only going to help you because I believe that, of all the fates you might deserve, being locked away for nearly being murdered is definitely not one of them," Ravi declared.

"I don't particularly care how you choose to phrase your motivations to make yourself feel better, as long as the end result is my freedom. I do have one final question for you, though," I said.

"I absolutely will not become a pawn in whatever larger game you're playing," Ravi stated firmly, his stance and tone leaving no room for negotiation.

I nodded approvingly. His assertion was actually quite enjoyable to hear.

"Who are the other prisoners locked down here with me?" I asked, gesturing toward the darkness beyond my cell.

"The king has been systematically gathering anyone suspected of practicing ancient magic or harboring vampiric tendencies and imprisoning them in this dungeon. He intends to have them all executed together in a grand public display as some kind of memorial for Prince Altair." Ravi's voice carried disgust. "That's all the information I have about the situation."

He walked away with purposeful strides, moving like a crimson knight who remained fundamentally unsure whether he truly meant to help me or ultimately destroy me.

The uncertainty in his departure left me with more questions than answers, but at least now I had hope that escape might be possible.

Chapter Twenty-Eight
An Oath and a Fish

Ravi

I needed to write two letters before I dealt with anything else that would unfold at the end of my day. I sat at King Valen's ornate desk and used his ink and parchment, feeling like an intruder in his private space. The weight of what I was about to do pressed down on my shoulders like a heavy cloak.

Niyla,

I will be home soon. I'm bringing you several gifts that I hope will remind you of this journey. A dried sunflower with petals like spun gold. A spice called ginger—it's bitter at first taste, but I think you will grow to love its warmth. I've also convinced Queen Blair to let me bring you a sparrow. She keeps many birds and often speaks of how she relates to their need for freedom. I thought of you immediately when she shared this sentiment.

I know the timing is poor, but I need to ask another favor of you. Will you look into someone named Ash? All I know is that he was set to become a high priest for the Temple of Time. I'll explain everything when I see you again.

Love, Ravi

I folded the letter carefully and placed it inside a cream-colored envelope. I sealed it with my own stamp but used King Valen's deep red wax, watching as it pooled like blood on the parchment. It felt strange, as if I had somehow taken over what was once his rightful place. If he were in his right mind, I would never have been allowed to so carelessly use his personal belongings as if they were my own.

I pulled out a second sheet and dipped the quill back into the dark ink, its metallic tip scratching against the parchment.

King Orn,

I can confirm that I do not require many more days before making my return home. I have found no sympathizers within their court, nor any practicing witches. I have discovered no viable way to convince King Valen to strengthen our diplomatic relationship. There may have been an opportunity once, but he has been completely unreachable on any rational level since his eldest son's death. Princess Sala has also perished. The failure is entirely my own, and I will accept whatever consequences await me upon my arrival.

Regarding the other intelligence you requested: it is indeed true that Queen Blair originates from Ruby Wake. She was married into Emberrella's royal line, but it appears they maintain no formal alliance or agreements. Quite the opposite, in fact. They have ruled so firmly against any alliance that anyone discovered visiting from Ruby Wake is to be executed on sight.

First Blade, Ravi

I didn't understand why King Orn wanted such specific information, but I was far from being in a position to question his motives. I was already facing enough consequences upon my arrival home; I didn't need to add insubordination to my list of failures. I had failed in everything I was sent to accomplish, and I had done so willingly. I could have created a vastly different outcome if I had never laid eyes on Lanira.

I left the study and handed both letters to a trusted guard, ensuring my personal seal remained intact and my words would stay secret. I walked with studied casualness past the clusters of advisors' wives, not wanting to give them any additional reasons to whisper about my activities.

I was on edge about everything; every small detail felt magnified and suspicious. Even the way my hands rested naturally at my sides as I walked seemed wrong somehow, a thought that never would have occurred to me under normal circumstances. I wasn't accustomed to planning the assassination of royal family members from the shadows. What Lanira had asked me to do made logical sense; she was brilliant in that regard. If I managed to pull it off successfully, there would be no accusing fingers pointed back at me. Suspicion would land in a hundred other places before anyone ever thought to investigate her or me.

I slipped into the kitchen, where my fingernails immediately found their way to my mouth. I bit nervously at the skin around the edges of my fingers, a habit I thought I had abandoned years ago.

Was she worth the inevitable fallout? Would she assist me in the same way if our positions were reversed?

Could I live with myself if I denied her this aid? Could I live with myself if I provided it?

Was King Valen even worth saving at this point? It had taken far longer to reach the position where I had to ask these questions than I had anticipated. The King had barely made time for proper meals since Lanira was imprisoned, eating only scraps when reminded.

It was strange to witness the effect she had on him. Valen claimed to despise the girl, but the knowledge of Lanira rotting in a cell seemed to add another layer to his suffering and madness.

I wasn't entirely sure I could execute Lanira's plan successfully at all. If she were doing it with her own hands, I had no doubt she would succeed flawlessly. I wasn't someone who typically moved in shadows to scheme and manipulate. I had the power and authority behind my name to kill openly if I chose to kill.

I had no reason to do it in secret, which made this infinitely more dangerous.

I would have no home to return to if I were caught acting in secret like a common assassin.

Who was I trying to fool? I was going to do it. I knew I wouldn't be able to look at myself in any mirror if I didn't help her. If I left her locked away to slowly starve and die in that horrible place. I knew she was growing weaker by the day, and every time I considered giving her blood to sustain herself, I flashed back to my sacred oath.

I flashed back to the only other vampire hunter I had ever seen caught helping one of the creatures. Both the hunter and vampire were pulled apart at each limb and neck until nothing remained attached. It was done in the public square of our capital city, performed as a clear and brutal message about the consequences of breaking the oath to protect our realm from vampires.

Their bodies were torn apart piece by piece to the enthusiastic sound of cheers and thunderous applause from the gathered crowd.

Every time I got a little too close to Lanira emotionally, I could see that gruesome scene play over again in my mind. Our kingdoms weren't alike in their methods. Valen would simply forget her existence in the dungeon. My homeland would torture her slowly, playing with her as if she were an amusing toy.

The desire to help her and the mental gymnastics I had to perform to convince myself not to do it terrified me.

I should never have allowed myself to reach a point where I questioned the nature of my feelings for her. It put both of us in mortal danger.

I bit down too hard on my already far-too-short fingernail and jolted from the sharp pain. The kitchen was eerily silent around me. It might be the only opportunity I would have to make any decisive move.

I lunged for the pufferfish and deliberately ruined its chance of being safe for consumption. There was only one fish in the entire kitchen, and I knew it would be prepared exclusively for the king's dinner.

I left the kitchen as quickly as I could move without appearing to flee in panic. I forced myself to slow my pace and clear my throat as I entered the dining hall only a few steps away. I took my usual seat at the dinner table beside Princess Invidia, trying to appear as normal as possible.

"Maybe we're wrong about everything," Queen Blair was saying, her voice heavy with doubt. "Maybe Valen can see something that we're blind to. Maybe Lanira truly is guilty of these crimes."

"Don't you ever say that again!" Princess Invidia slammed her fork down on the table with enough force to make the plates rattle.

"Invidia, please," the Queen sighed wearily.

"No! Don't ever speak those words again!" The princess's voice rose to near-screaming. "You call her your daughter, the same as you do me. Are you actually suggesting that if Father decided I needed to be sent to the dungeons for weeks at a time, you would simply agree? With nothing more than his word to support the decision?" Her voice cracked with emotion. "You would discard me like some worthless, toss-away item?"

"You're absolutely right. I was only trying to lessen the crushing guilt I feel for allowing her to be sent away like that." Queen Blair's voice broke slightly. "I wish she were sitting here eating with us even now."

"I also believe her imprisonment is unnecessarily cruel. No one has asked for my opinion, but I'm offering it anyway," I interjected carefully. "She had no book in her possession when I found her. If it's common knowledge that she takes evening walks, then she did nothing out of the ordinary to warrant being locked away."

Princess Invidia raised a curious eyebrow in my direction.

"I only speak as someone who operates according to principles of justice," I clarified quickly.

King Valen entered at that moment, and his evening meal arrived behind him on silver platters. Maids carrying multiple elaborate dishes moved gracefully through the doorway like a choreographed dance.

His presence immediately silenced our conversation, and I was genuinely grateful for the interruption.

"King Valen, will you be holding a proper funeral for the guard Koen?" I asked, trying to sound casually interested.

He looked up at me as if I had lost all intelligence. "Why in the seven hells would I do such a thing?"

"I was told that he had been a trusted part of your household for a long time," I added.

"A guard is still nothing more than a guard," King Valen grumbled dismissively.

"Will you be releasing Lanira from the dungeon any time soon?" Princess Invidia asked with barely contained hope.

"I will not. I see no difference in our day-to-day life with her rotting down there, which means she serves no useful purpose to me," King Valen answered coldly.

The King made no attempt to strike up any other conversation. He attacked the fish as if he had never eaten before in his life, tearing into it with disturbing enthusiasm.

My bites were deliberately much slower as I watched him carefully. He took one substantial bite of the fish, then three bites of other foods scattered across his plate.

I wanted to shout at him to just finish the damned fish completely. I had to shovel food into my own mouth to keep myself from speaking the words aloud.

I felt Queen Blair's eyes studying me intently, but I couldn't risk acknowledging her scrutiny. The king only consumed enough to make himself ill rather than die, and the thought made my heart pound so violently I was sure others could hear it. I wanted to reach across the table and force the rest down his throat myself.

"Another group of villagers was sent off to fight at StoneDale this morning," Princess Invidia reported sadly. "I'm told most won't survive the journey there, and the ones who do won't make any meaningful difference in the fighting."

Queen Blair glanced between the king and me before focusing entirely on Princess Invidia.

"The war was doomed from the very start with the kind of leadership it's been given," Queen Blair declared boldly.

She was being far bolder than I was accustomed to seeing from her. They both were, actually. I looked toward King Valen, expecting him to be furious at her criticism. He had recently called her useless and threatened to lock her away while remarrying.

The king suddenly groaned loudly and dropped his fork with a clatter.

The entire table became instantly alert, everyone hyper-focused on his distress. My palms began dripping with nervous sweat.

"What was in that food?" he moaned, clutching his stomach.

"Are you feeling alright?" the Queen asked with genuine concern.

The king leaned further back in his chair and groaned again, this time more loudly.

"Get him to his chambers immediately. Someone call for the royal physician," Queen Blair commanded as she rose to her feet.

The room erupted into a chaos of panic and frantic activity. No one knew what was wrong except for me, but they could barely help him effectively because of his considerable weight.

I knew I must look suspicious to anyone watching carefully. I was always the first to offer assistance in any crisis.

My feet refused to move, and my hands shook visibly. I was far too committed to this course of action to stop now, yet part of me desperately didn't want to proceed.

Every available guard rushed to help carry him from the room. Princess Invidia stood back in obvious horror, her face pale with shock. She was my perfect excuse, my reason for not acting according to my usual character.

"Are you alright?" I asked, reaching for her trembling form.

"I—I—" she stuttered helplessly. "I can't bear to watch someone else die."

A maid quickly grabbed her other arm and pulled her away from me. The slow-motion quality of the world around me snapped back into sharp focus, and I hurried after the king's entourage.

If I was going to go through with this plan, I would at least ensure I didn't fail in the execution. I wasn't a failure. I wouldn't get caught.

I climbed the stairs two at a time, skipping every other step to move faster.

"Everyone out of this room!" I shouted with authority. "As the official hunter from RuneHold, I'm taking command of this situation. Everyone out until proper medical help arrives. Trust is a luxury we cannot afford right now. Escort the Queen to her chambers and post guards at her door. I will maintain watch over the King. No unnecessary risks will be taken."

The guards looked uncertainly between me and each other from their positions around the king's bed. Queen Blair hesitated at my orders as well, confusion clear on her face.

"Go! Now!" I shouted again with more force.

Maids quickly ushered the Queen away while the guards followed behind her for protection. I slammed the king's heavy door closed and turned the lock with a decisive click.

King Valen leaned over the side of his ornate bed and vomited everything he had eaten onto the expensive carpet below. He hadn't consumed nearly enough of the poisoned fish. He wasn't going to die from this. He was going to suffer temporarily and then recover completely. He absolutely could not be allowed to recover.

I bit down hard on my finger until blood welled up, then hesitated with my hand poised over his prone form. Once I made the irreversible choice to use forbidden cursed runes on a mortal man, I could never take it back.

I lowered my hand and took a deep, steadying breath. I flashed back to the horrific moment when that other hunter lost his limbs in the public square.

The next image that filled my mind was Lanira, crying over her ancient book in the candlelight.

I lifted my hand back up and firmly grabbed the king's thick wrist. I drew the curse rune on his skin using my blood, then flicked it with my other fingers. Crimson light rippled through his entire body like liquid fire, and I quickly scrubbed the evidence away.

He gasped and choked violently on his own air, his body convulsing.

I unlocked the door and stepped outside into the hallway. I wanted to wait for the physician's arrival without having to witness what was about to happen to him.

The king would begin convulsing uncontrollably within minutes. His brain would heat up until it was nearly destroyed. He would technically remain alive after this; his heart would continue beating, but he would be nothing more than that. He would become a lifeless, convulsing shell of meat from this day forward.

I had broken my most sacred oath for the sake of a vampire.

I had made a choice that could never be undone.

The weight of that reality settled over me like a burial shroud as I stood guard outside the door, listening to the sounds of approaching footsteps echoing through the corridor.

Chapter Twenty-Nine
THE WITCH

Lanira

The dungeon itself wasn't the truly painful part of being locked away. Princess Invidia had brought me thick blankets and heavy clothing that smelled of lavender and home. Being locked away and surrounded by watching eyes while slowly starving, that was the real strain. I had no way to feed properly. I had no energy left to maintain even the simplest pretenses.

Ravi was taking far too long to act.

It had been two days at first, then eight. Soon, it stretched into fourteen endless days of waiting.

The mornings brought visits from the princess, her footsteps echoing down the stone corridor like a lifeline. The evenings brought visits from Ravi, his presence both comforting and torturous. She brought me food that served little purpose for the specific hunger I was dying from, and his moral conflicts about feeding me blood kept him from delivering what I truly needed to survive.

They both held their chins high and spoke of hope while I slowly withered away before their eyes.

We had yet to say the word vampire aloud, but he knew the truth. It was the fact that it remained unspoken that allowed him to maintain his sanity. I could see the knowledge written across his face every time we spoke through the iron bars. He never asked about what had happened at the ocean, either.

He wanted to remain physically close while keeping himself mentally distant. I wanted him to return home and leave me to whatever fate awaited, because having this invisible wall placed between us was far harder than being complete strangers had ever been.

"You look absolutely dreadful."

I tilted my head toward the voice from the cell beside mine. Even that small movement required tremendous effort.

"You don't look much better," I mumbled, my voice barely audible.

My lips were so dry and cracked that speaking split them open, sending tiny drops of blood onto my tongue.

"I told myself I wasn't going to speak to you. That we'd all be dead soon anyway, so conversation didn't matter." Her voice started calmly and hushed. "But I couldn't shake the feeling that you looked familiar. Then I caught sight of that mark on your arm. I want to examine it more closely."

By the end of her statement, she was commanding me rather than requesting.

"You want to see my birthmark?" I asked, confusion threading through my exhaustion.

"That's exactly what I said, girl. Lift your arm up." She moved like a spider toward the bars that separated our cells, her movements unnaturally fluid.

I lifted my arm into the air with tremendous effort. The limb felt impossibly heavy, but her predatory movements terrified me enough that I didn't dare resist.

She grunted as she examined the mark closely, then retreated back into the shadows of her cell. The two of us sat in heavy silence for several long breaths.

"I bet you look so terrible because you haven't been eating the right things," she observed matter-of-factly.

"What would you possibly know about it?" I grumbled, irritation flaring despite my weakness.

"You're accustomed to that fake priestess up there who was never properly taught the things she speaks about, but I'm a real witch. I can see the red bleeding through your eyes." The witch's voice carried ancient authority.

"You aren't much of a witch if you're still locked down here with the rest of us," I tilted my head back toward her.

"You aren't much of a vampire," she shot back without hesitation.

"I'm here because I choose to be," I declared, though the words felt hollow.

"Does telling yourself that make your failure easier to swallow?" Her voice was almost gentle now. "You're nothing like the girl I remember. I admit none of us ever thought to check the castle for survivors. We all assumed you were burned alive with the rest of your family."

I tried to sit up straighter, but my body utterly denied me the strength.

"I'm just a handmaid to the princess," I assured her, though my voice lacked conviction.

"Ash would be deeply disappointed to hear you deny your true name," she murmured, shaking her head sadly.

"Who are you?" I demanded, though it came out more as a plea.

"Take this," she replied, tossing a freshly killed rat through the bars to land in front of me.

The scent of warm blood immediately filled my nostrils, overwhelming every other sense. I threw my body forward desperately and slammed into the cold stone floor. The aching in my shoulder didn't bother me nearly as much as the violent growling in my empty stomach. I grabbed the rat with shaking hands and drank from it until it was completely empty. The precious liquid felt like only precious drops against my desperate thirst.

"Looks like you still have some fight left in you," she mumbled with what might have been approval.

My throat felt moistened for only a fleeting second. The satisfaction was so minimal that it was hardly better than having nothing at all.

But I kept going anyway.

I kept going until I had chewed through its flesh, consuming small bits of fur and everything else. I licked each finger methodically until I could be absolutely certain there wasn't even the faintest scent of blood remaining.

I couldn't remember where the bones had gone. I couldn't recall hearing any crunching while the rat was in my mouth.

I suddenly became aware of the witch's eyes studying me intently. I felt the horrible realization settle in my stomach that she had witnessed everything I had just done. I wanted to become smaller than I already felt, to disappear entirely.

I must have looked like a rabid animal. Wild and completely without manners or humanity.

I tucked my knees up against my stomach and curled into myself as tightly as possible. I couldn't bear to look at her. She claimed she knew who I was, who I had been. She must think I was completely unrecognizable now.

It was surprisingly easy to cry without having to force or fake the tears when I felt like nothing more than a starving beast.

Part of me no longer carried the same burning desire to escape that had once consumed me.

Part of me wished, harder than I had ever wished for anything, that I could simply join my family in death instead of continuing down this dark path I was traveling.

Would I have been happier if I had died before witnessing myself become what I was moving closer to? Just another mindless animal?

Would my brother be disappointed in what I had become? Would Ravi look at me now and think I was exactly the monster he had been trained to hunt?

I glanced up at the small barred window set far too high to ever reach, watching as it became covered in shadow. The grotesque raven from the ocean lowered itself down and released a harsh caw into the opening. It was mocking me, I was certain it was mocking me.

"You brought it back? You actually managed to do that?" The witch spoke in obvious disbelief.

I didn't care anymore. If she wanted the raven, she could have it. I didn't bother answering her question. I was finally able to drift in and out of restless sleep after the worst hunger pains subsided. It was such a small amount of blood, but it provided just enough relief to function.

The raven cawed endlessly through the night and into the day. Guards swatted at it futilely. They shoved their swords through the window opening, hoping they might pierce its flesh. Several other guards and the priestess Minala came specifically to observe the bizarre creature. They couldn't believe that anything so grotesque could possibly exist in their world.

Minala declared it the first unmistakable sign of the prophecy coming to life. She warned ominously that there would be many more signs to follow. She sang eerily of our coming downfall and destruction.

She didn't even notice my presence crouched in the shadows.

I began to consider that I might have become completely forgotten. If it hadn't been for the raven's constant presence, that might have been acceptable.

"Do you know who that raven actually is?" the witch asked after days of silence.

"Who are you to ask? You still won't even give me your name," I pointed out.

She wouldn't reveal her identity, but she had fed me again with small creatures until I regained enough strength to move around my cell.

"It's a deity, locked away in that twisted body for daring to turn against its divine parents. Forever cursed to exist in that form," she explained with reverence.

"Parents?" I mumbled to myself, pieces clicking together. "When I performed the ritual, I witnessed a pink-haired girl being sent to the bottom of an ocean."

"The Goddess Helia and the God Thann, yes. The deity you saw disapproved of Helia's brutal methods. High priest Dominic earned his coveted place in the promised realm by assisting in the ritual that transformed her into that raven." Her lips curled as if she smelled something putrid. "You won't find that particular story written in any book."

"How do you know all of this, then?" I asked, leaning forward despite myself.

"I'm far older than you are, child. Far older than you would ever believe possible," she answered mysteriously.

Heavy footsteps approached, and a guard unlocked my cell door with a rusty key. He stood aside respectfully.

"Let's go," Ravi commanded from the doorway.

I hesitated, unwilling to leave. I was sitting beside the only person I had ever met who might possess the answers to everything I had ever wanted to know.

"Let's go. We don't have time to waste," Ravi demanded more forcefully.

He grabbed my arm and pulled me from the cell with gentle but insistent pressure.

"I'll come back for you," I promised the witch as Ravi guided me away.

Ravi continued pulling me along, and he leaned close to speak quickly and quietly.

"The king is gravely unwell. The pufferfish plan didn't work as intended; he didn't consume enough of it. I had to resort to using a cursed rune." His voice was tight with stress. "He's little more than a breathing shell now. You need to devise something brilliant, and it needs to involve a very quick exit strategy. You thought King Valen as a ruler was problematic; you've seen nothing yet. When Queen Blair saw his condition, something fundamental shifted inside her. Something forged from pure grief and rage. She has declared herself acting ruler of the kingdom."

His words sent ice-cold dread coursing down my spine. I hadn't anticipated that Queen Blair would carry enough raw emotion to transform into a tyrant.

Princess Invidia suddenly appeared and ran toward us, wrapping her arms around me in a fierce embrace. "Lanira! I'm so incredibly happy to see you free! I convinced Mother to release you as her very first official act. Father is desperately ill, and the physicians don't know if they can heal him. Mother has sent urgent messages requesting aid from neighboring kingdoms."

I embraced her back tightly, breathing in her familiar scent. "I'm so sorry about your father."

"I don't want him to die, but I'm overwhelmed with joy that you're out of that horrible place," she sobbed against my shoulder.

I squeezed her even tighter. "We'll get through this together, no matter what comes."

I ran my hand gently through her half-up, half-down hairstyle and kept my other arm firmly placed around her trembling form. I stayed in that position until she was ready to step back. I wanted her to fall back into the comfortable feeling of being in control, of being the better person between us. The savior. Whatever she needed to feel completely at ease.

Ravi watched us from behind the princess, his green eyes studying not just the situation, but me specifically. He looked at me differently now that we both understood the complete truth about what I was.

I realized I was probably looking at him differently, too. Ravi was fundamentally unlike me in how he processed actions and consequences. I did what needed to be done because that was simply how the world worked. I didn't think about it again afterward. I didn't dwell on guilt or regret. I put those feelings in a mental box and set them aside permanently.

Ravi didn't take any action unless he could convince himself it served some greater good. Some necessary step on his path toward justice. If he had broken his sacred oath for my sake, he had to be suffering tremendous internal anguish.

Princess Invidia finally released me and stepped back. "We need to move quickly. The Prince of RubyWake has arrived unexpectedly. He claims he's come to discuss potential alliances and negotiate peace terms."

Ravi moved close enough behind us that if we stopped suddenly, he would collide with one of us.

We entered the grand main hall at the castle's entrance. Queen Blair was already waiting there, engaged in animated conversation with our royal visitor. I hadn't taken their earlier warnings seriously enough. She wore an elaborate headdress functioning as a crown and luxurious fur draped over her shoulders.

The display was lavish and completely lacking the same overwhelming grief she had worn when I was first imprisoned.

The prince leaned around her and looked directly at both Princess Invidia and me. I smiled at him warmly, ensuring our first visual contact would be pleasant and memorable.

I wanted my newest chess piece to look at me and see a lust-struck girl completely captivated by his presence. I wanted his ego inflated and his defenses lowered.

I wanted to miss no opportunity in taking yet another kingdom to complete ashes from the inside out.

I had nearly given up hope entirely, but I was outside the dungeon now. Seeing natural light again. Breathing fresh air that didn't reek of despair and death.

I felt a renewed and urgent sense of purpose burning in my chest.

Act Four

A Queen's Exchange

Chapter Thirty
A Shifting Board

Lanira

Princess Invidia tapped blush made from crushed roses into my cheeks with gentle precision. She watched me as though I were a precious puppy or a new toy she had just unwrapped. She looked at me through different eyes now ones that, though still carrying their familiar naïveté, had witnessed a harsher reality than before. I hadn't seen her with dry eyes in months. She had been red and swollen at all hours before I was locked away in that cell. Yet here she was, somehow harder now, her eyes clear and focused.

She pulled my hair away from my face and twisted it into an elegant bun with practiced movements. Maybe if she had carried this kind of strength my entire life, we would have grown genuinely closer. She felt like a true sister as she pulled and tugged gently on my skin and hair, performing all the right gestures. The things I had read about in storybooks. She smiled with genuine care whenever she noticed me watching her work.

It was as simple as that, though. It remained only a look, a pretty illusion carefully maintained. Even if I had wanted to play along with this fantasy of sisterhood, I had built walls so impossibly high and so impenetrably solid that she would never be welcomed inside. I had carefully placed each heavy slab of stone around myself specifically to keep her out and away from the truth of what I was.

I had felt enough crushing guilt and devastating loss to ever willingly allow myself to grow close to anyone again.

Princess Invidia stepped back and studied me for a long moment before shaking her head and pulling a few strategic strands from the bun she had carefully shaped.

"Perfect!" She clapped her hands together with satisfaction. "You'll need to wash your hair thoroughly tonight, though. You've got bits of something red tangled in it. We don't have time to deal with that now, so I've tucked it all away so you won't be embarrassed. The dungeon was no doubt rough on you. There's no need to carry those reminders."

"Embarrassed?" I asked, trying to keep my voice level.

I worked hard to pretend that her comment didn't make my heart drop like a stone.

"My hope is that I can convince the prince to take you away with him when he leaves," she admitted, her voice taking on a conspiratorial tone.

"Princess, don't you think that should be my choice to make?" I asked carefully.

She sighed deeply. "We've known each other nearly our entire lives. Why not simply call me Invidia?"

"King Valen would punish me severely for such familiarity," I stated simply. "Besides, I'd rather stay here. It seems as though Queen Blair needs someone trustworthy by her side during this transition."

I deliberately shifted the conversation so I could try to extract the information I truly wanted. If I would refuse Ravi's offers, of course I would refuse to leave with some unknown prince I had never met.

"Mother has taken to her new role remarkably well. It seems like she was born for this kind of power. She rules with an iron fist already, so soon after taking control. It's as if a version of my younger father has returned from the grave." She paused thoughtfully. "Except Mother has developed quite a bit more venom in her methods."

"I can't imagine anything venomous about her gentle nature," I lied smoothly.

I hadn't been prepared for this dramatic shift in power, for Queen Blair suddenly being in complete control. I never would have predicted that she possessed the capacity to rule with such a cold iron fist. When the reality was presented directly in front of me, though, I couldn't claim to be shocked. The idea of Queen Blair hiding so much calculated cruelty beneath her soft surface felt disturbingly fitting. Maybe I had unconsciously picked up behavioral hints from her and decided to follow in her footsteps.

Deep down, I knew I hadn't learned these darker impulses from Ash. My brother never would have stood for mindless revenge or cruelty. I was becoming increasingly skilled at twisting that truth whenever I needed to in order to feel better about my choices.

"Mother is already 'cleaning the grounds,' as she calls it. Four executions so far," Princess Invidia reported matter-of-factly.

"Four isn't particularly many compared to what the king accomplished. He claimed more than that number with just the suspected vampires alone," I replied without thinking.

I immediately wished I could bite my tongue clean off the moment those words left my lips. It was my first real slip since returning a significant one that revealed I held at least a twinge of resentment toward the royal family. The princess looked at me as if she sensed the same dangerous undercurrent.

"I only meant that if there were anyone I trusted to wield that kind of power responsibly, it would be her," I clarified quickly, rising to my feet.

Princess Invidia dressed me in a gown with a scandalously low plunge across the chest and a skirt so voluminous I needed to gather the fabric carefully when I walked. She, by contrast, was dressed far more conservatively, as if she wanted to hide every piece of exposed flesh from view.

I moved closer to the door to encourage her to leave. She held her furrowed, suspicious gaze on me for several long moments before she silently agreed to accompany me to dinner. I sighed with internal relief because if she truly thought I was a traitor or threat, she wouldn't have followed me out of the room so willingly.

We walked in tense silence until Queen Blair came into sight.

"Lanira! You look absolutely gorgeous," Queen Blair gushed with seemingly genuine enthusiasm.

"So do you. Your headdress is breathtaking," I responded with equally effusive praise.

I considered my words and movements far more carefully now. I couldn't afford another slip in front of her like I had made with the princess. I couldn't allow her to suspect I harbored even the smallest amount of frustration or resentment toward her.

"I've missed you terribly. You were gone for far too long," Queen Blair mused thoughtfully. "I'll admit, I had a brief moment where I wondered... what if it actually were Lanira? How could I corner her and make her properly afraid? What would she be capable of doing to Valen if she thought he was going to have her executed?"

Queen Blair laughed louder and more freely than I had ever heard from her before.

"Of course, it was only a fleeting moment of paranoia, and then I realized that would also mean you had killed both of my beloved sons, and you would never betray our family like that. So naturally, I had to have you released immediately."

My ears pounded with the thunderous sound of my own heartbeat. Had she made some calculated move that I hadn't anticipated? No, if she truly knew my secrets, I wouldn't have a head left to think with. I couldn't let her see my composure slip even slightly.

"I completely understood why I needed to be locked away, and I would have remained there longer without any complaint if it had been necessary," I declared with conviction. "It's not just the kingdom at stake here, but our family. I would gladly give my life for you."

I held steady eye contact until she smiled with apparent satisfaction.

"Good girl," she murmured approvingly, then turned and entered the dining hall.

Ravi immediately stood to greet us and pulled out Queen Blair's chair with courtly precision. With King Valen, he had always been so carefully hands-off, offering opinions but never pushing his agenda. With Queen Blair, he was already positioned so close to her seat of power that I thought he belonged there permanently, as if he were her personal Minala and had always been stationed by her side.

Ravi's jaw dropped slightly as his gaze traveled over my revealing dress. I instinctively crossed my arms to try to shrink away from his intense scrutiny.

I moved quickly to claim the seat between Ravi and Princess Invidia. The visiting prince sat directly across from me, flanked by members of his court whom he had brought along for the negotiations. Queen Blair had chosen not to invite anyone else to this intimate dinner.

I felt completely displaced, as if I had entered a room I had never seen before in my life. Like I had missed far too many critical moves in this deadly game.

"It's a pleasure to meet you, Lanira. I've heard quite a lot about you from Princess Invidia," he offered with a charming smile. "I'm Prince Nio of Saydeean."

A vivid flashback flashed through my mind, feet hanging from the decorative ceiling fixtures and King Valen's furious bellowing. Had Prince Nio been informed that his sister had taken her own life?

He smirked knowingly. "I can see in your expressive eyes exactly what you're thinking. I do plan to bring my sister's body home for proper burial. King Valen was unnecessarily harsh and completely irrational in his treatment of her. Your Queen has already proven to possess much more diplomatic sense."

"I'm deeply sorry for your tragic loss," was the only response I could manage.

Nio nodded solemnly. "As you can imagine, my mother is utterly distraught; she lost much more than just a daughter. My father had many angry things to say about the situation as well, until he received Queen Blair's carefully worded letters. The timing seems almost divine. My father was certain we'd never find agreeable terms with your previous king, but then Valen suddenly fell gravely ill."

The way his words lingered deliberately over 'suddenly' sent an icy shiver through my entire body while simultaneously turning my stomach. Had I been played for a complete fool? I didn't believe in divine timing or convenient coincidences.

"I can't imagine how devastated she must feel," I replied carefully.

"No, you truly can't," Prince Nio agreed bluntly. "She lost a child,a daughter, and our kingdom values girls above all else. They rule, they create new life. There's no higher form of being in our culture. She had hoped there would be grandchildren soon to share between our kingdoms."

He ended this statement with a callous laugh that made my skin crawl. He was far more cold-hearted than Princess Sala had ever been.

"Of course, we still have several important matters to resolve," Queen Blair interrupted smoothly.

She raised her hand and signaled to the guard stationed outside to enter. He was followed by several additional guards, who escorted a line of dirty, chained prisoners into the dining hall. I sat straighter in my chair, my heart racing. I had been given no time to make any strategic moves, let alone develop escape plans. I hadn't been able to even attempt securing freedom for anyone who remained locked in those horrible dungeons.

My foot began tapping nervously against the floor as I frantically searched the faces of the condemned.

"Bring the girl forward first," Queen Blair commanded coldly.

The guard roughly moved Priestess Minala to the front of the group. Her desperate eyes searched between all of us at the table, silently screaming for mercy. The guard grabbed her shoulder and shoved her brutally onto her knees before us.

"When the king regains consciousness, he will make you pay dearly for this betrayal!" Minala shrieked.

Queen Blair lowered her hand with casual indifference, and the executioner's blade hacked into Minala's neck with a wet, sickening sound. Her scream of agony filled the air and echoed off the stone walls. A second brutal chop into her flesh made me jump involuntarily. Ravi's warm hand suddenly appeared on my thigh, squeezing firmly to snap me back into my body. My leg continued shaking beneath his touch.

It brought me no comfort that I couldn't locate the witch's face among the remaining prisoners.

The reality of beheading was that it was never accomplished with one clean slice, never.

Minala's head hung connected by only sinew and skin after five violent strikes. The guard unceremoniously dropped her twitching body, and the other executioners forced the remaining prisoners to their knees without waiting for the queen's command.

Queen Blair lifted her wine cup and took a leisurely sip, the grin spreading across her face resembling someone enjoying an entertaining theatrical performance. The guards grunted in unison and raised their various weapons, swords, axes, and cleavers.

"There's the first step in properly mending our diplomatic relationship," Queen Blair announced to Prince Nio with satisfaction. "No witches, vampires, or other supernatural beings will be tolerated in this kingdom."

One swing, two swings. A grunt from the axe men, then three. The metallic smell of iron mixed with sweat filled the air. Four strikes.

Princess Invidia flinched beside me and held back her own tears with visible effort. I had no time or emotional capacity to comfort her.

The witch's severed head suddenly rolled under the table straight toward me, and I jumped up from my chair in horror. It didn't stop rolling until it came to rest directly at my feet. The witch's eyes blinked up at me once, and I nearly screamed aloud. Her tongue darted out to lick the top of my foot before her eyes finally closed forever.

I shivered in complete disgust and fought the overwhelming urge to kick the grotesque thing away from me.

A guard casually moved to collect the head, grabbing it by the hair as if it were nothing more than refuse. A trail of bright blood followed behind him as he carried it away, and Ravi pulled me forcefully back into my seat as though he were the next person in line to make the rules around here.

I had never felt more utterly trapped in my entire life.

He slammed me down with such force that it ignited a flame of rage within me. I kept my mouth tightly closed and didn't dare allow myself to become snappy or defiant. I felt my fangs release involuntarily, a dangerous sign that I was losing control. I was slipping badly. No, I had already slipped completely.

The witch had been all that I had left. The only piece of my past I had discovered in all the time I had searched that might have contained answers to my endless questions. She was my sole connection to my people, my former life, my true identity.

She had been all the hope I had dared to allow myself to feel.

And now she was dead.

Queen Blair and Prince Nio clinked their glasses together in a toast before taking another celebratory drink, completely oblivious to the pieces of my world that had just been shattered at their feet.

Chapter Thirty-One
The Raven and the Rune

Lanira

I wrapped the raven carefully in a soft blanket because looking at its grotesque feathers made my stomach churn violently. They appeared as if someone had methodically stabbed each one into the creature's flesh individually, like tiny black needles. They looked as if they caused constant, throbbing pain.

I offered it a piece of bread roll that I had secretly tucked away from dinner, the crust still slightly warm against my palm. I had no idea what such a bizarre creature might eat, but it seemed content enough with my offering.

"Blink once for yes and twice for no," I instructed clearly. "Are you a vampire?"

The raven studied me with wide, unnaturally dry eyes that seemed to hold depths of ancient knowledge. Instead of responding, it reached its head down and snatched the remaining roll from my hand with surprising quickness.

"Very well then," I sighed with mounting frustration. "Caw once for yes. Are you a demon?"

It finished consuming the bread as if I hadn't spoken at all, then tossed itself dramatically onto its side, still wrapped snugly in the blanket like a petulant child seeking comfort.

"Are you useful for anything at all?" I asked with barely restrained exasperation.

Caw.

"So, you do understand me!" I exclaimed, reaching for the blanket with renewed interest.

I grabbed the fabric and rolled the bird unceremoniously out of its makeshift cocoon.

"If you aren't going to help me accomplish anything, if your only purpose is to annoy me with your incessant loud cawing, then you must leave my room immediately."

I reached up to shove the creature away, and it pecked sharply at my outstretched hand with vicious precision.

My jaw dropped as I jerked my hand back, a small bead of blood welling on my knuckle where its beak had struck.

"You'll pay dearly for that assault. I could easily turn you into a soup."

A firm knock echoed at my door before it opened without invitation. Ravi entered and looked between the two of us with obvious curiosity, his green eyes taking in the strange scene.

"There's no privacy in this place whatsoever, is there?" I asked through gritted teeth.

"Not for you," he replied bluntly, closing the door behind him. "What exactly is this thing?"

"A raven that I resurrected from an ocean of fire," I answered with complete honesty.

Ravi regarded me with his lips pressed into a thin, disapproving line and his eyes narrowed with deep suspicion.

"What are you attempting to accomplish with it?" he pressed further.

"Clearly I'm trying to establish some form of communication with it," I snapped, my patience wearing dangerously thin.

Ravi studied the raven again before glancing back at me and ultimately resting his gaze on the stone floor between us, as if avoiding direct eye contact.

I was suddenly reminded that although I had once shared space with a man who wasn't entirely certain of who or what I truly was, that dynamic had shifted completely and irrevocably. I had once stood beside Ravi when there was still an air of mystery surrounding both of us and our respective goals.

As he stood before me now, I became acutely aware that Ravi possessed all the confirmation he needed about my true nature. He was no longer someone I could cautiously trust, even when circumstances demanded it. He was someone who literally held my life in his hands in a way no one else could. He was precisely the person I should have been most guarded around.

He knew that I was the very creature he had been raised from childhood to hunt and destroy. Every conversation I shared with him was essentially a coin toss between continued existence and death.

This stark revelation made me hesitate to speak to him about anything of real importance.

It created an uncomfortable churning sensation deep in my stomach.

"I've already broken so many sacred rules, I suppose I may as well break one more," he decided aloud, his voice carrying a note of reckless resignation.

The spoken admission made my heart flutter with unexpected anxiety.

He pulled out a small silver pin and deliberately pricked his finger until blood welled up. He drew what I recognized as a rune in the air, holding the glowing symbol only briefly, and a shower of small golden glitter struck the raven directly in the chest.

Violent coughing suddenly filled the space between the raven and myself, echoing off the stone walls.

"It is wonderfully good to have a voice again," the raven spoke, stretching its damaged wings with obvious relief.

I immediately pressed my hands over the raven's beak. "Thank you for your assistance, Ravi. I won't require anything else from you."

He shook his head firmly. "If I leave this room, my rune goes with me."

I rubbed two fingers against my temple in small circles to ease the pounding headache building behind my eyes.

"Who are you?" I demanded of the creature.

"I am Alio," she replied with unmistakable dignity.

"And who exactly is that supposed to mean to me?" I snapped impatiently.

"You don't know who I am?" Alio asked, her voice dripping with obvious disgust and disbelief.

"Should I?" I grimaced.

"I don't know who you are either," Ravi admitted with a casual shrug.

"I am the Goddess of Dawn. My twin brother, Elio, is the God of Dusk." She flapped her sparse, damaged feathers and stood as tall as her broken form would allow.

"That explains why we don't recognize you. You're a deity of the vampire pantheon. You aren't worshipped by anyone anymore," Ravi stated matter-of-factly.

"Wait, just a moment, you know vampiric history and mythology and didn't think to share this knowledge?" I turned to glare at him accusingly.

"Of course I do. It's essential knowledge for understanding one's enemy," he replied without any trace of apology.

"What do you mean I'm not worshipped anymore?" the raven cawed indignantly.

"It seems both of you have significant gaps in your knowledge, but only one of you will have an easy time filling those gaps," Ravi spoke with infuriating confidence. "Alio, you aren't worshipped because there aren't any vampires allowed to move freely in this world, let alone participate in religious rituals. Lanira, you've already forced me to break enough rules and cross enough moral lines. Why would you ask for even more assistance?"

I thought his tone should have been recognized as pure audacity or false arrogance, not genuine confidence.

"I didn't force you to do anything," I pointed an accusatory finger directly at him. "I didn't make you break your precious rules or lie to me about your intentions. You chose to do those things entirely on your own, and you did so because you lack true honor. Don't you dare blame me for your choices."

"Where is my twin brother? I know you're lying about the vampires. You claim there aren't any, but I already took flight and saw—"

Ravi abruptly pulled the glowing rune away from the raven, and the only sounds that emerged from her beak were frustrated, wordless caws.

"Put it back immediately!" I commanded.

"Absolutely not. I finally have something that you desperately want, and since I apparently have no honor, as you so eloquently stated, I won't give it to you so easily. Perhaps I'll be truly honorless and play your manipulative game for once." Ravi's voice carried a dangerous edge. "Maybe I'll make you apologize properly and ask nicely."

"I'll tell Queen Blair that you're the one who murdered Koen," I threatened coldly.

"A great deal happened while you were locked away rotting in that dungeon. Queen Blair leaned on my shoulder quite heavily during her time of grief and need. I think if I told her I had grown suspicious of Koen and his potential involvement in her son's death, she would forgive my actions completely." He smirked with obvious satisfaction.

I rose from my position and moved closer to him, rage building like a storm in my chest. I wanted to hurt him badly. I wanted to tear his throat open with my bare hands or gouge out his eyes with my fingernails. I wanted to strangle him slowly until I heard his heart stop beating forever.

I kept my hands firmly at my sides because even though that violent urge was overwhelming, the sharp sting of feeling betrayed hurt far more than my anger burned.

I had foolishly thought that maybe the two of us, at the very least, understood each other well enough to avoid causing deliberate, unnecessary pain.

He watched me intently as if he could read every emotion racing through my eyes like an open book.

"Lanira," he began, his voice softer than before.

I shook my head firmly and forced myself to swallow down the pain threatening to surface. I shoved down the sharp tinge of hurt I felt and mentally consumed the word betrayal, stuffing it into the same emotional box where I kept everything else that threatened my focus. How could he betray me when neither of us owed the other anything substantial? I was a complete fool for allowing myself to think like a naive child.

I knew better than this.

I needed to pull myself back together immediately and remember my ultimate goal.

I was going to avenge my family and create a world where they could live freely again.

Even if achieving that meant I would have to kill him.

"Leave now, Ravi. There is nothing you need from me, nor do I require anything from you. Please follow the established rules of our court and stop putting my reputation at risk by visiting my room alone." I pointed directly toward the door. "If we are going to make threats and use Queen Blair as leverage against each other, then we should at least commit fully to that path."

He hesitated for a long moment, his usually stoic expression cracking slightly around his eyes. Good. The hint of his pain gave me exactly the emotional boost I needed to push forward with resolve. If I allowed myself to absorb his emotions and match them to my own, I might never escape from their grip.

When Ravi finally turned to leave, a folded letter barely clung to his coat pocket, threatening to fall. I nodded meaningfully to the raven, and she seemed to read my mind perfectly.

She swooped down and grabbed the letter from his pocket with her sharp talons, and he didn't notice the theft before shutting the door behind him. I immediately clicked the lock into place.

The raven dropped the letter into my waiting hand, and I opened it with trembling fingers.

How are things at home? I received word confirming that I am to return soon. Are you still looking after the pom-pom? I've met a girl here that I hope to bring home with me soon. I think she will die if I leave her in this place. If I bring her back, I may be able to protect her better. I've sent a letter to the king, and he responded with permission to come home. Do not send Boris. He will scare the girl I'll bring. Her worldview or knowledge is small. I'm not sure how to put a word behind what I think of her. She smells like when you cook a pot of soup with chicken, and the smell is finally strong enough to fill the air, so you need to take in a full breath of it. She looks like when both moons rise and you can see them at the same time, just as the tips come over the snowy mountain.

Lately, when I sleep, I dream of her. In my dreams, the two of us are together without a care. She smiles at me. Not with the one she uses in our waking conversations. The one where her eyes tell me that she's calculating her next move. In my dreams, she smiles at me with a joy that I was convinced she never truly knew in the waking hours.

I worry that I've been here too long, and I'll pay for the slip of my thoughts once I'm home.

I closed the letter abruptly and shoved it back inside its envelope. I pushed it out through the crack under the door, not wanting to read any further. I would add "two-faced" to the growing list of unflattering things I could call him. He wrote about me as if we were close friends, but spoke to me as if I were his sworn enemy.

I turned around to find Alio the raven lounging on my bed again, her grotesque form a constant reminder of everything I had lost.

I missed the simpler days when I was completely alone and had nothing to worry about except pursuing my singular goal.

Chapter Thirty-Two
A Board Change in the Name of Peace

Lanira

I existed as a small golden orb of pure light, weightless and ethereal. I possessed no hands, no feet to propel myself through space. I was so diminutive and light that I could traverse the entire world in the blink of an eye. The world I hovered above appeared different, newer, more vibrant with possibility. The Temple of Time in my homeland was still under construction, scaffolding and half-built walls reaching toward the sky like skeletal fingers.

The statue that decorated the front of the temple was already complete, though. Crystal-clear water surrounded the base of the carved marble feet, teeming with tiny neon fish that darted between the stone like living jewels. A crowd had gathered around the monument, their faces upturned in reverence or curiosity.

I spotted the witch immediately and knew it was her by the distinctive small scar marking her left cheek. She appeared decades younger than when I had known her, but she was bound by glowing shackles that looked impossibly heavy. The chains seemed to burn her flesh where they touched, leaving angry red welts.

"One day, I hope to live long enough to see this statue reduced to nothing but crumbling rubble," she declared with bitter determination.

I drifted closer, seemingly invisible to everyone present.

"On that day, you'll be the one forced to piece it back together entirely alone," came a cold, divine reply. "If something were to happen to me, if I never returned again, you would still remain here. Hesperia won't come to save you because she doesn't know of your location. If you thought I'd come here without having a plan for dealing with the sisters, you're a complete fool. You'll remain in this place, staring at my world, my legacy, until you die."

"Helia, stay or go as you please, I would sooner lose both my hands than help you build anything," the witch replied, her face contorting with disgust.

"Stop being so pig-headed and stubborn. Do exactly what I ask of you, and you can finally go home," Helia's voice carried the weight of divine authority. "It can be that simple for you."

"I've done everything you've demanded of me. I've had no choice with these accursed fate chains binding me. How much longer do you expect me to believe that hollow promise?" The witch spat the words like venom.

"Once Nikola successfully combines Shivani's essence with mine, you may have your precious freedom. Until then, I require a witch who was trained by one of the fate sisters. Help me learn how to create more vampires from these specimens. I know there has to be a way to make them stronger, to fully harness the blood magic they possess." Helia's demand echoed with imperial arrogance.

"I cannot help you with that!" The witch's anger flared like wildfire. "The vampires exist because you triggered some kind of ancient curse by wielding blood magic that was never yours to command. No matter if I were truly taught by a fate sister, even if I were a fate sister myself, I still couldn't undo your mistake or replicate it." Her voice grew more heated. "The only person who could accomplish such a thing is long gone. Quade, the Blood Weaver, has been nothing but a memory of the distant past. The Gods distanced themselves from him eons ago. He was your only hope for something like this, not me. Now you're just a failure who has to deal with the fallout of your own arrogance." The witch's laughter was sharp and mocking.

"Keep trying regardless!" Helia's scream echoed off the temple walls. "If he were able to be locked away by others, then he can't be anything truly special." Helia seethed with barely contained rage.

The witch screamed back with equal fury. "They won't save you from what's coming! You're no match for the sisters of fate. Even if you flee to this remote realm, the Creator will eventually find you!"

Helia stepped through a portal of swirling purple mist that she conjured in the air, its edges wreathed in exotic flowers that seemed to glow with their own inner light. When the magical doorway closed, a blinding radiance filled every corner of my vision.

I blinked, and suddenly I was the golden orb again. The statue before me now lay in ruins, crumbled and covered in thick green moss. The witch had aged considerably and stood beside my brother, who appeared much younger than I remembered. I couldn't have been born yet in this timeline.

"I'll be entrusting you with all of my accumulated knowledge," the witch spoke solemnly. "It will be your sacred responsibility to guard the blood magic carefully. There are many who covet it, many even in other realms who would kill for such power. Helia won't be returning in the way you might expect. She's been missing for so long, the fate sisters have no doubt gotten to her by now. If she has died, she will become a wandering soul. You will never be able to let your guard down." The witch stood in contemplative silence for a moment. "Even if I'm wrong and she disappears completely, the people of this realm won't give you any peace. They are never satisfied with what they have. Even with the willing donations of blood, the alchemists and RuneHold grow increasingly greedy for more."

Her head suddenly spun around as if she knew I was watching, and the sickening sound of vertebrae cracking filled the air like breaking kindling. The witch's eyes found me somehow before her severed head hit the ground and rolled directly toward my position. She blinked once at me before extending her tongue in that same grotesque gesture from the dining hall.

"Protect yourself, girl. Change is in the air," she whispered with haunting finality.

I shot upright in my bed, frantically pushing damp hair away from my face. My heart hammered as if I had sprinted for miles without rest. I felt as though I had barely slept at all. Every time I closed my eyes, I was plagued by dreams of that ancient witch.

She must have done something to me with that obscene tongue contact, some sort of magic to make me hallucinate these visions. I didn't understand why she was showing me these glimpses of the past. I possessed no knowledge that would allow me to fully comprehend the things she revealed.

I threw my blanket off my legs with violent force, and the raven sleeping in my bed didn't even stir. She slept without any apparent care in the world. I wanted to grab her and hurl her straight out my window.

I dressed quickly so I could spend my day exploring the castle and gathering intelligence. If I were to take anything meaningful from the visions she had shown me, it would be her haunting message about the future. I wouldn't dwell on dreams of my brother and neglect any more precious time.

I would channel all of my grief and mourning into my nightmares. Daylight was reserved for revenge.

I deliberately avoided seeking out Princess Invidia or Ravi. I wanted to move through the shadows undetected, to observe from a safe distance. I walked purposefully toward the lower levels, keeping my head down and my movements casual.

The castle buzzed with unprecedented activity compared to when I had last walked these halls freely. Women filled the kitchen spaces, all wearing elegant shades of lavender and deep plum instead of the drab, colorless garments mandated under the king's rule. The maids moved past me with obvious happiness, all dressed in the same regal purple color scheme.

I dodged several dogs wearing ornate vests emblazoned with the royal seal as they trotted importantly through the corridors.

The familiar cadence of Queen Blair's voice grew steadily louder as I approached my destination. She was holding court in the throne room. I positioned myself carefully at the doorway, hidden but able to observe.

"Do you recall when Valen and I were preparing to marry? For the entire two weeks leading up to our wedding, you spent your days and nights trying to convince him it was a terrible idea. You were absolutely relentless in your opposition." She laughed, but the sound held no warmth, and no one else dared join in. "I also distinctly recall that after my marriage was finalized, you moved into the castle and gained Valen's ear quite easily. If I whispered suggestions about chicken for dinner, you would somehow convince him we needed pork instead. I never got the chance to tell you how truly impressive your manipulation was."

I leaned carefully into the doorway just enough to catch a glimpse of Queen Blair sitting regally on the throne. Two of the king's former advisors knelt on their knees beneath her elevated position, trembling with obvious terror. She flicked a single finger dismissively, and the guards immediately raised massive axes. She had prepared more efficiently this time, the weapons were large enough to fell ancient trees.

"Please, Your Majesty, wait! Please wait!" one of them yelled desperately.

The two men panicked and tried to speak, but they had almost no opportunity to voice any pleas before both axes were embedded deep into their necks with wet, sickening sounds. I startled and jumped backward, though I wasn't certain if my reaction was due to witnessing what Queen Blair had become or to Ravi suddenly grabbing me and pulling me forcefully away from the scene. His grip was tight enough that I would definitely bruise.

"If you ever listen to anything I tell you, let it be this: stay completely out of sight," Ravi warned urgently. "Queen Blair has developed a taste for bloodshed. She represents a far greater threat than you realize. You no longer have any solid plan in place, and the king will be walking free again as soon as I remove my rune. I'll be removing it soon, if only to halt the Queen's reign of terror."

"I thought you couldn't undo a curse?" I asked, confusion threading through my voice.

"Every moment that I haven't been stationed at the side of your new Queen, I've been studying extensively and sending letters back and forth to my homeland to find a way to reverse what I did to him." Ravi rubbed his forehead wearily. "My personal dealings matter little in this larger conflict."

Ravi's expression suddenly turned to panic, and he pressed his hand firmly over my mouth before pulling me deeper into the shadows of the doorway where we stood concealed. Queen Blair and Prince Nio walked out of the throne room and passed directly by us.

I felt Ravi's heart thundering against his ribs. He no longer felt trustworthy or honest to me. I didn't want to hear his carefully chosen words anymore. I wanted to know exactly what situation I had walked into. I wanted to see with my own eyes and hear with my own ears precisely what moves were being pushed into place on this deadly game board.

I didn't need information withheld from me or haunting dreams clouding my judgment. I needed the truth grounded in cold reality.

I bit down hard into his hand until I broke through skin and tasted copper. He jerked back and gasped while cradling his injured hand. I left him standing there despite his attempts to restrain me and moved closer so I could eavesdrop on their conversation.

"I've given this considerable thought, and I believe the solution is quite simple," Prince Nio announced. "I want Princess Invidia as my bride. Peace between our kingdoms will still be achieved through this marriage alliance, exactly as it was originally meant to be."

"She is far too young for such an arrangement!" Queen Blair protested with genuine concern.

"Actually, she's a bit older than I typically prefer," he countered casually. "She could have already been bearing children by now. My sister was considerably younger when she was promised in marriage."

If the prince wanted a bride and I needed to escape this kingdom before the king regained consciousness, I could offer myself as an alternative. I would gain control over their military reinforcements. Their kingdom would live in constant fear before an inevitable revolt erupted under Queen Blair's increasingly tyrannical rule. The plan could work out perfectly for my ultimate goals.

Ravi attempted to grab my wrist as if he had anticipated exactly what I intended to do, but I shoved him away forcefully and stepped into the light of the hallway.

"I will go in her place," I offered, lowering myself gracefully to one knee in a gesture of submission. "This war has destabilized everything, and even though Princess Sala took her own life, I can still help forge a strong alliance between our two kingdoms. I won't dare claim any personal benefit from this arrangement. I would like to see Princess Invidia remain safe at home while also offering my adoptive mother some small measure of repayment for her kindness."

Queen Blair remained silent while I struggled to control my facial expressions at calling her my mother.

"I will give your offer serious consideration," Queen Blair replied slowly.

She studied me with an intensity I had never experienced from her before. She looked at me with unmistakable suspicion and cold calculation. Her eyes seemed to peer into my very soul instead of simply looking at my surface. In all the ways I had imagined my chess pieces might be repositioned, I had never anticipated that she would begin to consider me a genuine threat until it was far too late for countermeasures.

I had originally wanted her to live long enough to witness her daughter's death as well, but I might need to drastically alter that particular aspect of my plan.

"Call for Invidia and the remaining advisors. We are to hold an important meeting," Queen Blair commanded a nearby guard. "Have everyone meet me in the throne room immediately."

I watched her march away with Prince Nio and felt a rush of triumphant joy. Ravi was far too uptight and unfamiliar with the political dynamics of our kingdom. I still held the upper hand in this game, and Queen Blair still liked me enough for it to matter significantly.

It felt like endless hours that I waited in the throne room. I watched as the space filled with advisors, villagers who still roamed the castle, and even guards and soldiers who were summoned from their posts. The room grew uncomfortably hot and stale with so many bodies pressed together.

Queen Blair finally entered with Princess Invidia, and the Queen directed the two of us to stand on opposite sides of her throne like living chess pieces.

Princess Invidia appeared completely unsure of how to react to this formal arrangement. I watched her fiddle nervously with her fingers and the delicate lace on her dress. I noticed her anxiety, as well as I noticed that Queen Blair continued to glance back at me with calculating looks. She was adamant about our specific placements. We were positioned on her board as king and bishop. Princess Invidia represented her king, and I was clearly her bishop.

What exactly was she planning? Was she sending a silent message that she would protect Invidia at all costs? Invidia was a weak player in this game. She was too spoiled and naïve even now to accomplish much alone, but with proper assistance? She was an incredibly important final piece. Without her, Queen Blair would lose everything. The Queen was too old to recover in terms of producing heirs. There were plenty of bastard children waiting in the wings to fight for the throne that she had worked her entire life to maintain control over.

Did she mean to tell me that I was meant to protect the princess? That I had the potential to make many more dangerous moves, and she was going to put a definitive stop to it?

Queen Blair stood regally and motioned both of us closer to her elevated position.

"I wanted the entire court to attend and hear directly from my lips about our kingdom's future," she announced with imperial authority. "Princess Invidia will marry into the kingdom of Saydeean, and we will build a strong alliance not only in military matters but also in profitable trade agreements. I still fully intend to crush StoneDale, but not with poorly trained farmers wielding farming tools. I want StoneDale to become nothing but a distant memory, the same as the vampires. Soon we will disband our makeshift militia, and everyone will return to their farms and shops. Lanira will be formally adopted and become an official member of the royal family. She will marry into RuneHold as my second daughter, Princess Lanira Leblanc, and form a formal diplomatic alliance between our two kingdoms as well."

My knees trembled violently, and my breath caught painfully in my chest as if I had completely forgotten how to breathe.

"She's not of royal blood!"

"She's cursed!"

"We won't allow this travesty!"

"She manipulates you! Why would this mere maid help create such a bond?"

"She has been my daughter in all but name; she owes me a great deal of loyalty and service. I see no reason why she would not follow through with this arrangement. She offered her hand in marriage already. She's willing to do more for this court than many of you have ever done." Queen Blair settled back onto her throne with satisfaction.

She motioned her guards to seize the advisors who had spoken out against her, and daggers were buried in their chests before anyone else had time to react or protest.

My mind reeled in complete shock. I had never offered to be married into the very kingdom that had spent their entire existence dedicated to hunting and killing creatures like me.

Ravi entered the room at that moment, and I realized he hadn't been in attendance for the announcement. He refused to look directly at me, not so much as a small glance in my direction. He moved to Queen Blair with obvious haste and leaned down to whisper urgently in her ear from beside Princess Invidia.

Queen Blair's eyes widened dramatically, and she rose to her feet with sudden alarm.

"There is nothing left to discuss here. My word is absolute law."

She rushed out of the room with Ravi as if something were literally on fire.

Princess Invidia did not move from her position beside the throne. Her skin had turned deathly pale, and she barely blinked.

It seemed neither of us had truly understood what this morning would bring us.

I didn't want to stay and offer comfort to her. I didn't want to pretend to care about her emotional state. I wanted to know what was so urgently important that the Queen and Ravi needed to rush away in private.

I gathered my dress and ran after them through the corridors.

Ravi stopped and positioned himself outside the king's chamber like a sentinel, and I stopped directly in front of him. He stood tall and eerily quiet. For the first time since I had met him, he seemed like a true vampire hunter, cold, calculated, and utterly dangerous. He held out a muscular arm to prevent me from entering, but I had no intention of attempting such a thing.

Ravi had removed the rune from the king. Valen wasn't just awake, he was furious. He yelled and threw objects from his bedside table at the wall with violent force. Was this Ravi's master plan? To wake the king and have me locked back up in that horrible dungeon? I wouldn't go willingly. I wouldn't be put back into that cold, damp cell to slowly starve.

"I found your letter, Valen!" Queen Blair's scream echoed from inside the room with raw fury.

The sound of a heavy vase crashing into pieces filled even the hallways. I leaned past Ravi and peered into the doorway. Queen Blair looked absolutely feral. She straddled Valen with a pillow clutched in her hands, her knuckles turning white with effort, and her arms shaking with rage. The broken pieces of the vase lay scattered around Valen's head like sharp confetti.

She was trying to smother him to death with her bare hands.

Ravi grabbed my arm firmly and pulled me back away from the gruesome sight.

"Do not involve yourself in anything else that happens here. I'm warning you only once more," his voice carried deadly seriousness. "You are completely unaware of how many pieces have shifted away from your favor. Leave now and keep absolutely quiet about what you've witnessed."

Chapter Thirty-Three
A Bit of Magic in the Air

Lanira

I sent the raven to snoop around the palace, desperate for any scrap of intelligence. I wanted her to bring back word of anything; it didn't matter to me what information she discovered. I needed something tangible to grasp onto in this increasingly chaotic situation. Queen Blair had sent orders demanding that everyone be confined to their rooms; those who dared to leave were to be executed on the spot without question. The punishment seemed far too extreme for something simple.

There had to be a much bigger secret unfolding behind closed doors.

The raven came barreling through my window like a black cannonball and tumbled across my bed before stopping flat on her back. She tossed her wings out dramatically and flopped her tongue to the side in an exaggerated display.

Several long moments passed, and she didn't move a muscle. I reached down and poked at her side cautiously, and she shot upright with startling energy.

Caw caw, and she threw herself down again with theatrical flair.

"What in the seven hells are you doing?" I asked with growing irritation.

She jumped up and bit my hand sharply before dropping dead again.

If she thought I would play some foolish charades game with her, she was gravely mistaken. I would toss her into the fireplace and attempt the resurrection ritual again if I had to. I would.

"You're trying to tell me this is about the king's death!" I exclaimed as understanding dawned.

The realization hit me like a physical blow. She was acting out the information she had gathered.

She jumped up and flapped her wings before puffing out her chest and prancing across the bed regally. She used her other wing to point dramatically before releasing another sharp caw.

"The Queen?" I asked for confirmation.

Caw caw.

"The Queen has everyone locked away so she can hide his death! She's more cunning than I thought she would be. If everyone discovers the truth, they'd push harder to crown someone else immediately."

My door slowly creaked open, and I quickly shoved the raven off my bed and onto the floor, where she would be hidden from view. Princess Invidia slid inside like a ghost and closed the door with careful precision.

"You should not be wandering about," I cautioned her.

"I'm sure you won't tell on me," Invidia replied with tired confidence. "How are you feeling about everything?"

She moved to my bed and sat beside me, her weight making the mattress dip slightly.

"Devastated," I lied smoothly. "Nothing has felt right since Prince Tillo died. I don't sleep as well anymore, nightmares plague me constantly. The idea of us being separated, sent away from each other. I never imagined such a day would come." I let my voice stutter convincingly.

Princess Invidia turned and embraced me tightly, her arms trembling slightly.

"Me either. When I do manage to sleep, I dream of how they must have felt in their final moments. I dream of Father dying too, alone and afraid." She cried into my shoulder, her tears dampening the fabric. "I will miss you more than words can express."

I embraced her back, keeping her close with my arms wrapped securely around her. Many things might have changed in recent days, but I remained exactly the same. I felt absolutely nothing for her tears or her pain. A few small lapses in my judgment hadn't altered the fundamental truth. She wasn't my sister. They weren't my family. The word adoption had only entered my world because Queen Blair had run out of viable options.

No one had cried for my murdered family. I wouldn't mourn hers.

Princess Invidia pulled away from me, wiping her eyes. "Mother's transformation has terrified me. She has the same face, but even her words to me have become harsher and more cutting."

I stopped her spiral of self-pity. "She only has your best interests at heart. Everything she's doing is for you and securing your place in this kingdom. If the king dies and you aren't properly married, you'll lose absolutely everything."

Princess Invidia stared at me as if this thought had never crossed her mind, as if she were so certain that no matter what chaos erupted around her, she would always remain a favored and protected princess.

"If the king dies, she cannot remain on the throne legitimately. Both princes are dead, which means the advisors will select someone else, or the bastard sons your father sired will fight viciously for that throne. They may even decide to kill you as a precautionary measure. The situation will become far more dangerous than Queen Blair has ever been." I made my words harsh enough to leave a lasting impact. "You should return to your room immediately. The queen has changed dramatically; neither of us can predict how she will react if you break her direct orders. I can't risk seeing you punished severely." I smiled at her with practiced warmth.

I kissed Princess Invidia gently on the cheek and gave her a soft, reassuring smile. It didn't wipe away the horror that was now written clearly across her pale features. She walked out of my room slowly, as if her entire world were crumbling around her feet. Her expression was harsh and deeply contemplative.

My smile grew wide enough to show teeth the moment I heard the doorknob click shut. I leaned over to grab the raven and bring her back up to the bed, but the door opened again unexpectedly.

"Princess, you can't stay here." I sighed heavily and dropped the raven back down again.

Alio, the raven, looked up at me with unmistakable rage burning in her dark eyes. I kept my hands far enough away that she couldn't bite at me again.

"Don't look so disappointed to see me. It wasn't that long ago you were practically begging to touch my lips," Ravi observed, crossing his arms as he leaned against my shut door.

"I distinctly recall it being the other way around," I snapped defensively. "Why are you here?"

"I wanted to see if you were holding up all right," he replied simply.

"You wanted to check if I was all right after you acted as though I didn't exist? After you refused to even look at me, and then decided not to protest my betrothal to your kingdom?" I growled. "Last I heard, there are no available princes, which means I'm destined to marry your king."

"Leaving this place is the best possible thing for you," Ravi said seriously. "I learned that Queen Blair has been exchanging letters with my kingdom for several weeks now. They've been negotiating back and forth on the price for acquiring you." His expression darkened. "I don't know the further details, but I do know that you cannot stay here any longer. You witnessed for yourself that she murdered Valen."

He raised his hand and pointed at me emphatically, but I stopped listening when his sleeve fell back. A small red star was etched deep into his wrist like a brand. I got off my bed and moved closer to him for a better view.

"What is that mark?" I asked as I grabbed his hand firmly.

He pulled it away quickly, but it was too late; I had already seen it clearly.

"I already saw it. What exactly is it?" I asked again with growing insistence.

"It doesn't matter to you. Did you hear anything I just told you?" He pulled his clothing back down to cover the mark.

"I didn't listen to a word. What is that mark?" I pressed again relentlessly.

"It's what happens when we break our sacred oath. When we use a cursed rune on a human being. Nothing in this world is without serious consequences, Lanira. You just haven't had to pay yours yet." His voice grew urgent. "Listen to me when I tell you not to argue about this. You need to get out of here immediately. Queen Blair knows far more than she's even willing to tell me."

He lingered on me for a long moment, his gaze shifting between my eyes and mouth with obvious conflict. I didn't understand him at all. I was supposed to believe that he was so powerful and wise, yet he didn't have the courage to stand up and speak the truth openly. He was supposed to be a hunter of the highest honor in his homeland, but he played elaborate games with me even after learning exactly what I was.

I didn't understand why he thought I would blindly trust him. He made no logical sense to me, and he didn't try to explain himself properly. He acted as though I were a part of his court and beneath his station, that I had to take orders from him without question.

"Put the rune back on the raven, and I'll make that mark disappear completely," I offered as a bargain.

He looked at me in complete disbelief. "What did you just say?"

"You heard me perfectly. I can't fully explain it, but my blood can heal scars, even permanent blemishes." I stated matter-of-factly.

He sighed heavily. "It won't work. We're taught in our training that—"

"Aren't you also taught that sunflowers hurt vampires? That's not true, is it?" I grabbed Ravi firmly by the chin, forcing him to meet my gaze. "Put the rune back on her, and I'll save you from that mark."

"Prove to me that you can actually do it," he challenged, his lips hovering tantalizingly above my own.

I bit the inside of my lip deliberately until blood welled up, then pulled his face down to mine. Our lips met in what was supposed to be a simple transaction, and I let the blood drip into his mouth while pressing my thumb over the small rune burned into his wrist. He would only need a few drops before he witnessed the truth. Before my end of the bargain was completed, he would have to restore the rune to Alio.

I hesitated to pull back and separate us, the moment stretching longer than intended. Ravi kissed me as though he had forgotten this wasn't meant to be real or meaningful. His hand came to rest on the small of my back so gently that if I weren't already paying such close attention to him, I might have missed the tender touch entirely. He pressed his lips back to mine as quickly as they had parted.

My breathing quickened involuntarily, and I nearly forgot the practical reason we were positioned so intimately. I dropped his wrist when he lifted his arm and tangled his fingers in my hair instead. Our bodies held no space between them now. We moved so close together that I could feel his heart thundering beneath my palm, though I couldn't recall when I had placed my hands on his chest.

Ravi placed both of his hands on my thighs and lifted me against him with surprising strength. He was far more powerful than his lean frame suggested. He kissed my cheek and chin before moving to my neck, and I felt his unmistakable arousal pressing against me. He guided us both onto my bed, and his hands found my bare thighs before the mattress had even stopped shifting under our weight.

Caw. Caw!

The raven flapped her wings in obvious distress, and I lifted my shoulder to free her from beneath us. Ravi had inadvertently pinned her when we fell onto the bed, and I hadn't noticed in my distraction. I had been too focused on his hands, his breath against my skin, the heat radiating from his body.

Ravi's hand still rested high on my thigh, his thumb tracing small circles on my skin. If he moved even slightly higher, he would discover far more than I would ever admit aloud.

"The rune on your wrist should be completely gone by now," I whispered breathlessly.

Ravi kissed me one more time, slow and deliberate, before he lifted himself off of me. I hated myself for wanting him to stay pressed against me so desperately.

"It did work," he spoke with wonder as he held his arm up for inspection. His dark hair was still thoroughly messed from my fingers. "But I won't be returning the rune to her."

"Yes, you absolutely will!" I shouted, sitting up abruptly. "What happened to your precious honor? To keeping your word?"

I scrambled to look him directly in the eye.

"I've done numerous things today that go against everything I'm supposed to be. Why not add another transgression to the list?" He spoke with casual indifference that infuriated me.

"Why won't you honor our agreement? Why?" I demanded loudly.

"I cannot allow you to get into any more trouble or make any moves on your own. It's for your protection," he said with infuriating calm.

"You don't get to make choices for me! Put the rune back and return to your own business," I commanded.

I got back to my feet, trying to pretend that nothing significant had just happened between us.

"Are you going to hurt me if I refuse, Lanira?" he asked with genuine curiosity.

He reached out and fixed my disheveled dress and hair with a knowing grin playing on his lips before giving a satisfied glance to his unmarked wrist.

He ran his fingers through his hair to smooth it back into place and left my room without another word.

I couldn't have formed a response to give him even if I had wanted to, because it was that simple question that made me realize a devastating truth.

No. I wouldn't hurt him.

And that realization terrified me more than anything else that had happened.

Chapter Thirty-Four
The Unraveling

Lanira

I stood outside Queen Blair's bedroom door, my hand hovering over the ornate handle. It was a deeply uncomfortable sensation to be truly hesitant about anything. Queen Blair had always been a pawn that I smiled at politely, a piece that I had carefully calculated plans for. She had always been a woman I kept at a safe distance and considered of low strategic value.

I was having tremendous difficulty wrapping my head around the way she made me feel since my release from the dungeon. I never would have predicted that I would see her as someone capable of laying an axe into the neck of a person whose only crime was speaking too loudly. No other transgression, simply raising their voice.

Princess Invidia was meant to die next, directly in front of the queen. I had meticulously planned to make Blair watch as Invidia took her final breath. I had wanted to see the exact look in the queen's eyes when she realized there was absolutely nothing she could have done to save her only remaining daughter. I had fantasized extensively about the way she would scream helplessly into the wind.

I had a sinking feeling that somewhere in my careful planning, I had missed the smallest hint that would have revealed who she truly cared about, and what would have actually caused her real pain.

Somehow, beyond my control and understanding, she had shifted from an easy target to a genuine problem. She was far from being my equal, but she now possessed a much stronger and more dangerous aura than she had once carried.

I turned the door handle slowly, and she sat there, dressed down from the elaborate gowns she had worn since my release. On the edge of her bed, Queen Blair sat beside what was supposed to be the king's body. But it wasn't, it wasn't his corpse at all. It was some kind of doll or mannequin. There was no pulse, no blood flow that I could detect.

She must have locked us all away to properly dispose of his actual body. Not even the telltale smell of rot lingered in the air. She sat calmly beside a doll posed as the deceased king so that no one could legitimately take the title of ruler from her grasp. If I killed Princess Invidia now, Queen Blair would be all that remained of the royal line. Her carefully constructed alliances would crumble immediately. She would have no strings left to pull when the advisors were finally alerted to the king's death.

I internalized my smile of satisfaction at the prospect. Queen Blair's sharp eyes were fixed on me, searching my face intently for any hint of emotion that she could extract and analyze.

Queen Blair tapped the open spot on her bed beside the false corpse. I absolutely did not want to sit beside whatever grotesque thing lay next to her. I had no desire to examine it any more closely.

"Come, child. Let us speak as mother and daughter should," she requested, continuing to tap the spot beside her.

The very idea of being her daughter disgusted me to my core. I sat beside her only because I didn't have a solid plan for what I would do if I killed her in that precise moment. I would no doubt be blamed immediately, and I didn't know if I could count on Ravi to help me escape alive. I wasn't certain I was strong enough to fight my way out against the entire royal guard by myself.

Queen Blair placed her hand gently on mine, the touch feeling unnaturally cold. "I hope that you don't think less of me after receiving the news about the marriage arrangements. I only want what's absolutely best for both of my daughters. Invidia is a much softer girl, and as such, she will need a gentler kingdom to thrive in. It makes perfect sense for her to marry into Saydeean's more peaceful court. You have always been tougher, more resilient. I believe that you'll be able to handle the harsher environment of RuneHold quite well."

She paused, studying my reaction carefully.

"Ravi agreed enthusiastically with the idea of this marriage alliance. At first, I wasn't entirely sure about the arrangement, but after considerable thought, I agree that it makes strategic sense. If you truly love me as a mother, if you genuinely care for Invidia's wellbeing, then you will do your absolute best to secure a happy marriage and gain another powerful army in RuneHold." Her voice took on a sharper edge. "If you happen to be a vampire and you did murder my boys, then I can think of no better place for you than in the very heart of those trained specifically to hunt and kill creatures like you."

My heart skipped several beats in rapid succession. I didn't need her brutal reminder of where I was being sent. I understood exactly what it meant for me without her spelling it out so bluntly. Queen Blair was the only person who had ever made me feel as though I was a pawn being moved against my will, instead of the other way around.

The weight of potentially gathering RuneHold's army didn't feel heavy or burdensome to me. It didn't feel as though I was being given a responsibility that only a good daughter could fulfill. The idea of leaving this kingdom to travel to another didn't frighten me, not even the prospect of being surrounded by vampire hunters. I had survived this long because I was intelligent and careful.

What truly scared me, what felt crushing and overwhelming, was this complete loss of control.

I hated the suffocating feeling of not being able to make moves myself. Of not being in charge of my own destiny. Of someone entering my life and systematically taking everything away from me.

Queen Blair looked at me as if she had successfully caught me in some kind of trap. As if she had made me slip up and reveal something crucial.

Had my face betrayed my internal thoughts?

I cleared my throat and looked down at the floor. "I apologize. The full weight of it didn't hit me until this very moment. I didn't have proper time to truly consider that Invidia and I will be permanently separated soon. Of course, I will do everything within my power to help my home kingdom. I also completely agree that Princess Invidia should go to the safer, more gentle land. I'll do whatever I can to help bring lasting peace."

Queen Blair tapped my hand several times before releasing a low, knowing laugh.

"No, my dear. It's not peace that I want, Lanira. I want total war. I want StoneDale to fall completely and burn to ashes. Our army is going to combine with Saydeean and RuneHold, and then we will march decisively on StoneDale before we turn our attention to RubyWake. The king of RuneHold desires this as well. I think destroying a second kingdom in exchange for burning the one that murdered our boys is a very small price to pay." Queen Blair smiled at me with cold satisfaction.

It was truly a shame that she and I needed to stand on opposite sides of this conflict. We would have made a formidable team if she had remained filled with the kind of righteous rage she held during that conversation. She was taking me for a complete fool, and I could see it clearly.

"Isn't RubyWake your homeland? Why would you offer it up for destruction?" I asked with genuine curiosity.

She smiled with secretive knowledge. "We all have our own carefully laid plans. Our own desires and ambitions. We all hold our own dangerous secrets. Some of us play an incredibly complicated game where we constantly stand on the edge of life and death. RubyWake is where I was born, but it was never truly my home. I've patiently waited a very long time for my own plans to finally come together, as have certain others. You only need to focus on getting yourself ready to depart. Something tells me we won't see each other again after this." Queen Blair patted me firmly on the shoulder before giving me a decisive push toward the door. "Go on now, make sure you are properly prepared for departure."

I stood and walked as casually as I could manage out of her room, though I felt her piercing eyes following me. I felt her taking in every detail of my posture and movement. I knew that she was reading as deeply into the way I carried myself as I was analyzing her. Her parting words had sent an ice-cold chill down my spine. How much of our current situation had she actually planned in advance? She spoke as if I had missed a significant handful of moves in this deadly game.

I took slow and deep breaths, focusing on the rhythm. In through my nose and out through my mouth. I needed to refocus my scattered thoughts immediately. I would do myself no favors by spiraling into a pool of negativity and doubt. Queen Blair thought that she had successfully cornered me. She believed that I was completely trapped with no escape.

She wouldn't have made such pointed comments about my true nature if she didn't at least strongly suspect me, but suspicion without decisive punishment was ultimately useless. If she and Ravi were only going to point accusatory fingers without taking action, then I would keep moving forward with my plans.

I was still in control of this situation. I was still several steps ahead of her machinations.

I flung the door to the king's study open with barely contained fury and closed it just as forcefully. She was absolutely right, I needed to prepare to leave this place. There was nothing here for me to say goodbye to that I would genuinely miss. Nothing except the remnants of my past that might still be hidden with King Valen's possessions. I would find anything valuable left in his prized private room before the queen could go through it herself.

I would gather anything important left to discover and take it with me to RuneHold.

I lit a candle with shaking hands and looked around at the overwhelming amount of items scattered throughout the room. I had far too much to search through in what was likely a very short amount of time.

I tossed papers and scrolls off his massive desk with growing frustration. I flung drawers open violently and moved aside rings and gold coins with careless hands.

Nothing of value. Nothing useful.

I pulled books off the shelves and thumbed through pages with increasing desperation. Information about the neighboring kingdoms. Agricultural records. Books filled with children's bedtime stories and detailed royal family lineages. I could have screamed with frustration.

I threw a heavy book at the wall and collapsed into the king's ornate chair. I tapped my finger anxiously against the polished arm of the chair. It was a foolish move that made me look like a petulant child. I didn't feel any better after throwing the book. I only felt more frustrated and defeated.

If I were a piece of truly important information, where would I be hidden?

I pushed the chair back and crawled under the king's massive desk to examine it thoroughly. A small brown button was placed precisely in the center, barely protruding from the wood. It hardly stuck out at all, and if I weren't specifically looking for something hidden, I might not have noticed it. I pressed the button firmly, and out dropped a thick pile of papers.

King Valen was far from being a mystery or puzzle. I scanned the pages quickly, not wanting to linger but determined not to leave anything crucial behind. If I was going to be sent away against my will, then I wanted to depart with a solid plan and all of the important information left in the castle.

I stopped abruptly on a page with an intricate mirror drawn on it. The accompanying writing spoke of being able to communicate with people in distant places through its reflective surface. The record showed it had been traded specifically to the vampire hunters of RuneHold. Several other pages discussed "deity artifacts" in detail, but they didn't list specific locations like the mirror entry did.

Why would such powerful items be in the possession of RuneHold?

Heavy footsteps stopped directly outside the door, and I quickly shoved the papers into my dress before it opened.

"Why am I not surprised to see that it's you causing all this commotion," Ravi observed as he closed the door behind him.

"Me!" I gasped with false innocence.

"Yes, you. I received urgent word of someone slamming doors and throwing books around in the study. Did you honestly think that you were being silent?" Ravi chuckled to himself with obvious amusement. "For someone so incredibly smart, you can be remarkably careless. How did you survive so long without my protection?"

"I could never be as silent as you are. Moving in the shadows to arrange a forced marriage alongside the queen!" My heart raced with anger and betrayal.

At first, I had been momentarily distracted by his warm laugh and the light-hearted way he had approached me. I had betrayed my own common sense and better judgment. Flames of betrayal grew steadily in my stomach. He didn't owe me loyalty or honesty, but somehow I had thought he should have given them to me anyway.

"I did arrange it. I convinced her to have you married off to my kingdom. You're becoming increasingly reckless, and if you're going to continue that way, then I'd feel much better if you were in a kingdom that I understand completely. Where I can properly watch out for you and your safety. I can help you far better that way." He tried to speak gently and reasonably.

"Don't you dare," I growled with rising fury. "Don't treat me like I'm some hopeless girl who desperately needs saving. How am I supposed to know that once we arrive at your homeland, you won't simply abandon me? How am I supposed to know that you won't realize the true depths you've gotten yourself into and leave me to fend for myself? As much as you think I haven't considered, I believe you also haven't thought through all the critical details." I pushed past him roughly. "You've talked extensively about your sacred oath and all of the ways I've forced you to cross your moral lines. Are you truly willing to do that in your own kingdom, directly in front of your king and all of the people you swore that oath to? I honestly don't think you would have the courage."

Ravi grabbed my arm firmly to stop my retreat. "You can be upset with me for as long as you need to be, but do it quietly. Do it while appreciating the fact that someone actually wants to have your back, even when they know exactly what you are."

I pulled my arm away from his grip forcefully. He was lecturing me, but we weren't truly that different from each other.

"What I am? Not who I am, but what," I scoffed at his choice of words. "I should be grateful for the way you speak about me? As though I'm not a living, breathing being, but rather a monster who happened to get lucky enough to meet the one man among the hunters who's operating on a guilt trip." My finger was pointing accusingly in his face before I even realized I had raised it.

Ravi grabbed me firmly by both shoulders and pushed me backward until I was pressed against the king's chair. He guided me down until I was seated and then knelt directly in front of me.

"I think that you should be genuinely thankful to have friends in places that you couldn't reach on your own. I think that you should be grateful in whatever way you can manage to have someone firmly on your side who thinks highly of you, despite having every conceivable reason why I shouldn't." Ravi's voice was steady and serious.

I looked down at him, and all I could feel was my heart pounding violently against my ribs.

"Do you want me to thank you profusely? To grovel pathetically at your feet? Would you like me to scream from the rooftops that someone finally thinks I'm only partially a monster?" I glared down at him with burning intensity.

"I cannot change the way you see yourself, though I desperately wish that I could. I can only tell you that the only person in this room who would use the term monster in connection with your name is you yourself." He replied with quiet conviction.

The flame from the candle danced hypnotically in his green eyes, casting shifting shadows across his face.

"What exactly do you want from me?" I whispered, feeling a strange tightening sensation in my throat.

"I want you to care about whether you live or die as much as I do. I want you to stop being so recklessly self-destructive and truly consider the things that are happening around you, genuinely consider all the consequences." Ravi's voice was filled with sincere concern.

"You don't even truly know me, and we aren't close. A few stolen kisses don't mean—"

"You're absolutely right. I don't know all of the parts of you that I'd like to understand. But I know enough. I've watched you carefully enough. It's been the only thing I've been specifically tasked to do since you killed Tillo." His admission hung in the air between us. "I think I can say with certainty that you aren't a monster. I think I can say that even through your resistance and walls, I'll help you as best I can. So, I repeat my request, please, Lanira, move quietly until we leave this place."

Ravi placed a hand on each of my thighs and pushed himself up from the ground with fluid grace.

He didn't give me a second glance or any chance to argue with him again. He held the door open expectantly for me to leave, and I found myself agreeing. I stood and walked out of the study, leaving behind whatever secrets might still be hidden there.

I hated that I desperately wanted to believe him. I carried a sour taste in my mouth from breathing in his sickly-sweet words and promises.

I longed to simply enjoy the idea that someone I also desired was willing to see me for who I truly was beneath all the darkness.

But I knew, deep in my gut, that once he was back in his home-land, in the place where he would face real judgment and serious consequences, I knew that he would abandon me completely. That I would be nothing but a fool with nothing left except the ability to swallow his empty words in bitter silence.

Chapter Thirty-Five
ONE FINAL CEREMONY

Lanira

Ravi stood beside me close enough that with a single flinch, I could have driven my elbow deep into his ribs. Queen Blair positioned herself with her new head advisor by her side, a girl who looked barely twelve years old. They huddled around ornate chalices while the child's hands trembled visibly as she poured deep red wine.

Guards stood stationed at every doorway and window throughout the ballroom. The space had been decorated elaborately from floor to ceiling for this particular occasion. We were here to celebrate Princess Invidia and Prince Nio's union. Our kingdom traditionally held pre-wedding send-off ceremonies. I wouldn't be receiving one because my husband-to-be remained in another kingdom entirely. I would have an armed escort from this moment until I arrived safely with him, ensuring I reached my destination untouched and intact.

Princess Invidia wore gold thread woven into every inch of her elaborate clothing. Her exposed skin had been painted with gold dust as well, making her shimmer like a living statue. Prince Nio didn't wear a traditional veil, but he was adorned as lavishly with gold as she was otherwise. The two of them walked hand in hand toward the raised podium where Queen Blair stood waiting.

The musical jingle of Princess Invidia's jewelry chimed melodically with every careful step. When the pair stopped directly in front of Queen Blair, a guard moved to flank each side of them. The guards held blazing hot iron brands, glowing red-hot and radiating waves of heat. Without ceremony, they pressed the burning metal into the sides of both their ankles simultaneously.

Prince Nio barely flinched at the searing contact, but Invidia sobbed openly at the excruciating pain.

They were each branded permanently with the opposite kingdom's sacred symbol. They had no choice but marriage now that they were marked irrevocably with each other's emblems. The two of them accepted the chalices from Queen Blair and drank deeply from them while the acrid scent of burning flesh still hung heavy in the air.

I stepped backward instinctively. The smell was absolutely terrible, making my stomach churn. I desperately wanted to be near an open window. Ravi grabbed my arm firmly and pulled me back to his side. I ground my teeth together in frustrated response.

"Stay exactly where you are," Ravi whispered urgently.

"It seems I don't have any choice in the matter," I replied, pulling my arm back from his grip.

Queen Blair began blessing the couple and completing their ceremonial union. She started speaking in ritual phrases, but I didn't bother listening to the familiar words.

Ravi leaned close and whispered under the Queen's ongoing speech, "I have no choice in this. The Queen specifically told me that I was to remain by your side from now until we depart. Just tr—"

"Trust you. Just trust you," I cut him off sharply. "I hear you every single time you say it, but you never actually give me a real reason to trust you, do you?"

Queen Blair made a subtle hand motion toward Ravi, and he immediately grabbed me by the arm. His grip was iron-tight and relentless. He dragged me forcefully from the ballroom despite my resistance.

"You have no choice in this either?" I asked as I clawed at his restraining hand.

"You can keep fighting, but you know perfectly well that I don't have any other option," he replied, maintaining his firm hold on my arm.

I stumbled over my own shoe from the rapid pace at which he was dragging me through the corridors.

"What would you have me do? Tell her no directly?" Ravi still spoke in low, careful tones.

"I'd have you stick to your own words. The ones where you claimed that you were on my side," I snapped back venomously.

"I'm sorry, Lanira. Please, don't act as though you don't understand the situation. You and I both know that if I tell Queen Blair no, it doesn't end well for either of us." He sighed heavily with obvious frustration.

I laughed bitterly in response. "You know, I could rip your throat out right here and now."

Ravi's eyes softened at my violent comment, and it only sent me deeper into rage.

"I know you could easily accomplish that, but I'm still not afraid of you, Lanira. No matter what threatening things you say, I still see something in you that is softer than you want to admit to yourself." He wiped blood from the scratch marks I had left on his hand and casually wiped it on his pants.

Ravi held me firmly at the main entrance of the castle. I watched as carriages arrived one after another in the courtyard. Two vastly different-looking vehicles approached. One was constructed of gleaming silver and pristine white woods. The coachman looked as if he were royalty himself, especially considering how he was dressed in elaborate jewels and fine fabrics. The second carriage was made of wood so dark it appeared almost black. Dark blue accents trimmed its edges, and mysteriously, no coachman was anywhere in sight.

"Does that carriage command itself?" I whispered with genuine curiosity.

Ravi glanced at me from the corner of his eye but remained stubbornly silent.

"You can't ignore me with jokes or arguments forever, Lanira," Ravi spoke quietly. "You'll need a trusted partner if you want to be the hero who brings peace."

"I'm not aiming to be any kind of hero, nor am I looking for everlasting peace," I whispered back. "I'm looking for complete control. If I'm the hand of choice, if I hold the hammer of justice, then no one will ever leave me without options again. No one will ever take from me without paying dearly for it."

"Lanira, I had hoped that you were still here. I wanted to say a proper goodbye," Queen Blair announced as she walked outside to join us.

I closed my eyes and took a moment to compose myself before turning to greet her with a respectful bow.

"I would have refused to leave unless I got the chance to say goodbye to you," I replied with a practiced smile.

Queen Blair barely returned what could be called a sarcastic smile.

"Keep your head down and your mouth closed once you step foot outside these walls, unless you're prepared to deal with the consequences. If there's a need for them, they will be swift and absolutely merciless." Queen Blair's words carried an unmistakable threat.

She looked at me with what appeared to be pity before showing me a cold, fake smile and departing. Guards moved around me after her departure, and though I initially thought they were my escorts, instead, they locked heavy iron chains around my wrists. One of the guards shoved me roughly into motion and pushed me past Ravi.

Ravi stared at the ground like a coward, refusing to meet my eyes.

The guards that I had known my entire life paraded me through the courtyard as though I were a condemned criminal. The crushing weight of every set of eyes in the castle beat down on me mercilessly.

My only regret was not killing both Queen Blair and Princess Invidia before my departure. Not leaving some sort of deadly poison behind for them to discover. I should have done something final and decisive.

I stopped in front of the dark carriage with wide, startled eyes. There stood what appeared to be a massive bear who somehow also looked like a man.

"I sent specific instructions that you weren't supposed to come, Boris," Ravi called as he shoved the creature toward the front of the carriage.

Guards pushed me inside the carriage roughly, and I nearly slammed my head into the opposite wall. Ravi shouted angrily at both guards, but I didn't find his belated protection endearing. He looked pathetic to me as he climbed inside and shut the carriage door with finality.

"Boris is completely harmless," Ravi assured me.

"It was a talking bear," I stated flatly.

"He's half human," Ravi corrected with a frown.

"I was just threatened and then marched around in chains like a prisoner, but you think I'm most concerned about your man-bear?" I scoffed. "Sure, he was strange, but there are much bigger things happening. Am I a prisoner or a bride-to-be? You truly are unbelievable."

We sat in heavy silence for several hours. He watched the passing scenery from the window, but I watched him intently, studying his every expression.

"I understand that you're upset with me," he finally started to speak.

"I understand that you're a coward," I shot back immediately.

"I thought that of all people, you would be the one to understand having to do what you need to instead of what you want to," he replied. He unlocked the chains from my wrists with a small key. "You will have to trust someone eventually. You don't have to be alone forever."

"Maybe I want to be alone. At least I'm honest with myself. That's more than I can say for you!" I spat venomously. "Why would I want to surround myself with people who can't tell the truth?"

Ravi knocked firmly on the side of the carriage, and it came to an immediate halt.

"You want the truth? We're far enough away from your Queen now, let's talk openly." His voice became serious. "Queen Blair and my king, King Orn, have been exchanging letters for weeks. I intercepted several of them when it was safe to do so, and they discussed a specific price for acquiring you. It was always my king's intention for you to end up in this carriage. There is no prophecy. The vampire hunters planted it themselves after the slaughter. The vampire hunters don't hunt vampires to kill them, they hunt them to collect and bring back to the alchemists."

"What?" My voice shook uncontrollably.

If I were to believe him, it meant everything I had held onto, everything I had planned my entire life around, was a complete lie. I had never believed in the prophecy personally. I had never thought of myself as some chosen one, but I had built my entire strategy around the idea that I could convince others it was real enough to matter.

"I can see the realization dawning in your eyes. I tried to warn you repeatedly. You're entering a kingdom where exploiting the idea of a prophecy will put you in the spotlight as someone who doesn't understand even the surface of what they deal with. Only those of us who have worked our way to the top or are alchemists know it's fabricated. You might succeed in convincing the lower ranks, but once word reached us that you were pulling those strings, you'd be in a predicament not easily escaped." He continued relentlessly.

The carriage remained stopped, but my head pounded as if the wheels were hitting rock after rock. He kept speaking even though I desperately wished he would stop.

"No one could locate the LastBorn. You were all but erased from history deliberately. They tested blood after blood from survivor after survivor. They wanted to use the prophecy to push another kingdom to start the war, and then keep it alive as an alert system in case someone thought they had stumbled onto the LastBorn." Ravi ran his hands wearily over his eyes. "We thought we were looking for a boy. It wasn't until I heard the detailed story of how you were found that I became suspicious something was wrong.

The raven was going to tell you everything, and I needed your mind to stay clear and focused."

Ravi grabbed my trembling hand, but I didn't know where to begin organizing my chaotic thoughts. I had been playing into someone else's elaborate game all along. I had thought I was winning decisively. I had been so certain that I was on track to bring everyone back to life. The only suspicion I'd harbored was near the end, and it had been about Queen Blair. I had never considered that my strings were being pulled from another kingdom entirely.

I shoved the carriage door open violently and stumbled down the steps. I leaned over the large wheel and vomited everything in my stomach. It was enough to help me calm down slightly and take slower, steadier breaths.

Ravi walked down the steps behind me and gently caressed my back. He offered me a clean cloth for my face.

"We can make camp any time you'd like. You can rest properly, eat something substantial," he offered kindly. "I wasn't sure if I should have told you the truth, but I couldn't let you walk into the kingdom without the knowledge you needed to survive."

I wiped my face clean and moved my hair out of the way. "I don't understand any of this," I mumbled weakly.

"The prophecy was never about the last vampire alive. It was always about the last one to be born with blood magic before the slaughter occurred. There was only ever one specific line of vampires who could wield blood magic effectively. Alchemists can use vampire blood for many basic things, certainly, but the truly good things? The real advancements? They need you specifically for that." Ravi grabbed my wrist and carefully drew a rune on my skin.

I felt a powerful pulse surge through my entire body. A wave of ice-cold sensation before I felt my blood literally boil within my veins. Streams of blood began forming from my fingertips, flowing freely.

"So it is true," Boris observed with his mouth gaping open in amazement.

Ravi and I both jolted at his voice. He quickly removed the rune from my wrist, and the blood retreated back inside my fingertips.

"Boris," Ravi pointed firmly toward the front of the carriage. "Return to your position."

"I want to keep traveling," I declared as I climbed back into the carriage with shaking legs.

Ravi followed, and we resumed moving along the road.

My breath still trembled noticeably on the way out of my lungs.

"Why didn't you kill me from the very start?" I asked. "Were you lying to me, too? Was this entire thing just an elaborate setup for you to bring me back to my death with the least amount of struggling?"

"I told you before, I wasn't sure at first. I was suspicious, and I was confident a few different times. I was never completely certain. Believe me or not, I do not enjoy killing just to kill." Ravi's voice was steady. "If I had known for certain, I'm not sure if I would have been so determined to bring you back alive. It wasn't until I intercepted those letters that I started truly thinking about all the pieces. It hit me then, you've had a rune on you the entire time.

That's why you passed all the blood tests easily. Runes didn't react to you because the blood magic and all the vampirism, except the hunger, was locked away deep inside. It's why you aren't faster or stronger than a normal person. You're nearly entirely a mortal woman."

It struck me painfully that if what he was telling me was true, then everything I had done to hide myself, the jars of blood I had hoarded to keep safe, all my careful deceptions, it had all been for nothing because I was already hidden by magic.

I appreciated him for constantly reminding me why I never trusted anyone completely.

I needed this harsh realization that I was not operating at my best. That I had so much more to learn. That I needed to become far better at this deadly game.

It would be much easier to rule effectively if I never allowed myself to love the pawns I planned to crush.

Chapter Thirty-Six
The Carriage

Lanira

My thoughts felt like they were drowning me in an endless, churning sea. I had so many things that I wanted to scream at him, but I refused to speak. The words burned in my throat like swallowed fire.

"I really thought you would have said or done something by now," Ravi observed as he ran his hands through his dark hair. "It's going to be a long ride in this suffocating silence."

I hardened my gaze on him like steel, refusing to blink as if it made some sort of meaningful difference. As if we were wild animals locked in a territorial standoff, neither willing to show weakness first.

"Don't you have any questions? Anything at all you want to ask?" He spoke as if my murderous look meant absolutely nothing to him.

"I don't have an interest in anything you may have to say," I replied simply, my voice flat as winter stone.

He handed me a small fur-covered container, its soft surface warm against my fingers. "Drink," he urged, pushing it closer to my face. "If you won't talk to me, then at least hydrate yourself."

I snatched the furry jug from his hand with deliberate force. I wanted my message to be loud and crystal clear. I wanted him to understand that there was no grace, no forgiveness waiting for him in my heart. He and I were like a tree caught in a violent windstorm; we whipped back and forth, changed directions so quickly that we created irreparable snaps in our bark, and grew in opposite directions even though our roots might have looked similar to outside observers.

Ravi took in a deep, steadying breath and prepared to continue speaking despite my obvious desire for him to remain silent. The sound of his breathing filled the cramped carriage space.

"At first, I really wasn't certain who had killed Prince Tillo. Your perfume lingered in his room like a ghost, but there were so many ladies in attendance that evening, who was to say it was only you who smelled of sunflowers and honey? Who was to say that your scent shouldn't have been in there for innocent reasons?" He paused, studying my unchanging expression. "At first, you had set things up so brilliantly. You would have remained much further down on my list of suspects if it weren't for that single piece of fabric I found caught on the door frame. It was such a small thing, a sign of a hurried, panicked exit, and I spent endless hours comparing it to the gowns of every other lady in the house. When it matched only yours, I was still able to convince myself you were innocent because no one had a single ill word to say about you.

Everyone spoke of your kindness, your devotion." His voice grew quieter. "It wasn't until I caught sight of the red shimmer hidden in your hair that I knew exactly what you were. There was nothing I could tell myself to write that damning evidence away. There was no denying it then, no matter how desperately I tried. I wrote to the king of my homeland that I needed an extension, that I needed to stay longer because I believed there might be more than one vampire in the court. It was the first outright lie I told to my own kingdom, my own blood. I didn't and still don't fully understand why I did it, why that specific deception made sense out of all the things I could have reported."

Ravi paused, the silence stretching like a taut rope between us. The carriage wheels rumbled over uneven stones, jolting us with each pothole.

I wanted him to stop speaking entirely. I wanted to reach Rune-Hold and face whatever fate awaited me there. I didn't want to hear another word of his justifications or explanations. It all meant the same thing in the end: he had lied to me and betrayed my trust.

"Queen Blair agreed to send you back with me, and I foolishly thought it was due to my powers of persuasion. It wasn't until I intercepted those letters that I realized it probably wasn't the first lie she had fed me." Ravi continued relentlessly. "I told her the chains weren't necessary, that you would come willingly without a fight. She called me a naive fool. She warned me that if you really were a vampire who had been hiding in the shadows of her court, then it would be far safer to transport you in chains because there was no one more skilled than you at the art of deception. She told me that I was putting my own life on the line by underestimating you. That you'd eventually catch on to the truth. I still believe the chains were unnecessary and cruel."

"Do you honestly think this confession will make me forgive you?" I snapped, my voice cutting through the air like a blade.

"No," Ravi admitted without hesitation.

"Good, because it absolutely won't. You could have warned me at any point during this entire charade. You could have kept your distance from the very beginning. You could have done literally anything except act as though you were genuinely on my side and then betray me when it suited your purposes. No one held a sword to your throat and forced you to deceive me." My words poured out like bitter bile from an uneasy stomach. "You could have warned me the moment you discovered the truth."

He looked at me with deeply pinched brows before he sucked air sharply through his teeth and expelled it slowly, as if trying to center himself.

"All of that is to say, your kingdom and mine operate very differently. I'm telling you this now not to beg for forgiveness, but to give you the best possible chance at survival. My kingdom is more cunning, more inherently cruel than anything you've experienced. It's nothing like the court you're used to navigating. You'll need to plan your moves far more carefully and wisely. You won't be able to get by on charm and quick thinking anymore." His voice grew more urgent with each word. "You'll need a reliable ally, Lanira. I know you don't trust me, I know I've destroyed any faith you might have had, but you don't need to trust me to allow me to help you. Just like you didn't need to love Koen to use him effectively. Keep your guard up. Hold fast to your walls. I actually want you to maintain them."

His words fell with increasing desperation, and each syllable sent panic and rage rising in my chest like a flood. I felt sweat forming on my palms as my hands began to shake with barely contained fury. The idea that he could still consider himself honorable and helpful after everything he'd done, the audacity of thinking he understood the dynamics between Koen and me, it all sent me spiraling into white-hot anger.

How dare he? I had never needed him from the very beginning. He had only succeeded in delivering me to a place far worse than where I'd started, and somehow I was supposed to be grateful for that betrayal?

Supposed to want to keep him by my side? To show some sort of admiration for his twisted logic?

I balled my fist and raised it with lightning speed to slam into his jaw. The impact sent shock waves up my arm, and it felt better than anything I had experienced in weeks. My mind went completely blank for the first time in days, and a rush of satisfaction ran through me, leaving chill bumps across my heated skin. I balled my other hand into a fist and let it crash into him as well.

"I'm sorry," Ravi declared as he caught my third swing, blocking it with surprising gentleness. "I deserve every blow you want to give me, and if it makes you feel better, then continue. But you also deserve to hear a genuine apology."

"Stop talking," I yelled as I struck him in the chest with my free hand, putting all my weight behind the blow.

He didn't pull away or lift his own hands to defend himself that time. He simply absorbed the impact and let me hit him a fourth time, then a fifth. His acceptance of my violence only fueled my rage further.

"I am truly sorry, Lanira," he repeated, his voice steady despite the abuse. "You deserved so much better than what I gave you. You do deserve better."

His lip had split open and was bleeding freely now, and even through the haze of my anger, the sight cracked something deep inside my chest. It broke me ever so slightly in a place that only ever ached when I thought of my lost family.

Ravi reached up slowly and wiped away a tear from my cheek with surprising tenderness. I hadn't even realized I was crying until his rough, calloused fingers slid the moisture away.

He pressed his lips gently to my cheek where the tear had been, then moved to kiss my chin with the same careful reverence.

"You won't get my forgiveness," I whispered through shaking breath, my voice trembling like autumn leaves.

"I don't deserve it unless you feel ready to give it freely," he agreed quietly.

His response only made the fire in my stomach burn hotter, and my fist balled up again instinctively. Who did he think he was to be so understanding, so reasonable?

Without thinking, without planning, I kissed him. I didn't know why the impulse struck me so suddenly. Maybe it was because he was too close, his breath warm against my face. Maybe it was because I couldn't think straight with all the conflicting emotions boiling over inside me. Maybe there were simply too many feelings running through my system at once.

It certainly wasn't because I had forgiven him or even because I particularly liked him in that moment.

He kissed me back with more intensity than he had ever shown before. There was a raw sense of desperate desire that I hadn't felt from him previously. I tasted the copper tang of blood on his split lip, and I expected it to be bitter and unpleasant, but it wasn't. It was hot and sweet, exactly as it should have been. The carriage hit a particularly violent bump that shoved me closer into his solid warmth, and I didn't resist the momentum. He seemed to read my body like a familiar book and smoothly pulled me from my hard wooden seat onto his lap.

His lips wandered away from mine, trailing kisses along my chin before he found my neck and collarbone. My breathing became so heavy it was audible in the confined space. Ravi's was even louder as his mouth pressed a burning trail down toward my chest. He pulled at the intricate strings of my corset with one skilled hand while keeping me steady and secure on his lap with the other. The word "experienced" was the only thing that came to mind as I watched him work.

A soft moan slipped past my lips when he had my corset completely undone and open, the restrictive garment falling away like shed armor. Only the thin silk of my dress remained between his eager mouth and the sensitive skin of my breasts. He slid his tongue over my cloth-covered nipple so gently that it sent electric shivers racing across my entire body. He carefully lowered the silk to expose my breast fully and took it into his warm mouth. His tongue swirled over my hardened nipple with deliberate slowness, as if he wanted to memorize every sensation, drawing another helpless moan from deep in my throat.

"Tell me to keep going," Ravi whispered against my skin, his breath hot and urgent. "Tell me that you want this as desperately as I do. If you don't, if you have any doubt, then we can stop right now and pretend this never happened."

My rational mind screamed at me to stop everything immediately. If we continued down this path, there would always be a part of our relationship that would be fundamentally changed, and we could never return to what we were before. But my body was telling me something entirely different; it pulsed with an overwhelming need to finish what we had started. My heart ached for me to allow myself just one moment of pure desire, just one small instant of feeling genuinely wanted because someone cared for me, rather than viewing me as another need to be satisfied.

I knew with absolute certainty that I would regret this decision later.

"Keep going," I whispered in return, sealing both our fates.

Ravi took my words as permission and ran with them like a man possessed. He spread my legs wider and tore a deliberate hole in my stockings with more force than I expected. The aggressive act took me completely by surprise and revealed a feral side of him I hadn't seen before. The sight of his barely controlled passion allowed me to join him in abandoning restraint. He didn't hesitate to put his hands everywhere he could reach, caressing and exploring every inch of exposed skin. I wanted desperately to do the same to him. I pulled at his leather belt until it finally came unfastened, and he lifted himself up just enough to lower his pants and free himself.

The full length of his arousal pulsed hot and insistent against my inner thigh. He was hard and throbbing with the same intensity that I was, wet and aching for him to be inside me. He pulled my dress straps off my shoulders so that both of my breasts were finally completely exposed to his hungry gaze. He played with my sensitive nipples between his fingers as if he wanted to tease and torment me deliberately. He lowered his head and flicked his tongue over one peak before slowly circling it with maddening precision, as if he wanted to savor every single moment of my response.

I didn't possess the same patience that he seemed to have. I needed him inside me immediately, needed to feel complete. I reached down and grasped his length firmly, running my hand up and down until it throbbed eagerly under my touch. The sensation was the final straw; I couldn't wait another second. I lifted myself up and guided him inside me with a gasp of relief and pleasure. His deep moan sent shivers racing down my spine, and I instinctively tightened around him in response.

"Lanira," he groaned my name like a prayer.

Hearing him say my name while he threw his head back in ecstasy felt like winning some precious prize. His strong hands cupped my backside possessively, and he looked as though he were savoring every sensation without a single coherent thought in his head. The sight of his abandon made me ride him faster, chasing the building pressure inside me. He bit his lower lip and squeezed my flesh more firmly. His grip grew harder and more demanding the faster I moved above him. I felt myself building steadily toward my climax, and he must have sensed it too because he shifted my legs even further apart and grabbed my hips with both hands so he could take control of our rhythm.

He buried his face in the valley between my breasts and drove himself as deep inside me as our position would allow. He pushed into me with increasing force and speed, and every powerful thrust drew another helpless moan from my lips. I clung desperately to his broad chest and finally let myself fall over the edge. I throbbed and pulsed around him while my entire body shivered with the intensity of my release.

"I can feel you," he groaned against my skin, his voice rough with need.

I felt him reach his own peak in several hard, deep pulses before his thrusts gradually slowed to a gentler pace. His grip around me didn't loosen even slightly; he held me as close to his chest as if he wanted us to meld into one being. I felt him twitch and move inside me again, and the sensation caused another wave of pulsing pleasure to wash over me.

My breath still came in hard, uneven pants, but my mind had suddenly cleared of all the chaotic emotions I'd been drowning in before. I had given in completely to him, to my own desperate wants and needs, but the only thing I felt once rational thought returned was an overwhelming sense of foolishness.

Koen had been easy to manage because I hadn't felt anything meaningful for him at all. He had been nothing more than a physical need and a bit of entertaining fun combined.

But in that moment of vulnerability, I had thought, however briefly, that I genuinely cared for Ravi. That perhaps the two of us could have found some common ground or mutual understanding despite everything that had happened between us.

That hope, that moment of weakness, had been a terrible mistake.

Chapter Thirty-Seven
The Camp

Lanira

I sat on my knees between Ravi's legs, feeling every small bump and jolt the carriage took through the worn wooden floor beneath me. The discomfort was almost ignorable with the way he used his gentle fingers to brush through my hair. He braided it as carefully as he could, his touch feather-light against my scalp. The simple task could have been completed quickly, but he moved with deliberate slowness. He touched me as if I were made of delicate glass, as though he didn't want to cause me even the slightest pain.

Neither of us spoke much, but the air between us seemed heavy with unspoken promises. It spoke of its ability to keep dangerous secrets. The two of us were operating on the silent agreement that what had happened between us in the carriage could remain there, locked away from the outside world.

Ravi tied off the finished braid in my hair and gently pulled me back against his chest. I could hear his heart beating steadily through the fabric of his shirt. If I hadn't been able to hear that telltale rhythm, I might never have known he was nervous about anything. He rubbed my tense shoulders with practiced ease, as if he couldn't have been calmer about our situation.

I struggled to let myself fully enjoy the intimate moment. Maybe if the two of us had met in another life, or at another time entirely, we could have been something meaningful together. I was making a terrible mistake by allowing myself even this one moment of softness. My parents hadn't been able to enjoy such simple pleasures. My siblings, I was certain, had wanted far more than one stolen moment of happiness. Why was I allowed a grace that they had never been granted?

"Do you want to talk about it?" Ravi asked quietly, his voice rumbling against my back. "I can feel how tense you are, even now."

"No," I replied simply, not trusting myself to say more.

Ravi helped me settle back into my seat before he knocked firmly on the wooden side of the carriage. We immediately pulled off the main road and came to a gradual stop.

"We're going to make camp for the night. We can't possibly travel the entire distance in a single day." He stretched his arms above his head. "I'll get everything set up properly. You can stay here if you'd prefer, or you can explore a bit, just stay close to the camp. Not because I don't trust your judgment, but because there are dangerous things in these woods that might try to hurt you."

The way he looked at me when he spoke was softer than I had ever seen him before. I hadn't imagined such gentleness was possible from someone in his position. He leaned forward and kissed me with surprising tenderness. It was a lingering touch, completely devoid of the desperate lust we had shared earlier. He pulled back slowly and looked directly into my eyes with an intensity that made my breath catch.

I sat straighter and felt an overwhelming urge to flee. All of this unexpected tenderness made me deeply uncomfortable. How was I supposed to respond to such openness? I genuinely didn't know.

"The red in your eyes really is beautiful," he murmured before opening the carriage door and stepping out into the evening air.

I rubbed my hands across my skirt to clear the nervous moisture from my palms. The facts remained unchanged: Ravi had lied to me about fundamental things. He had known I was destined for his kingdom before I did. Those truths couldn't be erased by gentle touches or sweet words.

Caw caw.

My heart dropped for a moment before I quickly swung the carriage door open myself.

"Alio!" I exclaimed as the raven landed gracefully on my outstretched arm. "You're absolutely disgusting, but I'm genuinely glad to see you."

She pecked sharply at my hand before abandoning my arm for the ground. My eyes traveled upward to take in the massive bear wearing ornate armor that stood casually beside the carriage. I had to crane my neck back to see his full height.

"I ain't gonna bite," Boris declared in his rough voice.

My eyes must have been as wide as they felt in my skull.

"Oh, come on now, I ain't more shockin' than your meaty bird!" he added with what might have been amusement.

"Boris, I specifically told you to introduce yourself slowly," Ravi grumbled as he began unpacking supplies.

"So, this is the person you wrote about in that letter?" I asked, curiosity getting the better of me.

"You read my personal letters?" Ravi stammered, color rising in his cheeks.

"I happened upon one letter by accident. I didn't deliberately steal them," I muttered defensively.

"With what I heard from inside the carriage, readin' a letter is the least a your worries," Boris interjected with obvious amusement.

"The camp is ready. Let's move," Ravi announced, pointing us both toward the cleared area.

When I rounded the side of the carriage, I was surprised to see three elaborate tents and a crackling fire already set up against the backdrop of the setting sun. The tents weren't anything like the crude shelters we had used during hunting expeditions back home. Ravi's tents looked like miniature houses, complete and sturdy. I could see they were made of fabric, but I would have been convinced they were suitable for year-round living. They appeared to be constructed of far more than simple cloth.

"Runes make many things much easier," Ravi chuckled, noticing my amazement.

The three of us each claimed a seat around the warm fire, and I leaned my hands closer to the dancing flames. It wasn't particularly cold outside, but the heat was deeply comforting after the day's revelations. Boris skewered a fresh fish on a pointed twig and then sat motionless for a moment, studying me with obvious uncertainty.

"Do ya eat food?" Boris asked bluntly.

Ravi's eyes shifted between the bear and me with obvious shock at the direct question.

"Do ya just drink the blood from things, or? Do ya have fangs?" Boris continued with genuine curiosity. "I'm not sure what to offer ya."

Ravi must have written far more letters than I had initially realized. The level of detail Boris possessed about my nature was startling.

"Would you like to see them?" I hissed playfully.

Boris immediately dropped his fish and leaned backward. His eyes widened to an almost comical degree. I rose gracefully to my feet and approached him with predatory movements, as if I were a wild animal stalking prey. I deliberately bared my fangs, three sharp points on each side. Boris tumbled off his log and scrambled backward across the ground like a frightened child.

I stood calmly and brushed my dress back into place. I retracted my fangs and returned to my seat with dignity intact.

"Yes, Boris, I do eat normal food. I'm not particularly fond of fish, though I can certainly manage it without complaint," I stated matter-of-factly. "I'm also not the monster you're imagining."

At least, when I had killed Prince Tillo, I hadn't felt like a monster. It had felt satisfying and justified. It had felt like proper justice, an eye for an eye. That feeling had been less strong when

I killed again later. During those subsequent deaths, I had indeed felt dangerously close to becoming something monstrous.

"That wasn't funny," Boris protested loudly.

"It was a little funny," Ravi laughed, his tension finally breaking.

"What about you, then? If we're going to be asking personal questions like this, shouldn't you be out in the woods rubbing against a tree or something equally bear-like?" I asked with mock innocence.

"The alchemists enjoy creatin' us. You'll see a lot more once we get to RuneHold," Boris replied as he resumed his position on the log. "Hunters are tortured into submission; they remain loyal ta the king outta fear. Alchemists remain loyal only to knowledge. Offer them a better chance at open experimentation; they'll be sure ta change sides. Remember that while ya stay in RuneHold. Emberrella doesn't know cruelty."

His words carried a warning that made my blood run cold.

"You keep calling him my king but then referencing the king of your land as if he's not yours. If you know what I am, then you would also know that the king of Emberrella was never my king," I pointed out logically.

"How did ya manage ta do that for so long? Stay with not just the man but the family that murdered yours?" Boris asked with startling directness.

If Ravi had looked shocked before, he appeared absolutely horrified after that blunt question. I felt equally taken aback by such brutal honesty. I had never been asked such a thing so directly before. I had never experienced speaking openly about who and what I truly was in a group setting like this.

"It wasn't easy. I made a detailed plan, and I stuck with it religiously," I admitted slowly. "I turned my emotions completely off, and then I focused entirely on how much I hated them and how much peace my family would feel once the royal family was dead."

"What was it you was plannin'?" Ravi asked, his voice barely above a whisper.

To make the King and Queen watch helplessly as their children died one by one. To drive them both completely mad with grief. To burn their kingdom to the ground before moving systematically to the next one that had played a role in killing my family. To create endless piles of rubble and then rebuild something better, stronger, with higher moral standards and unbreakable principles.

Instead of voicing those dark thoughts aloud, I only offered a mysterious half-smile.

"It doesn't matter now, does it?" I found a suitable stick-on the ground and pierced one of the fish that Boris had placed in a woven basket beside the fire.

My gaze suddenly jolted toward the tree line beside our camp. A shadow figure moved past so quickly I almost missed it entirely. Neither of my companions looked up or so much as flinched at the movement. It was as if my eyes were playing elaborate tricks on me. But the hair standing upon my arms told me I had indeed seen someone, or something.

"I don't know what would a been worse if I was you," Boris mused as he flipped his fish in the flames. "To know my plans failed or to know that I was actually the pawn the whole time. I think I'd feel even more set on my goals if I knew that I was used, not once, but multiple times."

"Enough," Ravi declared sharply.

"I'm just sayin' is all. I'd be upset if I were her. I'm not privy to all the details, but it seems to me that at least the Queen had to have known what you are. How else would you have a rune that stops you from using your blood magic? Seems like you were a means to an end," Boris continued relentlessly.

I hadn't made that particular connection before. I hadn't considered the situation from that angle. But Boris was missing too many crucial pieces to form the complete picture. He hadn't witnessed the way Queen Blair and King Valen had mourned the genuine loss of their children. I was far from being merely a means to an end. My legs began shaking involuntarily, and my fish started to burn in the fire.

"What does the king of RuneHold actually want with me?" I blurted out, unable to contain my growing anxiety.

I had to be better prepared for what awaited me. I had to find something that made logical sense in the middle of all this chaos. I desperately needed something solid to ground myself in reason.

"I'd guess to have the ultimate weapon. To breed you out. To let the alchemists experiment on you," Boris replied with casual brutality. "It's why I live. There are others like me, too. We're all just an attempt at creating a living weapon as strong as what you are. You're weak now, but what your line can do—" He shook his massive head grimly. "Devastation doesn't come close to the right word."

"Enough!" Ravi shouted, his patience finally snapping.

"You ain't got to yell," Boris grumbled in response. "It's only fair someone be honest with the girl. You think I can't see? You keep lookin at her like you're in love. May as well give her a fightin' chance."

That particular idea struck me as almost comical. I was completely surrounded by liars and manipulators.

I had only myself to rely on. Only myself to trust completely.

I jolted violently as another shadow figure breezed directly past my face. I felt the cool breeze from its movement against my skin. I saw it clearly for a brief moment before it vanished. It moved too quickly for me to understand exactly what it was.

"Do you two see that? Please tell me I'm not losing my mind," I demanded as I shoved myself to my feet.

Boris looked up toward the dark tree line with knowing eyes. "Shadow people. The further from Emberrella we get, the more of them we will see."

The casual way he spoke suggested there was much more to this story than he was revealing.

"Why aren't they in Emberrella?" I asked, dreading the answer.

Boris shifted his gaze meaningfully to Ravi, and the two of them exchanged silent words with their eyes. It was a conversation I definitely wasn't invited to participate in.

"You weren't taught much, were ya?" Boris shook his head sadly. "All I'll say is that shadow beings are what's left of the people that didn't make it through the alchemists and all their experiments. They didn't mold with whatever they was supposed to become, but they couldn't cross over into whatever our afterlife is."

Boris ended his explanation with a second meaningful glance at Ravi, clearly indicating there were deeper secrets still hidden.

I had felt so powerful once, so completely in control of my own destiny. But now, at only the beginning of my time outside of Emberrella's borders, I felt as though I was a tiny, insignificant speck in a much larger world that I possessed no real knowledge of. That realization sent my mind spiraling completely out of control.

I never wanted to feel this helpless and ignorant again.

Chapter Thirty-Eight
The Ship Set Sail

Lanira

The carriage came to an abrupt halt, and I listened to the heavy sounds of Boris and Ravi jumping down from their seats on either side. The door flung open with a creak of worn hinges. Boris positioned himself at my side while Ravi was forced to sit with him during the journey, granting me a precious moment of silence. I needed it desperately, even if it would be short-lived.

I accepted Ravi's offered hand and descended the worn wooden steps. A magnificent ship waited on the shore before us, its presence dominating the entire coastline. The vessel looked as if it could have comfortably housed an entire village, complete with all their possessions and livestock. It seemed like excessive luxury for transporting only the three of us to RuneHold. Silver sails billowed dramatically in the ocean breeze, their metallic sheen gleaming even brighter against the rich, dark grain of the ship's hull. If this impressive vessel was any indication of what RuneHold would look like, I might actually enjoy my time there despite the circumstances.

There might have been barnacles and sea growth clinging to the ship's bottom, but everywhere my eyes could reach, the craftsmanship was breathtaking. It appeared as though skilled artisans had spent countless months carving intricate designs of sunflowers and mysterious runes into every visible surface.

I was as surprised by the heavy silence that hung in the salt-tinged air as I was by the magnificent sight of the ship itself. I had expected hundreds of bustling people to be swarming around such a massive vessel, but it remained eerily quiet with only the three of us present. Ravi walked purposefully in front of me while Boris maintained his position behind, creating a protective formation. I was being guarded as if I were genuine royalty rather than a political prisoner. I didn't allow myself to settle into the comfortable feeling of importance. Queen Blair might have declared me a princess in name, but that empty title mattered to absolutely no one else in the world.

I still didn't fully understand why the King of RuneHold thought such a meaningless designation held any value. Why would he possibly want me as a wife based on a fabricated royal connection?

Once we had climbed the steep wooden ramp onto the deck, Boris effortlessly pulled the entire structure on board with his massive strength. I had assumed he would be physically powerful since he was a bear hybrid, but witnessing it in action was genuinely fascinating. He didn't frighten me in the slightest, but he captivated my attention completely.

A sudden rush of crew members came pouring from below deck like water from a broken dam. They pushed and shoved each other out of the way in their eagerness to reach the surface. I couldn't understand why I had initially thought of them as people; not a single one was remotely human. They were an exotic mixture of lizards and foxes, wolves and cats, their animal features seamlessly blended with human characteristics. The entire ship was apparently managed and operated by alchemist-created hybrids.

They crowded around Ravi and Boris as though the two men were precious prizes to be examined and celebrated.

"This is the second princess of Emberrella," Ravi announced, turning to gesture directly at me.

A wave of nausea washed over me as I felt the weight of every curious gaze, as if a blazing spotlight had been trained directly on my face.

Ravi skillfully pulled some of the ship's crew members away with him toward other parts of the vessel, but several others remained behind with me. They immediately began tugging at my elaborate gown with obvious fascination.

"It's so much softer than it looks!" one exclaimed with genuine wonder.

"I'm gonna have Anne make me one exactly like this when we get home!" another declared while tugging more insistently at my tightly laced corset.

They all wore similar outfits of tan leather, some in full-length pants and others in practical shorts, but the material remained consistently the same. Plain, sandy-colored baggy shirts appeared to be their standard uniform as well.

"I have several more dresses packed with Boris if any of you would like to try one on," I offered generously.

They looked around at each other with uncertainty and hesitation, except for a cat-girl with striking blue eyes. She sprinted away faster than they had originally appeared on the surface.

The ship caught me completely off guard when it suddenly lurched into motion. I was jolted around unsteadily, stumbling because I hadn't expected such tremendous force from the departure. A wolf-hybrid with narrowed green eyes caught me firmly by the arm before I could fall. The possibility of sharp claws flashed through my mind, but her touch was surprisingly gentle and careful.

The heavy silence returned as they continued studying me with obvious curiosity. The rhythmic rushing of water against the ship's hull was the only sound that broke through the symphony of their collective breathing.

"Can we ask you a question?" the wolf-girl finally ventured.

"Can we exchange names first?" I requested politely.

The four of them looked between each other with sudden realization of their oversight.

"Come," the wolf-girl directed.

She guided me toward the back of the ship, where large wooden barrels had been placed and nailed securely into the deck to make a sitting area. She gently pushed me down to sit on one of the makeshift seats.

"I am Seela. That is Natasha, a fox-hybrid. Ner is our lizard friend, and Mio is the lion," Seela explained as she settled beside me.

It didn't matter who sat directly beside me, though, because all four of them leaned in toward me as if I were about to tell the most captivating children's story they had ever heard.

"So is it true?" Natasha asked with breathless anticipation. "Is your King truly ruthless and filled with intimidating muscle?"

I couldn't stop the burst of genuine laughter that escaped my lips. "What exactly have you heard?"

"The man who led an entire war has to possess such a commanding aura to be around," Mio spoke dreamily, her eyes filled with romantic notions.

"If you enjoy the overwhelming smell of bile and the constant sound of a loud, unpleasant voice, then certainly," I answered honestly.

They all looked at me with obvious displeasure and disappointment.

"You must be joking with us," Seela declared with a completely blank expression.

I shook my head firmly. "Not at all. He is old, fat, and thoroughly unimpressive."

He is also dead, is what I should have added, but didn't.

"What about your Queen? We hear she's absolutely terrifying. That one wrong move around her and—" Ner made a dramatic slicing motion across her throat.

"I'd say she possesses more of that commanding 'aura' you mentioned than King Valen ever did," I agreed thoughtfully.

"What is it like being constantly around someone originally from RubyWake?" Seela asked with genuine curiosity.

"I only just learned she was from RubyWake," I admitted honestly. "Of all the monsters I encountered in that court, she seemed to be the smallest and least threatening one until very recently."

I felt an uncomfortable twist in my stomach. Something warned me that I might regret speaking so openly to complete strangers.

"Now I don't believe you at all," Mio declared, shaking her head dismissively. "King Valen is fat and weak, and the notorious trash from RubyWake is kind and gentle? Absolutely not, you're obviously lying to us."

"We have a traditional saying," Ner interrupted, leaning forward conspiratorially. "In RuneHold, we say 'beware of any God who may set foot in our lands, for they've come to wield a power as great as ours.' But in RubyWake, they say 'beware the Goddess, so blood-thirsty that she'd drain all of your children and still devour more.' They claim she bathes in blood and is never satisfied with her destruction."

I couldn't help but smirk at the dramatic description. "I've never witnessed such a thing. She bathes in milk and lavender quite often, though."

"Hmm," Mio huffed as she stood abruptly. "This princess is hardly worth talking to if she won't share any interesting stories."

She marched back toward the main deck of the ship with obvious irritation, but I only offered the remaining three a casual shrug.

"I can't offer you exciting ghost stories that simply don't exist," I explained reasonably.

Ner and Natasha exchanged glances before standing as well. "Then there's nothing entertaining for us to share with the others."

The two of them joined their disappointed friend, leaving me alone with only Seela for company.

"They've done nothing during the entire journey except discuss how they'd return home with the most impressive gossip. You'll have to excuse their childish disappointment," Seela explained with an understanding smile.

"I won't think twice about their reaction," I assured her honestly. I glanced around to see if Ravi was within sight before turning back to Seela with renewed interest. "Can you tell me about Rune-Hold instead?"

She leaned to her side to follow my searching gaze. "Are you asking me to provide you with information you were previously denied?"

I sighed heavily. "No one will give me anything truly useful or practical."

I bit my lip nervously as I tried to read her expression and gauge her willingness to help.

"You've definitely come to the right person. What exactly do you want to know?" Seela smiled widely with obvious enthusiasm.

"Anything, everything. Who is your king? What is he like as a ruler? What is your land like? What are the important rules and customs?" My questions poured out of my mouth in an eager rush.

Seela nodded thoughtfully as she organized her thoughts. "Well, I don't think we have sufficient time for a complete history lesson, but I can certainly give you the most important parts so you're at least somewhat prepared. I honestly can't believe a princess was sent to a kingdom she was meant to unite through marriage, yet remains so completely blind to our customs and history."

"Seela," I prompted gently.

She cleared her throat and refocused. "As I was saying, you definitely came to the right person. I have an impressive natural ability where I can hold my breath long enough to speak for extremely long, detailed sentences."

I cleared my throat more loudly than she had, and the sound jolted her back on track.

She pushed herself back on the barrel to sit up straighter with renewed purpose. "All right, here's what you need to know. Long ago, in a time not actually that far in the past, to be completely honest, vampires and alchemists lived together in relative harmony. Mortals formed the kingdom of Emberrella and grew a powerful army. Saydeean developed and focused on mastering the arts. StoneDale was established next, and they dedicated themselves to education and learning. They all excelled in their own chosen areas of expertise. StoneDale still maintains the finest schools and universities in all the known lands. The witches of Lunadur were extremely strict about the proper use of magic. They held certain rituals they deemed too dangerous close to their chests, refusing to share the knowledge. Plenty of others didn't find that restrictive idea appealing at all. They stole magical secrets from the witches and used that stolen knowledge to form the alchemists and establish RuneHold."

"I hadn't imagined RuneHold to be such a relatively young kingdom," I mused.

"It's actually the second youngest kingdom in existence. Ruby-Wake was the very last to form as an independent nation. They were originally part of RuneHold at first, too. Some of the people eventually left our kingdom. They called themselves Vitalists and loudly condemned the way the alchemists conducted their research and experiments. Vitalists are dirty, no-good lunatics who harm and torture innocent people. They kill without mercy or reason. You stay far away from them if you value your life. No one wants to venture to Emberrella anymore for fear of your Queen and her connections to RubyWake. There's excellent reason to fear her, too! Once RuneHold was finally rid of the destructive Vitalists, we became the absolute best kingdom at revival techniques, deadly poisons, and creating hybrids. The things we've made genetically possible are nothing short of miraculous achievements. We don't have sick children or any defects in our population," Seela beamed with obvious pride when she spoke.

Her enthusiastic words made me increasingly anxious. No sick children? I could only imagine that would be possible if they were systematically killed before they could be counted in any official tally. How could there be shadow people wandering the lands if no one was ever considered ill-equipped for life? Wouldn't that mean everyone successfully made it through the alchemists' procedures?

"That does sound like something to be genuinely proud of," I managed to say.

I desperately wanted to shift our conversation in a different direction. At first, I had liked Seela; she had seemed curious and refreshingly light-hearted. The more we spoke, however, the more her tone became disturbingly close to fanatic devotion.

"Your King Orn will certainly know of King Valen, then? They would have fought together during the wars, no doubt," I suggested.

"Oh, no. King Lorn was the ruler during that time period. It was told to us from sources inside the castle that he died peacefully in his sleep. Anyone who actually saw his body was either murdered or still remains beside King Orn. Whispers and rumors say that King Lorn was actually killed by his own son. We heard stories of how King Lorn was growing more concerned with filling his own pockets and less concerned with the welfare of his citizens. We have heard that Prince Orn, at the time, killed his father for the betterment of all our lives," Seela spoke as though she were drifting off into a pleasant daydream.

"You're all truly content with that violent transition of power?" I asked with genuine surprise.

"Of course we are. How can we possibly argue with a king who keeps our best interests at the forefront of his thoughts and decisions?" she replied as if the answer were obvious.

"I don't mean to sound foolish, but it seems like none of you receive your information directly from him?" I pressed carefully.

"No one except a very carefully selected group is allowed to set foot inside the castle, and most of them never leave again once they enter. We all eagerly look forward to the day when we might be assigned an important position there," Seela explained with hopeful longing.

"Lanira!" Boris called loudly from across the deck.

He waved me over with urgency, and I looked back at Seela with reluctance. I genuinely wanted to stay and continue our conversation. I wanted to keep her talking and sharing information. She was like a waterfall of knowledge, bursting with eagerness to give it all to me. Boris had ruined her desire to speak freely, and she immediately took the opportunity to leave my side.

I stood with obvious displeasure and joined Boris at the edge of the ship. He pushed me closer still to the railing, close enough that the ocean spray could reach us.

Magnificent orange whales suddenly leaped from the dark water and twirled effortlessly in the air like graceful dancers before crashing back into the sea with tremendous force, spraying us with cool, salty water.

"That's a sight ya won't see back on the mainland," Boris smiled with genuine appreciation. "Enjoy the peace and beauty the ship brings. I'm afraid it won't be nearly so calm for ya once we land."

His words felt like the clearest possible warning every time he spoke to me. If there was anyone I had learned to trust during this journey, it was Boris. It was simply because he and I both shared the same fundamental value: the absolute importance of being properly prepared for whatever lay ahead.

Act Five
THE KNIGHTS' REBIRTH

Chapter Thirty-Nine
RuneHold

Lanira

Seela made it abundantly clear, loud and persistent, that she was the one to provide me with stories and lessons instead of the others. I was kept under a watchful eye for the remainder of my time on the ship, as if I were valuable but dangerous cargo. Ravi smuggled me off the vessel and into the waiting carriage as though I were a prisoner whose every movement needed to be controlled.

The carriage ride that followed was suffocatingly silent. I had no desire whatsoever to speak to Ravi. I didn't even want to look at him or acknowledge his presence beside me.

I wanted desperately for the carriage to be ambushed by ruthless bandits so that I could force Ravi to play the self-righteous hero he constantly pretended to be. I wished fervently that I could strangle him slowly with a rope made from twisted fabric. I could have torn strips from my dress and wrung them until they formed a tight, deadly cord. That would have accomplished the same murderous goal. I wanted the carriage wheel to break completely so that while he labored to change it, I could slip behind him and slam his eye violently into the sharp wooden peg.

I would finally be rid of another problem, a much bigger one than I had dealt with yet. I had never truly cared about King Valen, and the brief moments when I had cared about any of the others were so small, so fleeting that they were easily forgettable.

But as I watched Ravi and the way his thick black hair tapered so perfectly around his strong forehead, I realized with startling clarity that I was looking at the most beautiful man I had ever seen. That he represented much more than just a small tug at my heartstrings. That, despite everything he had done to betray me, I didn't actually hate him. My heart skipped erratic beats at the dangerous thought that maybe I understood him on some fundamental level. That maybe he and I could have found common ground. That maybe my beloved brother would have wanted something different for me than endless revenge.

"We're here," Ravi announced, his voice cutting through my turbulent thoughts.

His unexpected words startled me from my internal conflict.

He grabbed my arm with firm insistence and pulled me until I was forced to look outside the carriage window. Massive stone carvings stood like ancient sentinels guarding the entrance to the kingdom. Knights carved from solid stone bore tablets across their chests, their weathered faces stern and imposing. Rune symbols were etched so clearly and deeply that they remained visible even where parts of the stone knights had faded with age and weather.

"What do those carvings represent?" I asked with genuine curiosity.

"The tablet tilted to face those entering is for cleansing and purification. The tablet that faces those leaving is for protection and safe passage," Ravi explained with the tone of someone who had memorized this information long ago.

We crossed a sturdy stone bridge to enter the bustling town below. Buildings were clustered together so tightly that if it weren't for the crooked chimneys pouring steady streams of smoke into the air, they might have appeared completely melded into one massive structure. Merchants navigated the sloped, winding pathways with practiced ease, and elaborate stained-glass windows sparkled like precious diamonds in the filtered sunlight. The wooden frames supported dramatically slanted roofs that looked as though they held rooms reaching as high as the endless sky stretching in the background. The buildings were constructed of darkened, weathered wood, but the brilliant colors of every decorative accent made the entire scene breathtaking to witness.

It wasn't anything like the kingdom I had grown accustomed to living in. Genuine laughter filled the narrow streets of RuneHold, echoing off the close-packed buildings. Children moved quickly out of the way of passing carriages and horses. People argued loudly over fruit prices at market stalls, and others called out enthusiastically to sell miracle potions they claimed to have brewed, elixirs that could cure the beards off even the most stubborn mother-in-law.

The bustling town gradually faded into the distance behind us, leaving only floating lanterns suspended in the air like captured stars. Then a castle so magnificently large came into view that I was certain it could have comfortably housed an entire town within its walls. The stone bridge we traveled on suddenly ended, and I felt a surge of panic when I realized there was nothing but empty air beneath us.

I sat straighter in alarm at the sight of us apparently plummeting to our inevitable deaths. Ravi reached out and touched my leg in what might have been reassurance, and I immediately slapped his hand away with force. I didn't have the chance to demand why he wasn't acting concerned or to question why I hadn't taken action myself when brilliant blue and purple lights suddenly illuminated the ground beneath us as we continued moving forward. We were traveling on an invisible trail, supported by magic I couldn't comprehend. The entire magnificent castle sat suspended on a surface that my eyes simply couldn't detect. A separate floating garden filled with vibrant red and pink trees hovered gracefully on one side, while an elaborate bathhouse floated serenely on the other.

The village had been placed firmly on solid ground, but the castle floated impossibly above the vast sea below.

"Even if you don't want to speak to me, I need to warn you before you're thrown into a completely new way of life," Ravi began urgently. "You aren't allowed to speak to the villagers. Any of them, under any circumstances. Even if you encounter one and they try to convince you otherwise through friendliness or familiarity. We are two completely separate worlds existing in this kingdom. To the villagers below, we hunt and kill vampires to protect them from an evil much greater than they could possibly understand. Inside these castle walls, the correct vampiric bloodline fuels our entire way of life, our studies, our advancements, our very existence. Inside these castle walls, you're a prize if you prove to be what they desperately want." Ravi's green eyes held no room for jokes or exaggeration in their depths.

His grave warning felt like a physical punch to my chest. Everything about this situation felt fundamentally wrong. My entire world felt backwards, twisted into something unrecognizable. I felt as if I were stuck inside a snow globe and someone kept shaking it violently, never allowing me to find solid ground.

"I don't need your unwanted advice," I hissed through gritted teeth.

Ravi grabbed my chin firmly and forced my gaze to meet his intense stare. "You aren't letting your new reality sink in properly. You aren't thinking clearly about the danger you're in. We don't hunt vampires to kill them outright. We hunt vampires to capture and cage them for experimentation. If you attempt to pull a stunt that conceals your true blood again, you won't be freed, you'll die slowly and painfully."

The carriage came to an abrupt halt, and I shoved the door open with desperate force. I wanted to escape from him, to find space away from the way he made me feel as though my carefully constructed world was crashing down around me in ruins.

I didn't stop to think about the fact that there was no solid ground beneath the carriage. I stumbled forward blindly, genuinely fearing that I was going to plummet to my death far below, before a small, twisted man grabbed my arm with surprising strength.

Half of his weathered face was horribly scarred as if it had been touched by intense fire, and one of his eyes had been replaced with glass that caught the light eerily. Like an insect, he studied me with what appeared to be a hundred tiny pupils reflecting in the artificial orb. I straightened my posture at the unsettling sight of his pronounced hunch. He was a grotesque and awful sight set against the ethereal beauty and glow of the castle behind him. The structure was luminescent even in the soft light of the rising morning sun, constructed of shimmering and glossy materials I had no words to describe. It looked so delicately designed yet so far ahead of anything I could have imagined seeing in my lifetime. The castle stretched so impossibly tall that it seemed it might pierce the sky itself.

"Yes, 'tis quite the magnificent sight, aye," the hunched man slithered in a voice like oil over stone. "You are quite the sight in life as well, my dear. We only had your portrait till now, and justice, it did not do you proper service. Fine fruit you will bear for our purposes." He spoke these disturbing words while rubbing my stomach with his gnarled hand in a way that made my skin crawl.

I shivered in complete disgust at his inappropriate touch, but he maintained his unsettling half-grin with obvious satisfaction. He waved a commanding hand toward the building's interior, and guards dressed in armor that seemed to glisten like liquid metal marched outside through the open archway of the castle. Like the invisible ground beneath us, if there hadn't been a telltale shimmer in the air, I wouldn't have known they wore armor at all.

Two of the armored guards grabbed me roughly, one seizing each of my arms, and lifted me completely off the ground as if I weighed nothing. I would have willingly followed them if they had simply asked, but instead, they dragged me like a dangerous prisoner. They gripped my arms so tightly I was certain they intended to tear them from my body entirely. They carried me down curved, glowing stairways that seemed to pulse with inner light, descending into an area thick with the metallic scent of old blood. I was shoved unceremoniously into a cell, and they sealed bars made of actual flames behind me, the heat washing over my face.

I didn't understand why I was being locked away any more than I understood the bizarre kingdom and the impossible things I had witnessed.

"Our Master won't be home till morning arrives. Master needed to retrieve another vampire from distant lands. Master is not convinced about the girl's authenticity. Master left specific word for Ravi to keep his guard sharp on the womb bearer. We test the blood then," the hunched man announced to his companions in that same slithering tone.

The twisted man limped away with his uneven gait, and a floating lantern followed behind him like an obedient pet before the guards joined their grotesque leader.

Heavy silence settled between Ravi and me while my heart slammed violently against my ribs. I was locked away in a cage for the second time in my life, and both instances were directly because of him. Ravi drew a glowing rune in the air with practiced movements and used it to open the flaming cell bars that imprisoned me. He moved as if to sit beside me on the cold stone floor, but I held up my hand in a sharp gesture to halt his approach.

"Don't even think about it. Go guard me from a much greater distance," I growled with barely contained fury.

"I'm sorry for the way things have to be conducted here," he offered quietly, his voice heavy with what sounded like genuine regret.

"If you continue to speak, I will make you my next meal," I declared with deadly seriousness.

Ravi stared at the stone ground in front of us for several long moments before he reluctantly got back to his feet, the movement slow and defeated.

"I'm not scared of you, Lanira. I will give you the space that you need, but I'm doing it because I respect your wishes, not because I fear what you might do to me." Ravi's brows couldn't have been pressed together any harder, creating deep lines across his forehead.

My treacherous heart skipped a beat at his sincere words. The unwanted feeling made me even more displeased with my own emotional weakness. I was already tired of the way his words affected me so profoundly.

I dozed off eventually, my exhaustion finally overcoming my anxiety. Being surrounded by oppressive silence with absolutely nothing to occupy my mind made me realize how truly tired I was after everything that had happened.

I thought I was still caught in a dream when I felt the unmistakable weight of a presence hovering over me. When I felt hot breath against my skin, carrying the scent of something ancient and otherworldly, I knew with certainty that I had to be awake. I opened my eyes just enough to allow light to enter, but there wasn't any illumination to be found. My heart dropped into my stomach, and I shot upright in alarm.

I recognized the figure from our encounter in the woods during our travels. He was shaped like a man, but his outline blurred and shifted like smoke. He was nothing but living darkness, a shadow given human form. Night itself in the shape of a person. His eyes, which should have been white, were instead a dull grey, and what should have been colored irises were only the pale shape of a white moon. The sparkle of a distant star sat suspended inside each otherworldly orb.

"I had to see for myself that it was true. That you were actually here and truly what they claimed you to be," his voice resonated as a deep, otherworldly hum that seemed to come from everywhere at once. "We've been waiting for you for so very long."

I pressed myself closer to the cold stone wall behind me, the rough surface scraped against my dress. I desperately wanted distance from the supernatural being. Ravi's urgent warning echoed through my head like a repetitive drum.

"I can sense it in your blood," the shadow continued. "The prophecy will come true, regardless of what you've been told."

"There is no prophecy," I stated firmly, though my voice trembled slightly. "It was all an elaborate lie."

"The origins of the prophecy stopped mattering the moment it brought hope to those who believed in its promise. Divine meaning or not, it's still very much alive in people's hearts and minds," he stated with unwavering conviction.

"Who are you?" I asked, though I dreaded the answer.

"I'm a part of the resistance, just as you are destined to be," he replied with certainty. "We are the same, you and I." His form suddenly shifted as he glanced toward the entrance with obvious concern.

My head followed his gaze instinctively, turning toward the source of his alarm.

Voices rang out clearly from the entrance, echoing off the stone walls and growing louder with each passing second. The shadow moved smoothly into the wall as if it were nothing more than an open doorway. He molded into the stone as if it were soft as silk, and within moments, the room appeared as empty as it had been before. As if the entire encounter had been nothing more than a vivid dream.

Ravi appeared first, his familiar face wearing what I could only describe as a smugly satisfied expression. The hunched man hobbled in next, followed closely by Boris and several mysterious figures dressed in elaborate golden robes. The heavy fabric hung down over their faces, concealing their features, but their jaws were clearly visible beneath the hoods. Golden mechanical brackets were attached to their lower faces in place of natural bone. Had they actually removed their human jaws and replaced them with intricate machinery?

Additional guards entered next, their armor clanking softly against the stone, followed by a man dressed entirely in gleaming silver. The diamonds adorning his jewelry caught the flickering light and blended seamlessly with the metallic fabric. His hair was bright gold and artfully tousled around the strong frame of his face. Dark golden eyes studied me with predatory intensity, as if I were a specimen to be examined and catalogued.

The area around my cell quickly became crowded with bodies pressing close to the bars. There was no possible exit for me to attempt. No gap that I could have squeezed through, no space that I could have woven between to escape. Only person after person crowded around me as though I were nothing more than a fascinating experiment to be observed and discussed.

The man I could only assume was King Orn smiled at me with obvious satisfaction. He bared all of his perfectly white teeth in what might have been meant as a welcoming expression, though it felt more like a predator showing its fangs.

What was I doing? Was I going to forget who I truly was simply because strangers wanted to intimidate and frighten me? Was I going to forget my family, my beloved brother, because I found myself in an unfamiliar place? This was what I had wanted all along, after all. I had wanted to seize control of Emberrella and systematically tear through the other kingdoms until justice was served.

I was getting exactly what I had wished for. It just wasn't happening in the way I had originally planned it. If something like an unexpected change of circumstances was enough to completely shatter me and send me running away in defeat, then I didn't deserve to avenge my murdered family.

I got to my feet with renewed determination and stood as straight as possible. I lifted my chin proudly and shook my hair away from my face with defiant grace.

"Lanira, I'm going to request that you excuse my poor first impression. Such treatment is quite unlike my usual manner. When someone is suspected of vampirism, they're usually either cleared of suspicion or killed immediately," King Orn spoke with casual authority.

A guard lowered the flame bars that stood between us with a gesture from the king, and King Orn stepped closer with predatory confidence. The two golden-robed figures moved inside the cell around him with synchronized precision. They moved in perfect unison as if they were twins who had rehearsed this ritual countless times. They each grabbed one of my hands and held it up for inspection. The figure on my left produced a golden pen and drove it deep into my palm until it could penetrate no further into the flesh.

I winced involuntarily, and my knees shook from the intensity of the pain. The shock that shot through my arm was pure agony, like lightning traveling through my bones and setting every nerve on fire. The figure on my right allowed his golden jaw to drop open with a mechanical whir of intricate gears. Golden fangs emerged, perfect imitations of my own natural weapons, and he bit down hard on the side of my hand with brutal force.

I screamed in pain and shock, the sound echoing off the stone walls. He didn't bite delicately to extract a few drops of blood for testing. He bit down with savage intensity, designed to cause maximum pain while watching me bleed freely onto the floor. Ravi stood silently behind King Orn, staring at the wall behind me as if we were complete strangers who had never shared a single moment of intimacy.

The first figure removed the golden pen from my palm and stepped to the side with practiced efficiency. The other figure unhinged his mechanical jaw from my wounded hand and held my blood inside his mouth like a living receptacle. A guard grabbed me while blood still flowed from my injuries and pulled me roughly up the glowing stairs, my feet barely touching the steps. He dragged me outside to the same entrance I had arrived through, but the scene had been completely transformed. A new floating island now sat suspended in front of us.

The surface was completely flat, and carved deep into the sand was an elaborate rune of considerable size and complexity. Surrounding the island were floating seats arranged in perfect rows, rising up like an amphitheater. Thousands of faces watched me intently as if I were a public spectacle designed for their entertainment. The guard threw me to the ground at the beginning of the rune and shoved my bleeding hand into the carved symbol with unnecessary force.

"Its not enough, open her up further." King Orn called out.

The guard looked frustrated, as if my presence was a personal inconvenience that was delaying his other duties. Without warning, he grabbed my wounded hand and sliced it open from wrist to elbow with a razor-sharp blade that glinted in the strange light. Blood gushed freely into the carved symbol, filling it as quickly as I became lightheaded from the sudden loss. A brilliant red glow emanated from the rune and traveled back into my arm like liquid fire coursing through my veins.

My other arm gave out completely, and I nearly drove my face into the rough sand below, saved only by my instinctive attempt to catch myself.

"Perfect," King Orn declared with obvious satisfaction, clapping his hands together as if he had just witnessed a delightful performance.

The figure who had held my blood in his mechanical jaw had mysteriously disappeared, vanishing as quickly as if he had never been there. The remaining one poured a thick, translucent liquid over my wounded arm, and my skin immediately became alive with supernatural healing. The flesh reached out like living fungus, extending fingers to grab onto the separated edges and pull itself back together with disturbing efficiency. When the process was complete, there wasn't even a scar remaining. No visible sign of what I had endured, except for the emotional trauma that would remain with me forever.

My mind spun chaotically with confusion and terror. No answers were being provided to help me understand what was happening or why. I couldn't see the crowd's reaction to the spectacle from my position on the ground.

King Orn held out his hand for me to take, as if offering assistance to a lady at a formal gathering. I would not give up at this crucial moment. I would not allow myself to be taken down so easily by intimidation and pain. I grasped his hand firmly and pulled myself to my feet with as much dignity as I could muster.

"Forgive me for the harsh treatment. Having you sleep in a cell was a poor way to begin our relationship. Let this moment be our true first impression of each other instead," he declared as if the entire brutal show he had orchestrated had never happened. "We will have breakfast together, yes? I'm sure you have many important things to ask me. Many requests regarding your upcoming wedding ceremony."

King Orn waited expectantly for my response, acting as though the torture I had just endured was completely irrelevant to our conversation.

"Of course," I replied, keeping my voice steady despite the fear and rage coursing through me.

He was clearly insane. He was utterly full of himself. He was surrounded by people and beings just as spine-chilling and dangerous as he was.

But I would be the one to kill him before he had the chance to hurt me again.

Chapter Forty
The Letter and the Shadow

Ravi

I stood concealed in the shadows of the doorway on the upper levels of the castle, my back pressed against the cold stone wall. Working alchemists in their distinctive golden robes huddled around the second princess of RubyWake, Queen Blair's younger sibling, born after the queen had severed all contact with her homeland. The Princess had been intercepted on her way to StoneDale several years earlier, captured like a prize to be claimed. King Orn had demanded so much protection for the princess of Saydeean because of his own crushing guilt over past actions.

He knew how disturbingly easy it truly was to take something that didn't belong to him because he had done it himself countless times before. Orn was of the twisted mind that nothing was beyond his reach, and if he had to use brutal force to obtain what he wanted, it was his divine right to do so.

Cluttered desks were scattered haphazardly around the room in front of me, their surfaces overflowing with glass jars filled with mysterious substances and intricate mixing equipment. Leather-bound books surrounded each desk, stacked in precarious towers that threatened to topple at any moment. Still, even in the midst of all the overwhelming clutter, there was not a single speck of dust to be found anywhere. The alchemists maintained their workspace with obsessive precision.

Lanira couldn't have known that her machinations had sent even more fire raining down on a land that was already drowning in conflicts with RubyWake. RuneHold had also spent considerable time and resources systematically tormenting StoneDale through subtle warfare and political manipulation.

StoneDale never stood a fighting chance when Lanira pointed an accusatory finger at them because they were already worn dangerously thin from constant harassment. Not many people knew that King Orn had been holding RubyWake's lost princess captive as his personal project. If StoneDale had discovered it was Orn behind their troubles, they would have sent RubyWake's army to our gates in an instant. RuneHold was particularly skilled at spreading rumors like wildfire to point fingers and stir chaos in neighboring kingdoms. In that calculated regard, Lanira would fit right in with our methods.

The StoneDale Princess served as Orn's mistress in the most disturbing sense. She remained by his side like a devoted pet and showed up obediently for her so-called "medical appointments" without protest. I didn't consider it genuine consent when the alternative was a slow, painful death, but if asked directly, she was always insistent that she was deeply in love with him. She refused to entertain even the slightest idea of leaving Orn's side for freedom.

Alchemists dressed in tight-fitting golden clothing scurried around like busy insects to retrieve a syringe of blood from a specially designed bag they kept chilled with ice. With practiced efficiency, they inserted the thick needle into the swollen belly of the pregnant princess, their movements clinical and detached. They were hoping desperately to succeed with their experiment this time around. They were running dangerously low on the precious blood; they murmured to each other, blood they claimed was the only viable sample for their purposes. They were attempting to breed blood magic-wielding vampires directly from Orn's bloodline through forced artificial means.

They wanted their own never-ending source of supernatural power.

The princess screamed in agony, and her entire body convulsed violently as the needle was withdrawn from her womb. The needle was thick enough that even I shuddered involuntarily at the gruesome sight. Watching horrific procedures like this was what had initially started my questioning of everything I had sworn to uphold. I had sworn a sacred oath, but to what end? I had sworn to be the hand of justice, but the underlying message was that I had actually sworn to uphold the alchemists' ability to be utterly inhumane.

I had sworn to protect my kingdom and its people, but the common people had no clue about the truth, and the inner kingdom was filled with unspeakable horrors. The words I had spoken during my oath ceremony sounded noble and righteous, but the carefully hidden subtext was that I was expected to turn a blind eye to one group while being the hand that allowed them to retain all-encompassing power over life and death.

Where exactly was I supposed to draw the moral line?

"I heard you've been looking for me," Vex's familiar voice emerged from beside me, though I hadn't seen him approach.

He moved effortlessly through the walls like flowing water. He was made of pure shadow, and as such, if I stood within those shadows, then I was temporarily in his domain.

"I have been searching for you," I nodded, keeping my voice low. "I found a letter while I was away in Emberrella. One with your name clearly written on it. You had written to someone named Ash, telling him specific RuneHold secrets that could have destroyed us. I can't seem to find much reliable information about who this Ash person is."

"The blood the alchemists are using to inject inside the Ruby-Wake princess, it's the blood of Lanira's older brother," Vex revealed quietly.

My heart plummeted into my stomach like a stone. The way our lives intertwined in such twisted patterns sent violent shivers down my spine.

"When I served as your father's right hand, I was completely loyal when your father deserved such loyalty. I did exactly what I was commanded until he took his descent into absolute madness. Until he started teaching young Orn that the deepest and darkest parts of the alchemists' minds were acceptable ideals to act upon without question." Vex paused in his explanation, and I could hear the weight of old pain in his voice.

I detected in his tone that he was struggling to hold back tears. I had known Vex for my entire life, and I had hardly ever seen him show such raw emotion.

"You mentioned powder?" I asked, confused by the reference.

I hadn't heard of any such thing before in all my training.

"We needed an army that truly believed vampires were dark and twisted creatures that deserved no mercy. The problem was that our hunters hadn't witnessed any such evidence on their own," Vex explained with bitter resignation.

The alchemists in front of us finished their cleanup and escorted the pregnant princess out through the back entrance as if it were just another routine day. They hadn't noticed the two of us lurking in the shadows. They didn't need to be cautious; they were free to do whatever they pleased without shame or consequences.

"A mind-altering powder was the easiest method to use for mass manipulation. We mixed it into their water supplies, drinks, and food. We put it in their medicines. It was disturbingly easy to distribute without detection. We only needed to convince one generation of hunters that vampires needed to be rounded up and caged like animals before they would pass down the fabricated stories to their children on their own. They never questioned us, not once. They were completely convinced that they had seen the proof with their own eyes." Vex's voice grew distant with memory. "I became genuine friends with Ash during diplomatic visits to Emberrella. I met his sister, Awsha. She was absolutely gorgeous, stunning in a way that took your breath away. When I look at Lanira now, she has Awsha's exact eyes. They all shared the same distinctive nose shape. I remained loyal to your father until he no longer deserved such loyalty, Ravi."

"The same nose? Are you trying to tell me that Ash is related to Lanira?" I shook my head in disbelief. "That doesn't make any logical sense."

Vex continued speaking as if he were recounting cherished memories from another lifetime. "I fell deeply in love with Awsha, and she returned my feelings with equal intensity. I was planning to marry her, and Ash would have become my brother-in-law. Lanira was so incredibly small then, just a child. I had a crucial choice to make, and I still live with my decision in complete peace. My last gift to the family I nearly had was leading everyone searching for the lastborn to believe that there was a younger little boy in their bloodline instead of a girl." His voice grew heavy with the weight of sacrifice. "The alchemists tortured me on your father's direct orders until my physical body gave out entirely and I became nothing but a shadow, but it was a small price to pay to continue ensuring they looked for a boy and not Lanira."

"Then you were the one responsible for feeding out all of the intelligence that was leaked from RuneHold," I repeated slowly, trying to process the magnitude of his betrayal.

I understood what he was revealing to me, but it was incredibly difficult to process all the implications. It was easier to understand why Vex had once been a prized addition to my father's inner court, and then suddenly declared dead and relegated to the shadows. Still, the idea that Vex was a traitor was hard for me to fully accept. He had been my personal idea of loyalty and duty made flesh.

The illusions that surrounded my entire life were never exactly a shock when revealed, and yet somehow they still managed to surprise me.

"I also tried to organize King Orn's assassination," Vex admitted with quiet pride.

I remained silent because a significant part of me would have considered that a tremendous blessing. If my sister Niyla had become queen instead, RuneHold would have been immeasurably better off under her rule. The thought still sent an uncomfortable ripple through my stomach. I wanted desperately to be a strong, loyal hand of truth and justice. I wanted to be a genuine protector of the innocent. I had strived so hard to reach my current position because I wanted so badly to help people and make a real difference.

I couldn't openly sympathize with Vex's treasonous actions. In the end, no matter his noble reasons, he could have cost our entire land everything for the sake of one girl.

"I only have one more question before I leave," I stated firmly. "Do you intend to speak with her?"

"With Lanira? Do you mean, do I intend to tell her who I really am? Who she truly is?" Vex's voice remained steady and strong.

I nodded, dreading his answer.

"Of course not," Vex replied without hesitation.

I didn't believe him for a second. He walked back through the solid wall that we stood next to without another word, leaving me alone with my churning thoughts. I ran a weary hand through my hair and sighed heavily before taking my own steps away from the alchemists' chambers and back into the main halls of the castle.

The central kingdom was designed to be very open and welcoming. I had only taken a few steps into the center walkways when I spotted a group of women pushing and pulling at Lanira like she was a doll to be dressed. They tugged at her hair and spoke over each other about all the work they claimed they needed to do to transform her appearance.

She looked absolutely miserable, and it brought an involuntary smirk to my face. A few more vibrant strands of red were peeking through in her hair, and even from my distant position, the cherry color reflected the light differently than the dull brown dye. The deep frown on her face didn't stop her from being the most stunning woman in the room.

She was so perfectly created by nature that even when she smiled and the small smile lines around her eyes presented themselves, it was like watching a precious gift being given to the world.

It would be a significant adjustment for her to navigate this new life. She wouldn't need to dye her hair anymore to hide her true nature. She didn't need to conceal who she was as long as she stayed safely inside the walls of RuneHold. If she truly was the lastborn, she represented the biggest prize RuneHold had ever gotten its hands on.

And I was falling in love with our most valuable prisoner.

Chapter Forty-One
The First Move

Lanira

Four girls met me with fire in their eyes. They clutched brushes and fabrics like weapons and charged at me without mercy. Their fingers tore at my clothes until I stood as nothing but bare skin before them, the cool air of the chamber raising goosebumps along my arms. I tried my best to resist them, but they shoved me into a bath before they took turns holding me down so that they could unleash sponges heavy with water onto me.

So much water poured over my face that I could hardly breathe. The soap stung my eyes and filled my nostrils with its sharp, floral scent.

They scrubbed my skin until it felt raw and tender. They lifted each arm and worked at my flesh until they deemed it clean to perfection. I was ripped out of the bath and dried by two others, their rough towels chafing against my already sensitive skin. I was pulled and tugged as if I were a rag doll, my joints protesting with each sharp movement.

I wanted to scream, but the unknown stopped me. I wasn't aware of the punishments or guidelines well enough to make a scene. My heart hammered at a speed that spoke to the realization that I was out of my element, completely at their mercy.

They pulled white fabric over me that dragged along the ground with a whisper of silk against stone. They took strips of silver silk and spun them around my waist before they pulled the material over my shoulder and tied it off with practiced efficiency. Jewels bigger than any I had seen in Emberrella were placed against my collar as a necklace, their weight unfamiliar and cold against my throat. They brushed at my hair with firm strokes and pulled it into a bun before they stuck more jeweled pins inside, each one sharp against my scalp.

The girls didn't speak a word to me. They didn't show any signs that my resistance bothered them in the slightest. They finished their duty with a few dabs of pink rouge on my cheeks, the powder tickling my skin, and shoved me out the door and into Ravi's waiting arms.

He gripped me with intent. He didn't catch me and help me stabilize before moving away from me, like one would expect. He clung to me like a lid on a dinner plate, his fingers pressing into my arms through the silk. He looked at me like he did the first night we met at the ball, as if I were dressed up and ready to be gazed upon for his enjoyment alone. He watched me as if he were mesmerized by me, his dark eyes drinking in every detail.

He made my hands shake every time his gaze lingered on me for too long.

"You're touching the king's future concubine," I declared as I shoved him off of me, my voice sharper than intended.

I needed distance between the two of us. I was controlled and held together until he was too close. Then I only thought of his lips, of the way they had felt against mine.

"How do you know our customs don't declare you shared property?" Ravi asked with a raised brow, though something dangerous flickered behind his casual tone.

He silently agreed to the distance between us and kept his hands to himself, but it didn't stop the horror that washed over me. A frown overtook his features when he saw my expression.

"I'm not serious." He gestured for me to walk ahead, his voice gentler now. "Let's go."

"Why are you still around? Don't you have a duty to get back to?" I snarled at him as we moved through the halls, my silk slippers silent against the polished stone.

"I'm doing it now," he replied simply. "My orders are to ensure you get anywhere you are needed until otherwise ordered." The smirk he wore, the one that showed a hint of a dimple, crept onto his face. "I thought you'd be more comfortable this way. After all, I have been closer to you than anyone else present."

Heat flooded my cheeks at his words, and I quickened my pace.

"I'll have to ask the King to find someone else for the job." I shot a glare at Ravi over my shoulder.

"It wouldn't be wise, but sure. Lanira can do whatever Lanira wants. She hasn't seen enough to feel the need to tread lightly and must need to learn a few lessons the hard way," he mocked, his tone cutting.

I walked faster, my dress rustling with each hurried step. I wanted to be away from him and the way he made my pulse race.

"Are you going to also tell him that I've had my hands on you? My lips on you?" Ravi moved as fast as I did, easily keeping pace. "Will you tell Orn that the reason you want a new guard is because you enjoy me too much?"

The truth in his words made my stomach clench. I needed to pull myself together. I didn't need to enter my first breakfast with the man who would determine my life, worked up over the one who had already tried to end it by bringing me to his land.

Ravi moved ahead of me and opened two oversized doors, their hinges groaning softly. He clearly wanted me worked up before I entered, and I hated that his strategy was working. The doors opened up to a room covered in stained glass windows instead of walls, casting rainbow patterns across the floor. A dark wood table for two sat in the center of the room, its surface polished to a mirror shine. A black chandelier hung above it with purple balls of flame that danced and flickered, filling the air with an otherworldly glow.

Ravi entered but did not speak. He assumed his position like a well-trained dog at the doorway. His eyes stood as still as his arms, fixed on me, unblinking and intense.

The sight made a rush run through my body from the top of my skull down to my toes. Despite everything, I wanted to toy with him.

King Orn walked in with a strut that announced he owned the world. He sat in the chair across from me and grabbed his napkin with deliberate movements. He shook it out and tucked it into his buttoned blouse. He entered and completed his routine to ensure he was ready for his meal, but never once laid an eye on me, as if I were nothing more than furniture.

It must have been the arrogance of kings, something that was chemically altered when the crown was placed on their skulls. A switch was flipped that allowed them to feel so far above and re-moved from the average person. If kings had ever known empathy or love, I had yet to believe it.

It felt familiar. The treatment I received at a royal breakfast was only a different setting and face, but the dismissal was exactly the same.

"Do you know much of my kingdom?" he asked, finally deign-ing to acknowledge my presence.

"I do not, but if a wise ruler is willing to educate me, I am willing to listen," I replied with a smile that made my cheeks ache.

I had to start somewhere. Even if I made myself sick with the performance, I needed to know something about him to under-stand what moves to make.

He shook his head and contorted his face into a look of disgust.

"The prettier they are, the lower their intelligence," King Orn muttered, loud enough for me to hear every word.

A woman in a diamond bra and metal underwear entered with two trays of food, her movements mechanical and precise. A lock on her undergarments shimmered in the same purple light that adorned so many things in RuneHold. I began to connect the pieces well enough to understand it was the shimmer of alchemist creations, magic bound into metal and stone. She placed a tray in front of each of us and left without raising her eyes from the ground, disappearing as silently as she had come.

The sight of her made my stomach turn, but I forced myself to remain composed.

King Orn lifted his tray and grabbed his fork with greedy fingers. He dug into his eggs and moaned at the flavor as though he had nothing to hold back for, the sound obscene in the quiet room.

"I think you're smart enough to understand that some things are clearly different inside my walls," he began between bites. "My kingdom proudly took over the duty of keeping the world clear of the rituals and practices the vampires partook in from resurfacing. We also keep control of the population of other abominations that accompanied them, like witches. It came with a few downsides, like shadow spirits. They were created after some alchemists failed in their goals." He paused to shovel more food into his mouth. "Without a specific line of vampires, we cannot keep our current progress on track. The entire world would be devastated without our advances."

King Orn took another bite of his eggs, yolk running down his chin, before he caught it with his tongue in a display that made my skin crawl.

"That's enough information for you to understand what needs to be understood in order for us to proceed. The Ambrose bloodline was never confirmed to be cut off. We thought we were looking for a boy, that's what our whisperers told us, at least. If that line were to rise again, it would send the kingdoms into a spiral. Some would have the idea that they may wield a larger power than we do." He gestured vaguely with his fork. "You get it. It is my duty to find that line and breed it out in a controlled environment where they will be used for good, protected."

The word 'breed' hit me like a physical blow, but I kept my expression neutral.

The breakfast wasn't the only thing that was similar to home. He was, too. He was just another man who thought he was smarter than everyone else, righteous and justified in his cruelty.

"I do understand. I admire your drive to be an aggressively active leader. It's a refreshing change from what I'm used to," I responded, the lies coating my tongue like honey. "You see that some things need guidance to thrive, and you are taking up the task for the greater good of the people."

He nodded with satisfaction, pleased with my response. "What are you used to?"

"Where I'm from, the ones in charge sympathize with the abominations of the vampiric past. They tell us to hold secrets close and not tell a soul what they keep in the dungeons. There are so many tunnels and supplies there." I took a careful bite, buying myself time to weave the lie. "They are called supernatural, and we are told to protect them. I'm beginning to see that maybe Queen Blair puts on a good outside appearance so that no one questions the things that go on inside her walls."

The food was bland and tasteless, nothing like the rich flavors he seemed to be experiencing. Maybe it was that I was riding lines I didn't know where the edge was, and it affected me more than I gave it credit for.

"Interesting. You're so willing to give up your homeland," King Orn observed, taking a drink with a loud slurp that echoed in the chamber.

He acted as if we were having any other casual conversation, but I could feel him studying me. He made no slip for me to latch onto, no crack in his armor.

"I see what you've built here. I can see in your presence that you're strong and you have a mission you believe in. It makes me think that you deserve to know." I kept my voice soft, almost reverent. "You can also call it gratitude for healing my arm. You didn't have to heal it or allow me the gift of eating in your presence, but you did. The least I can do is give you something that shows you I want to help."

I kept my chin low and my shoulders slumped down just enough to appear as no threat, pulling from the lessons Princess Invidia had taught me about playing the part of a submissive woman.

He nodded slowly, apparently satisfied with my deference. "As long as you eat with your mouth closed and don't mind the loss of respect you've earned for throwing your own land over the bridges so quickly, then you are welcome to eat with me for dinner as well."

He looked me in the eyes then, his gaze sharp and calculating. He narrowed in on me and tried to dig into my thoughts, searching for cracks in my facade. He was analyzing me as much as I analyzed him, and I wanted him to think that I was weak and foolish.

I pushed my bottom lip out and let it quiver ever so slightly. I shifted my gaze to the ground and let my eyes fill with moisture, summoning tears that weren't entirely false. He was pathetic, not a leader, but only a ruler because he induced fear and control.

King Orn turned around and called to Ravi. "You can join us, too, brother."

"Half-brother," Ravi corrected, his voice flat.

He spoke but didn't break his stance, remaining perfectly still by the door.

Half-brother? Ravi was a bastard son of the king? The revelation hit me like cold water, pieces of the puzzle suddenly clicking into place.

"For now, I must excuse myself." King Orn stood, brushing crumbs from his shirt. "A ruler's schedule is always filled," he declared with a smug smirk.

I got to my feet as soon as his back turned, my chair scraping against the stone floor. I didn't want to be alone with Ravi, not with this new knowledge burning in my mind. I scurried out of the room like a rat who smelled cheese, my silk dress whispering against my legs. I was on a mission, and I would complete it.

"There she is!" a girl whispered as I hurried down the corridor.

"She doesn't have red hair, though," another mumbled, disappointment clear in her voice.

"Does it really matter? If she's still here, it must mean the alchemist tested her."

A girl stepped directly into my path, forcing me to stop. "I've heard rumors that there's a hunter who follows you a bit too closely. That he kissed you once."

"Swayed by the blood, we heard," the second added with obvious relish.

I tried to hurry past the two, but they made me anxious. Their voices made me uncomfortable, a reminder that I wasn't home any longer. There were people around who knew what I was, but I had never given them permission to hold that knowledge. When I quickened my pace, so did they. They pushed me down the hallway as if I were cattle, their voices growing louder and more insistent.

One grabbed my arm and pulled me back to face the group, her fingers digging into my flesh through the silk. "Your skin is so soft," she breathed, her hand moving to my cheek.

I slapped her away, the sound sharp in the corridor.

"Don't be rude! You're supposed to save us. You're meant to be the start of King Orn's godly line. It's only natural that we want to look at you," the woman snapped, her eyes flashing with indignation.

"Where I come from, you don't just put your hands on people," I retorted, my voice steady despite my racing heart.

"They should have taught you how to be grateful," another girl spat, venom dripping from her words.

I hadn't stopped moving, walking backwards while they grabbed at me with increasing boldness. When I finally had the door to my room in sight, I shoved the nearest girl into the wall with all my strength and ran for my sanctuary. I heard her body hit the stone like a sack of grain before I yanked open my door and slammed it shut behind me.

I clicked the lock with trembling fingers and gripped my chest, trying to steady my breathing. My heaving breath and shaking hands needed a moment to recover. I needed a moment to compose myself and process what had just happened.

Of all the things that I thought I'd have to prepare for, that was not it. It had never crossed my mind that I'd have to fight off court ladies like they were flies and I were something rotten they wanted to feast upon.

The comparison made bile rise in my throat, but I forced it down. This was only the beginning.

Chapter Forty-Two
It Must Be Believable

Lanira

My room was vast; an entire home could have fit inside these four walls. There wasn't an entire wing like Emberrella provided, only this single chamber. But it was sufficient for a temporary stay, and temporary was all this would be. King Orn declared that I was to be a concubine, but I wanted the title of queen. He was driven by the need to feel in control, in charge, by making me feel small and weak.

He didn't consider strongly enough that I was used to that treatment. That it wouldn't break me to pretend to be weak. I'd be as stupid as he needed me to be to get what I wanted. I'd never look down on myself for the performance. In the end, I was still in control.

Ravi opened my bedroom door and moved inside without invitation, his boots silent on the marble floor.

"Turn around and go." I pointed him toward the exit, my voice sharp.

"No," Ravi challenged, crossing his arms. "Are you not going to fight him? Deny the marriage? Challenge anything?"

"I'm not. I want to marry him," I asserted, keeping my expression neutral despite the lie burning my tongue.

"Stop playing with fire," Ravi warned, his voice dropping to something dangerous.

"What does it matter to you? You didn't mind watching me be harmed earlier. You didn't mind watching me sleep in a cell. I know the air between us has become mixed, so let me make it clear." I took a breath, steadying myself for the words I needed to say. "We aren't anything. We never were, and we won't ever be. You and I won't see each other again once I am queen. Go back to your duties and pretend you know nothing."

I tried my best to keep my voice low, but emotion crept in despite my efforts.

"Do you believe it when you say it? I don't. You don't sound convincing to me." Ravi moved closer, his eyes searching my face. "When I say I don't want to see you marry someone else, I believe it. When I say my duty to this kingdom is important, I don't think I believe that anymore. Can you hear it in my voice?"

The honesty in his words made something twist in my chest. I backed away from him, needing space to think clearly.

"It's none of my concern what you believe, or what you want. You made your choices," I replied, though the words felt hollow.

"Have you pieced it together yet?" Ravi asked, his tone shifting to something more urgent. "What's really going on here?"

I held my lips shut, refusing to give him the satisfaction of an answer.

"They know exactly who and what you are. They're testing your blood now to see how potent it is and to ensure you are on the correct line. That rune in the sand told your secrets." His voice grew harder with each word. "The next step is locking you away to have children until your body gives out. If you're going to play against him, you may as well understand that you are already five moves behind."

The weight of his words hit me like a physical blow. I moved past him and left the room, my silk slippers whispering against the stone. I didn't want to be alone with him, not when the realization was crashing over me that I had been bought from Queen Blair and was being played with. That I was going to be used as nothing more than a womb. That it was all real.

My hands shook as the truth settled into my bones.

I passed through feeling sorry for myself and into something harder. Instead of despair, I felt a growing fire inside of me. I felt my blood boil and my heart grow colder, more determined.

I followed the sound of voices to find my way through the halls, letting the noise guide me like a beacon. Vampire hunters stood at every single door I passed, their weapons gleaming in the purple-tinted light. The castle was guarded beyond what I could have imagined. The colors were bright, and the staff wore smiles, but the air was thick and tense, like the moment before a storm breaks.

A large arched doorway surrounded by etched columns came into view, and the voices were at their loudest. I leaned into the room, pressing myself against the cold stone, and saw King Orn draped over his throne with a girl on his lap. She wore the same metal-locked undergarments I had seen before, the alchemist shimmer catching the light. The hunched man I remembered from my first day stood beside the throne like a faithful dog.

I hadn't been noticed; I couldn't have been because the conversation continued without pause.

"She should be Queen! Her bloodline would create a new age of technology!"

"Yes! With her as Queen, RuneHold would become the strongest of all the kingdoms! It's what makes the most sense!"

"In order to do that, we must alter the course of our kingdom. The citizens have no idea. They'd riot, at the very least!"

"She doesn't need a crown to produce her bloodline!"

"Exactly! She'd become too dangerous. Who is to say that she's not vengeful?"

The group of advisors continued to yell over one another, their voices growing more heated with each exchange. I didn't know how they got anything done with the way they acted, but it hardly mattered. I understood the things that they were debating. I was losing what little freedom or influence I may have had before I could even touch it.

The girl on the king's lap shifted, and the chains around her ankles clinked softly, a sound that made my stomach clench.

"Shouldn't you be settling into your room?" King Orn's voice cut through the chaos, hushing the room as his eyes locked on me.

"I'd rather be with you. If I'm going to help the kingdom, then I have a lot to learn," I announced, stepping fully into the doorway.

"The girls here can teach you what you'll need to know," the hunched man, Lee, laughed, his voice crackling like old parchment.

"Now, Lee, I didn't give you permission to speak," King Orn replied coolly. "If she wants to help so badly, I think she should join us."

He tossed the girl off of him without warning, and she hit the ground hard on her elbows, a small cry escaping her lips. King Orn stepped over her prone form as if she were nothing more than discarded clothing, and I followed him out. I gave the girl, who remained on all fours on the floor, a second glance. Her hollow eyes met mine for just a moment.

She was my future if I failed.

King Orn led us outside through a side door instead of the main entrance. The flowered courtyard, which had seemed so beautiful before, opened up to reveal a group of people on their knees, covered in chains that scraped against the stone with each tremor that ran through their bodies.

They were lined up in perfect formation. Dirty and naked, their skin pale and bruised. They shook and shivered at the sight of us, terror etched into every line of their faces. A man in golden robes drew the same rune beneath them that had been drawn under me, his movements precise and practiced. A large man with a scythe double his size stood beside them, silently waiting like death incarnate. The row of people were already bleeding into the carved symbol, their blood creating dark rivulets in the stone.

My hands shook along with my breath, and I tried to hold them steady behind my back. I pressed my palms together, hoping the contact would stop their trembling.

"They are my prize from my travels. It was thought to be only one vampire when I went," King Orn announced to me, his voice filled with satisfaction.

The rune lit up grey before it shimmered golden, the light pulsing like a heartbeat. King Orn lifted his hand and dropped it in a casual gesture. The executioner followed his signal and took three heads with one fluid motion. He didn't need to hack away at them; one smooth slam and their heads rolled across the stone, leaving trails of crimson behind.

My stomach turned violently. I had known what was coming, and yet somehow it still surprised me. The sudden and careless way life was extinguished in RuneHold had an uneasy air that I wasn't used to, even after everything I had witnessed.

Alio landed on the wall's edge, her black eyes fixed on me, and her presence made the situation feel heavier, more significant.

King Orn held out his arm for me to take, and I took it in an automatic motion. I didn't do it because I wanted to; my mind was hardly functioning. Guards ran around us to gather the severed heads and place them on waiting spikes, the metal points gleaming wetly.

"It's your turn," he declared, his voice cutting through my shock.

"What?" The word slipped out before I could stop it.

How many times would I be put in a position to kill in order to prove myself? How badly did I want to prove myself? Could I take them all if I decided that I didn't want to keep playing this long game?

King Valen and King Orn were alike, even down to the way they demanded loyalties be proven to them.

"Take an axe and take the last head. If you're loyal to us, it should be no problem for you to aid in our mission and help rid the world of a predator before it causes extinction," King Orn urged, his words dripping with false righteousness.

I looked from Orn to the man on his knees. The prisoner's eyes met mine, wide, terrified, and utterly human. I knew I had slipped, shown too much emotion. I knew Orn was winning this round. Alio cawed twice, then three times. Was she telling me to do it? Did she warn me not to proceed? I couldn't understand her message.

What kind of person did it make me to do this? Was this any different than the killings I had done before? If I killed this person, knowing they weren't a vampire, knowing it was all a lie to keep up appearances, what kind of look would my brother have for me when I returned home?

Had I already gone too far to stop now? If I denied Orn, would all the other things I had done be for nothing? Was one more life worth the prize at the end of everything I had sacrificed? How many justifications could I make before I became the very monster I was fighting against?

Did I care anymore?

My trembling hands nearly betrayed my resolve, just as my churning stomach nearly lost all of its contents. The taste of bile filled my mouth, sharp and acidic.

I grabbed the axe from the hunter that stood beside me, its weight heavier than I expected. Without allowing myself another breath to think, I brought it down into the man's neck. The blade bit deep, but not deep enough. I didn't think. I wouldn't think.

Would Ash forgive me? Would he understand why I did what I did? Would he tell me that, in the name of bringing our family back, sacrifices had to be made?

I brought the axe down again, harder this time. The sound it made was wet and final.

Bile rose in my throat, burning. I had to swallow hard to try and force it back down, my body rebelling against what my mind had commanded.

One last throw of the axe, and his head rolled to the ground at my feet, coming to rest against my silk slippers. The weight of what I had done settled over me like a shroud.

I had no choice in what happened next. My knees buckled underneath me, and I had to grip the axe handle to keep from falling completely.

I needed to pull myself together. I needed a stronger stomach and fewer emotions. I had known when I made the choice to start setting up pieces on this board that I would have to kill. That I would have to make impossible choices.

But knowing and doing were different beasts entirely.

King Orn turned to Ravi, who looked on in horror. His skin had gone pale as parchment, and his gaze burned into me with something that might have been disgust or grief, I couldn't tell which.

King Orn looked pleased with himself as he slowly took in both of our reactions, savoring our discomfort like fine wine. For a moment, I imagined taking the axe to him next, feeling the satisfying weight of it in my hands.

"I've sent a spy to your kingdom," he announced suddenly, his voice cutting through my dark thoughts. "I intend to find out if they are sympathizers. A solid world order requires everyone to be on the same page. I'd hate to form an alliance on false pretenses." His smile was sharp as a blade. "If they come back and say that they found nothing, you understand it means you lied, and I'd need to take your life, right?"

I nodded, forcing steadiness into my voice. "I'm not afraid. I know that I speak the truth."

I hadn't expected him to send spies to check the dungeons in Emberrella, but I could count on Queen Blair. She would round up whoever she could find that she considered supernatural and hold them captive. If they weren't there already, they would be by the time his spy arrived.

The game was still in play, even if the cost was higher than I had imagined.

Chapter Forty-Three
A Third Board Enters

Ravi

Moving around the castle was easy until someone wanted a change of venue. Then you'd need to understand how to manipulate the platforms that shifted and rotated throughout the structure. It provided an extra layer of protection if you needed to keep a secret, you conducted business on a platform, not inside the castle walls. It was worth the inconvenience of moving platforms because anyone who wanted to interrupt would alert you with the grinding of those same mechanisms when they arrived.

I sat at a small iron tea table on a thick silver cushion; the chair made of the same black iron that felt cold even through the fabric. The garden that surrounded me held trees with pink leaves and purple flower blossoms that swayed gently in the afternoon breeze, their sweet fragrance mixing with the metallic scent of the iron furniture.

My foot tapped against the stone ground with impatience, the sound echoing in the enclosed space.

Princess Niyla rounded the corner in a silver gown that sparkled like captured starlight in the sun. She excused her maid with a gentle wave and offered me a smile as she entered the garden. She settled into the chair across from me and poured us both a cup of tea, her movements graceful and practiced. Her nails gleamed with a coating of pink shine that caught the light with each gesture.

"What was it like there? I've been waiting for stories in person," Niyla asked, her eyes wider than her smile, practically glowing with curiosity.

"It was... different," I replied, choosing my words carefully. "Niyla, we both know that there's a lot to discuss, and none of it involves scenery."

Niyla sighed, her shoulders dropping slightly. "Are you sure that you want to go any deeper? You don't have to keep pushing into this."

"Don't you think that I should know the things going on around me?" I pressed, leaning forward in my chair.

"No," she answered bluntly between sips of her tea, the steam curling around her face. "In fact, I think this knowledge is best kept from you. Hold Vex's story close and move on with your life."

"I respect you not just as my sister but as a person. If there is something you need help with, something you may need protection from, I should be involved." I set my cup down without taking a single sip, the porcelain clinking against the iron table. "I could tell by your letters that you knew more than you admitted."

The frustration with our careful dance of words was building in my chest like pressure in a kettle.

"Listen carefully," Niyla began, her voice taking on a more serious tone. "You cannot take back something once you've learned it. I only hold things from you that I believe are best kept that way. It's for your own protection." She paused, studying my face. "If you insist that you want all of the information, then I'll give it to you because I respect you as well. But you must promise that you will take it to your grave and that you will mind your own business afterwards. Out of respect for me."

Niyla sat straighter, her posture becoming regal and commanding.

My mouth felt suddenly dry, but I nodded in agreement, knowing there was no turning back now.

"I had no idea that there were hidden passages in the castle until I saw your mother using them to sneak to our father. She was in love with King Lorn, desperately, completely in love with him. In fact, I think you were the only thing she loved more than him." Niyla took another sip of her tea, her voice growing softer with the memory. "When King Lorn gave in to his darkness, your mother was distraught. She loudly disapproved of the violence that began to cover the castle like a plague. Your mother was the start of a revolution."

I struggled to follow what she was telling me. The words felt disconnected, as if Niyla were recounting someone else's life entirely.

"When she died, she asked me to continue her work. That's when I was introduced to Vex. Father kept me shielded well enough that I only knew fragments of the truth. We were so young, after all." Niyla looked directly into my eyes, searching them for something before she continued. "I have been sneaking vampires, witches, and even hybrids out of the castle for years. We leave bodies in their place, corpses that Vex brings, along with a witch who uses runes to make the bodies look like the prisoners they're replacing."

The world felt as though it spun too quickly around me, the garden blurring at the edges of my vision.

"You've been doing all of this behind my back? While I was training to be a hunter? That's why you never pushed harder for us to leave this place," I whispered, my voice sounding so quiet to my own ears.

"I never wanted to come between you and your goals. It isn't my place to convince you of which side to choose," Niyla replied, her voice still confident and unwavering.

I felt as though I had been slapped across the face, the sting of betrayal sharp and immediate.

"Which side?" I mumbled, the words barely audible.

The idea that any of us were on opposing sides wasn't one I had explored deeply enough. Of course, I had questioned things. I had slipped in my loyalty, disagreed with decisions that had been made, but actual sides? Had I been working for the group that stood opposite to the only people I truly cared for? The thought made bile rise in my throat.

Had I dedicated my entire life to the wrong cause?

Had I wasted all of my efforts on something fundamentally wrong?

"Ravi?" Niyla reached across the table and laid her warm hand on mine. "A choice will have to be made eventually, but today isn't that day."

"A choice?" I could hear my voice shudder with the weight of implications. "You plan to take her, don't you?"

Niyla's face never shifted from its calm expression. She held a steady and confident smile that somehow made everything worse.

"I do. The prophecy gives so many people hope. They count down the days until the vampire destined to free us will arrive. She is the hope we all cling to, the key to loosening RuneHold's strangling grip on our world," Niyla explained, her voice taking on an almost reverent quality.

A choice will have to be made.

Between my oath and the other hunters, or my sister and Lanira.

Her words echoed through my mind like sounds bouncing in a vast tunnel.

"Niyla, the prophecy isn't real. It isn't some divine set of words left by gods long gone. It's fabricated," I protested, grasping for any solid ground my thoughts could find.

"It never mattered who uttered the prophecy first. Once it created hope, it took root and became truth. Whether spoken by a person or some divine presence, we can't understand it, still doesn't matter." Niyla's eyes took on a distant, entranced quality. "Ravi, you should see the way they talk about her, the light that comes into their eyes."

"Who are 'they'?" I demanded, leaning forward.

Niyla removed her hand from mine, the warmth disappearing instantly. "I think it's better that you get time to let these revelations sink in before we continue. It's a lot to absorb." Her voice grew gentler. "You should know that no matter what side you choose, I won't hate you. I won't raise a weapon against you, either."

"A weapon?" I scoffed, but the sound died in my throat as I took in her expression. "You—" My jaw hung open as the full weight of her words hit me. "You truly mean to start a war?"

"I do. We do," she confirmed without hesitation. "How long can RuneHold just take and lock away anyone they want to? Orn may be the visible hand of authority now, but his little hunched minion holds the true strings. Lee is magical in his own right, with the way his whispers infect Orn's mind and bend his will."

Niyla sat back in her chair, and the pink polish on her nails caught the light like tiny mirrors.

If there was anyone around who could possess such insidious power, it would indeed be Lee. He was an original alchemist, taught alongside the vampires when the Goddess Helia still walked among mortals. He never let any of us forget that distinction. His twisted appearance was impossible to ignore and a direct result of his own experimental hands.

No one else had been willing to endure the procedures he wanted to test, so he had used himself as the subject.

Niyla rose to her feet gracefully. "Remember your promise. These secrets stay between us. If you think, after sleeping on this for a while, that you'd like to know more, I'll happily tell you everything." Her expression grew more serious. "But I will take Lanira regardless of your choice. I know that you've grown fond of her; it's something that can't be helped. She doesn't deserve what will happen to her if she remains here."

I watched Niyla walk away, her silver gown shimmering with each step, but only for a moment. Then I found myself staring down at my untouched tea, stirring it endlessly while my mind raced.

There had to be more people involved than just her and Vex. What hunters helped them? Which guards were part of this? Something so complicated and dangerous couldn't be accomplished with such a small group under such intense scrutiny.

Was I truly going to consider abandoning everything I had worked so hard for? Everything I had believed in so strongly? If Orn were removed from power, didn't RuneHold have a chance to become something better under different leadership?

If the alchemists were pushed hard enough, wouldn't they want change too? They couldn't all enjoy the work they were forced to do. Yet my sister was preparing for a full-scale war as though there was no other possible solution.

Didn't Lanira deserve a say in her own fate?

I tossed myself back in my chair and slouched down, feeling suddenly exhausted. I hadn't expected my entire world to flip upside down today. At best, I had thought I would learn more about Vex and the vampires he smuggled.

Instead, I had discovered that everything I thought I knew was built on lies.

Chapter Forty-Four
Two Ravens Are Better Than One

Lanira

I hadn't thought of sleep in the chaos of my arrival, especially while watching people with animal faces come and go from the window of my bedroom. I hadn't considered rest until the sun was nearly gone and the growing darkness made my eyes feel heavy, weighted down by exhaustion and the day's horrors.

I wasn't sure if I'd be able to sleep at all. Every time my eyes closed, flashes of my brother filled my mind, ashamed of me, looking down on me with disgust. He'd tell me that he didn't help raise a murderer, that I had become something he never wanted me to be. His voice would snarl with disappointment, cutting deeper than any blade.

Disappointed isn't the word for it, he'd say in my nightmares.

I only did what I had to, I'd reply, desperate for his understanding.

Pathetic, he'd whisper with a cruel curl on his lips.

I was startled fully awake from my restless tossing and turning when the shadow man with moon-bright eyes walked through my wall just as Alio struck the window with her beak. The sharp sound made me bolt upright, my heart hammering. The shadow Vex opened the window for her to fly inside, cold night air rushing into the room and making me shiver.

"We have business to complete now that the sun has set," Alio declared, landing close to my face. Her breath was oddly warm against my cheek. "Elio is not far from here. He is buried beneath one of their floating islands. We will need someone to accompany us, someone to die."

The shadow man stood silently beside her as if he were her protector, his presence both comforting and unnerving. The sight made me realize that if I was going to survive this place, Ravi was right about one thing: I would need more than just myself.

"His name is Vex," Alio announced, gesturing with one wing.

"I'm Lanira," I responded, pulling my blanket closer around my shoulders.

Vex nodded but remained silent. I felt suddenly exposed, as though I were undressed in a crowded room. Even though his features were sparse and shadowy, I could feel the intensity of his gaze fixed on me.

I cleared my throat, trying to regain some composure. "I can't help you. Even if I had the book, which I don't, Ravi, does it can't be the right one. It's empty. There are no words on most of the pages."

"Did you bleed on it?" Alio asked, tilting her head with keen interest.

My eyes shifted between the two of them as if my brain had stopped functioning entirely.

"Did you bleed on the pages to give them permission to reveal their secrets?" Alio pressed, her tone growing impatient.

"I—I," I stammered, feeling foolish.

Alio tilted her disfigured head back and forth in mockery, her movements sharp and jerky. "Then, of course, it didn't show you anything. The BloodBorn must bleed on the pages, or else the words remain hidden from sight."

I pressed a finger to my temple, trying to process this revelation.

"Let's go," Alio demanded, her voice brooking no argument.

I nodded, wanting the spotlight off of me, and opened the door. Ravi stood there already, looking directly at me as if he had been listening to our entire conversation.

"Where are we going?" he asked, his voice carefully neutral.

"We are doing nothing. We aren't ever doing anything together again. You are a traitor," I declared, pointing an accusing finger at him. "You sold me off, and you deserve to hear it every time you lay eyes on me."

"You can't leave this room without me, so if we aren't doing something, then neither are you," Ravi replied firmly, shoving me back inside my room.

He closed the door in my face with a definitive click.

"If he must die, I will make it quick," Vex offered, his voice like whispered smoke.

"Yes!" I called out immediately.

"No!" Alio said in unison with my response, overruling me.

"He is either a traitor to us or a traitor to his brother. He can't be trusted because either way makes him a traitor," I pressed, my voice rising with frustration.

"You aren't in a position to be picky about your help yet," Alio replied coldly.

I bit my cheek hard enough to taste copper and pulled the door back open.

"We need to find a hidden chamber where someone was buried," I announced reluctantly.

"We will also need a sacrifice," Alio inserted. "And her book."

I wanted to rip Alio's ugly little feathers out of her body one by one. But I didn't hold my anger against her entirely. I understood the desperation of wanting a brother back. I would have done anything, even worked with Ravi, for Ash's guaranteed return.

"Let's go, then," Ravi said, gesturing down the corridor.

Vex moved in and out of walls like a phantom scout, staying steps ahead of us, and I understood immediately why he had come with us. He possessed an advantage far superior to anything we could have achieved alone. His ability to phase through solid matter made him the perfect lookout.

Ravi stopped us at the same side door we had used earlier that day. The memory hit me like a physical blow. I saw the naked man trembling beneath me in a flash of vivid recollection. I didn't ask what he had done wrong. I didn't want to know and feel the weight of additional guilt. Innocent or not, I had killed him.

Ravi pressed a hidden button, and invisible gears rumbled deep within the castle's mechanisms. A floating platform rose from the mist below, its surface solid and reassuring beneath our feet. This island wasn't as beautiful as the others I had seen during my stay. It was a solid concrete structure painted with arcane symbols, not a single flower or blade of grass growing anywhere on its barren surface.

Ravi used a torch to guide us across the narrow walkway, its flame dancing in the night breeze. Small red stones embedded in the path lit up as we stepped on them, creating a trail of crimson light behind us. Below us was nothing but swirling mist that seemed to go on forever.

Inside the structure, the air was thick and oppressive, making each breath feel labored. Every wall was covered in writing words that seemed to pulse with their own dark energy.

Blood chanted. Held by the goddess, locked in a cage. Far from rebirth. Hidden from the blessings of fate. The light you won't hold. Dusk and dawn forever gone.

Alio didn't stop to examine the inscriptions. She flew forward with desperate haste that left us running to keep up with her. At the end of the walkway, the room opened into a chamber containing a pool of blood. Orange chains glowed beneath the crimson liquid like captured fire, the only visible feature in the dark depths. Alio perched at the edge of the pool in complete silence, her usual chatter replaced by reverent quiet.

The room was small and empty beyond the red water and bloodied runes carved into plain stone walls.

In that moment, I shared her burden completely. I longed to see my brother again with the same desperate intensity.

Ravi entered behind us, bringing a castle guard with him. My stomach dropped. Had he betrayed us after all?

"King Orn will be pleased to know that you turned them in for this treachery. When we bring them back, he will reward you handsomely," the guard praised, his voice echoing in the chamber.

Without warning, Ravi pulled out a dagger and sliced the guard's throat in one fluid motion. The look of fear and shock on the guard's face was palpable, his eyes wide with disbelief as blood spurted between his fingers. Ravi tossed the dying man toward us, and he dropped to his knees with a wet thud.

The bloodied water showed our reflections with startling clarity. Neither of us looked the way I remembered from that first night at the ball. Neither of us retained the innocence we had possessed then. There was something dimmer in our eyes now, something that spoke of lines crossed and souls stained.

Ravi held out the book for me to take, and I accepted it with trembling hands. I hated myself for the way my chest fluttered when his warm fingers brushed against mine, hated that even now, even after everything, my body betrayed me.

I swallowed hard and opened the pages to the same spell I had used for Alio.

Alio flapped her wings frantically. "Like before! Like before! Invoke the sisters of fate!"

I knelt beside the pool of blood, the metallic scent filling my nostrils and making my stomach churn. I sliced my hand with my fingernail, watching fresh blood well up in the cut. Vex dragged the guard's body and tossed it into the water with a splash that sent crimson droplets across my face.

"Moonlight and Time. Blood of the Sun. Collide the Stars under Insanity," I chanted, my voice growing stronger with each word.

I let my blood drip into the already crimson pond, watching the drops disappear into the dark surface.

"I call upon the sisters of Seed, Water, Clock, and Death to bring back what was wrongfully taken."

The water suddenly glossed over with red fire that burned without heat, then extinguished as quickly as it had appeared. A second raven broke through the liquid's surface, rising like a nightmare given form. He had no feathers, only exposed bone and rotted meat that barely clung to his skeletal frame.

Alio flew up immediately, and the two ravens entangled in a spinning dance of reunion, their movements both beautiful and grotesque.

My heart felt heavier than it had in weeks. There had been enough chaos and urgency that I hadn't had much time to reflect on my past and my family. I had barely had time to think about the person I was becoming. I should have already had my brother back by now.

But there was something about this city, this kingdom, these two ravens. There was something in the very air that reaffirmed my commitment to carve out a place where we could be free to exist without being used as pawns in someone else's game.

Ravi guided us back to my room in silence, and I was surprised not to encounter a single soul during the entire journey back. He didn't put up a fight when I didn't offer him an invitation inside. He simply assumed his position as a guard outside my door, accepting his role without protest.

I pushed thoughts of him from my mind to focus on the issue directly in front of me.

"I need the two of you to explain exactly who you are and why you're not in physical bodies in full truth!" I demanded, pointing between the two ravens.

"We are the only gods to remain in this realm. We were punished for our choices. It's that simple," Alio replied, her voice losing some of its usual sharpness.

"Helia and Thann created us for one specific purpose, and we failed that purpose. As punishment, we were trapped in these forms, our divine abilities locked away," Elio explained, his voice raspier than his companion's. "In another realm, there was or is going to be a battle of power between deities. We wanted no part in that cosmic war. We have nothing to hide from you. Both of us will remain loyal to you, as we were loyal to you before you knew of our existence. We were loyal to the original of your bloodline, and we will remain loyal to your children. You are a unique connection to the sisters of fate. It doesn't matter to you right now, because this realm is your only concern today."

The reality of having gods, truly divine beings, standing before me was hard to comprehend. Having gods by my side as allies was even harder to wrap my thoughts around.

Yet here they were, as real as the blood still drying on my hands.

Chapter Forty-Five
The Next Horror

Lanira

I searched every corner of my room, checking behind curtains and under furniture. Yet I found nothing, not a single sign of another person.

I could have sworn I heard someone whisper my name with the soft whoosh of the door closing. I felt as though I was losing my mind, my nerves frayed from everything I had witnessed. I heard a woman call to me as though she knew exactly who I was, her voice casual and tempting, like honey laced with poison.

"Are you looking for something?" Alio asked, perched on the windowsill.

I shook my head, pressing my palms against my temples. "I just thought I heard something."

"There are many souls trapped around this castle," Vex murmured, his smoky form shifting near the wall. "They whisper constantly, seeking acknowledgment from the living."

"I wanted to ask a question, but," I grimaced, suddenly feeling overwhelmed. "Now I've realized that there are so many of you to consider."

"Elio is loyal to the bloodline. Speak freely," Elio declared, his voice deeper and more resonant than his companion's.

The sound of Elio's booming voice made me jump, my nerves already stretched thin.

I didn't want to ask if they had also heard the strange woman singing to them, calling for them, so I shifted to the second subject weighing on my mind.

"Did I make a mistake at the beheading? If I wanted to formally align with you and whoever it is you're working with, is it too late?" I asked, the words tumbling out in a rush.

Getting all of the words out caused a sharp pain in my chest and made my breath tremble. I felt weak, useless, overly reliant on others forguidance.

Vex regarded me with what might have been confusion, though his shadowy features made it difficult to tell. "Orn has done far worse, and the alchemists continue to commit greater atrocities daily. We have long accepted that death is part of our struggle. The prophecy may not be real in the way that you originally thought, but to most of us, it has become our hope, a very real way of life." His voice grew more intense. "We have been slowly gathering and hiding for years now. We knew that no matter the exact words or the way the prophecy was interpreted, it would bring you to the surface all the same."

The pressure his words placed on me offered no relief from my guilt.

"Their prophecy is whatever they want to make it. Ours is waiting for the lastborn for the one who can lead us, for the one who possesses the only power that can stand against what has been developed in this kingdom." Vex's form seemed to solidify slightly as he spoke. "Next time, I will offer myself as the sacrifice. I cannot die from a beheading; I can take forms far beyond my current one. Use me as you need."

Such an idea was beyond anything I had conceived. I could convince the king of my loyalty to him without him forcing me into situations against my will.

"Can I ask something else? A question and a demand?" I shifted my gaze between the three of them, trying to read their expressions.

"The mirror of sight?" Elio asked before I could finish. "I will find it for you."

I nodded gratefully. "My question is, is that why he wants Ruby-Wake? The deal King Orn made was to receive aid in an attack on them?"

"That is where we have managed to gather in secret," Vex confirmed, his voice carrying a note of pride.

The handle of my door suddenly shook violently, then a fist pounded against the wood with enough force to make the frame shudder. We exchanged alarmed glances before the room cleared instantly. Vex took Alio and Elio with him into whatever realm he occupied when he walked through walls.

I moved to the door and wedged the chair I had been sitting in under the handle. The door burst open with such violent force that it knocked me to the ground, the chair splintering against the wall. I stumbled backwards and fell hard onto my back, the impact driving the air from my lungs.

Lee limped inside my room with a smile that made my blood flow sluggishly through my veins. My heart nearly stopped beating from how desperately I wanted to hold my breath and disappear. He carried a small brownbag filled with metal tools that caught and reflected the purple light streaming through my window. Two guards entered on either side of him, their faces expressionless and cold.

They grabbed my arms with iron grips and held me down flat against the cold stone floor. Lee leaned over me, close enough that I could smell the sour stench of old sweat clinging to his robes. A scalpel bit into my arm until blood flowed freely, warm and sticky. He pulled a glass jar from his bag and held it carefully under the cut, making sure to catch every precious drop. He worked with methodical precision despite my desperate resistance.

I kicked and screamed until my throat was raw. I struggled so violently that I thought I might have broken my arm trying to pull it from the guard's crushing grip. It was all for nothing; my efforts accomplished absolutely nothing.

"This is what yer 'ere for. If ya think anyone'll come save ya, yer wrong. 'Old still," Lee growled, his voice like gravel scraping against stone.

He sliced my arm deeper, in a fresh spot, and pulled out another jar. I pressed my head against the frigid floor, tears streaming down the sides of my face and pooling in my ears.

There was nothing I could have done to stop the pain or the humiliating tears.

It was a sharp, brutal slap of reality.

The guards dragged me behind Lee until we reached the alchemist's chambers, my feet barely touching the ground. The room reeked of death and chemicals, making my empty stomach churn. They had a body chained toa wooden table, clearly lifeless, its skin waxy and gray. They crushed a mixture of powders and herbs in a mortar and rubbed the paste onto the corpse's limbs before they poured my blood over the preparation. Lee forced the jaw open with a sickening crack and poured what remained of my blood down the corpse's throat.

The body flinched at first but did nothing more, lying still as death.

Lee shoved a handful of the powdered mixture down its throat, and then the body began to shake uncontrollably, convulsing against its restraints.

Screams erupted before anything else, inhuman wails that seemed to come from the depths of hell itself. The body contorted and mutated into something that resembled Alio's twisted form. It grew extra limbs that lacked skin, revealing raw muscle and bone. Odd fingers were missing from malformed hands. Hair sprouted from random patches while falling out in clumps from other spots, leaving the scalp mottled and diseased. The face shifted and changed until it became one I recognized with horrifying clarity.

I was still held down by the guards, my arm bleeding steadily onto the stone floor, as my sister Awsha's face formed on the corpse that writhed before me.

"Kill me!" the thing that wore her face cried, its voice a broken parody of the sister I remembered. "Please!"

Lee looked proud of his grotesque achievement, but even the other alchemists stepped back in revulsion at the sight of the abomination that shrieked before us.

"This hurts, please, I can't take it. Kill me! Vex!" The creature's pleas echoed off the chamber walls.

The guards' grip loosened slightly in their shock, and I seized the opportunity. I grabbed a knife from one guard's belt and drove it deep into the thing that bore my older sister's face. I granted her the mercy she begged for because even I couldn't find any joy in seeing her again in such a nightmarish state.

She was worse than anything my darkest nightmares had ever conjured.

She was a cold shiver down my spine, a testament to the horrors that lay ahead. To the unspeakable things they planned to do with my blood.

To what King Orn had truly purchased me for.

Vex materialized through the wall beside me, his black, misty figure storming toward Lee like a vengeful spirit. He grabbed the alchemist by the collar and hurled him aside with supernatural strength. The vial Lee had been holding, half filled with my blood, tipped and smeared across the floor in crimson streaks.

The two guards scrambled backwards, terror replacing their earlier confidence.

"Touch Lanira again and I will rip your soul from its cage," Vex growled, his voice carrying the weight of divine authority.

Lee stared at Vex in stunned silence, his mouth agape.

Maybe it was the blood loss or the lack of food. Maybe it was the shock of watching a sister I hadn't seen in fifteen years mutate to life before my eyes, only to die again by my own hand.

I felt my head strike the cold floor as my vision faded to black.

The air was crisp and cold when consciousness returned. The sky was painted in brilliant pinks and yellows, like a sunrise captured in eternal beauty. I couldn't shake the feeling of dread that consumed me despite the breathtaking vista. My mouth was parched, and even though I looked down upon the most beautiful golden city I had ever imagined, it meant almost nothing. The entire town shimmered like captured sunlight and seemed to smell of fresh eggs and steaming tea.

The sight of the golden city couldn't diminish the sinking feeling in my chest. I knew I had to be dreaming or hallucinating because there was no such place in any realm I knew.

An arm wrapped gently around mine, warm and comforting. "It was never something that I experienced either. You and I only get to look at the golden city in distant memory. Both of us we are on the edge of greatness, but we will never be accepted as something worthy of the original home of the gods."

I recognized her voice immediately. I had heard it before, calling to me through walls and dreams. It had summoned me with its mysterious familiarity. I turned to look at her face, desperate to finally see who had been reaching out to me, but instead of meeting her gaze, my eyes snapped open to find myself back in my room.

I was in a place that was familiar, yet nothing felt the same anymore. I didn't understand who she was or why I was hearing her voice in my mind. I didn't even know what questions to ask or where to begin searching for answers.

I didn't know who to trust with which pieces of information anymore.

I only knew that, in the end, Ravi had been right about one thing. I had never truly understood what RuneHold would bring to my life or what it would take from me.

Chapter Forty-Six
Honor or Love

Lanira

I knew I was risking my life with the choices I was making, but I needed to push forward all the same. My desire to continue had plummeted after witnessing what they had done to my sister. I couldn't sleep, and food held no appeal. My motivation was crumbling like sand through my fingers.

I had spent fifteen years so certain that I could bring my family back, that we would all be happy together again. Now it was staring me in the face that if I brought them back, they would only suffer. The truth was a blade twisting in my chest.

I tossed King Orn's belongings around his chamber with reckless abandon. I didn't care if his things were out of order when he returned. I didn't care what he would do to me as punishment. I couldn't imagine it being worse than what I had seen happen to Awsha. In the drawer of his nightstand, beneath silk handkerchiefs and gold trinkets, sat a pile of letters bearing a seal I knew all too well. The royal seal of Emberrella they were from Queen Blair.

They were exactly what I had been searching for. I settled onto King Orn's bed, the silk coverlet cool beneath me, and opened the first letter with trembling fingers.

King Orn of RuneHold,

I've carefully considered your words, and if I did know where the BloodBorn is, what would you offer me in exchange?

Queen Blair

My heart hammered as I moved it to the back and read the next letter, the parchment crackling between my fingers.

King Orn of RuneHold,

I am pleased to hear all of my requests can be easily granted. When Ravi arrives with the Princess of Saydeean, I will be sure to introduce him to the BloodBorn. If he is as easy a pawn as you claim, then things should proceed smoothly and quickly.

Queen Blair

I rushed to the next letter, my hands shaking with growing rage.

King Orn of RuneHold,

Of course, I always knew who she was. Her brother and I spoke often—they share the same distinctive nose. I knew she would be the key to disposing of Valen and his useless children. I knew eventually you would come knocking as well. I have plenty of patience. She can serve us both by removing my husband and paving my way to the throne before I send her to you.

Queen Blair

I crumpled the page in my fist, the paper cutting into my palm, before I opened the final letter with violent urgency.

King Orn of RuneHold,

I sent Prince Altair out to meet Lanira this morning. He smiled at me so blissfully unaware that his death was on the horizon. I watched the horse from StoneDale approach from the tower window. I hung Princess Sala in the night and confirmed her death before I retired. Invidia will be placed on the throne of Saydeean, and we will control their kingdom from within. She won't defy me—I've made sure of that. When I tell her of Lanira's true identity and show her proof that Lanira killed her brothers, she will fester with betrayal and hatred. I deliberately let Invidia defend Lanira so that Lanira would taste the bitterness in every breath she takes when she learns the truth.

Now I want confirmation that my sister will die, and that Ruby-Wake is next on our list to fall.

Queen Blair

The door burst open, and I still clutched the letters with a grip that made my fingers ache and turn white.

"What are you doing in here?" Ravi demanded, his voice sharp with alarm.

"Your brother has been behind everything. Everything!" My words came out like whip cracks, each one laced with fury.

"Half-brother," Ravi corrected through gritted teeth. "What are you talking about?"

I thrust the letters toward him, and he scanned them faster than I had, his expression growing darker with each line.

"You found these here?" Ravi asked, his voice barely above a whisper.

"No, I brought them myself!" I shouted, sarcasm dripping from every word.

"If these were truly from this room, it means both of us are nothing more than pawns in Orn and Blair's elaborate game," Ravi concluded, the weight of realization settling over his features.

"It doesn't matter anymore." I lifted myself off Orn's bed, the silk sliding beneath me. "I won't be caught trusting you again. Do what you want with the letters."

"Did you ever truly trust me? It never felt that way," Ravi admitted, his voice carrying a note of genuine hurt.

I sighed and began tapping my fingernails against my crossed arms, the sound sharp in the tense silence. "Prove to me what you're claiming is true, then. Prove to me that I can trust you."

"How?" he asked, stepping closer.

"I need to prove to the king that I'm completely loyal to him and his mission. If I can gain control of the army here, I can make significant progress toward my goal. I can get back on track as if nothing had ever derailed me." My voice grew stronger with each word. "I still have the chance to make Queen Blair and King Orn pay for what they've done. King Orn is a violent man who respects only strength. Queen Blair isn't much different. There's only one way to earn their trust, and it's through death. If I can find someone worth capturing, maybe even someone to execute myself, he will trust me completely. I need to show him that I'm at least somewhat capable. I have a plan."

"Or we can leave," Ravi offered, lowering himself to sit in front of me. "I can take you somewhere else. There are other options, other ways to move forward. It doesn't have to end this way."

"You sound like Koen," I replied, the comparison hitting him like a physical blow.

The comment took him by surprise. I could see it in the way his eyes widened and his jaw tightened.

"You're asking me to break every vow I've ever taken," he whispered, the enormity of what I was suggesting finally sinking in.

"You have free will," I replied firmly. "I already have the plan and the person in mind. I only need you to arrange for the king and me to be outside the castle together."

Ravi was quiet for a long moment, warring with himself. When he finally spoke, his voice was resigned. "I'll let him know that you've requested a tour of the grounds. If I tell him he should do it to better evaluate your loyalty, it won't appear suspicious."

Something in his tone made me study his face more carefully. There was a shift in his expression, a hardness that hadn't been there before. The letters had changed something fundamental in him, just as they had in me.

"Ravi," I began, but he cut me off.

"I need to tell you something," he interrupted, his voice steady but strained. "My sister has been planning something for a long time. She and Vex, they're part of a resistance. They've been smuggling people out of here, saving lives." He took a shaky breath. "She asked me to choose a side. I thought I knew where my loyalties lay, but after seeing those letters, after watching what they did to your sister..."

He stood abruptly, running his hands through his hair. "If you're determined to go through with this plan, then I'm with you. Not because of duty or vows, but because you're right. They both need to pay for what they've done."

The weight of his decision hung between us like a bridge we would either cross together or burn behind us.

Chapter Forty-Seven
A Possession of Pieces

Lanira

I paced by the doorway, my bare feet wearing a path in the stone. It felt like hours since I had been waiting for Ravi. I couldn't sleep at all, so I tossed and turned through the endless night, my mind racing with possibilities and fears. I missed the restful nights I had enjoyed in Emberrella, where my biggest concerns were court gossip and avoiding Princess Invidia's sharp tongue. I had nothing to occupy my time in RuneHold, no hobbies, no books, no embroidery. King Orn would see me go insane from boredom faster than from his own cruel hands.

Vex materialized through the wall, carrying a mirror in his smoky grasp. It was small and delicate, trimmed in ornate gold that caught the morning light. He slid it carefully under my mattress before pausing to regard me with those hollow sockets that served as eyes.

"Company is approaching for you. Now is not the time to examine it. Elio found the mirror of sight as you requested. I am merely the deliverer," Vex murmured before vanishing as quickly as he had arrived.

Ravi opened my door moments later, and I quickly tucked my hands behind my back to stand at attention. Vex could have been more specific about the company already being at my threshold, but we would work on those communication skills another time.

"Let's go. He's waiting for you," Ravi announced, gesturing toward the corridor.

I followed him out, my silk slippers silent against the polished stone. I hadn't imagined that our arrival in his kingdom would drive us further apart rather than bring us closer. It must have been the universe telling me that we should never have grown close in the first place. I desperately wanted to stay and examine what was so significant about the mirror, but I would have to wait.

King Orn wasn't just casually waiting for me; he was watching intently before I even arrived. His dark eyes tracked my movement as I rounded the corner of the hallway. King Orn was immaculately dressed, as he had been every time I had encountered him since my arrival. He did not have a collared woman beside him this time, which somehow made his presence even more intimidating.

He didn't wait for me to reach him before he turned abruptly and made his way outside. He was fortunate that I had no other choices available to me. If I were a princess like Invidia, with actual power and influence, I would have made it my personal mission to ensure he never found a suitable wife. That his reputation became too notorious for any respectable woman to consider him.

"When Ravi told me you wanted to tour the grounds, I knew I needed to accompany you personally," King Orn declared from ahead of me. "I thought to myself, what would a girl like her be planning if she were allowed to roam completely alone? One never knows what mischief she might be plotting."

"Only things you would disapprove of, of course," I replied as if I were reciting a sweet lullaby.

I wanted to appear as nothing more than a simple girl with a sharp tongue and no other notable talents while I was in his presence.

"Of that I am absolutely certain," he agreed, slowing his steps just enough for me to catch up. "What is it you truly want out of this excursion?"

"Time with you," I answered without hesitation. "If we are to marry, should I not know the man I'm binding myself to?"

"You aren't destined to be a queen. You should only concern yourself with learning my preferences in bed," King Orn stated bluntly.

"Those interest me as well," I responded, quickening my pace to walk ahead of him. "If you think we have need of that knowledge already, the garden seems as good a place as any for such education."

His steps faltered as if I had caught him completely off guard. It proved he was movable, that despite his hardened exterior, he was capable of some form of emotion or desire. I waited patiently for him to fall into step beside me before I spoke again.

"I don't think that I truly understand how things work here. The alchemists transform the vampire hunters, but how exactly?" I asked, affecting the tone of a genuinely curious but naive girl.

"Hunters are trained from early childhood. They learn combat techniques and then fight in groups to the death until the required number of accepted students for the year is achieved. When their bodies and minds are proven sufficiently strong, the alchemists alter their physical forms." His voice took on a lecturing quality, clearly enjoying the opportunity to demonstrate his knowledge. "They receive a controlled amount of vampirism that allows them to tap into the natural magic present in some vampires' blood and use it to make the runes come alive. It's not enough to make them crave blood like true vampires. The runes themselves were developed separately, without vampirism, by witches. They were carefully studied from ancient texts the witches left behind. Everything we possess here was taken from our enemies. We have never passed up an opportunity to gain power or knowledge."

King Orn's voice swelled with pride as he spoke.

"So, they are some sort of man-made hybrid?" I wanted the words to remain in my thoughts, but they slipped out as a mumble.

"You can call them that if it pleases you," King Orn confirmed. "Why are you so interested in such matters?"

"The subject is simply so foreign to me," I explained with wide-eyed wonder. "The idea that you just create supernatural beings."

"I imagine that feeling of ignorance isn't new to you. You seem to be uneducated on most subjects of importance," he mocked, his voice dripping with condescension.

Unfortunately for him, I was a remarkably quick learner.

Without warning, a man in a black robe lunged from the dense trees beside us and tackled the king to the ground. He wrapped both hands around King Orn's throat and squeezed with desperate determination, his face twisted with hatred.

I grabbed the guard's sword from its sheath on his hip and drove it deep into the attacker's back. I wanted to keep pushing until it pierced through to King Orn's stomach as well, but that would only have earned me a place in the dungeons or on the executioner's block. I stopped as soon as I felt significant resistance from bone and muscle.

"Are you all right, my king?" I cried dramatically as I dropped to my knees beside them.

The assassin's body slumped off the king and landed heavily beside us, blood pooling beneath him. King Orn grasped at his throat and gasped for air, his face flushed red from the attack. He didn't look at me with gratitude; he fixed his furious gaze on the guard beside him, his eyes blazing with rage.

Ravi appeared in the garden as if summoned and beheaded the negligent guard without question or hesitation. He lifted King Orn from the ground and rushed him toward the castle. I knew he was taking him to be examined by the alchemists, exactly as we had planned.

I followed behind them, ensuring I maintained the expression of terror on my face and kept tears streaming down my cheeks. I positioned myself outside his bedroom door and waited for the physicians to arrive and depart. When the room was finally empty, I was granted permission to enter.

King Orn lay shirtless in his bed, purple bruises already forming around his throat like a macabre necklace. "If it weren't for your quick thinking, my failure of a guard would have succeeded in his plot to assassinate me today."

"I don't know what came over me. The sight of you being harmed..." I made sure my voice trembled and my words stumbled authentically. "I'm sorry for being so violent."

"I will finish my afternoon with rest. I'm sure you can understand why I won't be continuing our tour today. However, I never allow anyone to go unrewarded. Loyalty is the most important quality I value in others." His voice was rough from the attack. "Think carefully about what it is that you want, and I will grant it to you."

I bowed deeply, and Ravi escorted me back to my chamber.

"It worked perfectly," I whispered once we were out of earshot.

Ravi nodded but remained silent. When he attempted to enter my room, I pushed him back gently and shut the door. I wasn't permitted a lock, so I wedged my chair firmly against the door.

One goal was complete. Now I had time to focus on another crucial objective. If Queen Blair believed she could use me and emerge victorious, she was gravely mistaken.

I retrieved the mirror from between my mattresses and held it up to catch the afternoon light streaming through my window. It was intricately etched with delicate vines and orchids, the gold trim gleaming like captured sunshine.

"Seed, water, clock, death," I whispered into the mirror's surface.

I didn't know if it would work. The prolonged silence suggested it wouldn't respond to words alone.

I bit my finger until blood welled up and let several drops fall onto the mirror's surface. It rippled like disturbed water before clearing to reveal the image of a woman. She had flowing red hair, piercing red eyes, and skin as pale as fresh snow. I straightened involuntarily at the sight of her ethereal beauty.

"Well, hello there," her voice sang out like a melodic bell.

"Who are you?" I asked, though something deep inside me already knew the answer.

"You may call me Helia," she replied with a smile that seemed to hold secrets of the universe.

"The goddess?" I gasped, hardly daring to believe it.

"Place your finger upon the glass and I will grant you the gift of true sight," she coaxed, her voice so peaceful and hypnotic that resistance seemed impossible.

I obeyed without conscious thought. Her voice was so soothing, so compelling. My finger touched the cool glass, and a surge of electricity shot through my hand and up my arm like lightning.

I felt as though I was being pulled underwater, drowning, and then brought back to life in a different time and place entirely. I felt weightless, without physical form or limitations. In the vision, I saw myself heavily pregnant and chained to a slab of bloodstained marble etched with crimson runes. Alchemists with golden prosthetic limbs chanted in ritualistic circles around me as if they were performing the ceremony of their lifetimes.

I saw Ravi in the distance, watching the horrific proceedings unfold. He made no moves to save me, no attempts to intervene.

I snapped back into my own body, but something fundamental had changed within me. I could feel it in my bones, in my blood.

"You and I will have plenty of time to become properly acquainted," Helia announced with satisfaction.

"Are you inside my head? Part of my body?" I asked, fear creeping into my voice.

For a terrifying moment, the reflection smiled without any input from me. She reached up and touched her hair, my hair, but I felt nothing. I hadn't moved a muscle.

"It's our body now," Helia clarified with a tone of finality that chilled me to my core.

Reference Guide

Kingdoms

Emberrella

Saydeean

Lunadur

StoneDale

RubyWake

RuneHold

Notable Landmarks

HollowGrove—Burial Forest

Alter of Time—Ruins of Vampire Temple

Notable Mentions

Stone Tablet Prophecy—Stone Tablets that speak of an uprising that will eradicate mortals.

The Vampiric Grimoire—A book that holds the vampire's secrets, rules, and rituals.

Sunflowers—Said to repel and protect against Vampires.

Residents

Lanira—Vampire

Ash—Temple of Time priest, Lanira's brother

Awsha—Lanira and Ash's sister

Vex—Shadow man, once the right hand of the old RuneHold king

Helia—The old Goddess

Thann-The old God

Alio—An old Goddess

Elio—An old God

Ravi—First Blade of the Hunters

Princess Invidia—The only biological daughter of Queen Blair and King Valen

Prince Altair—The youngest son of Queen Blair and King Valen

Prince Tillo—The eldest son of Queen Blair and King Valen

King Valen—King of Emberrella

Queen Blair—Queen of Emberrella

Koen—Guard to Princess Invidia

Princess Sala—Princess of Saydeean

Prince Nio—Prince of Saydeean

King Orn—Current King of RuneHold

King Lorn—The Last ruler of RuneHold

Princess Niyla—Only daughter of RuneHold

Boris—Hybrid of RuneHold

Lee—Original Alchemist from Lunadur

www.ingramcontent.com/pod-product-compliance
Lightning Source LLC
Chambersburg PA
CBHW060600300726

48975CB00005B/1399